SECOND CHANCES

Author KM Mitten

BOOK 2

MGX BOOK SERIES

Copyright © 2019 KM Mitten

ISBN: 978-1-7345712-1-9

Book cover paintings by Argentina Nealson

Book cover graphics by Scott Mitten

Miami Generation X Second Chances Book Two

For more information go to mgxbook.com

To all of my friends and family.

I want to thank you for your love and support while I'm chasing my dream. I hope you all enjoy this story and the ones to follow. May each of you go back in time with me when life was a bit more exciting and the music was awesome.

Table of Contents

Chapter 1 The Phone Call

My name is Samantha. My family calls me Sam and my friends call me Sammy. Except for Tonya, she's like my sister and calls me Muñeca. Which means doll in Spanish. When I had a boyfriend, he called me his Corazón. Which means heart in Spanish. I loved it. He's long gone now, and he broke my heart when he left. His name is Julio and he has been gone about a month now to live in Anaheim California. I don't believe in long distant relationships, so that's why we're no longer together. I thought if we broke up on the day that he left, it would spare us from the inevitable heartbreak. Guess what? I was wrong. My heart broke into a thousand pieces the day he left.

Today I woke up to my mom and my brother Tommy discussing yours truly. My mom asked my brother to take Daisy out for a walk. His response was, "Tell Sam to get up! It's her dog, so Daisy is her responsibility."

My mom replied: "You're right, Tommy; but she's devastated right now, so I'm giving her time to heal."

My brother sounded completely annoyed when he asked, "Heal from what? It's just puppy love. It's not real. Come on. Sammy is only 15 years old."

My mom sounded completely compassionate and filled with understanding when she simply said, "Tommy, heartbreak is devastating at any age."

"Mom! Seriously! You can't let Sam continue to spend her entire summer in her room. She needs to get over it already and go outside and get some fresh air. Tell her to go walk Daisy."

I knew Tommy was right; I needed to start living again. I mean, what was I doing? I've been cooped up in my room feeling miserable over a guy who hasn't bothered to call me even once since he left. That's when I climbed out of bed and went straight to the bathroom. I took a shower and put on shorts and a T-shirt. That in itself was already an accomplishment. I have been living in pajamas every day for about a month. I brushed my hair and had so many knots that my head was tender. I looked in the mirror and saw my eyes were a bit swollen and pink. I said aloud: "No more tears for someone who has forgotten I even exist." I put my hair up into a ponytail and grabbed Daisy's leash off the counter.

I took Daisy outside for a walk. When I arrived back home, I called up Tonya. She didn't answer, so I left her a message on her answering machine. I called Daphne, and Arturo answered the phone. "Hey, Sammy. How are you holding up?"

"I'm okay, I guess. I just want to get back to normal. You know what I mean?"

"Oh yeah. I definitely know where you're coming from. Michael has been gone over two weeks now."

"Gone where?"

"He is in LA at his dad's house."

"That's right. Sorry I forgot."

"It's understandable; you must have been dealing with a lot. How is Julio? Does he like living in Anaheim?"

"I wouldn't know; he hasn't called me."

"Have you tried calling him?"

"Yes, but no one ever answers the phone."

"Oh, Sammy. I don't know what to say."

"Neither do I." I heard Arturo release a loud sigh and I said, "You know what?"

"What?"

"I need to get out of this house and quit feeling all depressed Arturo.

"Really? Me too. Let me go wake up Daphne. I'll call you right back."

"Okay. Talk to you soon." After I hung up the phone, I walked straight into my brother's room.

"Hey, Tommy. Do you want breakfast?"

"No. I'm not making my bonging waffles this morning Sam. You didn't even touch your plate the last time I made them for you."

"I'm sorry about that; I just didn't have an appetite. I do now Tommy! I can make you pancakes."

"No, I want my bonging waffles."

"Okay. Then I will try making you waffles Tommy."

"Nope! They won't be bonging."

"Okay, never mind. I'm sorry I bothered you."

I stood up to leave his room when Tommy said, "Wait." I stopped walking, and he said, "I'll make breakfast." He got up out of bed and we walked out to the kitchen together. I grabbed the mixing bowl and a whisk. Tommy grabbed the waffle mix and the milk. As he prepared the batter, he told me to take a seat. I took a seat at the kitchen counter. "Talk to me Sam, I'm your brother and I've been where you're at. What's going on?"

"I called him, you know, Julio. He never answers the phone."

"Has he called you?" Tommy asked with a surprised tone to his voice.

"No." I crossed my arms over my chest, I was suddenly feeling frustrated.

"Then who were you talking to earlier Sam?

"Arturo, he answered the phone when I called Daphne."

"How is he doing?"

"Not so good."

"Why? What happened?"

"Michael's spending the summer at his father's house in LA."

"Now is Michael the guy with blond hair?"

I nodded my head yes, and Tommy said, "Yeah, I remember him that's Arturo's best friend."

I let out a sigh and asked, "What's the big deal about California? It's sunny here year-round too and..."

"Forget about him and start having fun. It's summer and I'm home. Let's cruise the Grove tonight and we can eat at your favorite burger place." Tommy poured the batter into the waffle iron and set the bowl down on the counter. He walked back over to me and said, "They have one in the Grove, Sam."

"What do they have?"

"Your favorite burger joint Sam."

"Really?"

"Yes. Really."

"What do you say Sam?"

"Okay, let's go."

"You haven't ever cruised the Grove before at night, have you?"

"No. Why?"

"Oh, you'll see. It's where everyone goes to be seen."

"What are you talking about Tommy?

"You'll see tonight; just be sure to dress up and act cool. Everyone dresses up. It's hard to explain; except that it's just different."

"How is it different?"

"Well, it's completely different from the daytime atmosphere. Everyone cruises around in their cool ride. They have a mega sound system so everyone can hear it as they drive by. Some people even have neon lights inside their car.

There's people everywhere walking around checking everybody out. When you think someone is cute, and they're checking you out, you say, 'Hey. What's up?

Hopefully, you get a number or two.

When you're in the car, you wink and jam out to your sound system. You have to show off a little bit and look cool doing it. You need to have tons of confidence. When you leave there, you feel like a celebrity or something. It's an awesome feeling."

"Okay, but there's only one problem, Tommy."

"What's that?"

"We don't have a cool car or a mega sound system. We only have Mom's car," I said frowning.

"Okay, so we won't look cool cruising. We can park and walk around the Grove. It's the same thing, and we have to like strut, you know."

"I don't strut, Tommy."

"Then you just have to dress up and look cool. It'll be fun, Sam."

"Alright! then I'll go, but I don't care about being cool. I just want to eat my favorite burger and fries with lots of cheese."

"That you can definitely do, but first eat your waffle." Tommy placed a waffle in front of me. It was so big; it took up the entire plate. I was definitely hungry because I ate the whole thing, and it was bonging. When I was finished eating, the phone rang.

I grabbed it on the first ring. It was Arturo. "Hey, Sammy. I was unable to get Daphne up yet. When she does get up, I will ask her about going out tonight."

I looked over at my brother and asked, "What about cruising the Grove tonight? My brother's home for the summer, and he has been wanting to go there."

"Yeah, that sounds great, Sammy. I will ask Daphne when she wakes up." My brother suddenly had a surprised look on his face.

"Okay. Just give me a call back and let me know."

"I can totally do that Sammy."

"Great. Talk to you soon. Bye, Arturo." I hung up the phone quickly before Tommy could refuse. When I turned around to face Tommy, I noticed he was sulking with his arms crossed over his chest. He was still sitting down at the kitchen counter.

"What was that, Sam?"

"Tommy, to be honest with you, Arturo asked me to hang out first. The Grove sounds amazing, and I totally want to go. I even want to dress up and look cool with you.

"But...

"But what Sam?"

"But I also want to hang out with my friends. Plus, Arturo has the car and sound system for your cruising the Grove experience."

"Oh yeah! What kind of car does he drive?"

"He just bought a convertible Mustang. He even put a loud sound system in it. The trunk is filled with nothing but speakers."

"Now that will definitely get us seen," Tommy said smiling.

"Wow. Tommy, you are so vain, dude."

"No, I'm just confident." He stood up from the counter and dropped an ice cube down the back of my shirt. The ice cube fell out straight to the floor only after I danced around the kitchen. When I looked back at Tommy, he took off running to his bedroom. I banged on his bedroom door, and said, "Don't worry, Tommy. I will get you back tonight, coward."

Daphne called me about an hour later. She was all excited about cruising the Grove tonight. She knew all about it. She also called it the place to be seen. I told her that I wanted to eat at my burger place while we were there. Daphne was all excited about that too and said, "Greg can meet us there." Greg was at work until six o'clock.

Arturo called me back, and he said he would be over to pick us up by seven. I told him we would be ready. Tommy and I watched TV with my mom until it was time to get dressed, and that's when Daphne called. She wanted to know what I was going to wear tonight. I really didn't know yet, so we both decided to wear a dress. I wanted to wear my hair in a French braid since it was so hot outside. That's when Daphne offered to come over and braid my hair and spike my bangs.

Arturo and Daphne showed up by seven. Daphne got to work on my hair, and she offered to apply my makeup. I was surprised when I saw my reflection in the mirror. Daphne didn't go overboard with the makeup. My face still had a natural look with my eyes and lips enhanced with light colors of peach and tan. When I walked into my closet, I put on the first dress that caught my eye. The dress was turquoise with a thick black zipper that went down the middle. I put on a pair of black panty hose, black slouch socks and black leather boots that went just past my ankle. Daphne was wearing a blue spandex dress with a black short-sleeved jacket. She also had on black boots with a three-inch heel. We were totally ready for the Grove and to be seen.

I walked into my brother's room. Tommy had his back to me, and I could hear him trying to suck in his gut to zip up his jeans. "Tommy, those jeans are too tight." When he turned around, I thought I was going to throw up. "Dude, that's gross. You're totally bulging."

"That's what the girls like, Sammy."

"No, girls don't like that, Tommy. I'm not going anywhere with you dressed like that."

"Okay, fine. I'll take the sock out."

"You're wearing a sock?"

"I just wanted to see what it looks like. Lots of guys do that Sam."

"You look stupid, Tommy! That's what it looks like!"

Daphne walked in asking, "What's all the commotion about? Oh, Tommy," Daphne covered her mouth, and walked out of the room.

"You see, Sam."

"What did I tell you? Girls like that."

"Tommy, she had to cover her mouth because she was about to throw up. Now take that sock out, and let's go." He turned his back to me and threw a pair of socks on his bed.

He walked inside his closet for a minute and shut the door. When he came out, he was wearing an aqua tank top, tan jeans, and a tan cotton jacket. He was also wearing tan leather espadrille shoes. "How do I look Sam?"

"Better, now let's go Tommy." When we walked out to the living room, Arturo was patiently waiting for us. He didn't look bad, but he wasn't dressed up. He was wearing blue jeans, high tops, and a faded polo shirt. My brother saw what Arturo was wearing and said, "Dude, we're going to the Grove. Don't you want to dress up for the ladies?"

"No, dude. I'm gay, and my boyfriend is in LA for the summer."

"That's Perfect. More ladies for me," Tommy said sounding ecstatic. "In fact, you can be my wing man Arturo. What do you say?

Arturo had a confused look on his face when he said, "I guess that will be alright."

"Awesome, I like this night already," Tommy said as he rubbed his two hands together smiling. He walked back to his room and we heard him yell out, "Woo hoo."

Arturo leaned over and asked, "Is he serious?"

I looked back at Arturo and answered, "I'm afraid so."

Daphne smiled when she added, "That's just Tommy being Tommy.

"Daphne's right Arturo. My brother is always thinking about how every situation can be used to his advantage to get chicks."

"Good to know," Arturo replied with the same confused look on his face.

Tommy walked back into the kitchen and yelled out, "Mom, we're leaving now!"

"Okay. Have fun and bring your beepers."

"Got 'em, Mom!" Tommy responded as we walked out the door. Arturo waited until we were about two blocks away before he put the convertible top down. When he drove up the two blocks, it was like a huge traffic jam.

My brother was all excited and shouted, "We're here!" I looked around to see where here was.

The traffic jam had the cars moving inch by inch. The passengers in the cars beside us would say, "Hey! What's up?" or "Aren't you cute?" I quickly realized this was the 'Check you out ride' Tommy was talking about.

Tommy had put in his mixed tape of his favorite freestyle jams. We were all waving to the different cars that drove by us. Girls often yelled out to Tommy and Arturo.

My brother kept his hand on his chin and occasionally he would look over at the girls. He just posed the whole time looking cool with a stiff lip. I laughed a few times when he said his lines to the girls. It usually went something like: "Baby, you got room for me in that car?" or "Hey, beautiful. You're smoking. You want to hang out later?" But my favorite Tommy line was definitely: "If you like what you see, let me get your number." Every time he said that, I would burst out laughing in the backseat. It was so vain and totally Tommy. The whole time he had on his sunglasses, and it was nighttime.

The speakers were thumping in every car that drove by us. There were groups of girls dressed up like super models walking around everywhere. On every corner there were groups of guys checking them out. Some girls would stop and talk to the guys, and some would just smile as they walked on by enjoying the attention.

Arturo finally pulled into a parking lot. The parking attendant handed Arturo a ticket. Then he pointed out the last available parking space in the lot. Once he was parked, Arturo put up the convertible top. We walked down the sidewalk and I noticed several things. Everyone outside was in high school. There are plenty of nightclubs here, and the lines to get in were filled with college students.

Tommy suddenly stopped and said, "Sam that's the center of the Grove." I looked over to where he was pointing and saw this huge staircase. It led to a big open bar on the second floor. It was filled with tons of people laughing and drinking frozen drinks.

Daphne's eyes lit up when she saw it. "That's the best spot in the Grove Sammy. From there you can see everything and everyone. When we turn twenty-one, we're hanging out there."

That's definitely the place to be seen." Daphne was all smiles as I turned around to look back at the Bar in the Center of the Grove. I felt excited as I began to picture us hanging out there one day.

We finally made it to my burger place. We placed our order then headed for the game room. Over the intercom we heard, "Greg and Mig, your food is ready for pick up."

Daphne stopped walking and grabbed my arm. We walked back over to the counter; Greg wasn't there. I looked over at Daphne and she was already scanning the restaurant for Greg. I saw her eyes comb every inch of the place. Then suddenly her eyes lit up as she pointed toward the back of the room. "Let's check there." Daphne headed for the back doors and Greg spotted us as we walked outside. He was smiling and waving us over to his table. Daphne ran up to him and gave him a kiss. Greg just kept smiling up at her as she pulled her head away. You could tell he was so into Daphne.

I stood at the table beside Daphne. Greg finally took his eyes off Daphne long enough to introduce me.

"Hi Sammy, do you remember my cousin Mig?" I turned my head and looked over to my right and saw Mig smiling up at me.

"Yes, of course."

"Hello Sammy, you look beautiful tonight."

"Thank you, it's nice to see you again."

"Have a seat," Mig said as he pulled out the chair beside him. I sat down and felt completely nervous." Is this your first time here?" I looked back at Mig and noticed his smile. He had a dimple in his left cheek.

"Yeah, it is."

"So, what do you think Sammy?"

I took a moment to think over his question and answered, "It's packed and kind of cool I guess."

"Yeah it is. What do you plan to do after you eat?"

I started to feel a bit nervous and I bit down on my bottom lip before saying, "I don't know yet Mig, first time here remember?"

"They're going to head home after they eat," Greg retorted.

Mig gave Greg an annoyed look before asking, "Then what are your plans for tomorrow night Sammy?"

I smiled and said, "I still don't know yet Mig."

"We're going to be playing at the Bonfire tomorrow if you want to come. This time he was looking directly into my eyes when he was speaking to me. Mig has light brown eyes and brown perfectly set eyebrows. His eyes and smile were captivating. "If you want to go and need a ride —" Before he could finish his sentence, they called our names over the intercom.

Daphne stood up and said, "Let's go, Sammy." Mig was smiling as I stood up from the table. Daphne latched onto my arm and looked back at Greg. Then I saw her fake a smile as we began to walk inside.

Which made me stop to look back at Greg. He was sitting up in his chair with an angry expression on his face. "Daphne, what's up with Greg?"

"It's nothing, let's go." When we arrived at the counter, I saw our trays waiting for us along with Arturo. They were loaded with big juicy burgers and fries. I went to the veggie station first. Followed by the cheese station second and smothered my fries in delicious hot melted cheese. My brother finally showed up and grabbed his tray from me. Once everybody had everything they needed, we all headed back outside to join Greg.

Mig's eyes lit up when he saw me. I looked over at Greg, and he was frowning. Then I heard my brother say, "Let me introduce you girls to my sister Sam." I looked over at my brother who was standing between two girls. They were totally Tommy's type. They were wearing tight short skirts and tank tops that revealed tons of cleavage and of course, high heels.

They joined us at the table and sat on either side of my brother. One of them was sitting in the chair beside Mig, I felt bummed about that. Daphne sat down beside Greg and I sat beside her. Arturo sat down beside me and whispered, "There is no room for these girls in my car."

"Maybe we will get lucky and Mig will take the girls with him."

"I don't think so, Sammy. I have noticed him looking at you." I smiled and didn't comment. Then I felt like someone was staring at me. I casually looked over at Mig from across the table. He was looking back at me. Then I turned my head and attention back to my food.

My brother was talking to the girls about school. He told them he just finished his first year in college. The girls were all excited when they heard that. They both just finished high school and were starting college when summer was over. My brother and the girls were in the middle of a conversation when I stood up.

"Where are you going, Sam?"

"Oh, I'm going to the arcade room, Tommy."

"Do you need any money?" I looked over at him and rolled my eyes. My brother thinks that girls like when a guy shows he can be generous.

"No, I'm fine," I answered sounding complete annoyed and shaking my head.

Arturo, and I walked over to the arcade room. When we sat down to play a tabletop game, Arturo started to laugh.

"Why are you laughing Arturo?"

"Sammy, why were you so rude to your brother?"

"I don't know," I answered smiling and trying not to laugh.

"Oh, I think you do know Sammy."

"Really, why do you think I was rude?"

"Obviously, you wanted to sit beside Mig, and the blond girl took your seat." I erupted into laughter because I wasn't expecting that to be his answer.

"I don't know what it is exactly, but I feel it, Sammy."

That grabbed my attention and I stopped laughing to ask, "Feel what?"

"I don't know. It's like this strange feeling is in the atmosphere. Maybe it's the chemistry between you and Mig."

"No, right now what you're feeling is my brother's aggravation. He's going to get even with me for being so rude to him."

"Yeah, I'm sure of that, Sammy."

"It's okay, I can handle it."

"Excuse me Sammy, I'm going to the men's room."

We both stood up, and I walked over to the pinball machine. I inserted my quarter, and my first ball was released. That's when I pulled the knob all the way back and let it go. This sent the ball flying to the top of the table. Then a quarter was placed on the glass top in front of me. I looked over to my left and Mig was smiling at me. "I have next game." I couldn't help it, I smiled back at him.

Then I turned my attention back to the pinball machine. After I saved the ball by pressing the flippers and sending the ball flying back up the table, I said, "It's yours when I'm finished." He just stayed there beside the machine staring at me. When I looked over at him again, he didn't shy away or turn his head. I felt as though he wanted me to know he was staring at me. When I lost my last ball, Mig picked up his quarter off the glass top.

It was a small room and the pinball machine was long. There was just enough room for one person to stand in front of the machine to play. As I turned to walk out from in front of the machine, Mig and I both had to turn sideways. He slid in behind me as I was moving past him. When he placed his hands on my waist as he slid by, I stopped and looked up at him. My mouth was dropped open and my eyes were opened wide. I was about to ask him why he was touching me.

That's when he said, "I'm sorry." He put both of his hands up and continued to say, "I just didn't want to squish you against the machine." I just nodded my head to let him know I understood and moved the rest of the way past him.

That's when Arturo came back, and asked, "Are you ready, Sammy?"

"Sure! Let's go Arturo." I looked back at Mig and smiled, and he smiled back. I turned my head back around to face Arturo; he had a silly grin on his face. I knew what that silly grin was all about.

I rolled my eyes at Arturo and he whispered, "Chemistry." We both laughed the whole way back to the table.

When we arrived, the girls were gone, and Tommy had a grin on his face. He said, "Okay, guys. I got what I came here for." Tommy waved a paper with a phone number written on it.

"So, does that mean we can go now, Tommy?"

"Yes, absolutely. Let's go, Sam."

Greg stood up and said, "Wait here a minute." He came back two minutes later with Mig. "We will walk you back to your car," Greg told Daphne as he leaned down and kissed her.

Daphne just smiled and took Greg's hand.

Mig walked beside me as we headed back to Arturo's car. "It was nice seeing you again, Samantha."

"Yeah, it was nice seeing you too, Mig."

Arturo unlocked the doors, and Tommy pulled the seat forward. Daphne kissed Greg and climbed inside first.

When I was about to climb into the car next, Mig kissed me on the cheek and said, "I hope to see you again tomorrow." The minute Mig kissed my cheek, I stopped and looked up at him. My mouth dropped open, but I was speechless. It was intense; he just stared back at me.

"Sam, let's go!" My brother said, and that cleared my head instantly. I climbed in the car and sat down beside Daphne in the backseat. My brother sat down on the passenger seat. Then he asked, "Are we going to put the top down?"

"No!" Daphne and I both shouted at the same time. We waved bye to Greg and Mig as we pulled away.

Daphne sat back in her seat and whispered, "I want to invite Greg over to hang out tonight. You know, back at the picnic tables, since Greg's staying at his cousin's house."

Now that got my attention. I turned my head from the window to look back at Daphne. "Oh, that's right, you aren't aware that his cousin Mig lives just down the street from you."

"If you want to call him and invite him over for an hour, you can Daphne. We should be back at my place in another 20 minutes at the most."

"Yeah, let's do that. But don't tell my brother Sammy please. Arturo said he was dropping us off and going out to shoot some pool with Tommy and those girls."

"Those same girls from the burger place?"

Daphne nodded her head yes, and I rolled my eyes.

"So, what do you say? Can I invite Greg over?"

"Sure, that's fine Daphne. Just call him when we get home."

Arturo pulled into the parking lot and said, "Hey man, I don't think I'm going with you tonight. I just want to go home and call Michael. Tommy just sat there with a blank look on his face. That's when Arturo said, "You know because he's my boyfriend and I miss him."

"Oh dude, that's cool. I just didn't realize that Michael was your boyfriend. We can totally hang out another time. Tommy climbed out of the car and pulled the seat forward." We climbed out of the back seat and waved bye to Arturo as he drove away. Daphne walked inside and grabbed the phone in the kitchen to call Greg, I headed to my room to listen to the stereo. Daphne yelled out, "Sammy! Come here!"

I walked out to the kitchen and noticed she was covering the speaker on the phone with her hand.

"Who's on the phone Daphne?"

"Greg, of course. He wants to come over and he has to bring his cousin. Do you mind hanging out with Mig?"

"No, that's fine."

"Oh, that's great, Sammy. Thank you."

Daphne took her hand off the speaker and said, "Baby, get over here! I miss you already!" She hung up the phone and hugged me. "Now I need to touch up my makeup; they will be here in a couple of minutes." As Daphne and I walked into my room, the phone rang. I ran back to the kitchen to answer it.

When I heard "Hello Samantha." I stayed quiet, because I suddenly felt an explosion of emotions inside of me. I heard him exhale loudly into the phone before saying, "It's Julio, please speak to me Samantha." I took in a deep breath and let it out slowly.

"Why are you calling me now Julio? I haven't heard from you in a month. You obviously don't miss me anymore now that you live in California. I told you it was too far away and once you got there you would forget all about me. Now you're gone and I've learned to accept that. It took me a while, but I have come to realize that I meant nothing to you, since I haven't heard from you after you left Miami."

"Samantha, what are you talking about? I have been calling you everyday since the day I left. If you don't believe me then just ask your brother. I have been speaking to Tommy everyday until four days ago."

I was shocked and all I could think to ask was, "What happened four days ago Julio?"

"That's when Tommy told me the truth.

"What truth?

"That you don't want to speak to me anymore Samantha."

My heart and head started pounding and my mind was spinning. My own brother is sabotaging my relationship.

"Tommy told you that?"

"Yes, so I stopped calling you."

"I see, and why are you calling me now?"

"Tonight, I decided if you honestly feel that way, then I want to hear that from you not from your brother, Samantha."

Tommy walked in the door with Daisy, and he saw me holding the phone. By the look on my face, Tommy knew it was Julio on the phone. I just closed my eyes with tears streaming down my face and said, "Julio, I miss you so very much."

"I miss you too, Samantha. That's why I can't understand why you don't want to talk to me anymore."

I felt the tears drop even with my eyes closed. I took in a deep breath before saying, "Julio, just hearing your voice is making my heart ache."

"Mine too, Samantha. But if all I can do is hear your voice, then at least I have something to look forward to."

That's when reality hit me. "Julio, we have to accept that it's over between us. You live in California now and I live in Miami. I need to learn how to live without you."

"Samantha, please let us try to have at least some sort of communication. I just need to know that you and Daisy are alright."

"Then you can write to me."

"Fine, I will write to you, Samantha. We will be pen pals. That means I will expect you to write back to me."

"Of course, I will, Julio. I think this will make it easier for us to move forward in our lives instead of living for yesterday."

"Now I'm yesterday, Samantha?"

"Yes, and so am I in your world Julio. That's the way it has to be in order for us to accept what has happened and move forward."

"Samantha, I love you and that is not yesterday. It's today, tomorrow, a year, and a lifetime from now. My love for you will always exist."

"I'm the luckiest girl in the world to be loved like that by you Julio. I am also the unluckiest girl in world because I feel the same way about you."

"Then why can't we try to remain together even with the distance, Samantha?"

"We're both hurting already because of the distance Julio. It won't get better. It will only get worse."

I heard Julio's voice crack as he said, "You're right. I am hurting every day without you, and I am holding on to a relationship that is not possible anymore. I love you and I always will; but we can no longer be together because you said so. Goodbye, Samantha."

My heart felt like it had been ripped right out of my chest. I just stood in the kitchen with the phone in my hand and tears running down my face. Daphne wrapped her arms around me and let me cry on her shoulder. A minute later there was a knock at the front door, Daphne ran to answer it.

It was Greg of course. Daphne told him I just got off the phone with Julio. Next thing I know Greg was through the door with his arms wrapped around me apologizing. "Wait. What are you apologizing for Greg?"

"I'm not the one apologizing to you Sammy." Greg looked up from me, and said, "He is." I pulled away from Greg and faced my brother.

"Why did you do this Tommy?"

"Come on, Sammy. You know why. You remember what happened to me. I went away to college and my girlfriend remained here in Miami. I was faithful the entire time I was away. When school was over for Christmas break, I couldn't wait to come home so I could be with her. Only to get back here and find out she had been cheating on me the entire time. It took me a while, but I realized she's not a bad person. It's just that long-distant relationships don't work out."

"What does that have to do with me Tommy?"

"Sam, I just wanted to protect you and spare you the pain I went through. I wasted so much time on her, and for what? The inevitable breakup? I just thought with Julio gone, given enough time, you would bounce back from this."

I just stood there looking back at Tommy in disbelief and shaking my head. Finally, I asked, "What about all the calls I made to his house? Did you have something to do with those calls not getting answered?"

"No, Sam. Of course not."

"Then why didn't Julio ever answer the phone any of the times I called him?"

"Oh, I can explain that," Greg said.

"Please explain it to me then Greg," I had my arms crossed in front of me.

"Monica had the baby, and the baby cries every time the phone rings. Now they have all the ringers turned off in the house. You have to leave a message on the answering machine."

"Thank you for the explanation, Greg. I think I will go to bed now, I'm tired."

I turned around and walked into my bedroom and shut the door. I put the radio on and sat down on my bed. I opened the drawer to my nightstand and pulled out the box for my heart necklace. I took off the necklace Julio gave me and held it up in front of me. I read the words carved into the heart and felt the tears building. I kissed it once and quickly placed the necklace back into the box. I said to myself, 'That's it, no more tears.' I have made up my mind and I don't want to feel like this anymore. I placed the box now filled with my heartache back into the drawer and with it all the memories. I shut the drawer and climbed out of bed.

Just wanting the conversation, I had with Julio out of my head. Everything stopped making sense after Julio told me he's been calling me everyday; followed by Tommy admitting to blocking his calls. My head is still spinning, and I'm so frustrated.

All I know is that I don't want to feel like this anymore. I laid back in my bed and began to pay attention to the lyrics of the song playing on the stereo. The song was 'We Belong' by Pat Benatar. After a bit of crying 'Magic' by the Cars came on and I danced around my room. I was actual starting to feel better, and I just kept telling myself it was going to be alright. That I just needed to get some fresh air and enjoy the little things in life again.

I opened my bedroom door and grabbed Daisy's leash. "Come on, Daisy!" I uttered, and she came running down the hall and met me in the kitchen. I attached her leash to her collar, and we headed out the back door for a walk.

We walked down the sidewalk past the pool until I heard a loud whistle, Daisy stopped walking and looked over in the direction of the pool. Then I looked over toward the pool too. That's when I saw my brother, he was sitting down at one of the picnic tables.

Tommy yelled out, "Sam, over here!" I walked over toward the picnic tables with Daisy, Mig was sitting beside my brother.

"Hey. What's up? I asked as I approached the table. "Where's Daphne and Greg?"

"Oh, they wanted some alone time Sammy, so this gives me a chance to get to know your brother better," Mig answered.

"Would you like to have a seat with us?" Mig asked as he stood up and pulled out a chair for me beside him.

"I'm so sorry. I forgot you were coming over tonight Mig. I looked over at Tommy before saying, I received an unexpected phone call, and it was very upsetting, and again, I'm sorry."

"You have nothing to be sorry about Sammy. It's not like you cancelled out on our first date or something. You won't cancel out on our first date, will you?"

"Our first date," I said with a nervous laugh.

"Yeah, I would like to take you out on a date, Sammy."

"Wow. Thank you Mig." I looked over at my brother and he turned his head away from me. I turned my head back to Mig and smiled as I said, "I don't think I'm ready to go out on a date yet."

"I get it Sammy, and I'm not going anywhere. I live here in Miami with no plans of moving away anytime soon."

"Okay, well. Thank you for the offer Mig, but I'm not interested. So, whether you live here in Miami today, tomorrow, or the rest of your life it doesn't matter to me." I backed up my chair and stood up from the table, "Goodnight, Mig. Tommy, I will see you upstairs."

I took off with Daisy running around the back of my building toward the stairs. I stopped when I reached the staircase and saw Mig standing in front of them.

I thought to myself crap he must of took the short cut. I put on a fake smile and asked, "What do you want now, Mig?"

"Look, I'm sorry Sammy, I shouldn't have said that. I'm a total jerk, and if you don't want to ever speak to me again, I understand."

"Good, because I think you're right Mig."

"Right about what?"

"You're a jerk, Mig, and I don't want to speak to you again. You're a complete waste of time. Look how selfish you're being right now wasting my time with your fake apology."

"It's not fake. I'm really sorry that I upset you. Have a goodnight, Sammy." Mig leaned in and kissed me on the cheek before walking away.

I just stood at the foot of the staircase feeling a bit frustrated and totally confused. Then I heard Daphne and Greg walk up behind me. "Hey, how are you feeling, Sammy?"

"Your cousin's a jerk," I answered as I turned around to face Greg and Daphne, who both broke out into laughter from what I said.

Greg clapped his hands together with a huge smile before saying, "You're right, Sammy, and I'm glad you feel that way. I will take him home right now." Then he leaned down and kissed Daphne which left her smiling. "Take care of my girl Sammy, and I will see you ladies tomorrow."

"I will. Goodnight, Greg."

We both headed up the stairs behind Daisy and walked inside. "Now tell me what happened between you and Mig?"

"Your boyfriend's cousin is a real jerk. That's all."

"But why, Sammy? What did he do?"

"He asked me out on a date, and when I told him I wasn't ready for that, he told me he could wait, that he has no plans on leaving Miami anytime soon."

"Wait, that's my fault Sammy. I was at the pool and in front everyone, I told Tommy that you would still be with Julio if he didn't move away."

Daphne put her arms around me, and she hugged me tight. "Daphne, it's not your fault. Mig is just a jerk, and I'm sure he was well informed why Julio and I broke up."

"Yes, I know he was. Poor Greg has been doing everything to keep Mig away from you.

"From me?"

"Yeah. You know! Because Mig has been so hung up on you, and Julio is Greg's best friend."

"What are you talking about, Daphne?"

"Oops. Forget I said that."

"Daphne, you haven't said anything. I don't really understand what you're trying to say."

"Mig has seen you before Sammy. In fact, he used to play on the soccer team every Sunday. He saw you several times when you first got Daisy.

"Why was he looking at me?

"He just noticed you walking Daisy out by the field Sammy."

"Well that's not right.

"Why?"

"I should have been off limits since I was Julio's girlfriend."

"Actually, Mig noticed you before you were dating Julio."

"Does Julio know about this?"

"I think Greg and I are the only ones who know about this."

"Greg informed Mig that he doesn't approve of him flirting with you.

"When did Greg tell him that?"

"He told Mig tonight when we walked over to the picnic tables." Suddenly I felt embarrassed and turned my head away from Daphne. "Mig and Greg actually got into a huge argument about this and..."

"And what, Daphne?"

"Obviously, Mig doesn't care how Greg feels."

"Why would you say that?"

"Sammy, he gave up on flirting with you and just asked you out."

"Well, Greg has nothing to worry about, I'm not interested in his cousin or anybody else for that matter. I'm in love with a boy I can't see anymore. I just need to learn how to live my life without him."

"Knowing Julio, he will be calling you bright and early tomorrow morning, Sammy."

"No, he won't be calling me tomorrow Daphne. I told him not to call me anymore."

"Why did you do that Sammy?"

"Daphne, because it was so hard for me to hear Julio's voice again."

Daphne frowned before asking, "Does that mean it's really over with you and Julio?"

"Yes, because my brother's right. I need to love the memories and move forward to make new ones." She hugged me, and we both had tears in our eyes.

Tommy walked in my room and announced, "I'm making my bonging waffles in the morning if anyone is interested."

"Oh, yeah? Well, I'm making my awesome pancakes and apple juice tomorrow."

Tommy scowled at me and said, "Sam, I'm expecting Greg and Mig to show up around nine o'clock, and they will be expecting my waffles when they arrive here in the morning."

"No, they won't, Sammy. Don't listen to Tommy. Greg and Mig work tomorrow and don't get off until around six o'clock."

"You're right, Daphne. Your boyfriend does work tomorrow at 12, so he will be over here at nine o'clock to have breakfast with us before he heads off to work."

"Daphne sat up and asked, "Are you for real Tommy?"

"Yes, for real." Daphne stood up and ran over to my bedroom door and hugged my brother.

I crossed my arms over my chest and said, "Fine, then it's a cook-off tomorrow morning Tommy."

"You're on, Sam. See you in the morning. Goodnight girls."

Daphne started clapping all excited and said, "I can't believe it? Greg will be here in the morning for breakfast."

"Yup. I believe it along with his cousin Mig. A dream come true."

"Sammy, It won't be that bad; it's not like he's going to hit on you again after you called him a jerk and besides that Greg will be here."

"Yeah, right."

"Look. If it makes you feel any better, Greg and I won't leave your side. Not even for a minute. Pinkie swear."

"That would actually make me feel better. Pinkie swear. "We shook on it, pinkies locked.

"Let's get some sleep, Sammy. Greg will be over in the morning, and I want to look beautiful when he arrives."

"Daphne, do you want to sleep in the bunk beds like old times?"

"No, not really. Your bed is fine Sammy."

"Oh, come on Daphne it will be fun." I gave her my pleading puppy dog eyes.

Daphne looked annoyed and even rolled her eyes before saying, "Fine. Let's go ask Tommy to trade rooms."

We each grabbed a pillow off my bed and walked over to Tommy's room. When I knocked on Tommy's door he didn't answer. So, I knocked again, and he still didn't answer the door. "What's all that knocking about?"

"It's just me, Mom, I'm trying to get Tommy to answer his bedroom door."

"Well, he probably can't hear you with those headphones on that he's always wearing. Just walk in his room and talk to him." I raised my eyebrows in a question to Daphne. She just shrugged her shoulders with a weary look on her face.

I grabbed the knob, and on the count of three, I entered his room. Tommy was already in bed under the covers.

I saw his head bouncing around to the beat of whatever he was listening to. So, I walked over to him and tapped him on the shoulder. He jumped and was totally surprised by my intrusion.

"Tommy, sorry to bother you. I just wanted to ask you... Before I could finish my sentence, I noticed someone in bed with Tommy. Startled I jumped back and asked, "Who is that?" Tommy had a smirk on his face and that's when I also took another look and realized it was a blow-up doll.

"Tommy, why do you have this?" I grabbed the arm of the doll.

He snatched her arm away from me and yelled, "Don't touch, Tracy!"

"You named your doll Tracy?"

"No, that was already her name."

"Okay, fine. Whatever. Why do you have Tracy?"

"She keeps me company, and I won her the other night when I attended the bachelor party at Alex's apartment."

"Oh, wow. I forgot about the wedding, Tommy." I sat down on the foot of his bed as I held my head that was pounding again.

Tommy sat up and said, "Well, it's in two weeks, and we're still going to California to attend the wedding, right Sam?"

"Yeah, of course. Why would you ask me that, Tommy?"

"Because I know how hard it will be for you to see Julio again. "

"Tommy, I have no choice. I promised Mom, and she's looking forward to it."

"Mom and I will be there for support, and it's going to be a lot of fun."

I looked up at Tommy and he was smiling and wiggling his eyebrows up and down as he said, "California babes. I can't wait."

"Does that mean you won't be bringing Tracy as your date?"

"Very funny, Sam."

"I'm going to bed now," Daphne said from the doorway. "I need my beauty sleep if I want to look good for Greg in the morning."

"Okay, I'm coming with you Daphne." Tommy hugged me and said, "Everything is going to be alright Sam. Just go get some sleep, and we can talk about it again tomorrow."

As I stood up to leave, I looked back at Tommy and told him, "Don't get too touchy-feely with Tracy. You might pop her."

I took off running toward the door when Tommy yelled out, "Don't forget your pillow Sam," then I felt a pillow hit me in the back. I stopped running and bent down to pick up my pillow as another pillow hit me. I grabbed both pillows off the floor and took off running out of his room.

When I arrived back in my room, Daphne said, "A blow-up doll? Really? Your brother's nuts. I was just getting over the whole sock thing from earlier, and now it's a blow-up doll."

"Yup, that's Tommy. Now thanks to him I have an extra pillow to sleep with tonight."

"How did you get an extra pillow Sammy?"

"How do think? Tommy threw it at me of course."

"I love when your brother's home."

"Me too."

After we climbed into bed Daphne asked, "What exactly happened with you and Julio tonight on the phone?"

"Daphne, I don't even know where to begin."

"Start from the beginning."

"Okay, here it goes. Did you know that Tommy arrived home the same day after Julio left?"

"Yes. That afternoon I remember. That's when you were at your worst with no sleep and you had been crying the whole day non-stop."

"Yeah, it was just the worst day ever and that's when my brother decided to block all of Julio's call's."

"Are you mad at Tommy?"

"Truthfully, I was at first."

"If I was you, I would be mad too. At least now I understand why Tommy apologized to you in the kitchen. Come to think of it, I think my brothers would have done the same thing Sammy. Tommy wasn't trying to harm you, he just wanted to protect his little sister."

"I love my brother. He's awesome and has a big heart. I know he's really protective of me and that's why I'm able to forgive him."

"Well, I'm tired, Sammy. Let's get some sleep." I turned off the lights and Daphne was asleep within minutes. I wasn't so lucky, my mind kept running non-stop. I just kept thinking about the conversation I had with my mom about three weeks ago. Pilar is my mom's best friend and she's also Julio's mother. She called my mom a week after she moved up to California. She said her brother Juan just took the whole family out to dinner, and her brother introduced everyone to his fiancée.

Nobody even knew he had a girlfriend, so to find out he was engaged and getting married was a shock to everyone. My mom received a wedding invitation along with three plane tickets just a few days after she spoke to Pilar. I was upset when my mom first told me about the wedding in Anaheim. I told her that I hate that place because Julio has to live there instead of Miami. My mom hasn't mentioned the wedding to me since that day.

Now my mind jumped back to the conversation I had with Julio over the phone tonight. That's when the tears arrived, and I quietly cried myself to sleep.

Chapter 2 Tracy and Mig

I woke up to the feeling of water sprayed on my face and the sound of Tonya and Daphne giggling. "Oh, come on! Stop it!" I yelled and tossed a pillow at both of them.

"You better get up then, Muñeca, before this becomes a waterbed."

"Okay, Tonya. I'm up. Now stop spraying me with that squirt gun."

I sat up, and Daphne and Tonya jumped up onto my bed and they both hugged me. "Get off of me. Why are you both hugging me?"

"Muñeca, your eyes are pink and puffy again."

"Yeah, which means you have been crying again, Sammy," Daphne said with a frown.

"I'm okay. It was only a little bit when I was trying to fall asleep. I was overtired, and my eyes watered up."

Daphne and Tonya looked at one another with their eyebrows raised showing they didn't believe me. "Okay. I just didn't want to talk about it now. I was overtired last night and had a hard time falling asleep. The phone call, and everything we said to one another was hard on me. I'm alright now, and we need to make breakfast."

"What phone call?"

"You missed it Tonya, Julio called.

"He did?"

"Yes, he called last night and basically Sammy told him not to call her anymore."

"Muñeca, I don't understand you. I thought you were upset because he hadn't called you in a month. Now when he finally calls, you tell him not to call you anymore."

I climbed out of my bed and grabbed my bathrobe off the hook on my closet door. "I'm going to take a shower. Can you braid my hair when I get back, Daphne?"

"Sure, Sammy. I can do that. Oh, and about breakfast —"

"What about breakfast, Daphne?"

"Oh, never mind."

"No, just tell her. We don't need to make breakfast anymore because Tommy made it."

"Well, I don't have to say anything now. Since you just said everything Tonya."

"Sorry, Sammy. I know you wanted us to make breakfast."

"That's no big deal, Daphne. Tommy makes bonging waffles.

I'm going to take a shower now. I'll be back in a few minutes."

"Good, while your taking a shower Daphne can tell me what happened between you and Julio last night."

"Nothing happened Tonya, because he lives in Anaheim.

"Whatever Muñeca, you know what I mean."

"We all know what you your saying Tonya, and I will tell you everything." As Daphne began to tell Tonya about the phone call. I rolled my eyes and headed out my bedroom door for the bathroom.

Until I noticed my brother in the kitchen with a spatula in his hand. Tommy looked over at me and said, "Hurry up, and get ready Sam. Breakfast is almost ready."

"Will Tracy be joining us for breakfast Tommy?"

"No, unfortunately, she popped last night."

I started to laugh, and Daphne was apparently behind me, because I heard her cracking up. "Hey, it's not what you girls think. I fell asleep, and I must have rolled over onto her because when I woke up, she was flat beside me."

"What are you all talking about?"

"Oh, Tommy's girl Tracy apparently popped last night," Daphne said.

"What?"

"Oh, it's nothing, Tonya. I'm going to take a shower now, and I will explain it to you when I get out."

"Yeah, go take a shower already, and I will tell Tonya about Tracy and Julio."

"Oh, that's great. Thanks so much, Daphne.

"Hey, I know sarcasm when I hear it Sammy."

Yeah, I'm sure you hear it a lot Daphne. See you in a few minutes."

My brother was still blushing when I left the kitchen and headed for the bathroom. I could hear him telling Daphne that she really didn't have to tell Tonya about Tracy.

After I was out of the shower and back in my room, Daphne came in a few minutes later. She was laughing when she announced, "Tracy's back."

"Daphne, what do you mean she's back?"

"She didn't pop; she just deflated. The valve to the blow-up doll must have popped open. Tonya and I took turns, and we blew her back up and left her tucked in under the covers on your brother's bed."

"You haven't told Tommy yet?"

"No, we haven't told him anything."

"I think that we should invite her to breakfast." We both started laughing, and Tonya walked in and asked, "What's so funny?" I told her we're inviting Tracy to breakfast, and she loved the idea.

A few minutes later Tommy called out, "Girls, breakfast is ready, and don't forget Mig and his cousin will be here any minute."

"I knew it!"

"Knew what, Muñeca?"

"I yelled out, "Tonya, my brother only invited them over to annoy me."

Then Tommy yelled out, "What was that, Sam? You can't wait to see Mig again?" I could hear my brother laughing to himself in the kitchen.

"Tonya shook her head and I asked, "Do you see what he's doing?"

"Yeah, I think he's playing matchmaker Muñeca." I nodded my head yes, and Tonya shook her head and rolled her eyes.

"But Greg is coming too," Daphne said sounding as if she was about to cry.

"Daphne, your boyfriend doesn't annoy me; he's awesome. His cousin Mig is a bit of a jerk, and he's totally annoying."

"That's only because he likes you, Sammy."

"Whatever. It doesn't matter; it's time to get even with Tommy. Tracy's coming to breakfast."

"I'm in. What do you want me to do, Muñeca?"

"Tonya, go in the kitchen and keep Tommy distracted. I will grab Tracy from his room and have her in the seat at the far end of the table, so he won't see her from the kitchen."

"What about your mom? You can't have a blow-up doll sitting at the breakfast table. She will totally freak out, Sammy."

"Geez. You're right, Daphne. Oh, I got it. Get a breakfast tray set up, and we will bring her breakfast in bed."

"That's perfect. She loves that, and I can get started on that right now." Daphne opened my bedroom door and headed straight into the kitchen.

Tonya followed behind Daphne and went into the kitchen and started talking to Tommy.

I walked over to Tommy's room and very slowly opened the door, so it wouldn't make its usual loud squeak.

Once I was inside Tommy's room, I pulled down the covers and grabbed Tracy. I opened the bedroom door just a little and took a peek. I checked to see if the coast was all clear before heading out the door with Tracy. I could hear Tonya talking to Tommy in the kitchen.

When I was almost in the dining room, I heard Tommy ask, "Can you watch this for a minute? I need to go to the bathroom."

That's when I sprinted to the living room and left Tracy behind the main sofa on the floor. I walked over to the kitchen and helped Daphne prepare a breakfast tray for my mom. Tonya was on waffle duty while Tommy was using the bathroom. Once the tray was ready, we headed down the hall.

Tommy walked out of the bathroom as we were walking into my mom's room. "Hey, Mom! I made you breakfast!" Tommy said rather loudly from behind us.

"Oh, what a wonderful surprise. You kids are spoiling me."

"Here you go, Ms. Harris," Daphne placed the tray down on the coffee table. "I made the apple juice, and Tommy made the coffee and the waffle."

"Thank you. Everything looks delicious. I appreciate it."

"Okay. Well if you need anything else, Mom, just call us. We are at your beck and call, right, Daphne?"

"That's right, Sammy." My mom just smiled and reminded me to walk Daisy.

"Oh, definitely. I will make sure to take her outside right after breakfast, Mom."

"No, you need to take her outside now before you sit down to have breakfast."

"You got it. I'm taking her outside right now, Mom."

I left my mom's room and walked into the kitchen and grabbed Daisy's leash. As soon as she heard the jingle of her leash, she was at the back door waiting for me to go outside.

As I attached the leash onto Daisy's collar, Daphne asked, "What about Tracy?"

"I don't know. I forgot all about taking Daisy for a walk. Right now, she is behind the sofa in the living room."

I walked out the door and down the stairs. I met up with Mig and Greg on the staircase. "Good morning, Sammy," Mig said with a big smile that revealed the dimple on his left cheek. As soon as I saw them, I thought crap, after all that. I won't be able to get even with my brother after all. "So, I guess you're still upset with me."

"What?"

"Well, I said good morning to you, and you didn't respond. I'm guessing you're still mad at me."

"Oh no! I'm sorry, my mind was on something else. Good morning Mig and of course Greg. Go ahead on upstairs. My brother and Daphne have been waiting for you."

"Wait. Aren't you joining us?"

"Yes, in a little bit after I walk Daisy."

"Come on, Daisy. Let's go," I said, and we headed on down the stairs. I heard footsteps behind me. Then all of a sudden, they stopped, when I heard Greg grunt. It actually sounded more like a growl. I tried not to laugh as I continued on down the stairs and walked over to a big patch of grass.

After a few minutes, I headed back upstairs, and took the leash off Daisy and washed my hands. I asked Tommy and Tonya how I could help. Tommy asked me to set the table, and Tonya smiled. I headed to the cabinet and grabbed the plates, and I noticed Daphne was already grabbing the silverware from the drawer beside me.

Daphne and I headed into the dining room area together. I had to take a step back and cover my mouth to hold in the laughter. Sitting at the head of the table was Tracy. She had her big red lips, blonde hair, blue eyes, and was wearing my blue sundress with the spaghetti straps. "So, what do you think of our breakfast guest?"

I just tried to contain my laughter and kept my mouth covered with the palm of my hand. I could see Greg and Mig sitting down watching TV in the living room. Greg looked over at us and just shook his head smiling.

Daphne was walking around the table setting out the silverware and napkins in front of each seat when she looked up at me and whispered, "So, she had to borrow a dress from you. I hope you don't mind. It was that or naked Tracy at breakfast."

"What happened to the black cocktail dress she had on?

"That dress is way to flashy for breakfast, Sammy."

Just when I think I've heard it all Daphne goes and says something like that. It was so unexpected that I couldn't help it I started laughing. Daphne ran over to me in a panic and whispered, "Stop laughing before Tommy hears you."

That's when we heard Tommy tell Tonya to grab the plate of waffles out of the oven drawer. Daphne and I ran back into the kitchen. I grabbed the juice glasses, while Daphne grabbed the pitcher of apple juice out from the fridge.

"Hey, Tommy. Do you need help with anything else?"

"Nope. That should do it Sam; just get everyone to sit down at the table, and I will be out in a second with the butter and syrup."

"Sounds good. I can't wait to eat; I'm starving," Daphne and Tonya just raised their eyebrows at me. I nodded my head toward the dining room, and we all headed out to the table to have a seat.

Greg and Mig stood up from the sofa and joined us at the table.

We were all smiling at one another while we waited for Tommy to join us.

When he finally walked in, he just placed the syrup and butter down on table. He didn't even notice Tracy, until he leaned over to reach for the pitcher of apple juice. He jumped and snatched his arm back as he yelled, "What the heck?"

We all broke out laughing and Greg asked, "Is that Tracy?"

"Greg, how do you know Tracy?"

"Daphne, she was at the bachelor party Alex threw for his uncle. Tracy ended up becoming the biggest prize given away at the party. It was the joke of the night that she was the only girl invited to the party."

"Greg, who named her Tracy?"

"I don't know Sammy. That was what we were told her name was when we all took turns introducing ourselves to her."

"Well, actually we all had to take turns using the best pick-up line on Tracy, and I had the best pick-up line, so I won Tracy," my brother explained proudly.

"Dude," Greg said shaking his head.

"Wow. I've heard your pick-up lines, Tommy, and they are pretty bad. If you were the winner, then I can only imagine how awful the other guys' pick-up lines were.

"Gee, thanks Daphne."

Everyone started laughing including Greg, who was looking relieved that Daphne wasn't mad.

"Laugh, it's good for the soul. Besides, I get girls with those lines every day of the week."

"That's right Tommy, and don't forget you won your best girl Tracy with those pick-up lines, so you know they work." Daphne had all of us laughing with her crazy come backs to Tommy.

"Who all went to the bachelor party, and why was it held in Miami instead of California?"

"Well Tonya, all I know is that Alex wanted to throw his uncle Juan a party. Alex couldn't get any more time off from work. He's already taking five days off from work to attend the wedding. He called his other uncle Guillermo and told him he wanted to have the party in Miami. The following day both of his uncles and Eddie came down here from California to have the party here."

"Yeah, but who all went to the party Greg?"

"Your brother didn't tell you anything about the party Sammy?"

I looked up at Tommy and he said, "No, I only told her Julio wasn't there."

That's true he wasn't at the party. Alex invited a few of his uncles' friends that live here. He invited your brother Tommy, my cousin, and me. Julio and Lewis weren't allowed to come. His uncle Guillermo didn't know how grown up the bachelor party would be. When the party was nearly over, his uncle Guillermo told me he regrets that he left Lewis and Julio behind. That's when he invited me to stay at his house, so I could attend the wedding in California. I have to admit the party was a lot of fun, and I can't wait for the wedding."

"I think that the way the party started off from the very beginning is what made it so much fun. Everyone was laughing the entire night. You put Alex and Eddie together, and you know you're in for a great time."

"Why? What happened in the beginning, Greg?"

Sammy, the minute we arrived at the apartment, Mr. Sanchez kept asking for Alex. Eddie told his dad that Alex went to pick up his cake. His father kept saying, 'This is not a birthday party. Who has a cake at a bachelor party?"

"That's when the striptease music came on, and everyone began to look uncomfortable. Eddie takes off and comes back less than a minute later pushing this huge cake on wheels that gets stuck. Eddie shoves this cake as hard as he can, and it goes flying like a runaway car across the tiles straight into the living room. Everyone runs out of the way except for his father Juan. He stood there frozen like a deer in headlights. I ran in front of the cake and stopped it from crushing him. As soon as it stopped, Alex popped out of the cake and kissed me on the cheek yelling, 'My hero! Mr. Goalkeeper!' with this high-pitched, girl type voice. He sounded nothing like a girl."

"That's what made it so funny," Tommy said, laughing.

Greg laughed too and said, "That's nothing girls! Alex climbed out of the cake wearing a short red dress and heels. He had his uncle Juan sit down in a chair that was placed in the middle of the room.

Then the striptease music was turned up and that's when Eddie comes walking back out wearing a short black dress and heels too. Together Alex and Eddie performed this mock strip tease for Mr. Sanchez. They had everybody laughing the entire time.

"I can't even imagine Eddie and Alex wearing a dress. First of all, they are way too masculine to be wearing a dress and heels."

"Your right Tonya," Greg added, "and I can't agree with you more."

"Well I think the highlight of that moment was when Eddie slipped during the strip tease, and he grabbed onto Alex for support. They both lost their footing in those heels and ended up on the floor together."

"Oh, yeah. That's right, Tommy. That was so funny," Greg said while trying to contain his laughter.

"I'm telling you; it was the best party I have ever been to. We had so much fun, and I can't believe the wedding is in a couple of weeks!"

"I didn't even know you were going to the wedding, Greg."

"Yeah, I'm definitely going Sammy, and so is everyone who attended the bachelor party. Or at least they were invited to attend the wedding. The wedding is in California, so who knows for sure if anyone else will go?"

"We are going for sure. My mom already has our plane tickets, and we're leaving on Wednesday and staying at Pilar's brother's house.

"Tommy, are you serious? You're staying at his uncle Guillermo's house?"

"Yeah, Guillermo's house."

Greg jumped up out of his chair and said, "That's where I'm staying too." They each high-fived one another and Greg sat back down. "That's the uncle who owns all of those businesses in California. That guy is really nice, and he was so happy to be in Miami. He said it was his first time here."

"Yeah, he was pretty cool," Mig said. At that moment when Mig spoke, I realized Mig was the cousin that was invited to the bachelor party. That meant he might be attending the wedding to, and that was freaking me out.

I jumped up from my seat with a fake smile on my face and leaned over the table and grabbed my plate. "Where are you going, Sam?"

"I'm just going to clean up the kitchen. Thank you for breakfast, Tommy. It was great."

"Really, Sam? Because you haven't touched your waffle." I looked down at my plate and saw the untouched waffle.

"Sorry, I just don't have much of an appetite this morning, but I appreciate you making breakfast for everyone especially Mom."

"You're welcome, thank you for inviting Tracy to breakfast."

"Well, I didn't think you'd mind since you thought she was popped earlier."

"Yeah, that's right. How did you fix her Sam?"

"Tommy, I didn't fix her. Daphne and Tonya did," and they both started to laugh. Tommy looked horrified and I walked into the kitchen.

I broke off a triangle piece of the waffle and handed it to Daisy. She smelled the waffle and stuck her nose up in the air and walked away from me. "Sorry, they're not beef chunks Daisy!"

I threw the waffle piece in the trash along with the rest of the waffle that was on my plate. I washed my plate and the silverware and placed everything in the dish rack. I headed for the counter, and I sprayed and wiped down the waffle plates and put the machine away now that it had cooled down.

I walked into my mom's room and grabbed her breakfast tray.

My mom was on the phone when I walked in. I was about to head out the door when I heard my mom say, "Okay, Julio. I will let her know." Then she appeared to be on the phone with Pilar by the sound of the conversation.

My mom was talking about what she intended to wear at the wedding. I headed back out her bedroom door and into the kitchen with the breakfast tray.

When I entered the kitchen, Mig was in there rinsing a plate. As I walked up closer, I saw the whole sink was filled with plates. "What are you doing in here Mig?"

"I'm washing the plates from breakfast. It's the least I can do since I made you so upset yesterday that today you can't even stand to hear my voice."

"What are you talking about?"

"Sammy, I noticed you left the table the moment I began to speak. You hadn't even taken a bite of your food. It doesn't take an expert to realize how much you dislike me."

"It's not that, and I'm sorry that I made you feel that way Mig. Honestly that was not my intention. Although I didn't like the way you mentioned last night how you have no plans to leave Miami. It was kind of a low blow, and you know that."

"Mig turned around and faced me. He took in a deep breath and told me, "Honestly, I didn't mean it to sound the way it did. I just figured you would be hesitant to date anyone unless you knew they weren't going anywhere."

I sucked in my lower lip and walked up to the sink. I grabbed a sponge and began to scrub a dish in the sink while saying, "Although I appreciate your honesty, I'm just not interested. I have a lot to deal with at the moment."

"Mig grabbed a towel and began drying the dishes. We both remained silent for a minute, until Mig asked, "Are you looking forward to your first year in high school Sammy?"

I kept my face down focused on the dish I was rinsing off. I set the dish down in the dish rack before turning around to face him. He smiled at me as he handed me a dish towel to dry off my hands. I smiled back at him and said, "Yes, I am.

Mig laughed and asked, "Are you sure about that Sammy? The look on your face says otherwise."

That's when I rolled my eyes and admitted to Mig before anyone else the truth. "I'm actually feeling a bit nervous about attending High School." Mig shook his head and smiled at me.

I thought that was the end of our conversation, but then he asked, "Why?" I grabbed the bottle of 409 from under the sink and sprayed the kitchen counters. As I began to wipe down the counters, I told Mig why I felt so nervous. How last year, I had Julio to lean on most of the year that I was in school. This year it's just me in a new school.

Mig leaned back against the sink and placed his right hand up on the counter. He was facing me when he asked, "What about the two years before you were with Julio?

"How did you get through them? Who did you lean on?"

That's when I stopped wiping the stove and faced him again. I thought about what he said and just blurted out, "I had all my friends to lean on."

"Will any of your friends be attending high school with you Sammy?"

"Almost all of them will be attending the same school with me. I never even realized that before. Thank you Mig."

"Yeah, well it sounds like you have nothing to worry about Sammy. You'll be just fine." He leaned in and kissed me on the cheek before saying, "You're welcome." When I looked up at him, he smiled and added, "We make a great team. The dishes are all done. Now I'm going to the pool. My cousin and Daphne should be supervised at all times. Will I see you down there?"

"Maybe."

"Well, I hope you will join us at the pool. I really enjoy your company."

"Wow, I guess you're not that big of a jerk after all."

He smiled at me with the dimple appearing in his left cheek. "I will take that as a compliment, Sammy. Thank you."

"You should, and you're welcome." He kissed me on the cheek again and walked out the back door.

Just after Mig left, my mom walked in the kitchen. She poured herself another cup of coffee and said, "I thought you left to the pool."

"Everyone else did, Mom."

"Then what are you still doing here? It's summer. Don't you think it's time to get outside and enjoy what's left of it?"

"You're right, Mom. When I get back, can we discuss the trip to California?"

"Of course, we can. I was waiting for you to bring it up again, Sam." She was grinning as she took a sip of her coffee.

"Great. I have lots of questions, and I want to know everything."

"When you get back from the pool, Carmen will be here. That will be the perfect time for us to talk about the trip,"

"Is Carmen attending the wedding too?"

"Yes, and so is Daphne unless she has decided not to go."

"She didn't even tell me she was going, and that's really weird. Daphne would have mentioned it, Mom. At least once this morning especially when Greg said he was going to the wedding."

"Sam, in that case, don't mention the trip to Daphne. I have a feeling that Carmen has not told Daphne yet. If that's the case, I'm sure she has a very good reason for that."

All I could do was agree with my mom. I ran into my room and put on my bathing suit and grabbed a towel out of the linen closet. Then I yelled, "Bye, Mom!" and walked out the door.

When I arrived at the pool, nobody was in it. Then I heard Tommy say, "Over here, Sam." That's when I looked behind me and saw everyone seated around a picnic table.

I walked over to the table and said, "I thought everyone was going to the pool."

"No, not today Sammy. We have to be at work in an hour."

Daphne was sitting in her chair pouting. Greg put his arm around Daphne and told her, "I promise to make it up to you. I will take you to this really cool swimming pool. It's all made out of limestone."

"You promise, Greg?"

"Yes, Daphne. I promise we'll go before summer is over."

"Where is that?" I asked.

"It's in Coral Gables, and the pool has a cave, a beach, and this giant ledge you can jump off of. The water is very invigorating because it's spring water. You girls will love it. Truthfully, I have been wanting to take you there for some time now, Daphne."

"Oh, Greg. I can't wait to go there. I have heard of that pool before, but I have never been there. When are you going to take me there?"

"Most likely when I get back from California."

"How long will you be gone?"

"I will only be gone for three days. I leave Friday morning, and I will be back Monday morning. I have to work the early shift, so I plan to sleep on the plane. When I get off work, we can spend the rest of the day together."

"You promise?"

"Yes."

"What about you, Mig? Are you going to the wedding?"

"No, I can't afford it right now Sammy."

"Too bad. More California babes for me," Tommy replied, and we all began to laugh.

Mig looked down at his beeper, then stood up. "Thank you for having us over for breakfast."

Greg and Daphne stood up, and they hugged one another.

Daphne took hold of Greg's hand and said, "I'll be right back, Sammy. I need to walk with Greg to the van."

"We'll be here, Daphne." I looked over at Tommy and asked, "Where's Tonya?"

"She went back home, Sam."

"Why?"

"She said something about some guy coming over, and she had to get ready."

"Is this a guy she's dating?"

"I don't know, Sam. You need to ask her about that. I don't care about that kind of stuff."

"I know. Tommy it's just that sometimes she tells you things that she doesn't tell me or anybody else for that matter."

"Yeah, I don't understand why Tonya does that."

"Yes, you do, and I know that you like that bond you have with her."

"Yeah, I guess she is like family, you know. She practically grew up in our house. Tonya reminds me of that cat we once had. Do you remember him?"

"What cat? We haven't ever owned a cat, Tommy."

"Exactly. He wasn't actually our cat. Yet the cat came and went as if he lived with us. I'm talking about the orange cat that lived outside. When we were little kids, it would come to our door every morning and cry. Mom and Dad would let the cat inside. It would eat, then sleep all day. Once it was dark outside, the cat would wake up, go in the kitchen, and get something to eat. Then it would cry at the door until it was let back outside."

"Tommy, I do remember that cat."

"Yeah, well. Tonya reminds me of that cat." I just nodded my head yes and laughed so much that I had tears filling my eyes.

We saw Mig's van pulling out of the complex about a minute later. We waved bye as Mig drove past us. Daphne joined us back at the picnic table about five minutes later. Daphne sat down and announced, "My mom's here now."

"Oh, that's right. I almost forgot. We need to head back upstairs and talk to Mom about the trip to California, Tommy."

Tommy and I stood up, but Daphne remained seated. "Daphne, come on. We have to go now. I really need to speak to my mom."

"Go Sammy. I will be here. Just come and get me after you're done."

"Aren't you coming with us?"

"What's the point? Greg will be gone, and you will be gone, Sammy. That weekend is really going to suck for me. I'm having a selfish moment. Sorry. I will be fine if you give me a few minutes."

"Okay. Then just come upstairs when you feel up to it, Daphne." Just as I said that, we heard a car pull into the parking lot. The tires were squealing, and the music was blaring. The car was a white Camaro Z28, and it stopped in front of Tonya's building.

Tonya ran to the car, and a tall skinny guy got out of the car and greeted Tonya with a kiss on the lips. Then Tonya jumped in the car, and they left the complex with the tires squealing as he peeled out.

I looked at Daphne and Tommy, and they both looked back at me. We were all shaking our heads. "You know what, Sammy? Let's go talk about this wedding." Daphne stood up, and we walked back upstairs.

"Any minute now Sam, and I'm just waiting for him to call me or knock on the door. I beeped him just now, and Maria has his beeper. She told me he will be home soon, and she will have him stop by or call me back."

"Tommy, do you know where Alex will be staying?"

"Yes, as a matter of fact I do Sam. He will be staying at his mother's house. Alex has his own room at his mom's house. This will be the first time he gets to see it. Pilar is still hoping that Alex will come home to live with her."

"Tommy what do you need to talk to Alex about?"

Tommy rolled his eyes and answered, "It's guy stuff, Daphne."

"Yeah right, he wants to know about girls and who his cousins can introduce him to. That's my brother's whole world of wonder in a nutshell, Daphne."

"Let's go call Denise and see if she is up for going to the movies or hanging out at the mall, Sammy."

"Or you girls can just go to the mall with us now. We can shop for the dress you'll need to wear at the wedding and grab some lunch."

I turned around and saw Carmen standing behind us. "You know, Mom. That sounds great, what do you say Sammy?"

"Just let me get my shoes on Daphne." I ran into my bedroom and kicked off my chancletas. I grabbed my purse, sneakers, and my beeper. I met up with everyone back in the kitchen.

At the mall, we tried on tons of dresses and jumpers with jackets until we found the right two outfits. It was already time for dinner, and we were hungry. We had dinner at one of my mom's favorite restaurants in the mall. It has an awesome salad bar, and that's all I want. During the meal, my mom and Carmen began talking about the trip. Carmen asked me about Julio, and she wanted to know if I was excited to see him. I have to admit after that conversation, I was officially ready to go home. Carmen dropped us off after dinner.

My brother was sitting in the living room with Alex beside him when we walked inside.

"Hey, guys. How is everything going?"

"Good. I heard you finally spoke with my brother, Sammy." I took a deep breath and let it out slowly before I answered Alex.

"Yeah, I did," and I looked down toward the floor. I could feel the floodgates of my eyes getting ready.

"How was that conversation?"

"Truthfully, Alex, it was terrible. I felt instant heartache the minute I heard Julio's voice. It made me realize that I can't stand how much I miss him."

"Sammy, I'm sorry."

"Don't worry about it. We have agreed to become pen pals now."

"Wait. What? I'm sorry?"

I took in another deep breath and put on a fake smile, when I said, "We have agreed to become pen pals. Your brother will write to me and I will write back to him. This will help us to move forward in our new lives and still keep in touch."

"So, what's the plan when you see each other in two weeks?"

I stayed quiet for a minute; Alex and Tommy were staring at me just waiting for me to respond. I felt my cheeks warming up, and I turned my head and saw my reflection on the oven door. I had a sheepish grin and bright pink cheeks. I turned my head back to Alex and answered, "Truthfully, I don't know yet."

"Oh, this trip is going to be something else," Alex said grinning as his leg started bouncing up and down, and my brother was laughing.

"Is Maria going to the wedding?"

"No," Alex replied, with a look of disappointment.

"That's too bad, I was looking forward to hanging out with her."

"Sammy, I will definitely tell Maria that tonight."

"Thanks Alex. See you later. I'm going to my room to hang out with Daphne."

When I walked into my room, Daphne was already on the phone. "Why are you using that phone? It doesn't even work properly."

"Your phone works fine Sammy, if all you need to do is beep somebody."

"You know you're right. That's why I still have that phone plugged into the wall."

"I just beeped Greg, so he could pick us up, and we can all go out tonight."

"Daphne, you can go wherever you want. I already told you; I'm not going to the Bonfire."

"Nobody's going to the Bonfire tonight. It's raining."

"No, it's not." I looked out my bedroom window, and she was right. It was actually pouring outside. "Wow. We arrived home at the perfect time before it started to rain."

"Okay, great. Daphne, so no more talk about the Bonfire. Tell me where you want to go."

"I don't know. I thought I would leave that up for Greg to decide."

"As long as it's indoors, I'll go."

"Really, Sammy?"

"Yes." Daphne gave me a big hug, then ran out to the kitchen to use the phone. When Daphne came back in my room over five minutes later, she said that she just got off the phone with Greg. He's leaving work now, and he is on his way to pick us up.

I walked into my mom's room and asked if I could go out with Daphne. I told her Greg would pick us up if I could go. "That's fine, Sam, as long as you bring your beeper, and your back home by 11 o'clock." I gave my mom a hug and left her room.

Mig's van was already downstairs when I opened the door. Daphne and I quickly walked downstairs, and I opened my umbrella before we walked out into the rain.

When we arrived at the van, Mig slid the side door open, and he jumped out. He grabbed the umbrella from me, and he held it over Daphne and me. He helped us into the van and climbed inside behind us. He tossed my wet umbrella into a rubber boot, and he took his seat behind the steering wheel.

I thought to myself what a genius idea to throw the wet umbrella into the rubber boot. It was out of the way and kept everything dry in the van. Then I thought, who was the owner of the rubber boot? Did he have stinky, sweaty feet, or worse Athlete's foot?

Should I even touch the umbrella again? Could I get Athlete's foot on my hand? I started to giggle out loud with all of these amusing thoughts plaguing my brain.

That's when I found out Mig was a mind reader. "Sammy, don't worry about the rubber boot. It's not contaminated or anything. I just keep the boot in the van to hold my umbrella. It's actually the perfect place to store a wet umbrella."

I agreed with him and asked him if he ever wore the boot. He told me that he never had the chance. He lost the right boot a week after he purchased them.

"Well, maybe you should patent the idea and sell rubber boots as umbrella stands for automobiles around the world."

He laughed before saying, "I was about to throw the boot away until it started raining just about every day again."

"Can you tell me where we're going Mig?"

"I don't know Sammy, but I'm up for suggestions."

Daphne asked, "How about the arcade?!"

"Baby, I can't be spending money right now. I need to save everything for this trip to California. Remember, I will need money when I'm up there, and I will be short a day's pay when I get back."

"I know, Greg. I forgot. I'm sorry, and I don't have my allowance until next week."

Mig announced that he wanted to buy a box of hot chocolate and some whipped cream. Then go back to his house and watch a movie. Daphne stayed quiet and looked at me with her pleading eyes. I eventually smiled and said, "That sounds perfect, Mig."

Daphne clapped her hands together and she was smiling from ear to ear.

We stopped at the store before arriving at Mig's house. We didn't walk into his house through the front door. Instead Mig unlocked a wooden gate.

This allowed us access to the side of the house. There was a little porch in front of a white wood door. When we approached the door a porch light turned on just above the door. Mig unlocked the door, and we all walked inside.

It was a little studio apartment. Everything was so nicely set up with a wall unit on the main wall made of black Formica. It held a stereo, TV, and VCR. There was a sofa at the foot of his bed. It faced the wall unit along with two bean bag chairs. There was a little coffee table in front of the sofa, and everything was in black Formica with gold trim. Even the couch was covered in black fabric with gold trim. The floor had all white tiles, and a large area rug on the floor in front of the wall unit and sofa, which really made the area feel more like a separate space, and I loved the area rug. It was in a herringbone pattern in the colors of aqua blue and black.

I just kept thinking, Wow! This place is better than my brother's dorm room. I was impressed with how clean everything was and that a boy lived here. "Do you want to help me in the kitchen, Sammy?"

"Sure, Mig. Where is it?"

"On the back wall over here." I followed Mig past the living room area to the back of the room. On the back wall, there was a kitchenette. It consisted of some kitchen cabinets in white Formica. There were blue tiles on the backsplash and countertop. He had a white mini fridge, sink, coffee maker, and a mini stove.

"So, what do think, Sammy?"

"I think your place is amazing. You're 16 years old, and you have your own apartment."

"I meant about the hot chocolate. Should I use milk or water?" I turned to face Mig and saw him holding up a gallon of milk.

"Oh," I said blushing, and started to giggle. It was definitely my nerves, and I was totally embarrassed.

"I'm sorry, Sammy. I didn't mean to make you feel uncomfortable."

"It's not you – at least not this time," I replied with a smile.

Mig set the milk down on the counter, and he turned around and faced me. He placed his left hand on the counter, then his right hand up on the counter, leaving me standing in the middle of his arms staring up at him. "Then what is it, Sammy?"

I swallowed once, and I looked down at his waist until I found the courage to look up into his eyes and answered, "I have never been inside a boy's apartment before."

Mig smiled and said, "Follow me." He took me over to an area beside the kitchen that had a throw rug on the floor and sliding glass doors.

"These doors here lead to the main house, Sammy. That's where my parents are now. If it makes you feel better, I can slide the door open. I can even invite my parents to come in and hang out with us if that's what you need."

"Mig, can you just leave the sliding glass door open?"

"I can do that Sammy."

"Great, I think that should be good enough."

We walked back over to the kitchen area. Mig kept his eyes on me the whole time as he called out, "Now who's ready for some hot chocolate?"

Daphne answered, "We are, and we're ready to watch the movie too."

"Two hot chocolates coming up and give me another 10 minutes for the movie."

"Do you want to have a seat?" Mig pointed to the little round bistro table with two chairs that was off to the side in the kitchen area. "My microwave is very small and only holds two coffee mugs at a time."

We both sat down and discussed his music and playing in a band at the Bonfire. He told me how the Bonfire was preparing his band to play in front of crowds of people. They eventually want to play at real gigs where they will get paid to perform.

I suddenly felt my beeper vibrate. When I looked to see who was beeping me, I noticed that it was almost 11o'clock, which was my curfew. I looked back at Mig and said "I have to go. Can you drive me home now?"

"Is everything alright, Sammy? Did I say something to upset you?"

"No, nothing. I've really enjoyed hanging out with you. It's my curfew; I need to be home by 11 o'clock."

I rode in the passenger's seat in the van on the way home. "Mig, the time just flew by tonight. Thank you for inviting me over to your place. I really enjoyed getting to know you better and your hot chocolate was perfect with a spot of whipped cream."

He smiled before saying, "I hope you will come over again, and next time we can watch a movie."

"I don't know. Your place is really nice and all but..." I couldn't find the right words to tell him how being in a guy's apartment felt intimidating to me. Even if it was attached to his parents' house with a sliding glass door.

When we arrived home, it was five minutes after eleven. I ran upstairs and walked straight into my mom's room to let her know that I was home.

I put Daisy on her leash to take her out for her last walk. As I was heading out the door, Daphne was walking inside, and she set her purse down on the counter and followed me back outside.

As we walked Daisy, Daphne asked me what Mig and I were talking about. I told her we talked about him and his love of music. I told her how I couldn't believe he lived in basically his own apartment.

Daphne smiled at me and said, "I was totally shocked the first time I saw it.

I found out that the apartment was built on the side of the house for his grandparents. His grandfather passed away a week before they were scheduled to move here. His grandmother lives in the main house with Mig's parents."

"They didn't want her living alone on the side of the house. Mig has always kept his drums in the garage, which is now his apartment.

He was always in there playing his drums and falling asleep in there. Once Mig turned 16, his parents told him on his birthday that he could move into the apartment. However, he has to keep up his grades and pay $100.00 a month rent. That money actually goes toward his room and board when he goes off to college. If he fails to pay or his grades drop, he has to move back into his bedroom in the main house."

"Really? That's cool, and I can't believe that apartment was once the garage. They did a great job converting that space into an awesome apartment."

"Yeah, Greg said it made so much sense. They never parked their cars in the garage anyways. It was always used for Mig's drums and band practice.

"We can go upstairs now, Sammy. Daisy has done her business, and I want to get some sleep."

Chapter 3 First Time in California

I woke up to a crazy Tuesday morning. It was one day before we were to leave for California. My mom was headed out the door to get her hair done. Before she walked out the door, she handed me a list. On it were all of the things that we still needed to get done before we left.

First on the list, of course, was to take Daisy for a walk. Check mark; already done. Second, someone needed to make breakfast, and someone needed to clean the kitchen. Check mark. Check mark; already done. Tommy made breakfast, and I cleaned up the kitchen. Next help Tommy pack and view everything he intends to bring. Make sure he doesn't bring naughty magazines or Tracy. Tommy walked into my room right as I read that part on the list. I broke out laughing.

"What's so funny, Sam?"

"Mom is. How does she know about Tracy?"

"Why? What did she say?" I held up the list and let him read it for himself.

"Whatever, Sam. I already packed, and I don't need you or Mom to check my bag. I know what I can bring."

"Tommy, you still haven't told me how Mom knows about Tracy."

"Mom saw her lying in the bed above me the other day, and she totally freaked out. She told me to throw her away. I told her I wasn't going to. That's all. Truthfully, I thought she forgot all about her."

"Why don't you just get rid of her, Tommy?"

"I don't want to. It's the first thing that I have ever won before. I plan on bringing her back to the dorm with me. It's an all-male dorm, and she's a conversation piece. You know the way I won her at a bachelor party for the best pick-up line. It's not only a true story, but it's a cool story."

"Okay, Tommy. I get it. I'm going to start packing now. Mom left you her car, so you can take me to drop Daisy off at Mig's house."

"Why are you leaving Daisy with Mig while we're gone? I mean, how do you know you can trust him?"

"Actually, I don't. I told Mom he offered to watch her for me. Mom thought that's where she was going. I'm leaving her with Tonya while we're gone. Abuela loves her, and she has no problem with Tonya watching her for me."

"Cool, so I have Mom's car free and clear for a couple of hours. Later, Sam."

"Tommy, wait. I still need you to take me by Mig's house in a couple of hours."

"Why?"

"I need to pick up Daphne and bring her back here. She is over at his cousin's house hanging out with Greg, and Mig is at work."

"Plus, we need to pick up a medium sized bag of dog food to drop off at Tonya's house for Daisy."

"Why? We have a whole big container of dog food in the pantry closet."

"Tommy, I'm not bringing them that huge container of dog food for Daisy. That doesn't make sense."

"Okay, fine. Whatever. What time do you want to leave here to pick up Daphne and go to the store?"

"Like in two hours. Mom is with Carmen getting her hair and nails done at her salon, so we have plenty of time."

"Don't forget lunch. They always do lunch."

"You're right. I forgot about that, Tommy."

By the time my mom arrived back home with Carmen, everything on her list was done, except my mom still needed to pack. Daphne and Carmen left to pack and get some rest themselves before the trip tomorrow. We are all on the same plane, so we will see each other bright and early at the airport.

We dropped Daisy off to Tonya around nine o'clock, along with a medium size bag of dog food, and a box of biscuits.

Tonya hugged me, then Tommy, and she kept telling us how much she will miss us while we're gone. She promised to take good care of Daisy, and she was excited to have Daisy staying with her.

When we arrived home, we placed all of our luggage by the front door and went to bed.

It was already four o'clock in the morning, when my mom was knocking on my bedroom door, and then banging on Tommy's door to get up. We were dressed, and ready to go 40 minutes later. We were out the door, and on our way to the airport by a quarter to five.

Once we arrived at our gate. I saw my mom look at her wristwatch, and she had a huge smile on her face. She finally sat back in her chair and relaxed. I know that she was proud of herself at that moment. All of her planning paid off, and we are at the gate on time.

At a quarter to six, Daphne, Carmen, and Arturo were just walking up to the counter to check in. You could see the stress and frustration on Carmen's face. A couple of minutes later, they announced our flight over the intercom.

"Wow, thank goodness. We just made it," Carmen said, and she was shaking her head in disbelief.

My mom asked Carmen if she saw Alex. Carmen shook her head no and my mom had a worried look on her face.

We took our seats once we boarded the plane. Carmen and my mom sat together. Tommy and I sat together, and Arturo and Daphne sat together. As soon as the seatbelt sign was turned off, we traded seats. Tommy told me he was going to sit with Arturo and talk about car stuff. I replied, "That's fine. Send Daphne over here to sit with me."

Once Daphne sat down, she asked me how I was feeling about seeing Julio again. That's when I confessed that I was very nervous. Then she told me that Greg was disappointed he couldn't come with us today. He wanted to attend the luncheon with us, just to see the look on Julio's face when he saw me for the first time. I admitted that was what scared me the most. After everything that I said to him over the phone, I'm just not sure if he will even bother to acknowledge me.

We both fell asleep, shortly after that conversation. When we woke up, the plane was getting ready to land. We exited the plane and walked into the airport terminal. Alex was waiting for us, by the door.

"My mom spotted Alex, and she ran up to him, and hugged him. She had tears in her eyes when she said, "You made it."

Alex was smiling, and he answered, "Sorry, Ms. Harris. I had to see Maria one more time before I left Miami."

My mom shook her head, and she was smiling now. "Alex, she must really love you to be up at four in the morning. She's a keeper."

"Okay guys, enough of that. Let's go get our luggage. We only have five days here, and we have a lot to do yet."

"Okay, Carmen, lead the way," my mom replied.

Once we all had our luggage, we headed outside. We were all looking around, and Alex yelled out, "There he is." He pointed to a guy standing in front of a limo. I looked over at my mom, and she was squinting to see in the direction Alex was pointing to.

We just followed Alex to a limo and saw him whispering something to Tommy. The man was wearing a black suit and tie. Alex introduced us to him, as one of his uncle's drivers. The driver smiled at Carmen and shook her hand. Then the driver smiled at my mom, and he shook her hand too. He kept on smiling at my mom and holding her hand. I thought, what the heck is that?

I immediately leaned over my mom and said, "Hi, I'm Sammy," and I put out my hand in front of my mom's. The driver looked startled, and he released my mom's hand, and he shook mine. Then he quickly headed to the back of the car, and he popped the trunk open.

He took our luggage, and placed them all in the trunk, with some assistance from Alex, Tommy, and Arturo. After all the luggage was in the trunk, we all climbed inside the limo.

I had never been in a limo, and I don't think Tommy, Daphne, or Arturo had been in one either. We were all just looking around, and my brother kept playing with the button to the divider glass. He opened all of the compartments. He opened the sunroof, until my mom finally said, "Tommy, sit back, and stop touching everything."

Carmen closed up the sunroof and my mom was smiling. She turned her head and went back to looking out the window. I just thought to myself, why is my mom smiling like that when Tommy is being so annoying? Then Daphne asked, "What's up?" I whispered back and told her about the encounter my mom had with the driver, at the airport. Apparently, I didn't whisper low enough.

Carmen said, "That's a handsome man, Sammy, and your mom didn't seem to mind the attention."

My mom turned her head from the window and asked, "What attention? Sorry I missed what you said."

Oh, wow, I thought to myself, that's why my mom is smiling.

"Oh, Sammy, stop looking so worried. We're on vacation. It was just some innocent flirting. Your mom is a beautiful woman, and to tell you the truth, that man, up there driving this car, is drop dead gorgeous. If that man even noticed me, I would be weak in the knees."

"Okay, great, Mom. Enough of that, please. I want to be able to have an appetite for lunch, and you're killing it right now."

"Daphne, stop overreacting. I was just making a statement."

I looked over at Tommy and Arturo, and they looked back at me. I could tell they were just as uncomfortable as I was with this conversation.

For a few minutes, there was nothing but awkward silence until Alex rolled down the divider glass and said, "We should reach my uncle's house, in about ten more minutes."

I was starting to feel excited. I couldn't wait to see Julio again, and at the same time I was still very nervous.

When we arrived, in front of the house. The driver popped the trunk open. Then he headed for the front door. I just stood there staring at him. I thought I heard him say, "Pénible luggage," to Alex, before he got out of the car.

I gave Alex a strange look, but he quickly turned his head away from me, and began to grab the luggage from the trunk. Tommy and Arturo quickly jumped out of the limo and began to help Alex. Daphne and I walked to the back of the car. That's when I asked Alex, "Where is the driver?"

"The driver is unlocking the front door, so we can take our bags inside." Tommy handed me my suitcase. I slowly walked over to the house with my suitcase and Daphne. We were greeted by the housekeeper, when we arrived at the doorstep. She told us to come in and waved us inside.

We walked in and the housekeeper showed us to our bedroom. The room was super spacious and was decorated in cream and mauve tones. The furniture and comforters were all in a cream color, and the drapes and carpet were in mauve. The room had two full size beds, each with a matching nightstand. There was a dresser, with six drawers, that had a huge round mirror, perfect for applying makeup. There was so much room that it had two chairs that were in cream, with a matching ottoman and a purple throw blanket. In front of the chairs was a fireplace. The fireplace was all white, with a cream-colored mantle that held a painting of four ballerinas, of course, wearing mauve tutus.

Daphne yelled, "Come here, Sammy. You have to take a look at this." I walked up a little hallway, with two doors. When I reached Daphne, we were standing at the end of the room. It was a dressing area, with double vanity sinks. The floor and countertop were done in marble with mauve and cream-colored swirls. All the way to the right side, there was a built-in vanity with a white chair tucked in underneath. That end of the mirror was different and had round white bulbs that went around in a circle. I looked over at Daphne, and said, "Now that's a makeup station" as I pointed to the chair.

Daphne had a huge smile, and replied, "That's nothing. Look at this." She opened the door behind her, and it was a large room with a Jacuzzi tub and a separate shower. I was shocked. I hadn't seen anything like this before, except on TV. There was another door on the opposite side of the vanity area. I opened it to find a toilet and bidet.

I walked back over to the first door and spotted Daphne. She was climbing up the stairs into the Jacuzzi tub, and she sat down. She put on her sunglasses and laid her head back. I left her in there and she stayed in that jacuzzi fully clothed for over twenty minutes.

When Daphne finally joined me in the room. I was sitting down on my bed facing her. I asked, "Can you help me pick out something cute to wear?"

"Of course, Sammy." I stood up and grabbed the handle of my suitcase, and I placed the case on the bed. I unzipped the case and placed my outfits on the side of the bed.

Daphne went through all of them and told me, "You need to wear the cotton dress in black, with the green panels on the side. It will show off your curves, and you look great in it. I will give you a French braid and tease your bangs."

"Daphne, there is only one problem, I don't have any curves to show off."

"Yes, you do, and the dress looks really good on you. You want to look your best when you see Julio, for the first time."

"What are you going to wear, Daphne?"

"It doesn't really matter. Greg's not here yet."

Daphne took her shower first. Then I took my shower. When I came out of the shower, and walked into the dressing area, I was wrapped in a towel.

Daphne was waiting for me by the vanity, with the chair pulled out. "Here, Sammy, take a seat," she patted the cushion on the chair.

I walked over, and sat down, and she began to brush my hair and braid it. I looked up on the countertop of the vanity and saw my hair spray and makeup.

When my hair was done, she told me to get dressed and come back. I did, and when I returned, Daphne applied my makeup, light brown eyeliner, mascara, and a very light pink colored lip gloss.

"There you are Sammy. We're finished. What do you think?"

"Wow, I look pretty! Thank you, Daphne." I stood up and gave her a hug.

"That's because you are, and when Julio sees you, he will have a hard time keeping his eyes off you."

"Thank you, Daphne. I don't know what I would do without you."

"Sammy, let's go get our shoes on. It's time for lunch, and I'm starving."

Right as we walked out of the dressing area, Carmen knocked on the door, and asked to come in for a minute. She walked inside and sat down on the ottoman, facing us. Carmen said, "I know you're nervous, and I just wanted to give you these earrings to wear."

She handed me the earrings, with little angels on them. "What is that?" Daphne asked.

I opened my hand to show Daphne, and I told her, "They are little angels holding a bow and arrow."

Daphne laughed before saying, "My mom thinks they're good luck. Oh, but those are Cupid, not angels."

"Well, if they are good luck, I'm wearing them. "Thank you, Carmen, and I will make sure to give them back to you after lunch."

"No, Sammy, you wear them until we get back to Miami. They are yours until then. Cupid is love, and he will watch over you while you are here."

Daphne started laughing again, and added, "Yeah, okay, Mom. Just like my name."

Carmen replied, "Yes, just like your name, Daphne," and we all started laughing.

My mom walked in, and asked, "Is everybody ready to go? The boys and the driver are waiting for us in the kitchen."

"Yes, Lori, the girls are ready," Carmen answered.

"Great, come on," and we followed my mom to the front door. My mom opened the door, and called out, "We're leaving now."

Once everyone joined us at the front door, we all headed for the limo.

My mom reached for the handle on the door, and the driver grabbed it first and opened the door for her. She looked up at him and smiled. He just stood there smiling back at her. My mom didn't even try to get in the car until Tommy asked, "Mom, are you alright?" My mom no longer appeared lost, and she climbed in the car. The rest of us followed her inside and sat down.

When we were all seated, Carmen looked over at my mom and let out a little laugh. My mom just rolled her eyes, then gave her a pleading look. I looked back at Tommy, and he looked over at me. I shook my head and Tommy just turned his eyes toward the floor.

Arturo leaned over, and whispered in my ear, "Sammy, you look beautiful, and I understand how you're feeling. I'm feeling the same way about seeing Michael, and he will be meeting up with us at the luncheon."

I smiled at Arturo and took hold of his hand. "You are very lucky to have one another, and you have nothing to be afraid of because he loves you."

"Then why are you afraid, Sammy?" Arturo whispered.

"I'm not sure if Julio will even speak to me again." He squeezed my hand and I just sat back in my seat. Finally, we were stopped, which meant we were at the Hotel. I felt my heart racing inside my chest. The nervous knots in my stomach were back, and it was time for lunch.

Daphne took my hand and squeezed it. "It's going to be fine, Sammy. You'll see." Then the door was open, and Daphne was the first person to get out of the limo. I was the last person to step out of the limo. We were now standing, at the front entrance of the hotel. I watched as the driver handed the keys over to the valet.

"Come on, Sammy," I heard Daphne say. I looked over to my right and saw everyone walk inside. Except for Arturo, and Daphne, they were waiting for me at the door.

Finally, I caught up with them and the three of us walked inside together. We were in the lobby of the hotel, and there was no sign of my mom, Carmen, or anybody else. Then the driver came in from outside, and said, "You guys follow me."

Daphne and I both looked over at one another quizzically. We followed the driver over to the elevator. We got off on the second floor and followed the driver down a hallway. I noticed all the gold plaques on the wall that held the name for each of the rooms. All of these rooms appeared to have double doors. The driver stopped walking long enough for us to catch up to him.

When we reached the last room with double doors. The plaque on the wall read, Imperial 1. The driver reached for the brass handle on the right door. Just as the left door opened, and Pilar walked out.

Pilar looked at the driver, and asked, "Where have you all been? I was beginning to think my brother ditched us to take you kids to the arcade or something."

"No, Pilar, come on. I wouldn't do that until Thursday." I looked behind me, and realized the driver was actually Pilar's brother. He noticed me looking back at him, and he just smiled at me, with his eyebrows raised.

Pilar put her arms around me, and she gave me a big hug. Then she hugged Daphne and Arturo. She told us that she missed all of us so much and that everyone was here, and excited to see us. Pilar hugged her brother and thanked him for picking us up from the airport. He started to laugh, and said, "No problem. It was so much fun."

"Now what do you think of my friend Lori?"

That's when I realized he was not only her brother, but he was Guillermo without a doubt — the one Pilar had been trying to match my mother up with for a while now. It all came back to me the minute I heard the last question.

"Well, right now, your friend thinks I'm the driver," he answered laughing.

"What? Why?"

"I knew you sent me to pick up your friends, with the intention of trying to match me up with one of them. I always know when you are trying to play matchmaker. I just thought it would be funny if I showed up as the driver, instead. That way, it wouldn't be uncomfortable for either of us."

"Now how should I introduce you, as my brother or the driver, Gio?"

"The driver, of course, Pilar."

We all started laughing, and that's when Pilar placed her hand on her forehead, and she started shaking her head back and forth. "Well, lucky for you, my friends have a sense of humor. Now you kids will get a chance to finally see where Eddie gets his personality from. I promise you, Eddie is an exact replica of my brother Guillermo, and that's not even his son."

"No, but Eddie is my nephew, and he spent most of his childhood with me. Besides, we bring you so much joy. I love you, Pilar, and I will confess to your friends now who I really am." He was pouting like a little puppy dog.

"Okay, please do Gio. Now let's go inside. Everybody has been waiting to see you guys," Pilar was smiling at us.

Guillermo and Pilar each held a door open for us. It was like we were making a grand entrance. I was waiting for the trumpets to start blaring as we stepped inside.

As we walked in, I noticed two large round tables each covered with gold table clothes and a large candle in a glass case in the center of each table.

Eddie, and Monica, ran up to us and hugged all three of us. Monica was excited, and she kept saying, "I can't believe you guys are finally here. I can't wait for you all to meet my daughter Erika. She is at home with her nanny. I wanted to bring her, but the nanny said it's not a good idea for my daughter to be around so many people at once yet. After all, she's only five weeks old."

They walked us over to a round table, and Eddie pulled out the seat for Daphne. I felt Arturo tap my arm, and he nodded to the left. I looked over my left shoulder, and it was Julio. Instant butterflies filled me. He was talking to his uncle Guillermo, and his brother Alex. I saw Julio turn his head toward my direction, and I quickly turned my head back to face the table. Arturo and Michael were smiling at me, and Eddie was waiting for me to sit in the chair he pulled out for me. I quickly walked over to Eddie and sat down.

Michael was holding out a chair for Arturo, and once he was seated, Michael walked over to Daphne and gave her a hug. Then he walked up behind me, and he gave me a squeeze. He whispered, "You look beautiful, Sammy, and I know Julio is excited you're here."

Then I heard Julio say, "Tio, I can't believe you."

Alex said, "Believe it," and I heard all three of them laughing.

I was about to speak to Monica, who was sitting next to me, when I heard, "Hi, Sammy." I looked to my right and it was Lewis. He was already leaning over to give me a kiss on the cheek. He took a seat, on the other side of me, and the table was now full. Except for the two seats directly across from me.

Monica began to tell all of us about Erika. "She is so beautiful and was born with a full head of hair."

Lewis added, "Yeah, she's such a happy baby, and she smiles all the time. Her nanny told me that she's not smiling. It's just gas. So, I told her the baby must have a lot of gas."

Then there was a sound of a spoon clicking against a water glass, from the center of the room. Everyone stopped talking and began to look toward the center of the room. I saw Lewis and Alex run to the chairs on the other side of the table and sit down.

When I turned my head around, to see where the sound was coming from, I noticed Julio was sitting beside me, in the seat where Lewis had just been sitting.

Guillermo announced, "Now that I have everyone's attention, allow me a second to put these down." He set the water glass and spoon back down on the table. I quickly stood up, and I was about to turn my chair around, when Julio stood up beside me, and he turned my chair around for me.

I whispered, "Thank you," but Julio didn't acknowledge that he heard me. I went back to paying attention to Guillermo. Then I felt Julio gently take my hand in his. I squeezed his hand once, and he squeezed my hand back.

Then he turned his head, and he looked at me. Those big dark brown eyes were finally looking back at me again. I swallowed once, and he slowly blinked. It was like we were in complete awe looking at one another. Those eyes, that smile, and the smell of his cologne. I wanted to kiss him so badly that all of a sudden, without even thinking, I leaned in, and his lips parted as he leaned in toward me.

Then my brother yelled, "Hey, no public displays of affection. Come on, that's gross. We're about to eat here any minute." Everyone at our table started laughing.

I pulled away blushing, and whispered, "I'm so sorry I tried to kiss you."

Julio whispered, "I'm not. I wanted to kiss you too."

I just turned my attention back to Guillermo again. He was saying, "I'm so happy we are all here together today. I want to thank you all for making the trip to attend my brother's wedding. Can we all raise our glasses up, and give a toast to Julie and Juan?" All of us at our table raised our water glasses up in a toast. At the other table, they all raised their champagne flutes up. I couldn't help but notice Carmen's flute was already empty. That had me laughing to myself. He said, "To love, laugh, and happiness. May we all have that."

After Guillermo finished his flute of champagne, he walked over to stand in front of my mom, and he took her hand. "For those of you who don't know me, I am Guillermo, Pilar's brother, and not the driver. You can also call me Gio or Tio. I respond to all three." (Everyone was laughing.)

He went on to say in front of everyone: "Lori, I'm sorry. I meant no harm, and I was only having some fun. I hope you will give me an opportunity to take you out on a date, just once, while you are here. My mom smiled, and said, "Yes, I would like that." My mom was blushing, and everybody was clapping. Pilar and Carmen looked like two lightning bugs, with the smiles they both had on their face.

The food servers came over to the table and asked us what we would like to drink. I stood up, and Julio turned our chairs back around, to face the table. I sat back down, and I felt Julio push my chair in closer to the table, just how I like it. I just looked up at him and smiled. Once he sat down, I thanked him. Julio leaned in toward me, as if he was going to whisper something to me, and to my surprise he kissed me on the cheek.

That's when the server came over to us and asked what we wanted to eat. My head was spinning, and I was so elated that I couldn't speak. I squeezed Julio's hand asking for help. Julio smiled at me and said, "She prefers chicken over beef and salad instead of soup. He squeezed my hand and asked, "Did I get that right?" I smiled and nodded my head yes.

The server looked down and noticed us holding hands, he smiled at us and said, "Coming right up."

We heard Guillermo say, "More champagne," and everyone laughed at our table.

"You guys, are now going to see where my brother Eddie gets his long commentary, and sense of humor — from my Uncle Gio."

"Yes, he does, Lewis. He even has the same laugh as your uncle. You know that type of laugh that when you hear it, you start laughing," Daphne replied."

"That's because the man's awesome, and he is a lot of fun to be around," Tommy said.

"Well, I was shocked when Julio and Eddie came to my dad's house about two weeks ago. They pulled up in this blue, four door Mercedes, and I didn't know who it was?"

"What are you talking about, Michael? Julio called you and told you we were coming over."

"Yeah, but not sporting a new Mercedes Benz. That just knocked my socks off."

"Oh, stop it. Everybody drives that car here. It's not a big deal anymore, not when everybody has one. Now the van, that's what impresses me. Everything about her has been put together by us. All of the interior, lights, and sound system were put in by Alex and me. I miss her. Alex, please tell me you're taking good care of her."

"Of course, I'm taking great care of her, Eddie. If you ever want to trade your Mercedes for the van, you can take her. She is in Miami, waiting for you. Just drive the Mercedes down to Miami, and the van is yours. Not everyone has a Mercedes in Miami, and I wouldn't mind owning one," Alex answered with a smile.

Eddie grinned and said, "Deal" and stuck his hand out to shake on it.

Alex stood up and reached over the table and shook hands with Eddie. When he sat back down, he asked, "When are you coming to get her?"

"When the wedding is over, we can drive back down to Miami together."

"Eddie, there's the problem. I can't get any more days off from work. As much as I would love to cruise the highway with you back to Miami, I want to keep my job, so I have to be back at work in five days. Sorry."

"I can drive back to Miami with you, and we can take turns driving, Primo."

"That sounds good, Julio. Then I can see Denise."

"Yeah, and I can see both of my girls," Julio looked over at me and smiled, before saying, "I miss Daisy so much."

"Yeah, I know she misses you too." After I said that my eyes began to water up, and my nose was starting to run. I stood up, and everyone was looking at me. Julio looked over at me too, up and down. Then his eyes finally fell back on my face again. "Excuse me a minute. I'm going to the bathroom."

Daphne stood up and told me, "Okay, I'll go with you, Sammy." I walked out the door and took in a deep breath then let it out. I heard Daphne walk out the door behind me. I said, "Finally!" as I turned around to see that it was Julio not Daphne standing behind me.

"Yes, finally, we're here together, Samantha, and I have missed you so much."

He slowly leaned in toward me and I announced, "I have to pee." He leaned back and covered his mouth, trying not to laugh.

Then he took my hand, and said, "Come with me." He took me to the restrooms, which were just on the opposite side of the room. "Here we are, and I'll be out here waiting for you. Unless you don't want me to wait for you."

"Julio, I want you to wait for me." I noticed the relief on his face after I said that. I walked inside the restroom and saw my reflection in the mirror. I was wearing a big smile, and had mascara starting to run just a little at the corner of my eyes. I quickly ran into the stall, then washed my hands, and fixed the mascara. I kept cupping my hands and blowing into them trying to smell my breath. I couldn't smell anything, so I panicked and grabbed a piece of mint chewing gum from my clutch.

I heard Julio begin to whistle a tune, which he always does when I'm taking too long. I ran out of the bathroom, and straight up to Julio. He wrapped his arms around me and held me. I wrapped my arms around him, and I felt whole again. I laid my head against his chest, so I could hear his heartbeat. I just closed my eyes, and tried to take it all in. The feeling of his arms wrapped around me and his heartbeat, with the smell of his cologne. I hoped I would remember this moment, right here and right now, when I'm back home.

"Come on, guys. Let's go. The food just arrived at the table." I heard Julio sigh, and I opened my eyes and saw Alex. He was waiting for us in front of the double doors, on the opposite side of the room.

Julio pulled away, and he took hold of my hand. Julio and I walked back over to Alex. He smiled at us and said, "Okay, Kissing Bandits, let's get back inside" then he held open the door for us.

As we walked inside Julio frowned and said, "We haven't kissed yet, Alex."

Alex patted Julio on the shoulder and replied, "Don't worry, little brother, I'm confident the two of you will do a lot of that soon enough."

When we arrived back at the table, Daphne said, "Wow, you guys were gone a long time." I looked around the table, and I saw that everybody had already eaten. I looked over at Julio, and he had a surprised look on his face.

I whispered, "I didn't realize we took that long."

He whispered back, "Neither did I, Mi Corazón." I had chills the minute he called me his heart. My food was sitting in front of me, but I wasn't hungry anymore.

Julio didn't appear to have much of an appetite either. We both handed the server our plates. The server looked panicked and asked if there was something wrong with the food. Julio told him he was saving room for dessert.

"I never had a server so concerned about the food before," I whispered to Julio.

"He just wants to make sure there wasn't a problem with the food because of my uncle, that's all."

"Why is he worried about your uncle, Julio?"

"He owns the hotel, Sammy," Lewis answered.

"Oh, that's a very good reason," I said blushing. "Sorry, I didn't realize that."

"That's cool. You want to know something else?" Lewis asked looking around the table.

"Yeah, I do," Michael answered.

"The formal dinner and wedding reception are also taking place here at this hotel. All of my dad's friends and Julie's friends and family will be staying here. At least up until the wedding. My mom and all of us demanded you guys stay by us at my Uncle Gio's house."

"Your staying with Uncle Gio because the nanny made it clear that more people in our house means the baby is exposed to more germs," Monica added.

"That was when it was decided you would stay at my uncle Gio's house. Plus, that house is bigger than all of our houses put together. It definitely has plenty of room for everyone. Since nobody lives there except for my uncle Gio, and the housekeeper," Lewis said.

"Yeah, and even she goes home to her family on the weekends," Eddie added, laughing.

The waiter came back to our table, and placed a coffee cup, and another cloth napkin, down on the table with a spoon and dessert fork. He asked each of us if we would like cheesecake, chocolate cake, or sherbet. Julio told the waiter he would like a slice of cheesecake and chocolate cake.

As the waiter walked away, Daphne asked, "Who is the chocolate cake for? We all ordered cheesecake. That's the best."

Julio looked over at me, and I smiled before he answered, "The chocolate cake and the cheesecake are for us. They both happen to be our favorite, so we will share both of them." I just kept thinking how Julio knows me so well.

After our dessert arrived, all I could hear was the happy moans of Julio taking his first bite of the chocolate cake. He was over the top with it, and I knew he was just trying to antagonize his brother, and Lewis, with the chocolate cake. "Hey, Julio, is that chocolate cake any good?"

"Yup, it's delicious. Do you want to try a piece?"

"Yeah, man, let me get a bite of that." Lewis reached over the table with his dessert fork and Julio picked up the plate.

"Sorry, man, the rest of the cake belongs to Sammy. I'm now going to have some cheesecake, if you want some of that now."

"No, I'm fine. I already have cheesecake."

Everybody was laughing except for Lewis; he was now sulking in his chair with his arms crossed in front of him. I picked up the plate with the chocolate cake and told him, "Take it. Julio and I can share the cheesecake."

"Really, Sammy?" I nodded my head yes and Lewis took the plate from me. He stuck his tongue out at Julio before sitting back down. Julio just laughed, and he moved the plate of cheesecake between us to share.

When we were through with dessert, Guillermo walked over to our table. "I hope you enjoyed lunch. It's time for you all to have some fun back at the house. He handed Alex the tickets to give to the valet, and said, "Sobrino, be careful."

"I will Tio, and thank you so much," Alex replied.

Alex asked, "Are you guys ready to go?"

We all said, "Yes."

Michael asked Alex if he could come back to the house with us. Alex told him of course, and we all stood up and left. When we arrived downstairs, we walked over to the valet podium.

The valet handed Alex a set of keys, and told him, "This is to the white one. Then he handed Alex a second set of keys. "This set is for the black one."

Alex looked bewildered and asked, "Where are the cars?" The valet pointed to the two Lincoln town cars, parked in front of us at the curb.

Alex called Eddie over and asked him if he preferred black or white. When Eddie said black, Alex said, that's what I thought you would say. Then he handed him a set of car keys, and yelled, "White it is," as he ran over to the black town car and climbed inside the driver's seat.

Eddie just stood there shaking his head. Lewis, Tommy, and Monica followed Alex and climbed in the back of the black Lincoln.

Daphne climbed into the passenger seat beside Eddie in the white town car. Arturo and Michael joined them in the backseat. Julio opened the back door on the white town car and sat down beside Arturo. Then he pulled me onto his lap and shut the door. Eddie took off driving like a maniac. Julio wrapped his arms around my waist tighter. When Eddie nearly hit the curb on the way out of the parking lot, Julio told Eddie to slow down and be careful. Eddie was laughing and replied, "Sorry, I just have to arrive first to Tio's house."

"Great idea, Eddie, except we don't have the keys to get into the house."

"Yeah, and that matters why? The housekeeper is there, remember. It's only Wednesday, Julio."

"Oh, yeah, I forgot. It just somehow feels like the weekend or something."

"Don't feel bad. It feels like the weekend to me too," I added with a smile. Julio squeezed me, and he was grinning now. Julio kept his arms locked around my waist and he wore that huge grin on his face the whole ride back to his uncle Guillermo's house.

When we arrived, Eddie just walked inside. The door wasn't even locked. We all followed Eddie, and Michael and Arturo walked in behind us. "Wow," Michael said.

As we entered the family room, I was thinking the same thing.

The family room had a large wall unit, complete with a big screen TV on wheels, a VCR, laser disc player, and stereo with huge speakers with surround sound. There was even a Nintendo, with a tray of video games set up on one of the shelves. A large tan leather sectional sofa was on the opposite wall facing the wall unit. Behind the wall unit was a large stone wall. In the center of the wall was an open door. That door led us into another room that had five arcade machines, and two pinball tables. Then another sofa in brown leather with lots of pillows, sat in front of Julio's favorite — a foosball table. As soon as I spotted that table, I looked up at Julio, and said, "I'm sure my soccer player loves that table."

He was smiling back at me, and answered, "Not nearly as much as I love you," and he kissed the top of my head.

Then he took my hand, and I followed him out a sliding glass door. He took us out to the pool deck, and it was incredible. A tropical oasis, with palm trees and waterfalls pouring into the pool. A huge lawn with sensational views of the whole city of Anaheim below. Julio walked us over to these concrete steps that led us down to another large open lawn. There was a cobblestone path, and at the end of the path sat a large yellow and white striped cabana.

Julio walked us over to the cabana, and he stopped right at the opening and had me walk inside first. There was a two-seater bar to the left in white, and a large screen TV in the middle of the cabana. In front of the TV was a white and tan wicker sofa, with two wicker chairs and tons of pillows. Then I heard this zipper sound, and I quickly turned around.

Julio was bent down toward the floor. I realized he just zipped shut the two panels that were the opening to the cabana. Then he stood up, took my hand, and walked us over to the sofa covered in pillows. He began to grab the pillows and toss them one by one onto the chairs. Once all of the pillows were removed, we finally sat down.

"Samantha, you have no idea how happy I am just to be here with you right now. I've missed you so much."

"Julio, I just want to enjoy every minute we have together, right now."

He leaned in and wrapped his arms around me. He pulled me in closer to him and just held me. I closed my eyes, and I felt his breath near my lips. Then I felt his lips touch mine gently. He pulled away, and I felt him looking at me. I opened my eyes, and just stared into his beautiful dark brown eyes.

Then we heard *knock, knock.* We both jumped and pulled apart. Julio smiled and said, "It's just Alex."

"Go away. No soliciting here. You're trespassing on private property."

"Okay, but we're heading home now Julio, and Mom knows you're going to stay the night here. Now you can just sleep in the same room with Tommy, while he's in town.

Just so you know, Mom wanted to say goodnight to you, her baby boy.

You know, before she leaves to head back home."

"Wait, Alex." Julio stood up and walked over to the entrance and unzipped the flaps to the cabana. "Are you serious? I can stay here in Tommy's room. I didn't even think to ask her that."

"Well, little bro. I told mom that you would want to sleep over here."

"How did you know?"

"Come on, Julio, the two of you always take off, and cuddle in some private place like the lake. At least if the two of you are here, at Uncle Gio's, I will know where to find you in the morning. Oh, and don't worry. I won't tell anyone where your hideout is. However, if I were you, I would spend time with everybody at the pool now and use the hideout later on."

"You're right, Alex," and Julio walked back over to me, and said, "Let's go say bye to my mom and hang out by the pool." He took my hand, and I stood up. We walked out of the cabana and followed Alex around the yard to the front of the house. From there, we walked up the stairs, and back into the house using the front door.

When we walked inside, all of the parents were in the living room having drinks and talking. There was music playing in the background, Pilar wasn't going home now.

Carmen was the first one to notice us walk past the living room. She asked, "Where have you two been hiding?"

I just smiled, and before I could answer, Pilar walked up, and added, "Now you can't tell us you were out walking Daisy."

Alex walked up behind us, and answered, "I found them right outside the house." I thought to myself, wow, now honesty is the best policy. Alex was definitely telling the truth, and he didn't even give away our location.

"Well, I don't know how you do it, Alex. You always find my baby boy, and Sammy. Thank you, mi hijo. I couldn't have asked for a better person to watch over your little brother than you. You are just the absolute best big brother, and such a wonderful son."

"Thank you, Mom. I love you too," Alex replied.

"Oh, I love all my children, and this includes you, Sammy. Then Pilar reached around and hugged all of us in a group hug.

We eventually made it back into the family room, and nobody was in there. Alex, walked up behind us and said, "Everyone is outside in the pool."

Julio took hold of my hand, and we walked over to the sliding glass doors. Julio asked, "Are you coming, Alex?"

Alex smiled and answered, "Yeah, why not?" as he followed us out the doors to the pool area. Eddie, Daphne, Arturo, and Michael were in the pool. Monica, and Tommy, were nowhere to be found.

Alex, Julio, and I sat down at the table beside the pool. I asked, "Where is Monica and Tommy?"

"Oh, they left the house to check on Erika," Arturo answered.

"They should be back soon, since they left over an hour ago," Michael added.

"Good," I answered smiling. Then I looked back at Julio, and whispered, "I'm worried my brother is a horn dog."

Julio just laughed and said, "He's perfect for Monica. What are you worried about?"

I smiled, but told him, "That's not nice."

Julio took my hand and stood up. "Where are you going?"

"You're right Samantha. Let's walk to my house, unless you can still ride a bike."

"Ummm, I remember how to walk, and ride a bike, so whichever one you want to do is fine with me Julio."

"Great. Then let's go."

When I stood up, Alex asked us where we were going. Julio told him we were heading back to the house to check on Monica and Tommy. Alex started telling us that we would be wasting our time. That they took off in the golf cart over an hour ago. They left so Monica could get ready for her big date with Tommy.

After hearing that Julio and I sat back down, completely blown away. Then Alex began to laugh really hard. Julio and I looked over at Alex, and he laughed even harder. "I can't believe the two of you fell for that story. You should have seen your faces. The two of you looked absolutely pitiful. Seriously, you two bought that. I can't believe it."

Julio stood up and shook his head while looking over at Alex. "Come on, Samantha. Alex is just goofing around. Let's go to the house." I stood up and Julio took my hand as we walked back into the house. We walked down the stairs; then we walked out a door that led to the garage. Julio turned on the lights in the garage, and it was huge. It had parking for up to five cars, and to the far-left hand side, there were five bicycles all in a row in the very first parking spot. I picked the only girls' bike in pink and white. It was a beach cruiser. Julio grabbed a blue ten-speed. .

Once we were outside of the garage, we started peddling the bikes down the sidewalk. I just followed Julio, and he was going pretty fast. I had to yell, "Slow down," several times in order to keep up. We crossed a small bridge and entered another community of fancy houses. We turned right, at the next block, and the third house was his."

Julio dug into his pocket and pulled out a single key. It didn't even have a key chain, or anything. Julio unlocked the door and we walked inside. All the lights were off, and the house was very quiet. Julio turned on a light and walked me over to the living room. It was spacious with a large amber colored leather sectional. I sat down while Julio walked around the house. I saw a picture frame on the coffee table in front of me.

I picked it up and it was a picture of a baby. It had to be baby Erika with her purple lace outfit. She was beautiful with her dark brown eyes, long eyelashes and a head full of hair.

Less than a minute later, Julio came back out to the living room. He whispered, "Nobody's here, except for the nanny and the baby."

"Then let's leave so we don't disturb either of them." He nodded his head yes, and I stood up, and followed him back out the door.

As we rode away from his house on the bikes. I yelled to him, "Where do you think they went?"

"I don't know, but they aren't on a date, because Monica's car is in the garage."

"Where do you want to go now, Julio?"

Julio stopped his bike, and he set it to rest on the kickstand. He walked over to me, and he placed both of his hands on my cheeks.

He leaned in and kissed me with so much passion, he actually left me breathless. I felt a cool breeze, and I heard a low pitch clicking sound. I quickly turned around, and it was Tommy and Monica. They rode up on the golf cart. "Hi, guys, what have you been up to?" Tommy asked.

"We came to the house looking for the two of you," I answered.

"Oh, and where did the two of you take off to, when you arrived to Gio's house?" Tommy asked.

"We were just outside the house, hanging out."

"Oh, really? Well, we had a bet with Alex as to who would find you guys first. Please tell me he didn't find you."

"Yeah, he did," Monica said, smiling.

"How do you know that?" Tommy asked her.

"Simple. My little brother looked like a deer in headlights when you asked that question. Besides, Alex always finds my little brother and Sammy, when no one else can."

Julio just looked over at me, with his eyebrows raised, and I looked over at him. We were both smiling, and blushing. "Okay, so we lost the bet with Alex, this time, but can you do me a favor?"

"That depends. What is it Tommy?"

"When the two of you take off again, can you find a different place to hide? I just want to have a fair shot at beating Alex."

Julio smiled, and answered, "Sure, we can do that."

"Great, will see you back at the house." Monica waved bye to us as Tommy drove away on the golf cart.

Julio wrapped his arms around me, and just held me. He kissed the top of my head, and said, "Okay, let's go back to Tio's house."

When we arrived, everyone was getting ready to go to bed. Pilar and Monica hugged everyone before leaving out the front door. My mom and Carmen waved bye to us as they walked up the stairs to their room. Alex looked over at his uncle Guillermo, which made me look over at his uncle too. He had a big, bright, toothy smile. That smile was very familiar; his nephew Julio has often worn that same smile. I looked up at my mom, when she reached the top of the stairs. I noticed she looked back down at Guillermo and smiled at him. That's when I recognized the invisible energy in the room, and it was coming from my mom and Guillermo.

Alex looked over at his uncle Guillermo, and then back at Julio and me. He announced, "I'm sleeping over. Tio, is the guest room still available?"

"Yes, of course, Sobrino. Take it. It's always yours for as long as you like."

Then Alex walked upstairs, and when he was halfway up, he stopped, turned around, and asked, "Tio, aren't you coming to bed?"

"Yes, but first I just want to check on everybody, and make sure they don't need anything else before I go to bed."

"Okay, Tio, I'll go and do that for you. Why don't you go to bed now? I know you've had a very long day."

"Oh, Alex, you are so good to me. Gracias." Guillermo said goodnight to us, as he headed up the stairs.

Alex walked back down the stairs. He asked do you want to go to bed now or hangout some more?

Julio answered, "Hangout."

"Okay, let's go back to the pool."

As we walked toward the sliding glass doors. I saw Daphne and asked if Michael and Arturo were still here.

"Yes, they are out by the pool. Michael's dad beeped Michael about an hour ago. His father had to attend a dinner meeting, and as usual, he's running late."

"Wait — so is his dad coming to pick him?" Alex asked.

"No, my mom overheard Michael's conversation on the phone. She asked to speak to his father, and now he's staying here tonight. Gio offered to have his nephew Enrique drive them back to LA in the morning."

"Okay, so where is Michael sleeping tonight?" I asked Daphne.

"In the room with Tommy. Arturo offered to sleep on the pull-out sofa bed in the family room."

"That's where I was going to sleep tonight. I guess I have no choice but to sleep outside, under the stars, in the cabana."

"Really, Julio, because I know there are two sofa beds in the family room, so you don't have to sleep outside, under the stars, after all, cowboy," Alex replied.

Daphne looked over at Julio. Then I looked over at Julio, and we both couldn't help it; we started to howl. Alex tried not to laugh; he even went as far as to cover his mouth with the palm of his hand. But laughter is contagious, and he started laughing too. "Julio said, "Whatever. I'm going to the pool."

The three of us followed Julio out to the pool. Alex told everyone the sleeping arrangements, and he waved bye to everyone, as he walked back inside the house.

I stood up next, and told everyone, "Goodnight, guys. I'm going to bed." Julio followed me back inside the house, and he walked me to my bedroom door.

I kissed him on the cheek, and said, "Goodnight, cowboy. I'll see you under the stars." I left him smiling, as I walked into my bedroom.

Once I was in the room, I walked over to my suitcase and pulled out my pajamas. I took a shower, and was dressed for bed, in under ten minutes.

I said my prayers and fell right to sleep afterward. I was woken up to the sound of Daphne, walking back in the room. I kept my eyes closed, and I didn't move a muscle. Daphne took her shower and climbed into her bed. Once I heard her snoring, I tiptoed over to the sliding glass doors in our room which were hidden behind the curtains and headed outside. I, quietly, slid the door shut.

When I turned around and faced the pool, Julio was already standing at the foot of the stairs waving me over. I quickly walked over to him and took his hand. We walked down the stairs and over to the cabana. When we walked inside, we went straight to the sofa. There was now a soft blue blanket waiting for us, along with a note. I read the note out loud, "To keep you guys warm. I'll be down here in the morning, to wake you up, Alex." We both laughed and snuggled up on the couch together under the blanket.

Chapter 4 The Sunrise in Anaheim

I woke up to Julio's big brown eyes staring back at me and his arms wrapped around me. I blinked a couple of times thinking I was dreaming. Then I closed my eyes and snuggled up against him, that's when I felt him gently squeeze me. I could still smell his cologne that was lightly fragrant on his T-shirt. When I opened my eyes again, Julio was still looking at me smiling. "Good morning, Mi Corazón." I had instant butterflies, I placed my head on his chest and listened to his heartbeat. "We need to get up now, I have something I want to show you." Julio stood up and went behind the little two-seater bar. He handed me a bottle of orange juice and leaned over the sofa to grab the blanket. He took my hand and we walked up the stairs to the pool deck.

He walked us over to a set of lawn chairs that were at the pool facing the city below. We both had a seat and it was still dark outside. I had no idea what time it was. I looked over at Julio and noticed he wasn't wearing a watch. I whispered, "Do you have any idea what time it is?"

Julio looked at the sky, and said, "It's about a quarter to six."

"How do you know that?"

"Mi Corazón look over there," he pointed toward the sky. "Our show is about to begin." He was smiling at me and took hold of hand and kissed the top of it. The sun slowly rose up into the sky, with bright orange and yellow beams of light. Together we were watching the sunrise. It was so beautiful, watching the sun slowly rise up over the city. To watch the city, go from complete darkness into daylight. I loved it, and I knew this was a memory I would take with me.

"I don't think you'll need this anymore." Julio took the blanket off me and folded the blanket.

"Thank you for sharing this with me Julio."

"Of course, the blanket was necessary. It was still chilly outside."

"Not the blanket, the moment. Watching the sunrise together."

Julio sat down on the foot of my lawn chair, and he took my hand. I looked up into his eyes and he said, "I have wanted to share this moment with you since I first saw it. When I first moved here, I would watch the sunrise every morning thinking at least we share the same sun. I don't know why, but for some reason, I really appreciate the little things that I use to take for granted like the sunrise. Or maybe it's just the view from this house."

"It's funny, Julio. When we were watching the sunrise, I thought the sun brings light to everything that was in complete darkness. It made me realize how change is so significant. It can make a situation better or worse. Either way, change is necessary to appreciate and discover the difference."

"You're talking about our relationship, aren't you?"

"Yes, because when you left, I was living in complete darkness, and I have been completely miserable. Now that I'm here with you, everything is bright again. I am just happy, to be here with you. To smell your cologne, hear your voice, look into your eyes, and feel your hand holding mine again. I looked down at our hands that were nestled together.

Julio lifted up my chin and looked into my eyes. "I have been living in darkness this whole time the same as you. It's just feels amazing, to have you here Samantha. You are my heart, my everything and without you and Daisy my life hasn't been the same.

"Maybe being separated is like the darkness we have to endure in order to appreciate the light. We need to take the time now to enjoy every moment we have together; just until I leave and maybe one day, we can be together again."

I suddenly heard a door open, and Peter Gabriel was playing. I turned my head to the side, and I looked up. Guillermo was standing out on his bedroom balcony. He was smiling and looking up at the sky in the direction of the sunrise. He eventually looked down and noticed Julio and I staring back at him. He waved to us and said, "It's so great to be alive and to see those eyes again." He placed his hand over his heart and started singing and dancing to "In Your Eyes."

I looked back at Julio, and he appeared to be surprised. His mouth was covered with the palm of his hand and his eyes were huge. "I think Tio has fallen for your mom."

We both looked back up at Guillermo, and the same song was still playing, and his uncle was still singing and dancing. " I don't know your uncle very well, but I think you might be right, Julio."

Alex yelled out, "Hey, it's the Kissing Bandits. I'm surprised to see you both up, so bright and early. I was actually on my way down to wake you guys up." Then he stopped walking, and asked, "Where is that music coming from?" Julio and I both pointed up to balcony where Uncle Guillermo was still dancing and singing. Alex looked up and his mouth dropped open. When the song was over, Guillermo walked back inside. Alex started cracking up, and eventually asked, "What's up with Tio?"

Julio laughed as he shook his head and answered, "I don't know."

Alex looked back up towards his uncle's balcony and added, "Well, he's gone now, but I have never seen Tio up this early or singing, and dancing. This is all new to me."

"Come on, let's go inside, and make breakfast, for everyone. Wait, Alex, is there enough food, to even make breakfast for everyone?"

"If we're in need of something Sammy, I can run to the market and pick it up."

"That's perfect Alex, just show me to the kitchen."

When I walked into the kitchen, I was blown away. The entire kitchen was circular and had a cathedral ceiling. The ceiling has seven wood beams that go across the entire ceiling and meet up at the center.

The center has a skylight that allows natural light into the room. The kitchen has black tiles, from the backsplash to the countertops. The cabinets were in cherry wood, just like the wood beams on the ceiling. The cabinets above the counters have glass doors. All of the appliances were in black, even the trash compactor. There was a large island in the center of the kitchen. That was also covered on all four sides in black tiles, and the countertop, was cherry wood with six stools in cherry wood pushed up against it. The floor was black marble with white swirls.

The room was spacious, and there were sliding glass doors that led outside to the pool deck, from the kitchen. In front of the sliding glasses doors, there was a large round table, with 10 chairs in cherry wood. There were several pictures on the walls around the room. My favorite was the one of the matador holding a red cape in front of a bull. I turned to Julio, and said, "Wow, this kitchen is so masculine, and enormous." I walked over to the kitchen table, and said, "Now this is an eat-in kitchen."

He smiled, and asked, "Have you been in the kitchen before now?"

"Yeah, but not to actually cook in here. This is a real treat to cook in this enormous kitchen. I'm actually excited about it and I can't wait to get started." I opened the refrigerator, and there were a couple of cartons of eggs, two gallons of orange juice, and apple juice. I opened the crisper and found a large package of strawberries, blueberries, and blackberries. I took each package out and set them on the counter. I found a bag of raisins and set them out on the counter beside the berries.

I asked Julio to find me a pen, and paper, and I made a shopping list of the items I will need to prepare breakfast. When Alex returned to the kitchen, I handed him the shopping list. He said he would be right back with everything . Eddie was already outside to pick him up.

We were alone in the kitchen now. So, I asked him what happened to Eddie and Lewis last night. He told me they were out on dates, and Lewis actually had a girlfriend that I would meet at the wedding. While searching for ingredients to make pancakes. Julio saw me struggling to reach a box in the pantry closet. He walked over and grabbed the box down for me. "Thanks," I was pouting, when I said it.

"What's wrong, Sammy?"

"Nothing. Crap, now I'm lying to you. Julio crossed his arms over his chest and bit down on his bottom lip. "Okay, I just feel the need to ask you a question that's none of my business. I'm completely upset with myself, because I can't seem to let it go. Which is distracting me and not allowing me to enjoy this moment of cooking in this incredible kitchen."

"If it bothers you that much, just ask the question Samantha. If it pertains to me, I will answer it. If it has to do with anyone else like Lewis or Eddie, I may not be able to give you an answer."

I turned around and took a seat at the counter facing Julio. I said, "Fair enough. Do you have a girlfriend, or are you dating someone?"

Julio sat up closer to the counter and he placed his hand under his chin with his eyebrows raised. "Oh, you know, I can understand why you would ask that question, Samantha, since you have been pushing me away after I left Miami. You always said we would remain broken up. Unless, we end up living in the same city again. You are very aware that I need to get on with my life. If and when we are ever in the same place, at the same time, I will drop everything, to be with you. Even if it's just for mere seconds because no one in this world can make me feel alive but you."

All I wanted was a straight answer to my question. Instead he gave me the run around speech. "Thank you, Julio, I guess I have my answer." I hopped down off the stool and walked over to the stove. Julio walked up behind me and he wrapped his arms around me. He kissed me behind the ear and whispered, "There is no one else, Mi Corazón."

I turned around in his arms and faced him. I looked into his eyes and asked, "Do you enjoy making me feel bad?" Julio smiled, and shook his head no. I stood up on my tiptoes, and I placed my hands to rest on his shoulders as I leaned in to kiss him Tommy walked into the kitchen.

"Aw, gross, it's too early in the morning for that, Sam. Seriously, we haven't even had breakfast yet, and I'm already feeling sick."

I quickly backed away from Julio and told Tommy, "Good morning to you too."

"Yeah, good morning, Sam," Tommy retorted, with a scowl.

Tommy gave Julio, a once over glance and had a seat in one of the stools at the counter. He asked Julio about Lewis and his girlfriend's situation. Julio replied he knew nothing about a situation. Tommy said, I know she has a cousin. Julio stood up from the counter as Alex walked into the kitchen with all of the groceries. Eddie walked in right behind him.

Tommy turned to me and asked, "Do you want to have a cook-off, Sam?"

"No, not today, Tommy, I'm just going to make four different quiche. Tommy frowned as he looked over at Julio, then back at me. I'm also going to make some scones later on. Do you want to help me with making the scones? If we bake them today, we can have them for breakfast tomorrow."

"When do you plan on making them Sam?"

"Well, I need to prepare each quiche now. I guess after they are baking in the oven, we can prepare the scones Tommy. Just give me like 45 minutes."

"Okay, you got it, Sam. I'll be back by then."

"Wait, Tommy, where are you going?"

"I'm going to Monica's house, so I can feed Erika breakfast."

"That's cool. Be sure to tell Erika Tio Julio loves her."

"Will do Julio, and can you come outside with me for a minute?" Julio and Tommy left the kitchen, and I got to work.

When Julio came back to the kitchen he asked, "Why can't my sister find a guy like Tommy? She loves gringos. Why not him? He's cool and he loves kids."

"My brother and Monica — are you serious?" I started to laugh. Julio grabbed a seat at the counter and a knife along with a cutting board. "Are you really going to help me cook today, Julio?"

"Yes, I have to learn how to cook for you and our kids. Do you think you can teach me, Samantha?"

"We have kids now, Julio?"

"No, not now, but we will one day, and I need to know how to cook for them, Mi Corazón.

I couldn't help it. I laughed and he was giving me the pouty face. I finally said, "Okay, you can help me." He honestly had my heart melting and wanting to kiss him with all this talk about one day. I had Julio wash and cut up the green peppers. We cut up some ham chunks into squares. Breakfast was ready an hour later. Everyone wanted to eat outside by the pool.

Just when I was pulling out the last quiche from the oven, the timer went off on the stove. In walked Daphne as I set the quiche down on the counter to cool off. I noticed when Daphne grabbed the orange juice and champagne. I gave Daphne a quizzical look.

"Hey, I'm sure it's mimosa time for the adults." I just nodded my head yes and followed behind Daphne with two quiche. Julio came up behind me as I set a quiche down on the table outside. He was carrying the paper plates, napkins, and plastic ware.

All of the adults were at the table talking, laughing and having a great time.

Daphne asked, "Does anyone need anything else?" Everyone said no.

"That's great, enjoy."

"You kids are amazing," Carmen said with a great big smile. "Every time I see them, I'm just blown away. Thank you for this lovely breakfast."

"Yes, thank you, guys," my mom said, before we headed back into the house.

"What do you want to do Sammy?"

"About what Daphne?"

"Sammy, we ran out of paper plates."

"I guess we won't eat outside then. It's fine. We can just eat here in the kitchen."

"That's perfect! Julio said as he walked back inside."

"We have two dishwashers; so, all we need to do is rinse the dishes off and place them in the machine."

Daphne and Julio set the table in the kitchen, while I went outside to let the others know to come inside and eat. When I came back inside the two quiche along with a pitcher of apple juice were on the table. I was surprised to see a stack of bagels with cream cheese and chives also on the table. The three of us took a seat at the table and within seconds everyone came inside. "I can eat at the counter if there's not enough room."

"I began to count everyone: Michael, Arturo, Lewis, Eddie, Alex, Tommy, Daphne, Monica and of course Julio and me. That's ten people, and we have ten chairs, Daphne it's fine we all fit." Once everyone was seated Monica asked to say grace.

After breakfast was over, Monica and Tommy offered to clean up the kitchen for us. An hour later Monica called me into the kitchen. I was pleasantly surprised. Tommy and Monica had made the scones, for breakfast tomorrow. They made four flavors: raisin scones, vanilla scones, blueberry scones and strawberry scones.

"I never made scones before Sammy. Your brother taught me how make them."

"Thank you, Monica they look, delicious. Monica turned to Tommy and hugged him, and suddenly he went from grinning to wrapping his arms around her and pulling her in closer.

I looked over at Julio, and I couldn't help but wonder if Julio was on to something. We all walked out to the pool deck and I whispered to Julio, "Maybe the idea of Tommy and Monica getting together is not that crazy after all."

Julio turned to me and asked, "Why? Did something happen?"

"No," I answered laughing.

"Then why did you say that?"

" I don't know. I just see what you see, how they are both smiling more. Tommy just showed your sister how to make scones. They seem to enjoy each other's company."

"Yes, and he admires my niece. That I approve of a hundred percent. Now let's go get in the pool." Before I could protest, Julio picked me up, and jumped in the pool. We were still fully clothed, and the parents started laughing.

Daphne, Tommy, Arturo, along with Michael joined us in the pool fully dressed. Monica was the last one to get in the pool, but she took off her shorts and T-shirt before she jumped in. She had on a bikini and Tommy couldn't take his eyes off her.

Michael and Arturo left about 12 o'clock. That's when Michael's dad finally showed up. Carmen wanted them to stay here with us at the house. However, Michael didn't want his dad to feel jilted. Guillermo made sure to get Michael's address before he left. He's sending a car to pick them up on the day of the wedding.

We spent a good part of the afternoon by the pool. Then we finally came inside and hung out in the family room. It was more of a kick back and relax day.

Around three o'clock, Guillermo and Alex walked into the family room, to tell us they had to go out for a few minutes. Alex told Julio and I specifically not to take off anywhere.

At a quarter to five, Alex and Guillermo were back. Alex walked in carrying a duffel bag that he handed to Eddie, and he asked him to place it in Tommy's room. Alex asked Daphne if he could speak to her outside for a minute. Daphne looked startled by the question, but she answered yes. Alex and Daphne left the family room and walked outside.

Julio and I walked out to the living room and headed for the front door, when we heard Daphne scream. Then Carmen and my mom shoved Julio and me out of the way to get to the front door. When Carmen opened the door, Greg walked in carrying Daphne.

Greg said, "Hi! I'm here to go to the park tomorrow."

Carmen was beaming and asked, "Greg, what are you doing here?"

"Guillermo called me yesterday. He asked me if I could come up a day earlier to attend the dinner tonight. I told him I would try and here I am."

"I thought you had to work today, Greg?"

"I did, but I traded schedules with my cousin Mig. He offered to work for me today, and I'm going to work for him on Monday, a double shift."

He set Daphne down on her feet and she hugged him. "I'm so happy you're here with me now."

"Me too," Carmen said, and she gave him a hug.

Greg walked up to Julio, and asked, "What? You don't call me or write to me anymore. It's like I don't exist." Julio started to laugh, and Greg gave him a one-armed hug.

"Man, I have to show you something." Then Julio and Greg took off. Daphne and I went to look for them after speaking with Alex and Carmen. We found them in the family room, and they were standing in front of the foosball table. Daphne sat down on the sofa and watched them play. I decided to go outside and sit by pool.

Tommy and Monica were back in the pool, sharing a big floating lounge chair.

"Hey guys! how's the water?"

"Very funny Sam. We're not in the water. We are floating on it."

"That's true Tommy, so, is there anything going on between the two of you?"

Monica laughed before saying, "If he didn't tell you about the times before; I don't think he'll tell you anything now."

"The times before, Monica?"

"Sammy, if it were up to me, I would have told you everything a long time ago."

"Like what Monica? Tell me now."

"Like he's a very caring guy and he loves to cuddle, but it's not up to me. Monica said this with a big grin on her face and she was looking at my brother."

"What are you trying to tell me, Monica?" She sat up in the float facing Tommy. He was just looking down at his toes.

"Tommy, why don't you tell me?"

"Sam, I was dating Monica before I left for school."

"Wow, was she the girl that broke your heart?"

"Sam, can we talk about this later?"

"Does Alex know about this? Or Pilar or even Mom?"

"Yes, they all know," Monica answered. "Except for my little brother Julio and my cousin Lewis. They don't know anything. I cheated on Tommy when he was away at school. I told him the truth that the distance was just too much."

"Sam, it's like I told you before, a long distant relationship is impossible."

"Thank you, Tommy," I replied with a smirk on my face.

"Just learn to enjoy the time you have with Julio now. When you return home, you can only take the memories with you not the relationship. Long-distant relationships don't ever work out, Sam."

"I know, Tommy. You have told me this at least a hundred times already."

That's when the sliding glass doors opened from both the living room and the family room. Everyone walked out of the house onto the pool deck. Guillermo said, "I would like to have everyone's attention for just a moment."

"Tomorrow, the weather should be sunny, and I am suggesting we all go to the park. We could spend the day together outdoors it will be fun. What do you think?"

Lewis was the first one to answer, "Sure, let's go Tio."

"Absolutely," Greg said smiling and he reached up and high-fived Julio.

"That sounds great, Gio. Now it's almost six o'clock. Which means everybody needs to start getting ready for the dinner tonight." Pilar opened the sliding glass doors to the living room, and we all walked back inside.

Pilar walked inside behind me, and she shut the sliding glass door. Then I heard her say, "El amor es una cosa hermosa," which means "Love is a beautiful thing," and she stood at the door watching my mom and Guillermo.

When I walked back into my room, Daphne was already in the shower. I heard a knock on the sliding glass door. When I pulled the curtain away to see who it was, Monica was standing there waving to me. I unlocked the door and slid it open.

"I'm sorry Sammy."

"For what?"

"That I didn't ever tell you about me and your brother before today. Your brother didn't want you to know. I was afraid you wouldn't approve of me dating your brother back then. He was my first boyfriend, it ended over a year ago. Tommy will always be my first love and I think I'm his. Please don't be mad at us for keeping this from you. Monica leaned over and hugged me, before she was called away by Pilar.

I shut the sliding glass door and walked from behind the curtain. Daphne was walking back into the bedroom area.

"Hey. You're back, Sammy. Do you want me to style your hair for tonight?"

"Yeah, that would be great, but what do you mean, 'I'm back?'"

"Sammy, I was just teasing . You know, because you snuck out last night to be with Julio. Now you have to tell me everything, but first you need to take a shower."

"Wait. I thought that you were asleep when I snuck out?"

"Yeah, right. Since when do I snore Sammy?"

"Daphne, you were snoring last night."

"I was pretending to be asleep so you could sneak out and spend time with Julio. You're only here for five days; that's five days to spend every minute that you can with Julio the love of your life. Just tell me one thing: are you still a virgin?"

I threw a pillow at Daphne's head and yelled out, "Of course I am. We just held one another all night and fell asleep in each other's arms. Nothing else happened. Oh, except we watched the sunrise this morning. It was such a beautiful sight from the pool deck. You and Greg really need to do that tomorrow morning. It's beautiful."

"But is it romantic, Sammy?"

"Definitely."

"Greg kept asking me, 'So what happened when Julio and Sammy first saw each other?' I'm telling you; he is worse than us girls. He wants to know every little detail."

"Yeah, well. I can't help but wonder what Greg and Julio are talking about right now."

"Daphne, they're not going to speak about this stuff in front of your brother."

"Sammy, did you know that Lewis already has another girlfriend?"

"Yes, I heard about her earlier today."

"Yeah, but did you know we're going to meet her tomorrow? Along with her cousin because that's Eddie's date for the wedding?

They're also going to the park tomorrow."

"Well, that's cool, I guess. We can't expect them to never date again. Besides, Denise and Tonya have already moved on. Logically speaking, long-distant relationships never work out. You just have to enjoy the time you have together and move on."

"That's your brother talking, Sammy. Not you."

"Either way he's right. We are making new memories right at this moment. When I leave on Sunday that's all I get to take home with me to Miami: memories. I don't get to take Julio, so I hope I make some good memories."

Daphne was pouting with a sad look on her face. "Don't be disappointed, Daphne. I'm not. We knew this before we came here. Right now, I'm living in the moment. I'm on Day 2 with the love of my life. It's such an exciting time for me and the four of us are together again. Let's not focus on what's going to happen when I leave, please. Let's just focus on the moments we have right now in this amazing house with our amazing guys Julio and Greg. Can you do that for me, please?"

Daphne jumped up and answered, "Yes, of course, Sammy. Now go and take a shower."

I took a shower, and Daphne was once again waiting for me in the dressing area. I walked out wrapped in my towel and I took a seat in front of the vanity while Daphne pulled the two sides of my hair up and braided them together. The rest of my hair was put up into a ponytail. Then Daphne wrapped the braid around the rubber bands that were holding my hair into the ponytail. My hair is already curly, so Daphne just put some styling foam on the curls to keep the hair from frizzing up. Daphne teased my bangs, so they were puffy in front.

She also applied my makeup, and when she was done, I looked in the mirror and saw that I was wearing tan and light brown eye shadow with brown eye liner, mascara, and a very light peach lip gloss.

When I was finally dressed, I looked at myself in the mirror and twirled around once. I loved this dress. The color was emerald green, and the top portion of the dress was nylon, stretchy, and sleeveless. The skirt was in a bell shape and it was puffy. I had a black satin jacket to bring with me. My mom didn't want me to wear the jacket, but it gets cold here at night. I had on a pair of black pantyhose and heels. I was officially ready to go.

When I walked back out to the bedroom area, Daphne had on her dress, and it was in black satin with spaghetti straps and it had a gold ruffle in the center. She really looked very pretty.

Her makeup was done in pink and white eye shadow, black mascara, eyeliner, and a light pink lip gloss. She was also wearing black panty hose and heels. Her hair was down and held up on the sides with a gold sparkly beret. Her bangs were styled the same as mine just a bit puffier in the front.

"You look beautiful, Daphne. Are you ready to go?"

"Sammy, I can't begin to tell you just how excited I am. To be all dressed up and going somewhere formal with Greg. Are you excited, Sammy?"

"Yes, I'm extremely excited! I can't wait to see Julio all dressed up. Wearing that smile on his face and the smell of his cologne. Daphne, do you think I look pretty enough for him? Will he remember me, when I've gone back to Miami?"

"Sammy, don't panic. You look beautiful. Don't do this thing again where you get all insecure."

"I'm sorry, Daphne. I didn't mean to freak out! I'm just nervous. You know! They are going to be taking pictures at the dinner tonight. That means photos of us Julio will see which I will never see. That may be the very last memory he ever has of me."

"Wow! After you put it like that Sammy, I'm not sure if I want my picture taken."

"Okay. Now I'm going to be quiet because I'm starting to freak you out."

There was a knock on the door, and it was my mom and Carmen. "Girls, are you ready?"

"Yes, we are," Daphne answered, she looked back at me and smiled before opening the bedroom door. My mom and Carmen told us we had to get going now. We followed our mothers out to the living room.

Guillermo was walking down the stairs as he was speaking on the cordless phone. He hung up and placed the phone on the charger. "Is everybody ready to go? The cars are here."

He opened the front door, and there was a driver in a black suit standing in front of the limo. Guillermo looked over at Alex and said, "That one is not for you. These are for you," and he handed Alex two sets of car keys. "I know that some of you may want to leave early. Now with two cars that can happen. No one is to leave until after dinner."

We were all smiling at one another as we all practically ran out the door to get in the cars. Julio grabbed my hand and we ran off in the direction toward the white town car. Greg and Daphne followed behind us. When Eddie arrived at the car, he was with a tall girl who had beautiful long straight brown hair. She was wearing a long black dress with a slit on the side that showed a little leg, and black heels. We all climbed into the back seat. Eddie was upfront with his date.

Eddie turned around in his seat and said, "This is my date tonight, Heather." We each introduced ourselves to Heather. Then he asked, "How are all four of you sitting back there?

"Eddie looked in the back seat, and I smiled. Eddie realized I was sitting on Julio's lap. "Okay, Sammy. As long as you are all comfortable."

"She is," Julio replied with a grin. "Now let's go, Primo."

"I can't go anywhere Julio until the limo pulls out. Sorry, but I was told to follow behind the limo to the hotel."

"I didn't hear Tio say that Eddie."

"He didn't say that. Your brother Alex did." We all started laughing in the backseat. "What's so funny? Why are you people laughing?"

"Eddie, is Alex still in the driveway? "Greg asked.

"No, but he told me he was going to pull out and wait on the curb since the cars need to be black, white, black."

All four us started laughing even harder now.

"Eddie, Alex, tricked you; he just wanted to arrive first."

Eddie started yelling, "Retaliation is coming tonight! I have not pulled one prank on him in the two days since he has been home." We were all still laughing, when Eddie finally pulled out of the driveway.

Julio wrapped his arms around my waist, and he squeezed me. I looked back at him and he had his hair gelled back. He was wearing a black suit with a black tie. He really looked good and he smelled awesome. The cologne was different from the one he normally wore. Yet the smell was familiar, and I loved it. I had to put my nose to his neck and sniff him.

Julio jumped and quickly pulled his head away from me. His eyes were huge, and he said, "You can't do that to me, not when you're sitting on my lap." After a couple of minutes of complete silence, Julio leaned over and whispered in my ear, "I'm sorry I overreacted, but my neck is a sensor. I felt your breath, on my neck, and you're sitting on my lap."

I pulled my head away and just looked back at him. Julio whispered, "Do you get what I'm saying?" I nodded my head yes.

I whispered back, "I'm sorry about that, but the smell of your cologne is driving me crazy. Is that the same cologne you wore at Daphne's birthday party?"

Julio whispered, "Yes, and I wore it because I know it drives you crazy."

I pulled away from him to see his face, he smiled and winked at me. I thought to myself don't do it, Sam. It was too late. I had already leaned in toward his neck. I gently placed a wet kiss on his neck, and I blew on it. Julio turned his head down to look at me.

I just sat up to look back at him and smiled. By the look on Julio's face, he was definitely surprised. He just shook his head at me and smiled.

Eddie pulled up in front of the valet podium at the Hotel. He told us, "Heather and I will meet you upstairs." The four of us climbed out of the car and walked inside.

When we reached the elevators Daphne smiled before saying, "Now this brings back some memories with Uncle Gio." We both broke out into laughter, and Greg gave us a strange look.

Julio told Greg, "My uncle Gio picked up the girls from the airport and pretended to be a limo driver."

"Dude are you serious?"

"Julio laughed and asked, "Greg, would I lie to you?"

"Julio man, I can't wait to hear about this. Your uncle Gio is something else."

We all stepped out of the elevator and walked down to the same banquet room where we had lunch the previous day. Julio grabbed the handle on the door and held it open for everyone. I walked in second to last. I wanted to walk inside with Julio beside me holding my hand.

This time there were five round tables in the room set up for eight people per table. Each table was assigned with name cards. Greg and Daphne walked over to the station set up to view the seating chart. Julio already knew which table we were assigned to. We walked over to Greg and Daphne. Julio told them to follow him. We were all assigned to the same table."

Tommy, Monica, Alex, and another person were already sitting down at the table when we arrived. Alex stood up and said, "Allow me to introduce you to my cousin Enrique." He shook hands with Greg and Daphne.

When he shook my hand, he asked, "Are you Samantha?"

"Yes, I am."

"I have heard a lot about you from my cousin Julio. It's great to finally meet you." Julio hugged his cousin, and we all sat down.

I started to take notice of all the decorations in the room. There were baby pink colored roses as the centerpiece on each table along with four fat candles in a glass case. The tables were covered with silver tablecloths and a white lace on top. The tables looked beautiful, and there was classical music playing lightly over the speakers above us, which gave the room a very romantic atmosphere.

Julio asked, "Where is everybody?

Lewis stood up and walked over to our table. "Where are the parents?"

"I don't know Lewis, did your dad say anything about changing banquet rooms?"

"Alex do you think we are in the wrong room?"

"No, we're not. Our names are on the seating chart."

"Monica's right," Alex said.

"I want to double check just in case." Lewis left out the double doors.

Guillermo and all the parents walked inside around 10 minutes later.

Alex asked, "Where were you, Tio?"

Guillermo answered, "I'm sorry we're late; we just stopped off at the cocktail-reception upstairs. It started at six o'clock for Julie and my brother Juan. We wanted to meet all of their friends and Julie's family. We didn't join them at the scheduled time obviously. We were at the house with all of you."

"Okay, Tio, but what's with the classical music?" Lewis asked as he walked back into the room with Eddie and Heather.

"Oh, yes. I asked my staff to play this especially for you. I know how much you enjoy it Lewis." We all started laughing, and Lewis looked back at us visibly annoyed. "Do you want me to tell them to turn it up for you, Lewis?"

"No, Tio. Please ask them to turn it off. We're not in an elevator or a horror movie."

"Okay, no problem. Anything for you."

"Gracias, Tio," Lewis marched back to his table and sat down.

Alex said, "Oh boy, here we go. It's not over yet."

A couple of minutes later, the classical music was turned up even louder.

At that very moment, everyone at out our table simultaneously said, "Okay, no problem" in our best Guillermo accent, and we all began to laugh.

After a couple of minutes, the classical music was turned off. A man walked in the room carrying a guitar case. Then four more people walked in behind him. They all headed straight for the stage that was set up in the front of the room.

When Julie and Mr. Sanchez walked in the room, they brought up with them the rest of their friends and Julie's family. That's when the band began to play a song by the Beach Boys, and the waiters came around taking everyone's drink orders.

Lewis returned to our table with his girlfriend Amy this time. He introduced his girlfriend to all of us. She was very pretty with blonde curly hair, big brown eyes, and an hourglass shape (and what I envied most: a golden tan). She was wearing a silver sequined dress that ended right above her knee with silver heels.

I asked Lewis if they wanted to pull their chairs over beside us. Lewis looked back at his girlfriend before answering no. I thought that was odd, but he explained how he didn't want to leave Heather or Eddie alone. Amy hugged me and told me that she was so happy to finally meet me. That's when Lewis gave her a rather strange look. He didn't say anything after that, he grabbed Amy's hand instead and walked back to his table.

The boys were all talking about the bachelor party Alex had in Miami. Monica asked Julio to trade seats with her so she could speak to me. Julio kissed me on the cheek before he stood up and changed seats with his sister. He informed her that he wanted his seat back by the time his food arrived.

Monica sat down and turned her chair a little to the left, so she was facing me. Then she leaned over and asked, "What do you think of Amy?"

"She seems nice. I really haven't had a chance to speak with her much. Although she did give me a hug and told me she was happy to finally meet me. When she said that, Lewis gave her a strange look. Why do you think he did that?"

Monica suddenly had the same strange look on her face, and she turned her head to look over at Julio. Daphne said, "Well, I think Amy looks a lot like Tonya and she even has her booty and curly blonde hair."

"Right. That's the first thing I thought when I met her," Monica said. "Why didn't Tonya come? I mean she was invited. When she didn't respond to the invitation, Alex went over to her house to invite her in person. Lewis was all ready to ditch Amy for the week if Tonya made it up here."

"Truthfully, I didn't even know she was invited."

"Sammy's right, Tonya never mentioned a word to either of us." Monica appeared to be surprised to hear that.

"Did Alex tell you what happened when he went over to Tonya's house?"

"That's just it, Sammy. When Alex called, he said to tell Lewis to take his girlfriend."

"Well, that's what he did, so I guess it all worked out," Daphne said smiling.

"Okay, what's going on? What are you girls not telling me?"

"It's nothing Monica."

"Spill it Daphne."

Okay, we saw Tonya kissing some guy in the parking lot the other day. We don't know if it's her boyfriend; in fact, we didn't even know this guy existed until that day."

"Well, that's good. At least they have both moved on. It's not like they were madly in love with one another; it was just puppy love."

"Yeah, I think you're right Monica. They fought the entire time they were together. It was still so much fun to be around them when they were a couple though.

"Daphne, I have to admit my mom and I didn't think their relationship was going to last as long as it did. Now when Julio and Sammy got together, we knew they fell in love. My mom says they were just meant to be together."

"Monica, your mom said that?"

"Yeah, Sammy, and your mom agreed."

"Well, now there is only one problem?

"What's that Sammy?"

"Over a thousand miles between us."

Monica hugged me before saying, "Enjoy today Sammy and who knows what will happen in the future." The food arrived and Julio stood up and walked over to stand behind Monica. She stood up and moved back to her seat.

Julio sat down and whispered, "I missed you." He reached for my hand under the table.

When everyone had their food, Greg said, "Wait. We have to say grace." Everyone held hands, and Greg said grace. During dinner, we talked about where we could go after we finished eating.

Daphne mentioned the arcade. Greg mentioned bowling. Tommy was tired and Monica wanted to go home and check on Erika. That's when Lewis walked up to our table with Eddie.

Lewis asked, "What are you guys going to do now? We finished eating, so we can leave."

"Why? What do you want to do?" Alex asked.

"I just want to go back to Tio's house and watch a movie in his theatre room."

Greg sat up, and his eyes were lit up now. "Your uncle has a movie theatre in his house?"

"Not an actual movie theatre but a theatre room. You know, it's a room with a big screen and a bunch of leather sofas and chairs to kick back, relax, and watch a movie."

"Where is the theatre room in the house? I haven't seen it," Tommy asked.

"When you go down the stairs to the garage, instead of making a right for the garage door, you make a left, and the door is on that wall behind the stairs," Monica answered.

Greg stood up and asked, "Who wants to go back to the house and watch a movie?" Everyone stood up and said, I do."

That's when my mom, Pilar, and Carmen walked over to our table. "Where have you all decided to go?"

Alex answered, "We're just going back to Uncle Gio's house to watch a movie."

"Yes, because Guillermo told all of us that he wanted us to make it an early night, we have a big day tomorrow," Greg added smiling.

Pilar said, "Yes, Gio did say that. You all need to go straight back to Gio's house. Don't go running around town tonight. We do have a big day planned for tomorrow." I hugged my mom, and Daphne hugged her mom, and we left out the door with Greg and Julio.

When we arrived back at the house, it was already a quarter after ten. Tommy and Monica left the house in the golf cart to check on Erika. Eddie, Heather, Amy, and Lewis went downstairs to watch a movie. Alex went to his room to call Maria while the four of us (Greg, Daphne, Julio, and I) went to the game room to play foosball.

An hour later, Daphne and I went back to our room to get ready for bed. We left Julio and Greg playing one more game.

I took a shower and put on my pajamas and climbed into bed. Daphne told me she was going for a swim in the Jacuzzi as she headed down the hall carrying her bathrobe with a clip in her hair and a book in her hand.

Next thing I knew I heard a light knock coming from the sliding glass doors. Daphne and I jumped out of our beds, and we ran over to the door. It was Greg and Julio. They were smiling the minute we appeared in front of the glass doors.

Daphne slid open the door and we both stepped out of our room. Daphne shut the sliding glass door quietly behind us.

It was still dark outside, and I had no idea how long I slept for. I whispered to Julio, "I'm sorry. I fell asleep; I meant to come say goodnight to you."

"That's okay Samantha. We only hung out for another hour. After the parents arrived home, we went to bed!"

"Yeah, we had time to catch up," Greg whispered.

"Oh yeah. What did you do?" Daphne asked.

We all shushed her and told her to whisper.

Daphne whispered, "Sorry" and covered her mouth.

Julio took my hand, and Greg took Daphne's. The boys walked us over to the edge of the pool deck. The same two lounge chairs were waiting for us from yesterday. Each chair had a throw blanket neatly folded up on it.

Julio wrapped his arms around me and whispered, "I hope you don't mind if we sit out here and watch the sunrise again."

I reached up on my tiptoes and I wrapped my arms around him. He whispered, "The picture in the sky is never identical, Samantha. I thought we should share it with our friends."

"I can't wait to see it all again with you Julio."

He took my hand, and we walked over to the lounge chairs. Greg and Daphne were curled up together on the left lounge chair. I waited for Julio to sit down and I sat down between his legs and laid my head back on his chest. I looked up at Julio and whispered, "It's almost better than the lake."

Julio whispered back, "Nothing is better than our lake, Mi Corazón," as he wrapped his arms around me. That sent chills up and down my neck so quick that I was shivering. Julio grabbed the blanket and covered me up. He snuggled right back into me holding me and rubbing my back over the blanket.

A couple of minutes later we watched the darkness disappear under the bright star we call the sun. Daphne said, "Wow. I haven't ever watched the sunrise before. I mean, I have seen it like from the car on the way to school. I just haven't ever experienced it like this."

I noticed something caught Daphne's attention behind us. I quickly turned around to see what it was. At first, I didn't see anything; then I heard music playing.

I looked up toward the balcony and I saw my mom and Guillermo. They were holding one another as they danced out on the balcony together. The four of us just watched them in complete shock.

"Sammy, I don't think we should have left dinner early last night."

"Nope."

"I don't think we should have gone to bed early last night either, Sammy."

"I think you're right, Daphne."

"Now we missed everything that happened, that led up to this, Sammy."

"Yup," Greg said, and we all started laughing.

That's when I heard Tommy ask, "What are you guys looking at?" He was walking over towards us and suddenly stopped. "Mom, what are you doing?"

My mom and Guillermo pulled apart. They looked down at all of us from the balcony, and they each had a startled look on their face. I could see my mom had become upset. She turned her back to us and was frantically waving her hands around while speaking to Guillermo. He wrapped his arms around my mom and as she laid her head on his shoulder. He now had a worried look on his face, while he held my mom and stroked the back of her head. My mom suddenly pulled away from Guillermo. She turned around and walked over to the balcony door that led to her room. She looked back at him once, and he held an apologetic look on his face as she walked inside.

Guillermo turned around and faced us. He told us, "I asked your mother to come out on the balcony at a quarter to six to watch the sunrise with me. I was caught up in the moment and I turned on some music and asked your mom to dance." He looked out at the sky and continued saying, "Tommy your mother brightens up my day just like this sunrise."

Tommy looked from Guillermo to me. I was now standing beside Tommy right below Guillermo's balcony. I just smiled and my brother was smiling too. Guillermo turned his eyes away from the sky and he noticed I was standing beside my brother looking up at him. He smiled and asked, "Would the two of you approve of me asking your mom out on a real date?"

"Why are you asking them Guillermo? You need to ask me." Startled, I looked behind us, and saw my mom standing out on the pool deck looking up at Guillermo.

Guillermo clapped his hands together and replied, "Okay, Lori." Then he put his index finger up and said, "Just give me a second." He ran back inside his room.

"Mom, do you like this guy?"

My mom closed her eyes, and when she opened them, she answered, "Yes, I do, Tommy."

"Well, good! because I like him too."

"What about you, Samantha? Are you okay with me going out on a date with Gio?"

"Yes, Mom. Of course, I want you to be happy and I think he's cool."

Less than a minute later Guillermo walked out to the pool; and he was carrying a single pink rose. He walked up to my mom and bent down on one knee in front of her. He took her hand as he looked up at her and asked, "Would you go out on a date with me, Lori?"

My mom laughed and said, "I don't know, Gio. Let me ask my kids."

Tommy responded, "Sure. Why not, Mom? Just be home by curfew."

My mom looked down at Guillermo and answered, "I guess I can go as long as I'm home by midnight." Guillermo smiled, and he kissed the top of my mom's hand. He handed her the pink rose and he stood up. They walked back in the house holding hands.

Chapter 5 A Day at the Park

Daphne and I walked back into our bedroom through the sliding glass doors. Once Daphne closed the door she turned around and asked, "Now what do you really think about your mom and Guillermo?"

"I was shocked obviously to see them out on the balcony wearing their bathrobes. At first, I honestly had the wrong idea and was kind of upset."

"What do you mean by the wrong idea, Sammy?"

"I thought my mom had just spent the night in Guillermo's room and that sort of upset me."

"To tell you the truth, Sammy, I thought the same thing."

Luckily, I was wrong, and Guillermo explained why they were on the balcony. I know it's silly, but I felt so relieved."

"It's not silly! I was actually freaking out myself Sammy."

"Yeah. For the first time ever, you were completely speechless."

"Whatever! Sammy. You weren't able to speak either when you first saw them out on the balcony. Besides, your mom is like my auntie or something, so I care about her."

"Aw. That's so sweet of you to say that, Daphne. Now tell me, how was your swim in the jacuzzi last night?"

"It was awesome. I poured half the bottle of shampoo into the jacuzzi. I had so many bubbles that I had to take a shower after I climbed out."

"That sounds awesome. Do we have any shampoo left Daphne?"

"Yes, but you can't go for a swim in the jacuzzi now Sammy. We have to get ready to go to the park, remember?"

"Daphne, I'm not worried about going for a swim in the jacuzzi. I just want to wash my hair when I get back from the park."

"Maybe we should stop off at the store and pick up some more shampoo. You know just to be on the safe side."

I rolled my eyes as I stood up and headed into the bathroom to take a shower. We were both dressed and ready to go in less than an hour. We each had our hair in a braid. We decided to wear shorts and a tank top with slouch socks and high-top sneakers.

We headed straight into the kitchen and I opened the refrigerator to grab the trays of scones. I looked all around the refrigerator, but the trays were gone. That's when Tommy walked in the kitchen and said, "They're gone, Sammy."

Tommy had a seat in one of the stools facing me. "The parents came home last night and were hungry. I brought out a tray for the parents. Then Alex and Eddie wanted to try them, and before I knew it, they were all gone. Sorry, Sam. I know how much you wanted to try them."

"It's okay. We better get started making breakfast now. We all need to eat something before we head off to the park."

Tommy stood up and opened the refrigerator, "Look at all these tubs of yogurt. Gross. I can't stand that stuff. Now cottage cheese — that's the good stuff."

"Uh, Tommy! You don't eat yogurt, but you will eat cottage cheese!"

"Are you kidding, Sam? It's the best. I love cottage cheese with some fruit on top. It's the perfect breakfast when you're in a hurry and need to get to class."

"That's a great idea, Tommy. Find me a strainer."

I opened the refrigerator, and I grabbed a container of blueberries and a couple of bananas. I set them up on the counter and asked Tommy to find two bowls. Daphne joined us in the kitchen, and I asked her to start rinsing off the blueberries in the strainer. I grabbed three large tubs of yogurt out of the refrigerator and set them on the counter along with a container of cottage cheese.

Julio and Greg came into the kitchen and sat down at the counter. Greg asked, "What are you making Sammy?"

"A quick breakfast for everyone."

"Great. I'm starving."

"Of course, you are Greg."

Julio smiled after I said that and asked if he could help. I told him he could help me by setting the table and counter for everyone to eat. Julio set out some bowls and bread plates. Greg followed behind him with the napkins and silverware.

After the berries were washed, I cut up the bananas and placed them into four separate bowls. I placed two bowls of fruit on the counter and on the table.

Greg walked back into the kitchen with Julio and asked what's next. I tossed them each a bag of English muffins and bagels. Tommy stopped cutting up the chives and asked, "Do you guys even know how to use a toaster?"

When the boys weren't laughing, I looked up at Julio and Greg, "They both had a bewildered look on their face. "What's up? Why do you guys look like that? Of course, you guys know how to use a toaster. Tommy was only joking."

"Actually..."

"Actually, what Julio?"

"Samantha, I know how to use a toaster."

"Great, so what's the problem?" Julio rolled his eyes and placed his hands on his hips.

"Julio, out with it already!"

"I don't know if my uncle has one."

I couldn't help it I looked over at Daphne and Tommy smiling. I knew the answer, but I had to ask. "Julio have you ever seen a toaster in this kitchen?"

"He looked me square in the eyes and sounding completely aggravated answered, "No."

Tommy and Daphne nearly passed out from laughing so hard. Greg crossed his arms over his chest and asked, "Are you guys done yet?"

Daphne ran around the counter and told them to follow her. She walked back into the kitchen and they followed her to the end of the kitchen counter. She pulled the cotton cover off the toaster and said, "tah-dah."

Julio walked up to me and squeezed me around the waist. He nuzzled my neck and spoke in a low tone, "Mi Corazón we found the toaster. I had instant chills as I looked back at him and saw his devilish grin. "Now I'm going to show your brother who can really make bonging waffles, but not today I need to go to the grocery store first."

"Okay, you do that Julio. I tried not laugh as I went back to grabbing the butter and cream cheese out of the refrigerator.

After everything was prepared, Julio let everyone know breakfast was ready. Tommy made a pot of coffee and I set the bagels and English muffins freshly toasted on the counter and table.

When Julio walked back into the kitchen, he wasn't alone. "Samantha, I found everyone in the living room except for Monica and my mom. They will be over here in a few minutes."

"Thank you, Julio," I replied with a smile.

The parents all had a seat at the table; Alex joined them.

The boys all sat at the counter. Daphne and I remained standing on the other side of the counter.

Carmen asked, "What are we going to have today, guys?"

"Yogurt or cottage cheese with your choice of strawberries or blueberries, and we also have bagels with cream cheese and chives or an English muffin with butter and jelly."

"Oh, now that sounds perfect. You kids have done a fantastic job, and those scones we had last night were delicious."

"Thank you, Guillermo, but Tommy and Monica made the scones."

"Now, how many of you want coffee?"

Pilar walked in and replied, "I would love a cup Tommy." That's when my brother turned around and he saw Monica.

His face lit up and he had a huge smile on his face. "Coming right up Pilar." Julio was already in the cabinet grabbing down the coffee cups.

"Julio, be sure to grab at least five coffee cups from the cabinet. My brother should be here any minute, and he is always in need of a cup of coffee."

Daphne went into the refrigerator and grabbed the apple juice and orange juice along with the jelly. I walked over to the cabinet where Julio was standing. I asked him if he could hand me eight juice glasses. He said, "Wow. You're extremely thirsty, Samantha."

"Very funny Soccer player."

"Hey, what's going on over there, you two?" My mom asked in a happier than usual tone of voice.

Pilar smiled and answered, "Love. Now that is what is going on all around us Lori." She looked over at my mom and Guillermo continuing to smile.

Tommy handed Pilar a cup of coffee. Julio followed behind him and brought over four more empty coffee cups along with the pot of coffee. Daphne brought over the creamer and a serving bowl of sugar. A couple of minutes later, Eddie, Heather, Lewis, Amy, and Cousin Enrique walked into the kitchen. Guillermo asked, "Where is your father and Julie?"

"They're not coming with us Tio. They have plans to spend the day with Julie's family," Eddie answered. He sounded so disappointed and Lewis had a look of disappointment all over his face.

"Okay. Come sit down and eat so we can all leave here in 30 minutes." I could tell by the tone of Guillermo's voice and the expression on his face that he was not happy.

I had already finished eating, so I brought my plate and bowl to the sink. Daphne followed me carrying Julio and Greg's plates. We placed everything into the sink and wiped down the kitchen counters. Greg began to rinse off the plates, and Julio was loading them into the dishwasher. Daphne and I looked at one another stunned.

That's when Guillermo came back into the kitchen and said, "Thank you guys for breakfast. Everything was wonderful. Now Let's go to the park?"

When Guillermo opened the front door, Enrique quickly ran outside and grabbed the car handle and held the door open, for Carmen. Once she was inside the car, he smiled and shut the door. My mom and Guillermo were standing behind Enrique.

Guillermo looking very surprised asked Enrique, "Why did you shut the door?"

Enrique turned around, and he was bright red. "I don't even know Tio." He placed his hand on his forehead.

My mom started laughing, and Pilar walked up beside my mom. She was laughing too and told him, "I knew it Enrique. You have a thing for Carmen." We all stood there waiting for Enrique to respond, but he didn't say a word.

Guillermo finally said, "Okay, no problem. Please open the door Enrique, and let's all get inside."

I looked up at Julio and asked, "How old is your cousin?"

Julio raised up his eyebrows, and asked me, "Why does that matter?"

"Ummm, because it does."

"Enrique has an ex-wife that's 20 years older than him."

"Wait. What? He's been married before Julio?"

"Yes, why does that matter?"

"I don't know. Just tell me how old he is Julio."

"He's old enough to drink!"

" Come on, Julio. Why won't you tell me?"

"Hey you two."

Julio and I turned around and saw Alex standing beside the black town car. "Are you guys riding with me or what?"

"Yes," Julio answered, he took my hand and we quickly jogged over to the car and climbed inside.

Once we were situated in the car, and I was comfy on Julio's lap, I looked up into Julio's eyes and asked him to tell me now. Julio nodded his head forward, and I turned my head around to see Enrique sitting in the passenger's seat beside Alex.

"Hey, Enrique. I didn't know you were riding with us. I thought you would —" Julio squeezed me before I could finish my sentence.

"You thought I would what, Sammy?"

"Never mind. Oh actually, I do have another question for you Enrique."

"What is it, Sammy?"

"I wanted to ask you a personal question."

"What's the question?" Julio squeezed me and gave me a disapproving look.

"How old are you Enrique?"

"How old do I look, Sammy?"

"Truthfully, you look about eighteen." That's when Julio and Alex started laughing.

Julio whispered, "Now I know why you were so worried, Mi Corazón," then he continued to laugh. I just looked back at Julio, surprised.

Enrique said, "Thank you, Sammy. That's a very nice compliment. Even if my cousins don't agree with you."

"I am 37 years old and recently divorced. I moved from Texas to California right after my divorce was final a little over a year ago. I am very happy now, and I work for Gio."

"Wow! Well, I'm very glad to hear you're happy, and I hope you will continue to be so Enrique."

"Thank you, Sammy. I hope so too."

Whispering into Julio's ear I said, "There's only a two-year age difference. I don't think he likes Carmen."

"Enrique likes her very much, I saw them dancing together last night in the living room.

"Julio, when did this happen?"

He pulled his head away from me and whispered "Shhhhh." Then he leaned in closer and in a whisper answered, "When they came back to the house after dinner."

"No way. We missed that?"

Daphne and Greg looked over at me, so I must have been speaking rather loudly. Julio just smiled at me and nodded his head yes.

Julio continued to whisper and told me, "A lot of things happened last night. Greg and I witnessed everything. I can tell you all about it later on if you behave and don't ask Enrique anymore questions."

That's when I whispered back, "I thought your cousin is into older women."

Julio snuggled up close to my ear and whispered, "No, my cousin likes all women."

I looked back at him with pleading eyes and softly said, "You have to tell me everything, Julio. It's going to drive me crazy until I know."

Julio laughed and replied, "Later, Mi Corazón. I promise." He looked back at me with his sweet soulful eyes, and that's all it took. He had his arms wrapped around me and he pulled me in closer to him. I didn't ask another question about last night for the rest of the car ride.

Once we arrived at the park, Daphne asked, "Where are the parents?"

"They will be here in a little bit. They stopped to pick up food and drinks so we can have lunch out here."

"What kind of drinks are we talking about Alex?"

"The non-alcohol type of drinks if that's what you're worried about Daphne."

Daphne just smiled at Alex.

Eddie pulled up into the parking space beside us. He quickly climbed out and said, "This place is going to be so much fun."

Once everyone was out of the cars. I took Julio's hand, and we all followed Alex into a gazebo. "This is where we will have lunch today." The gazebo had four picnic tables and two barbeque grills.

"Looks good Alex, now where are the parents with the food?"

"They'll be here shortly Greg."

The parents arrived around 20 minutes later. We all helped them unload the car and brought everything into the gazebo.

Alex was setting up the barbeque grills with Guillermo.

Julio asked if we could walk down to the lake. Guillermo handed Julio some money and told him, "Go rent some of those little boats or bicycles for everybody. Just be back here in two hours."

Julio grabbed hold of my hand and we all headed towards the lake. "Where are we going?"

"Daphne, we're going to the lake. Didn't you see it when we drove into the park?"

"No, I didn't notice a lake Julio."

"That's okay baby, the lake is really a Julio and Sammy thing."

"Gee, your right about that Greg." Julio and I turned around and stuck our tongue out at Greg and Daphne.

Lewis shouted with excitement, "Look!" He pointed to the dock. We could see pedal boats in the water tied up to several poles on the dock. Lewis yelled out, "Let's race," and he released his girlfriend's hand and ran down the hill with Eddie behind him.

I looked up at Julio and asked, "Don't you want to race?"

"No, I just want to hold your hand and walk down to the lake with you."

I stopped walking and Julio turned around and faced me holding both of my hands. "What's wrong?"

I shook my head and answered, "Nothing. It's stupid."

Julio raised his eyebrows up and pressed his lips together waiting for an explanation. "I released one of his hands and rubbed my forehead. Julio was just standing there patiently waiting as I found my courage and here it came as an outburst. "Julio, I don't want us to get to mushy and romantic in front of everyone. Lakes tend to do that to us. I have some very romantic memories with you at the lake back home."

"Yeah. Me too," we heard someone say from behind us. Julio and I both stopped walking and turned around. Alex was standing behind us smiling. "You aren't the only ones who hid out by the lake."

"You and Maria hung out at the lake?"

"Yes, why does that surprise you Julio?"

"No, but it does explain how you always knew where to find us."

"Maybe it does," Alex replied with a grin. "Now this might be a different lake, but you're still the kissing bandits." The three of us just stood there a couple of yards away from everyone laughing.

Daphne and Greg walked up to us with Amy and Heather. "What's so funny?" Daphne asked.

"Oh, nothing," Alex answered. "I was just teasing my brother. Let's get down to the dock before Eddie and Lewis throw each other in." We followed Alex and saw two other stands by the lake. One rented bicycles, and the other one rented sporting equipment.

Lewis asked, "Can we rent a soccer ball Alex?"

"I don't have any money Lewis. You have to ask Julio."

"Okay, fine. Julio, can we rent a soccer ball?"

"No, Lewis. Uncle Gio brought his ball; I saw him carry it to the car."

"Alex, are you riding with us?"

"Yeah, I guess Julio. But just so you can take me across the lake. I need to get back to Tio and Enrique."

"Okay, Alex. We can do that," Julio said while smiling at me.

Julio rented four pedal boats in total. Once we were away from the dock, Alex stood up on the back seat and said, "Pedal faster Julio, you must get me back to the other side of this lake."

"You got it captain." Julio shifted this little knob, and now we were pedaling around in a circle. "Wait. It's stuck!"

"What's stuck?"

"The knob Alex, it wont move."

Alex reached down and grabbed the knob, and he forced the rusty knob back to the middle. We were back to pedaling straight again. We finally made it to the other side of the lake. Alex jumped out onto the grass and Julio jumped out beside him. Together they turned the boat around. Julio jumped back onto the boat and climbed up to the front seat.

"Are you ready to go, Mi Corazón?"

"Yes. Where are we going, Soccer Player?"

He smiled at me before answering, "I would love to take you to Hawaii someday, but right now I need to take this boat back to the dock. The knob's broken, so we need another boat. Or we can go find a spot under a tree."

"Whatever you want to do is fine with me."

Julio continued to pedal toward the dock; he didn't say another word. I could see a smile on his face, and I felt his hand reach over to hold mine. Then he said, "I guess we will get a different boat." At that moment, I was instantly filled with regret for not speaking up and telling Julio I would rather find a spot under a tree.

One of the employees noticed us coming in when we were close enough to the dock. He told us to throw him the rope to the boat. We did and he pulled us the rest of the way to the dock. We climbed out of the pedal boat and Julio told him about the broken knob.

The guy was really cool and said, "That's no problem," and he showed us to another boat. We stepped onto this other boat, and Julio had a look of disappointment on his face. We both sat down, and Julio checked to make sure the knob worked.

We pedaled out to the center of the lake, and Julio turned to me and asked, "Why didn't you just admit you wanted to go sit under a tree with me?"

"I just wanted to do whatever makes you happy." He bit on his lower lip and turned his head away from me. "Alright, Julio, I need to stop trying to lie to you, because I'm not good at it."

"No, you're not a liar Samantha, so just do what you have always done and tell me the truth."

"Okay, but it's embarrassing for me to admit this type of thing. Julio just blinked at me several times and he tilted his head to the side waiting.

Okay, I wanted to sit under a tree with you and be locked away in your arms. Kissing you, holding you, and just be able to talk to you alone. I just didn't want to look too eager."

"That's what I really wanted to do too, Samantha. I haven't even kissed you on the lips today. I just want to kiss you so badly." I leaned over and pop kissed Julio on the lips.

I pulled away and opened my eyes. At the same time as a white, two door Mercedes pulled up beside the lake, honking. I saw two people waving, but I couldn't tell who it was. "Look it's Monica and Tommy."

I'm glad Julio knew who it was because I didn't. Finally, I waved back and heard Tommy yell, "Wait for us to park. We're coming down to see you."

About a minute later Tommy and Monica were walking down to the edge of the lake. We pulled up as close as we could get. Monica was giggling and saying, "We had no idea this was lovers' lake."

"You're right, it's like the love boat experience except we each have our own boat."

Monica laughed at my comment and replied, "By the way, that honking Sammy was your brother Tommy. When we pulled up, he saw you kissing my brother."

"About that Monica, do you want our boat?"

"Of course, I do Julio.

 "Wait, where are you two going?"

"Oh, just for a walk Tommy."

"Cool, get out," Monica said, as her and Tommy jumped onto the back of the boat.

Julio started pedaling rather fast and told them, "You both need to have a seat." Monica and Tommy quickly sat down on the backseats. We were across the lake and at the dock within a couple of minutes.

We climbed out and waved bye to Monica and Tommy.

"Now let's go find that tree Mi Corazón." While we walked across the dock to the back of the lake Julio spotted a tree. It was perfectly concealed by the shed that holds all the sporting equipment for rent.

Julio sat down first. He held his hands up to me and helped ease me down gently onto his lap. Once I sat down, he laid his back against the tree. I curled up against his left shoulder and looked up at him. He leaned in towards me, so I closed my eyes. When I felt his lips softly press up against mine, I thought finally! I opened my eyes when I felt his arms wrap around me. I was facing the lake, and I could tell he was no longer feeling disappointed.

"I waited for you for hours last night Samantha, when you didn't come back outside, I was disappointed."

"I'm sorry, Julio. I had every intention of coming back outside after I took a shower."

"Really?"

"Yes, and I was thinking we could sneak away, just the two of us to the cabana tonight."

"I would love that, Samantha. Now can you turn around and face me?"

"Why?"

"I want to kiss you."

"So, kiss me Julio."

"Okay, but first I want to prepare you."

I began to laugh and asked, "Prepare me for what Julio?" He was blushing now, and I knew he wanted to make out.

"For our first real kiss of the day, Samantha."

I had to work hard to hold in my laughter and ask, "What do you call all the kisses you gave me earlier today?"

Julio smiled and said, "I would call all of them safe kisses."

"Oh really! So, what's an unsafe kiss?"

"Turn around and I will show you."

"Julio, that sounds scary."

"It can be scary at times."

"What makes it so scary Julio?"

"This type of kiss will make your adrenaline kick in, your heart will beat faster, and you suddenly feel alive." He caught me off guard, I was not expecting him to admit to still having those type of feelings for me.

"Wow, I've been able to make you feel like that?" Julio started blushing and nodding his head yes. That's when I stood up and said, "Yeah, but that was before when you were still living in Miami." He caught my hand and pulled me back down onto his lap.

This time I was facing him, and I was incredibly nervous. "Samantha, all of your kisses make me feel this way. I felt his arms around my waist, but his eyes never left my face.

He pulled me closer to him, and I took a deep breath. As he leaned in, I closed my eyes. My heart was already beating faster before our lips touched.

He went in for a deep kiss and I felt his tongue brush against mine. I had instant chills mixed with an intense tingling sensation from my head to my toes. When we pulled away from one another, I looked down and noticed my chest was pointy.

I looked back at Julio, who was also looking at my chest smiling. I kissed him behind the ear, and I heard him groan. Then I noticed goosebumps appearing on the back of his neck. I kissed him again right behind the same ear and whispered, "Now you know how it feels."

Julio placed his hands on either side of my face, and he kissed me again. This time he kissed me slower and longer. I had to pull myself away from him. Julio was looking over at me with a big smile on his face. "Julio, you did something to me." I was panicked and out of breath.

"Mi Corazón, what did I do?"

"I'm not telling you that."

"Why not? I should know what I did to make you push me away. He was smiling and sounding so proud of himself.

"You already know what you did and that's why you're still smiling."

"No, I don't, so please tell me." He said this with a huge grin on his face.

"I can't."

"Why?"

"Julio, it's too embarrassing."

"Really, that's funny, because when you whispered, 'Now you know how it feels,' I definitely knew what you meant, and why you did that to me, Samantha."

"There is nothing that you can't tell me. I will always keep what we discuss right here, right now, between us. You don't have to hide anything from me. I want to know everything you're thinking and feeling. Now tell me what happened."

"Your unsafe kiss turned me on, like really turned me on Julio. Not like the times before where my head was spinning. Now I felt like... Oh, forget it, I can't describe it."

Julio was smiling at me and he wrapped his arms around me. "Samantha, you have no idea, how many times you have made me feel that way." He was laughing and told me, "To hear you admit that I have the same effect on you makes me feel like a million bucks." He proceeded to kiss me over and over again on top of my head while snuggling me into his chest.

At first, I couldn't look at him, I felt so embarrassed. Now I was looking straight into his eyes and I actually felt relieved. Admitting to feeling like this was a huge step for me.

"Sammy, you turn me on all of the time. It's normal, and there is nothing wrong with that."

"Well, I'm glad you said that Julio. I should also admit that I really wanted to rip your shirt open and touch your chest on several occasions. Julio's mouth dropped open and he appeared to be caught off guard. I pretended not to notice and continued on saying, "Oh, and you should also know that I have a huge thing for your legs.

Julio looked as though he could barely speak when he uttered, "Really?"

"Yes, ever since the very first time I saw you outside playing soccer. Every time I see your legs, especially your thighs, I become completely mesmerized. I can watch you run around a field kicking a soccer ball all day."

"Wow, Mi Corazón."

"Do you think I said to much Julio?"

"No, but I don't think you should rip open my shirt right here, right now, but definitely later." We both started laughing, and he squeezed me before asking, "Do you feel better?"

"Yes."

"Are you glad you told me all of this?"

"Yes, but it was really embarrassing, and a bit scary to admit to having all of these strange feelings and reactions to stuff. Especially since it's all about your cause and effect on me."

"Well if you didn't tell me, who would you have told?"

"Daphne."

"You would tell this to Daphne?"

"Yes!"

"Even how I made you feel?"

"Of course."

"Why are you able to tell her and not me?"

"Julio, I don't always understand all of these feelings, and thoughts I have."

"But you wouldn't have a problem telling them all to Daphne?"

"No, because she's going through the same thing as me. It's all new to her too, so she completely understands what I'm going through."

"I get it now and I'm proud of you."

"Why are you proud of me Julio?"

"Well, I warned you it was a dangerous kiss and how it affects me. It had to take a lot of courage for you to admit how it made you feel."

"It did thank you, and you're right it was a very scary and dangerous kiss." We both laughed and I laid my head down on his shoulder.

He raised his hand up that was holding mine and said, " Samantha, I've always wanted to know something."

"What do you want to know?"

"How did you get Daisy?" My heart swelled the moment he asked about Daisy. I know how much he loves her, and she loves him too.

"Daisy was a gift from Tommy. My brother gave her to me during his final year in high school. It was his last week of school, when he came home with Daisy. He walked in my room and handed her over to me. He simply told me, 'she's all yours Sam.' He walked out of my room and straight into my mom's room. I heard my mom yelling: 'there will be no dogs in this house'.

I could hear my mom and Tommy walking down the hall toward my room. He was telling my mom that the puppy will love and protect me while he's away at school. Then my mom walked into my room. I was holding the puppy on my lap. Daisy turned her little head and barked at my mom. Tommy laughed and said, "I bet if you give her treats, she will love and protect you too mom." Then Daisy barked again and this time she looked up at my mom with her loving puppy eyes. That's all it took; my mom was out the door with Tommy. When they came back, she had bags of puppy chow, dog bowls, treats and a bed. My mom keeps Daisy's bed in her room by the way. She usually sleeps in her bed beside my mom every night, but I wake up with her in my bed every morning."

I tilted my head up and noticed Julio was smiling. I snuggled up into him and asked, "Is there anything else you want to know or that you're curious about?"

"Like I said before, I want to know everything about you Mi Corazón." He kissed me gently behind the ear. I had instant chills and I immediately pulled my head away from him. Julio shrugged his shoulders and said, "It turns me on too, Mi Corazón. Remember the car ride?"

I was about to respond when I noticed there were no boats out on the lake anymore. Then I began to hear everyone on the other side of the building behind us. Julio whispered, "Everyone must be coming back in." He helped me up and thanked me for opening up to him today. Julio stood up and whispered, "I love you, Samantha," he took one step towards me and I backed up against the tree. When I felt his arms wrap around me, I dropped my guard. I looked up into his eyes, but he was focused on the lake over my shoulder. I heard him take in a deep breath before saying, "All of my favorite memories are with you and Daisy beside the lake." He pulled me closer to him and kissed the top of my head. Then someone called out for us. He whispered; I think we need to go. I released a loud sigh and nodded my head yes as he released me from his arms and took my hand. We quickly jogged, around the lake, until we caught up to everyone.

Daphne stopped walking and turned around. She asked, "Where have you two been?"

"Why? Were you looking for us?"

"Yes, as a matter of fact I was."

"Well, we came running as soon as we heard you call out our names."

"You still didn't answer my question Sammy."

I leaned over and whispered in her ear, "We were beside the lake making out."

Daphne covered her mouth and she was laughing. Then she looked up at Greg and he bent down as she whispered to him. I looked over at Julio, and he was smiling and shaking his head.

When we reached the gazebo, my mom wasn't there, and neither was Carmen. Daphne asked, "Where's my mom?"

Enrique answered, "Your mom and Lori are down at the courts playing tennis."

Tommy rolled his eyes and replied, "That figures!

When are we having lunch? I'm starving."

"Greg we will feed you and everybody else in another hour. The barbeque isn't ready yet. For now, you can have chips and watermelon." Guillermo pointed to the picnic table behind us, and we all ran over to that table. We each grabbed a slice of watermelon and sat down to eat until Greg discovered the tray of devilled eggs; we all stood up to grab one of those too.

A couple of minutes later Mr. Sanchez showed up. He was walking over to the gazebo wearing cleats, long socks, shorts, and a polo shirt.

Lewis saw his dad and he took off running towards him. He hugged him and said, "I knew you'd show up dad. I knew it. You wouldn't let us down."

My mom and Carmen came back to the gazebo after playing tennis. They were both wearing shorts with a polo shirt and they each had a racket slung over their shoulders.

"Where is everybody?"

"We're all here, Mom. Who's missing?" Tommy asked, teasing.

"Fine Tommy, where is Guillermo and Alex?"

"Mom, Juan Sanchez showed up and Guillermo disappeared. The truth is we don't know where they went."

"Thank you, Sam."

"No problem, Mom. Where is Pilar?"

"She's still down at the courts with Chris. They'll be back soon."

Guillermo came back with his brother Juan, Alex, and Enrique. His brother Juan was carrying a soccer ball, and everyone was dressed the same in shorts, a polo shirt, long socks, and wearing cleats.

Guillermo, with his deep voice, called out, "Who wants to play soccer?" That got the attention of Lewis, Eddie, Julio, and Greg. When they turned around and saw everyone dressed to play soccer, the boys all instantly had smiles on their face.

Lewis jumped up from the picnic table and ran over to his dad. "Are you going to play with us for real?"

"Yes, for real. Now go and get dressed." His father tossed Lewis the keys to the car and he told him, "Everything you need is in the trunk."

"Thanks, Dad," is all Lewis said before he took off running toward the car. Eddie, Greg, and Julio were right behind him. I kept thinking, "Julio will beat everyone to the car."

That's when Pilar arrived with Chris. They sat down at the picnic table beside my mom and Carmen. Daphne and I moved to the parents' picnic table and sat down in front of them. Pilar told us, "This is a very big deal for the boys. When they were little, I would take them to watch my brothers play soccer on the weekends."

"From the time the boys started walking, they each had their own soccer ball. They would always run around outside kicking a ball. Eventually, my brothers taught the boys and Monica the skills of the game. From that day on, Monica and the boys were obsessed with soccer. When we moved to Miami, right after my mom passed away, Gio moved back to Spain. "

"How did Guillermo end up going to Spain in the first place"?

"Oh Lori, you still don't know? I thought I told you. Well, it's a long story, but it appears we have plenty of time, so let me tell you."

"My brother Gio went to Spain to attend school there. He always dreamed of becoming an Architect. He was working part time as a Laborer at a construction site. On one of the days that Gio was working the owner of the site showed up. He was upset that things were not being done correctly. Gio read the blueprints with his boss and he had a few suggestions. The owner overheard Gio and was impressed with his knowledge. He hired Gio to work for him full time but as a carpenter. It was a lot of work, and Gio loved it. He loves working with his hands as much as being an architect. Once he finished school, he was hired by the same owner to work as an architect, but he had to prove to the owner that he could really do the job."

"That's fantastic, he had a job lined up right out of school.

"Yes, it is Carmen. Gio was doing great and Juan was attending the same university Guillermo had just graduated from. Then my mother became sick and we were told she didn't have much time left. That's when both of my brothers moved back home.

Pilar laughed and shook her head as she said, "I can still remember when Juan came home. He didn't come back by himself; he brought his wife with him. My mother and I had never met her before. In fact, we didn't know that he was married.

"What?" Carmen cried out as her and my mom appeared to be stunned.

"Carmen, when it comes to relationships my brother Juan is a very private person. He met his wife in Spain while attending school and married her. I will always remember the first time I met her. She just walked into the house and my brother was about to introduce her to us before she had to be shown to the bathroom.

She was very sick, I thought it was her nerves. It turned out that she was pregnant with Eddie."

"My mother was very upset with Juan; how he got married and none of us knew anything about it. That was until the third day. That was the day when my mother noticed his wife was very round in the middle with her grandchild. My mother was so happy, she would sing and knit things for the baby every day. To tell you the truth, I think that is what made my mother live another 13 years."

"But when Juan's wife passed away, my mom passed away a few months after her. My mom loved her so much and her loss was just too much for my mother. Shortly after her passing, Gio was offered an amazing job opportunity with his former employer. This meant he needed to move back to Spain."

"My brother Juan wanted to move to Miami. His brother-in-law offered him a job after his sister passed away. Juan's in-laws wanted the chance to get to know Eddie and Lewis. I didn't want my brother Juan to come alone with the boys to the United States. When I told him this, he told me, let's all go together and that's how we ended up moving to Miami, all seven of us.

"It has been the best decision we ever made. Now Gio moved to the United States around a year after us. The owner of the company he worked for wanted to branch out and start a business here. The idea was to specialize in building Spanish Architectural Homes. Gio was sent here to oversee everything. The company was not doing well at first. There was a lot of competition and the overall cost was more expensive than originally anticipated.

"Gio came up with an idea and he started to buy up houses that were in great neighborhoods. He would buy these run-down houses at a very low price. Then he would tear the entire house down and build a new one in its place. A brand-new single-family home that he designed inside and outside in a very lavish Spanish architecture.

He would sell the house at twice the amount he invested. Little by little, he bought and built more of these houses. That's how he made a name for himself and the company in California.

"The owner did not approve. He wanted Gio to locate vacant land and build new homes. However, at the time, there just wasn't enough money in the budget to do that and deliver the quality. Gio wasn't willing to do anything different. Eventually, the owner told Gio he should go out on his own."

"My brother spent every penny he had and took out a loan from the bank. It was a big risk, and it managed to pay off. My brother convinced the owner to sell the company, he started here in California to him."

"Now my brother owns several companies and the hotel. The hotel was also run-down until Gio renovated the place. I am very proud of him. All of his hard work has paid off financially. It's romantically, where his life has suffered. He has never been married or had any children. I'm hoping one day he will fall in love and finally have happiness in that area of his life too."

My mom was smiling, when she answered, "Yes, perhaps one day, Pilar."

"I know of only one woman who has ever truly captured my brother Gio's attention. My brother told me this woman has more than he ever dreamed of — from brains to beauty, she has everything. I even heard my brother gets up early in the morning to dance on his balcony with her. We all broke out laughing, and my mom was turning bright pink."

"Oh Pilar, it was nothing. Stop teasing me."

"I know you two were meant for each other. I have always told you; this was the man for you, Lori. Now you have met one another, and you are both like two teenagers staring at each other, talking, and laughing, all the time together.

"It's okay, Lori, you don't have to admit it now, but you're falling for him," Carmen told her with a big toothy grin.

"We have to talk about this again later," Pilar told them in a very low tone of voice.

The Sanchez boys were back. Guillermo smiled at my mom and announced, "We're all ready to play soccer now. How do we look?" We all looked at the boys and everyone was dressed to play soccer the same as Guillermo and Juan.

Pilar was the first one to respond, "You all look very nice."

That's when my mom noticed Tommy. He was dressed to play soccer and she asked, "Are you playing soccer too?"

Tommy looked over at Guillermo and answered, "I don't really play soccer mom, but Guillermo asked me to play, so I will be playing on his team."

Julio put his arm around my brother and said, "You have nothing to worry about Tommy. It's not about how well you play. It's about having fun and playing the game with your friends, and family."

"Monica stood up and she looked as though she was about to cry. Julio caught her arm as she was about to walk out of the gazebo. Monica lifted up her head and she had the palm of her hand covering her mouth. "Hey, I have to tell you something."

Monica shook her head and asked, "What is it Julio?"

"You need to hurry up and get dressed." He tossed a set of keys to Monica. "Uncle Gio won the coin toss you're on his team."

"A coin toss?"

"Yes, the Uncles were fighting over who's team you were going to be on. They both wanted you on their team. Alex had them decide by a coin toss." Monica went from sulking to having a great big smile on her face.

Monica yelled, "Tommy, let's go."

My brother stood up and quickly followed Monica out of the gazebo.

I looked behind us to see what the moms were watching. The guys were all out on the grass, setting up little tiny orange cones, and soccer nets. My mom asked Chris, "Do you play soccer?"

"No, I don't play, but I love the sport and always watch the games on TV."

"Me too," Pilar said. "They kept it a secret from everyone except Greg. He needed to know, so he could bring his gear. Did you see the look on everyone's face? Those smiles made my day."

"Yes, mine too Pilar. Oh, and did you see Lewis? His face lit up like a light bulb."

"I did see that Lori and it warmed my heart."

"Julie must be disappointed that she couldn't come with Juan today."

"I doubt that Carmen."

"Why Pilar?"

"She has so many last-minute bridal things to take care of."

"Well, I can't wait to watch them play. I heard that Julio is the fastest runner."

Pilar turned around and asked, "Who told you that?"

Chris crossed his arms over his chest and said, "Pilar do you know how many times I've heard that comment?"

Pilar sat up and crossed her arms over her chest and asked, "How many?"

"At least a hundred times."

Pilar rolled her eyes and asked, "When have you heard that Chris?"

"Every time Monica challenges Lewis to a race.

"Chris, what race are you talking about?"

"The race to the car."

"When Lewis beats Monica to the car she tells him 'You might be faster than me, but no one is faster than my brother Julio.'

Pilar smiled and a little giggle escaped her before she admitted, "I honestly forgot about that, and I don't know how since Monica has been saying that for years."

Chris smiled and hugged Pilar. She sat back against him and replied, "Well my daughter's right you know," and Chris laughed.

When the field was finally all setup, we left the Gazebo and walked out onto the field. My mom and Pilar laid out a big comforter and we all took a seat .

After a few minutes, Heather and Amy sat down on the comforter beside us. Carmen said, "I told you Lori, all we needed was a king size comforter and we would all fit."

"I'm glad we listened to you Carmen." My mom leaned over and squeezed me once before saying, "I enjoy having everyone together on one blanket."

Daphne watched Greg like a hawk. He was the goalkeeper on one side of the field. On the opposite side of the field was Eddie, the other goalkeeper. Heather had her eyes glued to Eddie. This moment felt just like déjà vu. When we watched them play soccer at home with the moms for the last time.

I looked over at my mom and she was focused on Guillermo. She was smiling and laughing with her friends constantly. That's when I realized I haven't ever seen my mom this happy before. It all started when we arrived here in California. I looked back at Daphne and she was looking at her mom. Daphne whispered, "I think my mom is into Enrique."

"Oh yeah, if you think that's bad, take a look at my mom." Daphne looked over at my mom and raised her eyebrows up at me.

Then she whispered, "We better keep an eye on our moms tonight. They go to bed before us." I couldn't help it; I laughed, and Daphne started laughing beside me.

I was really enjoying the game. It was incredible to see Mr. Sanchez and Guillermo out on the field playing soccer. They were so good that they would outrun and maneuver everyone on the field. They mentioned they hadn't played in years, but it didn't appear that way.

"Look at the smile on everyone's face," Carmen said. That's when I noticed the boys were all smiling, but it was Monica who had the biggest smile.

Several times, I noticed Mr. Sanchez or Guillermo challenging the boys to take the ball away from them. They knew all this fancy footwork and would tease the boys with the ball. I was extremely impressed. You definitely knew who the masters were at this game. I looked over at my mom and she kept her eyes on Guillermo. Every time he ran across the field my mom would sit up and start cheering.

Juan lost control of the ball and kicked it right in front of Tommy, he was standing beside the net. Tommy kicked the ball right past the goalkeeper and into the net for the win. My mom and I looked at one another in utter shock. The game was over after that and Guillermo's team won. Juan Sanchez looked back at Tommy, and he instantly had this big smile on his face. I realized at that very moment Juan and Guillermo did not care about winning. It was all about having fun playing soccer with your friends and family.

Alex and Enrique were placing the meat on the grill. When Guillermo and his brother Juan returned to the gazebo, they took over the cooking. Alex and Enrique went to the bathroom to change and wash up. When everyone came back to the gazebo, Mr. Sanchez asked, "Did everyone have fun today?"

We all yelled out, "Yes!"

"Good. Let's eat."

After everything was picked up, and the cars were packed up, Guillermo asked if he could speak to me. Then he saw Tommy and called him over. We went for a walk with Guillermo away from the gazebo. We stopped at a picnic table; Tommy and I sat down. Guillermo remained standing, and he appeared to be nervous. He was pacing back and forth. When he finally stopped and faced us. That's when he said, "I would like to ask your mom out on that date just the two of us tonight. I wanted to know before I did this if the two of you are really okay with this."

Tommy looked at me, then back at Guillermo and told him, "You don't need our permission."

"Yeah, Tommy's right you need to ask our mom."

Guillermo rubbed his hands together and replied, "Okay, great! I will ask her tomorrow."

Tommy and I both spoke at the same time and said: "Tomorrow's the wedding."

Guillermo stopped and ran his hand through his hair. "Oh boy! you guys are right." Then he started pacing again. When he stopped for the second time, he placed his hand on his forehead and started shaking his head back and forth.

"Hey, you don't have to be so nervous. My mom is awesome, and she already agreed to go out on a date with you. It was all just a matter of when. Now, when you two are alone ask her out."

"Yes, I will do that. Thank you, Tommy." Then he turned around and looked at us and asked, "What if she says no?"

"I doubt that, but you will never know for sure unless you ask her."

"You're right Sammy. I will ask her out on a date tonight."

I looked over at Tommy, and he was now standing beside Guillermo. You could tell Tommy really wanted to help him. He looked back at me with his hands out and shoulders up. Which usually meant now what? I scratched the back of my head and asked, "Do you know where you want to take my mom on this date?"

"No," Guillermo admitted, and he sat down on the bench in front of me looking defeated. "Samantha I shouldn't ask her out. I have no idea what I'm doing,"

"Guillermo you're just nervous. You can totally do this. Just some insight: my mom loves the beach and Italian food. She enjoys red wine and margaritas with the girls."

Tommy sat down beside me. "Sam's right, and my mom loves music. Her favorites are The Beatles, Bee Gees, and ABBA."

"Oh, I love The Bee Gees and The Beatles.

We can definitely listen to them on the car ride," and finally Guillermo was smiling once again.

"Okay, that sounds good. Now where do you plan on taking her?"

Guillermo clapped his hands together and answered, "Samantha, I want to take her to my favorite Italian restaurant in Santa Monica. They have wonderful food and their wine is from Napa Valley."

"Now that sounds perfect Guillermo." Tommy agreed with me.

"Except we forgot one thing."

"What's that Tommy?"

"Guillermo you still need to ask my mom out on a date tonight." After a minute of complete silence, Tommy jumped up and said, "I got it. Guillermo you should drive my mom back to the house in one of the town cars and listen to The Bee Gees."

"That's a great idea Tommy, and I gave him a high-five."

"He's right, Guillermo; then it will be just the two of you, and that's when you ask my mom out on a date."

"Wait, how am I going to explain to everyone that I'm driving your mom home alone in the car?"

Tommy smiled and replied, "Don't worry about that; I will take care of everything."

We walked back to the gazebo. When Julio spotted us, he ran up to me. He took my hand and whispered, "Is everything okay?" I nodded my head yes and I tried to spot my mom and Alex from where I was standing.

I whispered, "I need to find Alex, we need to ride home in the limo. We also need to make sure Alex gives Guillermo the car keys." Julio looked puzzled . I whispered, "I will explain everything to you later," and I kissed his cheek before I pulled my head away. Julio and I walked up to Alex. I told him that we all need to ride home in the limo, and I need him to give Guillermo the car keys. He reached into his pocket and pulled out the keys. I walked over to Guillermo and handed him the car keys. When Alex saw Guillermo with the keys in his hand. He immediately yelled out, "Everybody, let's go!"

Tommy yelled out, "Alex get everyone into the limo." Alex waved us over to the limo and we all climbed inside. The car was now filled with Eddie, Lewis, Heather, Amy, Greg, Julio, Daphne, and me. Alex was sitting in the driver's seat. Monica pulled up in her car and Tommy climbed into the passenger seat.

That's when Enrique walked up to the limo. Alex called Enrique over to him. I heard Alex say "Sorry, but we're taking the limo back home. You can take the other car." Alex handed Enrique the keys to the other town car.

Pilar asked, "What's going on here?" Alex pointed to Guillermo helping Lori into the car.

What a moment, the look on Pilar's face was fantastic. Her mouth dropped open and her eyes were huge. She went to tapping Carmen on the shoulder and said, "Look at that," several times filled with excitement. The two of them stood there watching my mom and Guillermo until they drove away.

Enrique walked around the front of the limo and up to Carmen. He asked her if she would ride with him. He held up the keys to the other town car and Carmen looked back at Pilar smiling.

That's when Pilar leaned down and looked inside the limo at all of us. Alex already had his head turned toward us in the back and said, "Mom, Chris, hop in." Once everyone was inside the limo, I lowered the window and waved bye to Carmen and Enrique.

Pilar leaned back in her seat. She crossed one leg over the other one and placed both of her hands on her knee. She said, "I know what you're doing, mi hijo, and I love it."

Alex was stopped for a second at a red light, and he looked over at me, and I looked back at him. I felt her eyes on me and turned back around. Pilar was smiling at me when she asked, "Sammy, are you a part of this too?"

I answered, "Yes, but so is Tommy."

Pilar covered her mouth and she laughed. "Tommy too! I can't believe it." I just nodded my head yes, and Pilar was beaming.

"Enrique and Carmen were not apart of the plan, but it all worked out nicely don't you think?" Alex turned his head toward the opening wiggling his eyebrows up and down and smiling mischievously.

Daphne asked, "What in the world is going on? Why are we in the limo? What were you talking about with Guillermo for so long?"

"Daphne, I will tell you everything when we get back to the house."

"You better Sammy, because I don't like feeling left out." She was pouting and crossed her arms over her chest.

"Daphne, we just thought it would be fun to change things up a bit and ride in the limo."

"Yeah, right. Nice try, Alex," Daphne replied while still pouting.

When we arrived at the house, Pilar let us inside, and we all headed for the kitchen. We each grabbed a glass out of the cabinet and took turns filling up at the water cooler.

We left the kitchen and headed outside to the pool. Julio and I walked around the pool and sat down on the ledge when we caught up to Greg and Daphne.

While Lewis, Amy, Eddie, and Heather were on the opposite side of the pool sitting on the ledge and dipping their feet in the pool.

I took off my sneakers, and I put my left foot in the water. Daphne screamed, "Shark!" and I jerked my foot up and lost my balance and fell in the pool. I was holding onto Julio's hand, and he went in with me.

Daphne and Greg cracked up laughing. I felt like retaliating until I felt Julio wrap his arms around my waist and pull me over to him. He kissed me, and I climbed onto his back. He took a deep breath, and he swam underwater to the other side of the pool with me on his back.

We always did this back home, and we called it 'the turtle ride.' When we popped up on the shallow end, Eddie laughed and said, "I can't believe the two of you are swimming around in the pool with your clothes on."

"We fell in the pool, Eddie."

"Well, I don't think it's fair that the two you have the pool all to yourself Sammy." Eddie looked over at Lewis, and they both stood up and ran over to the deep side of the pool. Greg and Daphne were sitting on the ledge of the pool having a deep discussion when they were both shoved into the pool by Eddie and Lewis.

Eddie shouted, "Shark!" and was losing it laughing. Lewis ran back to the other end of the pool to sit beside Amy and Heather. Greg and Daphne were completely taken by surprise.

They weren't laughing when they were the ones in the water. Julio and I were cracking up, to the point my sides were hurting from laughing so much. Greg yelled, "Shut up!" and started splashing water at Julio's face.

Daphne yelled at Eddie, then I heard Lewis yell back, "Here!" and he shoved Eddie into the pool.

Less then a minute later, Greg and Eddie ran up behind Lewis. They picked him up and he was yelling and kicking. They had Lewis by his hands and ankles and on the count of three, they tossed Lewis into the pool.

Everyone was laughing, including Heather and Amy. They were smart; they decided to lay out on the lounge chairs farther away from the pool. Eddie yelled over to Heather and Amy to jump in the pool. He told them he wanted to play Marco Polo or Red-light Green-light.

Lewis told him, "They're not going to jump in the pool to play with you." That's when Heather stood up and walked over to Eddie. Amy stood up and walked over to stand behind Heather, and they both jumped into the pool fully clothed.

"I guess I was wrong," Lewis said, as he swam over to Amy.

Heather swam over to Eddie on the deep side. She tapped him on the shoulder and asked, "Which game are we going to play?"

Eddie turned around and smiled when he saw it was Heather. He asked her, "Which game do you want to play?"

"Marco Polo," she answered."

"Great. Let me tell Lewis to get the blindfold." We all turned around, and we spotted Lewis and Amy. They were already out of the pool and headed down the stairs to the second yard.

Eddie turned around and faced Heather and the rest of us. He clapped his hands together and announced, "Okay, I guess we can play Red-light Green-light."

Heather smiled and kissed Eddie on the cheek. "That sounds perfect Eddie. Now how do we play?"

Eddie explained the game and Heather said, "So, we just have to make it to the other end of the pool staying afloat and stop whenever you yell out red-light?"

"Yes," Eddie answered.

"Well that doesn't sound to difficult."

We all started playing and Julio grabbed Greg's leg, so he couldn't swim across.

Eddie stood over both of them while they were playing around under the water and just waited. Patience paid off; Greg and Julio both came up for air, and Eddie yelled red-light.

They both were tired and were dog paddling and couldn't stop moving. Eddie yelled, "You're both it, and that crap the two of you were doing was stupid. One or the both of you could drown playing like that."

"Yeah, but Eddie, we learned that from you and Alex. Remember?" Greg asked him.

"I don't care. That's stupid, and you don't need to be doing stupid stuff." We all started laughing, and Eddie yelled, "You're both pénibles!"

Carmen and Enrique walked out onto the pool deck. Carmen asked, "Who are you calling annoying, Eddie?" Eddie covered his mouth and started laughing and I finally knew what that word meant.

Daphne turned around and said, "Mom, you're back."

"Yes, I am and why are you in the pool wearing your clothes, Daphne? Did we forget to pack your bathing suit?"

"No, Mom. It's a long story."'

"No, it's not, I pushed her into the pool."

"Eddie, why did you push Daphne into the pool?"

"Your daughter scared Sammy and Julio, and they fell into the pool first and Daphne just laughed at them."

You could see Carmen slowly backing away from the pool now. I think she was afraid to be the next one in. "Mom, where are you going?"

"Daphne, I'm going to have a seat over there beside Enrique at the table." Carmen sat down and Pilar along with Chris joined them at the parents table.

Carmen and Enrique were constantly talking and laughing. "Sammy, they sure do seem to enjoy each other's company."

"Yes, it does seem that way Daphne."

Julio and Greg swam over to us. Greg placed his arm over Daphne to comfort her and Julio took my hand.

Chapter 6 Cabana Boy

Julio and I walked down the stairs. Daphne and Greg followed behind us to the second yard. We were walking up to the cabana and I noticed the flaps were down. When we were a bit closer, I noticed the flaps were zipped shut.

I whispered to Julio, "I think somebody is already in there."

Julio laughed, then said, "Hello? Is somebody in here?"

"Yes! Go away! This spot is taken!"

Julio smiled and Greg replied, "Oh, yeah. What are you doing in there Lewis?"

"Bro, go away. I'm busy. Go find Daphne and play with her."

Daphne's mouth dropped open, and you could see she was about to flip out. Greg grabbed hold of Daphne's hand, and we all followed Greg over to the lounge chairs that were on the other side of the lawn and away from the cabana. Greg wrapped his arms around Daphne, and he kissed the back of her head.

Daphne smiled and pulled away from Greg. In a matter of seconds, she jumped up and ran back to the cabana. She had it unzipped and was inside before we could stop her. The three of us tried to grab her arm before she entered the cabana. Instead, all four of us walked in on Lewis and Amy.

They were both shocked by the intrusion and their eyes were huge. Our mouths dropped open and Daphne was frozen in place. We had just walked in on them having sex. I looked up at Julio and I ran out of the cabana. Julio, Greg, and Daphne quickly followed behind me.

I ran down the path beside the house and entered the garage by the side door. The three of them followed me inside. I leaned up on the bumper of one of the cars trying to catch my breath. Julio said, "Wait. Let me get the lights."

When the lights were turned on, Daphne screamed. Then I screamed because she screamed, and it scared me. When I turned around, I saw that it was just Eddie and Heather sitting inside the town car. Eddie climbed out and asked, "What happened? Why are you girls screaming?"

"Sorry, man. You just scared the girls. That's all. Go back to whatever you were doing. We're leaving now." Greg took Daphne's hand and headed for the side door.

Eddie climbed out of the car and said, "Greg, you don't have to leave. Heather and I were just talking for a few minutes before I take her home. If you guys want to go with us for a ride and some scenery, you're welcome to come with us."

Daphne turned back around and told him, "That sounds perfect Eddie. We would love to go."

"Okay. Then get in the car Daphne, and let's go."

"Daphne, we can't go."

"Why not Sammy?"

"We're still wearing wet clothes." Daphne stared back at me with a blank look on her face.

Greg and Julio started to chuckle, and I was beginning to feel annoyed. I rolled my eyes and asked, "Daphne, do you remember going in the pool fully clothed?"

She looked down at herself and responded, "Sorry, but I don't care. I rather not be around when Lewis gets out of that cabana."

"Eddie, would you be willing to wait for us?"

"How long Sammy?"

"Just give us 10 minutes Eddie."

Daphne took my hand and dragged me into the house. I dragged Julio with us, and Greg followed.

Once we were inside the house, Daphne asked, "Where are we?"

Julio laughed before answering, "Inside the house."

"I know that, Julio, but how do we get to the main part of the house?"

He pointed to the staircase.

"Oh, got it," Daphne answered, and she ran over to the stairs and up into the main house. "We will meet up with you guys in 10 minutes." Daphne kissed Greg on the cheek and took off running towards her room. Greg was left shaking his head and walking back to his own room.

Julio and I stayed in front of the staircase. He took my hands and told me, "We don't have to go with them if you don't want to Samantha."

"I don't want to go but Daphne's right. I don't want to be around when Lewis and Amy leave the cabana."

"You're right, so hurry up. Go put on some dry clothes. I will meet you back here in nine minutes." I nodded my head yes and took off running to my room.

Daphne was walking out of the dressing area wrapped in a towel. She said, "There you are finally! You need to hurry up, Sammy, take a hot shower!" I ran into the bathroom and I threw all my wet clothes into the Jacuzzi. I ran into the shower and back out as quickly as possible. I threw on a pair of jeans and a tank top. Daphne grabbed my sweatshirt out of the dresser drawer. She tossed it to me as I opened the door."

We ran out of the bedroom and to the staircase. We met back up with Julio and Greg. Julio looked down and asked, "Mi Corazón, where are your shoes?"

I looked down at my feet and replied, "Oh, crap. We forgot them." I could hear Julio and Greg starting to laugh as Daphne and I ran back to our room. We slipped our feet into our clogs and walked back out to the staircase.

Julio and Greg were smiling at us when we arrived. "Okay, so is everybody ready to go now?"

"Yes, Greg. Let's go," Daphne answered in a rush as she grabbed Greg's hand. They headed down the stairs and we quickly followed behind them. Once we were inside the garage the lights were off again. Julio put his arm out in front of me and that stopped me from taking another step.

"Let me turn the lights on first." Julio reached over on the wall and turned the lights on.

We caught Eddie and Heather kissing inside the car. They quickly pulled apart after they noticed the lights were back on. "Eddie rolled down the window and said, "You guys didn't take enough time. Are you sure you're clean enough to get in the car?"

Daphne opened the back door and told him, "Yes, we took showers and put on clean clothes just for you, Eddie."

"For me guys, really? You shouldn't have."

Greg pat Eddie on the shoulder and added, "I did it all for you, big guy."

That's when Eddie turned around looking completely startled at Greg. He placed his hand on his chest and started to laugh. His laughter is contagious and soon we were all laughing. As Eddie pulled out of the garage he winked at Greg and told him, "I'm sorry bro but I think Heather is more my type."

Julio started to laugh, and he looked over at Greg and told him, "Better luck next time dude." We had been laughing since we got in the car. All of the panic I had been feeling was starting to fade away now.

Eddie was our tour guide and he pointed out all of the different places we passed along the way. We saw the movie theatre the boys go to and the arcade they hang out at. Eddie stopped at a red light and he told us to look to the right. He pointed to Julio's favorite Pizzeria. I turned my head and was able to spot the pizza place inside the shopping plaza.

A few minutes later Heather pointed out the window and said, "That's Megan's house."

Julio suddenly tensed up. When I turned my head to look at him, his lips were pressed together, and his jaw was tight. He was definitely angry about something and Eddie must have known what it was about. He kept looking back at Julio through the rear-view mirror.

I was about to ask Julio what's wrong, but Daphne interrupted by yelling out, "Eddie, take us there." She was pointing to a mall.

"Daphne, we have to take Heather home first. Remember she went in the pool just like you did."

"Eddie, I wouldn't mind going to the mall with you. If you don't mind waiting for me."

"Heather, I waited for everyone else so I can definitely wait for you."

"Great, all I need is ten minutes."

When we arrived at Heather's house. Eddie pulled up to the gate and pressed a button on the intercom; it started to ring. Heather leaned over Eddie and all I heard was what Heather said: "It's me, Daddy." Then I saw the gates open. Eddie slowly drove through the gates and up this long cobblestone driveway to the house.

It was a huge house with arched windows and a large archway over the front door. The house was tan with orange barrel tiles on the roof. The whole front of the house and even the driveway was filled with lush tropical foliage and several palm trees.

Heather climbed out of the car and said, "I will be right back." True to her word, Heather was back in less than10 minutes. Eddie was smiling the minute he saw her walking back to the car. "You really like her don't you Eddie?"

"Yes, I do, Julio."

Heather opened the door, and we all yelled, "Welcome back!"

"Thank you, guys."

"Oh, and just out of curiosity. How long has Lewis been dating Amy?" Greg turned to Daphne and gave her a dirty look for asking that question.

"Oh, like a month now," Heather answered.

"Do you still want me to take you to the mall Daphne?"

"No. What else can we do around here Eddie?"

"Daphne, there's a place with go-carts and an arcade about 10 minutes from here."

"That's perfect Eddie, lets go."

We spent hours there playing video games and racing go-carts. We all finished off the evening sharing a pizza at Julio's favorite Pizzeria. When Eddie drove Heather back home, Daphne and I climbed out of the car and we each gave her a hug. Eddie walked Heather up to her front door. She leaned in and kissed Eddie under the archway before walking inside.

When Eddie came back to the car, he was beaming with this incredible smile. On the drive home he thanked us over and over again for going out with him and Heather tonight. He even asked her to be his date at the wedding tomorrow. "

"Oh, I just assumed she was already your date for the wedding."

"No, Sammy. She was only my date for the formal dinner. Lewis invited Heather to come with Amy to the park today."

"Wow. You must really like her then. I thought you were just hanging out with her for Lewis."

"To tell you the truth Julio, at first, I was just hanging out with her because of Lewis. You know because of the whole thing where Amy is not allowed to go anywhere without a chaperone. Now the first chaperone was her cousin Megan. She was nice and everything. Don't get me wrong, but she's not my type."

"When Lewis asked me to go out again on a group date and said it was with a different cousin, I was not up for it. I told him no. Lewis was desperate and even offered to do my chores around the house for a week. I still said no. Then the formal dinner came up, and Lewis pointed out to me. Oh, never mind. Forget it."

"No. Say it."

Eddie took a deep breath, and said, "He just pointed out the obvious Daphne, you know.

"Pointed out what?"

"How you and Sammy are friends with Denise. You both would be here for the wedding. How it's going to look if I am the only person without a date at dinner? I thought about it and that's when I agreed to the date.

"I think you made the right decision Eddie, but maybe for the wrong reason."

"I realize that now Daphne, but I don't regret the choice I made for one minute. She really turned out be someone special."

"Okay, so now that I told you the truth about all of that, it's your turn to tell me why you don't want to be at the house."

Daphne's eyes became huge. Julio and Greg looked at the both of us and started smiling. I felt the alarms going off in my head again and felt the nervous knots tugging inside my belly. I looked over at Daphne. She had her arms crossed over her chest and her lips tightly pressed together. "Well, what are you waiting for? Go ahead and tell him, Daphne."

"I can't Greg. It's private. We shouldn't talk about that, it's not any of our business."

"Oh, but barging in on them was your business?" Daphne's mouth dropped open and she just looked over at me with a stunned expression. "Tell him Daphne. How Greg pulled you away from the cabana. We all had a seat on the lounge chairs where we had this incredible view and could relax. But no. You were mad at Lewis for what he said and furthermore, I think you just wanted to find out what they were doing in the cabana. Boy, weren't you surprised when you caught them having sex? Did you even feel bad for intruding on them, Daphne? Did you?"

When I stopped ranting, I realized the car was stopped and we were now in a parking lot. Eddie, Greg, and Julio all appeared to be shocked by my outburst. Daphne was on the verge of tears and I felt horrible. I opened the car door, and Julio reached for my hand asking, "Where are you going?"

"I just need to get some fresh air." I climbed out of the car and Julio was right behind me.

I walked to the back of the car. "Samantha, I know you didn't mean to go off on Daphne like that, and you were right. She shouldn't have barged in like that and it was horribly embarrassing for all of us." He wrapped his arms around me, and I laid my head against his chest.

"Julio, I just wish it didn't happen. It was so horrible, and I don't know how I can face your cousin. Like, what do I say to him or even Amy? She's a girl and I'm sure she didn't want all of us to see her naked. Or know that she went all the way with her boyfriend."

"Samantha, you're right."

"I am?"

"Yes, we shouldn't have seen that!"

"Julio, I just don't understand why Daphne allows her temper to ruin everything?"

"You know what I think?"

"No."

"I think that you're very tired Mi Corazón and you need some sleep. I also think that you're upset with Daphne and rightfully so. However, I know that she is one of your best friends and would not ever intentionally hurt you or any of us."

I held Julio a bit tighter and I wiped my tears away with his shirt. I looked up at him and smiled. "Are you ready to get back in the car now and head back to the house?" I nodded my head yes and Julio took my hand.

We climbed back into the car. Once I was sitting on Julio's lap again, he closed the door. Eddie turned around and said, "So, my little brother is no longer a virgin! Of course not, now that Lewis doesn't have to share a bathroom with six people. How convenient. Good for him. Now maybe he can take a shower like a normal person instead of taking over 40 minutes in the shower." Our mouths were all gapping open in the back seat. Eddie left us stunned by this new information about Lewis. This was nothing new to Julio and he found the whole conversation to be quite amusing.

When we pulled up in front of the house. Eddie told us, "Lewis is long gone by now. Amy has a curfew and she should already be back at home."

"Eddie, what time is it?"

He looked down at his beeper, "It's a quarter to one Sammy."

"Geez. Eddie, it's late."

Julio squeezed my hand before saying, "Yes, it is Samantha. We all better get to bed now."

"Tell Tio I will have the car back to him in the morning."

"Okay, goodnight Eddie." We all waved bye to Eddie and walked up to the front door. Greg and Daphne walked inside first. Julio pulled the front door shut and grabbed hold of my hand.

He walked us over to the garage and we walked inside through the side door. Once we were in the garage, he turned on the lights. "Julio, what are we doing in here?"

He bit on his bottom lip and released it long enough to smile and say, "You'll see." He grabbed hold of my hand again and headed for the main door to the house. We walked inside and went past the stairs and he opened the door to the theatre room.

We walked inside and he shut the door and turned the lights on. It was so bright that we were both squinting. I grabbed a throw blanket and throw pillow. While Julio turned the lights down on the dimmer switch. We both walked over to couch in the center of the room.

We curled up together and fell asleep in each others' arms. I woke up to sound of Alex's voice. "You guys have to get up now. Daphne and I can't cover for you anymore. The whole house is up." I sat up startled and opened my eyes instantly.

Julio was still sound asleep. I leaned over and kissed him on cheek. Julio didn't move and I leaned in closer to him and whispered, "Julio, wake up. We have to go now." He wrapped his arms around me and said, "No, don't leave me, Samantha. We are meant to be together. Don't leave."

Alex looked over at him with an annoyed expression. "Sammy, he's still asleep. Let me wake him up." I moved away from the sofa with my hands up.

Alex leaned over Julio and he shoved him a couple of times while saying, "Samantha is outside by the pool. Get up." Julio's eyes popped open and he sat up and jumped up and off the sofa.

Julio was blinking and staring back at me. "Julio, we have to go upstairs now. The whole house is up, and everyone will be looking for you soon."

"Okay, just give me a second Alex."

Julio wrapped his arms around me and kissed me. "That was the best night sleep I've had in months. I held you in my arms where you belong Samantha."

"That's cute, Julio. Really! it is but we have to go upstairs now before the rest of the house finds out you two were asleep together down here."

"Fine! Alex. Let's go!" Julio took my hand as we walked out of the room. "Samantha, you need to go out thru the garage and up the stairs to the pool deck. Daphne unlocked the sliding glass door to let you in your bedroom."

I hugged Alex and thanked him. Then I began to walk down the hall toward the garage door.

"Julio, you come with me."

"Alex, I want to go with her and make sure she's safe." When I heard that I started to giggle.

"No, we're going upstairs and when anyone asks me where I found you, I'm going to tell them the theatre room." Julio watched me until I made it inside the garage.

I quickly ran through the garage and out the side door to the yard. Walking up the stairs I noticed the coast was clear. I took off running when I reached the last step. As I slid the sliding glass door open, someone tapped me on the shoulder and asked, "Where are you coming from, Sammy?"

My heart was racing, I started to panic. I turned around to face Tommy and he had a smirk on his face. I knew that I was busted, and he was waiting to hear my explanation. I was squeezing on my bottom lip while my mind was trying to think of something to say.

"Well are you planning to say anything?" Tommy was clearly frustrated with me by the sound of his voice, and I was nervous.

"Tommy, I had to go for a walk to get some fresh air and clear my head. See you in a couple of minutes."

"Sam, wait!" My brother placed his hand on the handle of the sliding glass door to prevent me from opening it.

"Tommy, what is it now? What else do you want to know?"

Sam you were missing this morning, and Alex made another bet on who finds you first. Just tell me, did I find you first?"

I squinted my eyes at Tommy as I tried to look up at him. The sun was shinning right into my eyes making it difficult for me to see him. Finally, I just placed my hand up to my forehead to block out the sun. "I'm sorry Tommy for lying to you. That wasn't cool of me."

"Hey! Listen, Sam. I totally understand especially after the whole Lewis thing yesterday."

"Wait. You know about the Lewis thing?"

"Yes, of course. Everybody knows after Carmen and Enrique walked in on them."

"What do you mean they walked in on them?"

"Carmen and Enrique walked in the cabana when Lewis and Amy were having sex. Can you believe it? It was so crazy here after that Sam. I can't believe you missed it."

"Tommy, tell me what happened after that! What else did I miss?"

"Okay, let me start from the beginning. Carmen said she heard Daphne yelling from the second lawn. When she called out Daphne's name to check on her, no one responded. Next thing you know Carmen and Enrique ran down the stairs to check everything out and found Lewis and Amy in the cabana actually having sex."

"This whole thing blew up. Mom and Carmen went with Pilar to drive Amy home. Lewis was told to stay here until they returned. When they couldn't find you guys, Pilar called Eddie on his beeper and he called back and said you were all together at the go-cart park."

"Now, what did you think I was talking about, Sam?"

"Oh, it's just that we walked in on Lewis and Amy having sex in the cabana. When I say we, I mean Greg, Daphne, Julio, and me. We were so freaked out about it that we took off with Eddie and Heather. We just didn't want to stick around to face Lewis or Amy afterward."

"Oh, wow, and what about the other thing?"

"What other thing, Tommy?"

"You know! Where did you sleep last night and did, I find you first?"

"We hid in the theatre room and Alex found us first."

"I don't blame you for staying away Sam or hiding from Lewis. What he did was disrespectful and how he behaved afterward…

"What is it Tommy?"

"Nevermind, I won't bore you with those details."

"Tommy, I can meet you in the kitchen in about 20 minutes and we can have a cook-off."

"Actually, Sam, you have about 10 minutes and the parents are in the kitchen cooking breakfast now. I won't keep you anymore. You need to hurry up and get ready."

I slid the sliding glass door open and walked inside. Daphne was sitting on one of the overstuffed chairs in the bedroom beside the fireplace.

I ran straight to the bathroom and took a shower. When I opened the shower door to reach for a towel, Daphne handed me one as well as my bathrobe.

"If you hurry up and have a seat in the dressing area, I can braid your hair." I wrapped the towel around my head and slipped into my bathrobe.

I took a seat on the chair at the vanity. She stood there ready with a hairbrush in her hand. "Daphne, I'm very sorry for the way I spoke to you last night. I was overtired and I completely freaked over the whole Lewis thing."

"I know Sammy and I'm sorry for placing you in such a predicament. I let Lewis get to me and I paid dearly for intruding on him. I was and I still am, completely embarrassed by the whole situation that took place yesterday."

"Yeah, well! I wonder how your mom is handling it."

"Sammy, I didn't tell my mom about what happened."

"No, but you should ask her what happened after we left."

"What are you talking about, Sammy?"

"Okay, so Tommy just told me your mom was looking for you yesterday after she heard you yelling. She came downstairs with Enrique to find out if you were okay and..."

"And what?"

Your mom walked into the cabana and found Lewis and Amy having sex."

"Are you kidding me? So, after we walked in on them, they just went back to having sex again like nothing happened."

"Yes, well, Eddie did say it takes him at least 40 minutes in the shower." We both laughed until we heard footsteps right outside our door.

We both stopped laughing and I whispered, "I still can't believe your mom and Enrique busted them."

"Do you know what happened after they were busted Sammy?"

"All I know is that the moms went for a car ride last night."

"Where to?"

"They took Amy home."

"Where was Lewis?"

"Here at Guillermo's house. He was told to wait here until Pilar and our Moms returned."

"Then what happened?"

"I don't know."

"But the parents know we were out with Eddie last night. When they couldn't find us, they called his beeper. Eddie called them back and told them we were with him."

"Well that explains the comment my mom made this morning."

"What comment, Daphne?"

Daphne started to laugh as she said, "Oh, let me find you in the cabana like that and see what happens to you." Then she went on saying, "That girl is just a year older than you. What is this world coming to?"

"Seriously?"

"Yes, and I had no idea what she was even talking about."

"Now that's really funny."

"It is now, but this morning I had no clue what she was trying to tell me, and it was sort of freaking me out." We both laughed and I mentioned we need to hurry up. The parents are making us breakfast."

I ran into the bedroom area and quickly put on shorts and a T-shirt. "What time are we leaving here for the wedding?"

"I'm not sure Sam, we should ask that question during breakfast." I slid my feet into my clogs, and we left the bedroom and headed for the kitchen.

We walked in when Julio, Greg, Lewis, and Alex were eating at the counter. Daphne and I took a seat at the kitchen table with the parents. Pilar asked us, "What would you girls like to eat?" , "We have pancakes, scrambled eggs, bacon, and sausage. We also have some blueberry and raisin scones."

I squinted up my face and asked, "Scones?"

"Yes," my mom answered. "Last night was so stressful after we took Amy home. Pilar, Carmen, and I made some scones."

"Mom, I would like to have a scone, please."

"Certainly. Here you go," my mom handed me a plate of scones. I took one off the plate and Daphne took one as well.

My mom, Carmen, and Pilar were smiling at us. I looked at them and asked, "What's going on? Is something wrong?"

"No," Pilar answered smiling. "We're just waiting for you to try the scone to tell us what you think."

"Oh, yeah. Let me try it." I closed my eyes and took a bite. It was good.

I set the scone down on the bread plate in front of me and told them, "It's terrible."

I heard all of the stools turn and I looked over toward the counter and the boys were all facing me wearing a very shocked expression. I looked at the moms and smiled before saying, "Just kidding. It's actually delicious, thank you."

My mom was apparently holding her breath and she exhaled releasing a long sound of relief. Pilar was smiling at me and shaking her head. She was sitting beside me and leaned over to wrap her arms around me. "I love you, Samantha, and I can't wait for you to become my daughter-in-law someday."

Tommy stood up and retorted, "My little sister isn't getting married for a long time. She hasn't even started High school yet, and then she has to attend college."

"Yes, I agree with you Tommy, but I think it will happen one day."

"Lewis, are you being serious right now?"

"Yes. If they still feel this way about each other after college."

"Lewis, my sister is only fifteen years old. I don't want her head filled with a bunch of forever fairy-tales."

"Why? What's the big deal Tommy?"

"Lewis, I don't want my sister to be found in the cabana like your girlfriend Amy. That's what can happen after filling her head with that type of stuff."

"Tommy, no," I yelled, and I covered my mouth. I looked over at my mom and Pilar, "I'm sorry. I didn't mean to yell like that."

Pilar smiled and my mom responded with, "That's okay, Sam. Your brother is being overprotective, and he is completely out of line for saying such things."

Tommy stood up again and retorted, "Are you kidding me? Lewis just sat here telling all of us that he has no privacy. That everyone barged in on him yesterday in the cabana. Not once did I hear him apologize to anyone for what he did at his uncle's house. He is the one being totally disrespectful."

"Hey, let me ask you something, Tommy. What bothers you more? That I'm 16 and having sex already or that you're still a virgin?"

"Eddie, take your brother outside. I will be out there in a minute."

"Okay, Tio." Lewis, and Eddie stood up and walked outside to the pool.

Guillermo stood up and said, "I'm going to apologize to all of you for my nephew's behavior yesterday and today. We are all like family now and I will tell you the truth. Lewis is not happy that his father is getting married. In fact, he does not like Julie.

He has done everything possible to try and stop them from getting married. Now if you will all excuse me; I am going outside to speak to my nephew."

Guillermo walked over to the sliding glass doors and no one said a word. We just watched him walk out the door and slide the door shut.

"Oh, this is great. Monica is finally back on track and better than ever. Just in time for Lewis to completely fall off the tracks. He has totally derailed. My brothers and I are trying everything to get him back on track.

"Pilar, when did this all start to happen."

"Lori, it all started to fall apart the minute my brother announced he was getting married. I just kept praying this would all work out and Lewis would come around. Now I know that Guillermo has no choice but to have Lewis move in here with him. He obviously can't live in the house with Julie."

"But why?"

"Lewis of course has been doing everything possible to make Julie's life a challenge. It has in fact become a full-time hobby for him. He has been staying over at my house and sleeping in Julio's room this whole week. That seems to have helped with his attitude until his outburst yesterday."

"Pilar, he didn't sleep at your house last night. He slept here and maybe it's your house that he needs to move into and not Guillermo's house."

"Lori, I think you're right. When we even mention him moving into this house, Lewis becomes even more furious. Which doesn't make sense to me because he spends so much time here."

"That's not it, Pilar. You have been a mother figure to him since his own mother passed away. I think when he lives under your roof, Lewis is getting that mother nurturing that he craves and needs."

"Lori, I didn't even think of it like that, but I think you're right. His mother wasn't my sister-in-law after Eddie was born, she was my sister. There was a time I was devastated beyond repair. She found a way to put me back together. Just by making me realize that I had so much in my life. I had the love of my children, her children, my brothers, my mother and her. No matter what the cards were dealt to us in this life, we decided will sort them out and play this game of life together."

"What caused you to feel like that Pilar?"

"When my husband left me and the kids to be with another woman."

"Do you know that less than a year later I received a visitor to my house. It was my husband's sister and she had no idea that her brother walked out on me and the kids. She came over to tell me that my husband had passed away.

To this day she is the only one from his family who keeps in touch with me and the boys. Even after all of these years, she continues to write, send us pictures, and visit from time to time."

"Yes, my mom is a good woman and luckily nothing like her family," Enrique added."

"Your mom is her husband's sister?"

"Yes, she is Carmen."

"Wait, but you told me in the car yesterday that you work for Uncle Gio,"

"Yes, I did, Sammy, because I do. I look at Guillermo and Juan as my uncles. They have always treated me as part of their family. I am Pilar's nephew and cousin by blood to Alex, Monica, and Julio."

Julio smiled and told me, "We're Latin, Sammy. If someone is one of our cousins, he is now all of our cousins."

"Yes, that's true," Pilar replied, and she was smiling now herself. "He couldn't only be my nephew. When we arrived in the United States and met Enrique now as an adult, he was immediately known as our nephew. In fact, Juan and I were living in Miami and Guillermo had just moved to California. When we all flew to Texas to meet up with our nephew Enrique together."

Guillermo opened the sliding glass door, and everyone was quiet. Lewis, Eddie, and Guillermo walked back inside. Lewis walked over to the table and told Carmen, "I'm very sorry about what you saw yesterday and for my reaction."

"I accept your apology Lewis."

"Thank you, Carmen."

"I'm also sorry for speaking to you the way I did yesterday Greg. There is no excuse for the way I overreacted."

"Lewis, are we cool now dude?"

"Greg, I think that's what I should be asking you.

"Greg reached around and gave Lewis a one arm hug. "You're my family man, we're always cool."

Lewis looked over Greg's shoulder to Guillermo, and said, "Tio, again, I'm sorry for disrespecting your home. It won't ever happen again."

Pilar stood up, and said, "No, it won't. You're moving back into my house after today. I realize that you are out of control and you need supervision. I'm going to keep a close eye on you Lewis. From now on you better get used to living in Alex's room. Oh, and if you think for one second, you're bringing girls into my house, think again."

Lewis was smiling and Julio said, "Under the same roof again, primo."

"Yeah," and he high-fived Julio.

"Um, can I ask a question?"

"Of course, Sammy. What is it?"

"What time is the wedding today Guillermo?"

"The wedding is at three o'clock. Michael and Arturo should be here by noon."

"Okay, cool, can you and Tommy go outside with me to talk for a minute alone?"

"Of course, Sammy. Let's go." Guillermo, Tommy, and I stood up and we walked outside onto the pool deck and took a seat at the table.

Once we were all seated, Tommy asked, "How did the date go with my mom last night?"

Guillermo looked up and answered, "Good, good, I think," and he looked back at the two of us.

"Oh, wow, Guillermo, what happened?" I asked sounding worried, because I was, and I knew by listening to him it wasn't good.

"Nothing. Don't you guys worry about it. Everything is okay. There's no problem."

I looked over at Tommy and I rolled my eyes, thinking oh boy, 'This must be worse than I thought.' I nudged Tommy and he told Guillermo, "Just tell us what happened, so we can help."

Guillermo stood up and started pacing. He wasn't even saying anything at first. Then he stopped walking and faced us. "I think I'm going to suffer when your mother leaves here on Sunday night."

"Oh, wow, are you in love with our mom?"

"How would I know that Sammy? I haven't even kissed her."

"Are you serious? You haven't kissed my mom yet and you think you're going to suffer when she leaves here on Sunday?"

"Yes, Tommy, I haven't ever felt like this before so I'm not sure what I feel is love, but I know that I enjoy every minute that I am with your mom. Even if I'm not talking to her just being in the same room with her and being able to hear her voice makes me happy."

"The minute I picked your mom up from the airport and heard that voice I was under some sort of spell."

"A spell?"

"Yes, Sammy, that's what my sister calls it."

"Whoa, that goes to show you, love at first sight is real."

"Yeah, I think your right Sammy. It sounds like he's falling in love with mom."

"I am constantly happy, every minute of the day that I am near your mother. She makes my life exciting just with her smile. I want to take her everywhere, and experience everything with her.

"Seriously, Guillermo."

"Yes, Sammy. This is the first time ever in my life that I have felt this way about anybody."

"Guillermo, you need to tell my mom how you feel."

"I don't know how Tommy, and I'm scared of my feelings for her."

My mom popped her head out the sliding glass door and asked, "Is everything okay?"

"Yes, Mom, everything is better than okay. Why don't you come out here and join us?"

"Are you sure I'm not intruding Sam?"

Tommy replied, "Mom were sure, join us but shut the sliding glass door behind you." I heard my mom shut the sliding glass door and she walked up to the table and sat down.

"So, what's going on, Sam? Why are the three of you outside?"

"We're just talking mom."

"Does this have anything to do with Lewis?"

"Tommy answered, "Mom, it has nothing to do with Lewis and everything to do with you."

"With me? What about me?"

"We just wanted to know how your date with Guillermo went yesterday. I know you're going to say that it's none of our business, but we just wanted to make sure you had a good time."

My mom looked over at me then Tommy and told us, "I had a very good time, but you should have asked me and not bothered Guillermo with questions about me. Only I can answer questions pertaining to me and how I feel. Next time, when you want to know something about me or anybody else you should ask that person. In this case that would be me, right?"

Tommy looked down at the floor and answered, "Yes, Mom."

I frowned, and replied, "Mom, we also wanted to know how Guillermo was doing and how he's feeling. I learned he has a huge crush on you, and I think he may even want to kiss you. Anyways, that's pretty much the deal Mom and we're going back inside now. Come on, Tommy."

We both stood up and walked back inside using the sliding glass door into the kitchen. We left my mom and Guillermo alone at the table.

As soon as we walked inside the kitchen Carmen and Pilar asked, "Where is your mom?"

"She's outside talking to Guillermo. I'm sure they'll be back inside in a couple of minutes."

Carmen frowned and removed her hand from the handle on the sliding glass door. She sat back down beside Pilar and Enrique at the kitchen table. I looked up at Tommy and he looked back at me. We both looked over at Pilar and she gave us a thumbs up.

Pilar asked, "Why don't you two join the others in the family room?" We both left the kitchen and walked over to the family room. We played some video games. An hour later Monica arrived at the house. Tommy walked over to Monica and asked her to join him outside on the pool deck. They both stood up and headed outside. A couple of seconds later they both walked back inside, and Tommy suggested we all go downstairs and watch a movie.

We all walked downstairs to the theatre room. Pilar, Chris, Carmen, and even Enrique followed us down. Alex came downstairs around an hour later and announced, "Arturo and Michael are on their way now. They will be here in less than an hour. Oh, before I forget, Uncle Gio and Lori left. They said they would meet us at the church."

"What are you talking about, Alex? Lori and your uncle are supposed to be going with us to the wedding. Why would they leave now and meet us there?"

Alex laughed and answered, "I got you, Mom. They are still out on the pool deck talking."

Pilar took off her chancleta, and Alex ran for the door. She stood up and threw her chancleta across the room. It hit Alex before he made it out the door. Pilar stood there and crossed her arms over her chest. She yelled out, "Got you, mi hijo" and we all started laughing. Alex was cracking up, and he ran over to his mom and hugged her.

"Mom, just be sure to remember no pranks during the wedding or reception— you promised." Pilar reached down to take off her other chancleta as Alex was laughing and running for the door again. This time he managed to get out the door and the chancleta hit the back of the door.

Pilar was still standing up and facing the door. "I know you can hear me Alex, and when I said no pranks, I meant you and Eddie, not me!"

Alex opened the door and saw both chancletas on the floor. He bent over and picked them up and smiled at his mom. He called out, "Mom, I don't know what you're going to do without your flip-flops. These belong to me now. Pilar ran toward the door and Alex ran back out the door with her flip-flops. We were all laughing so hard and Pilar had the biggest smile on her face.

Alex came back a few minutes later, with a glass of water for his mom and her chancletas. They sat on the couch together and Pilar held onto that smile, the whole time the movie was playing. When the movie was over, we all walked back upstairs, and headed outside to the pool.

My mom and Guillermo were still at the table in the same seats. They were talking to Enrique and Carmen now. Pilar eventually joined them with Chris beside her. Daphne said, "Well, that's it! The table is officially the parents' table, once again." Monica and I started laughing. Lewis walked by and asked what's so funny.

"Oh, Cabana Boy, can you get me a towel?"

"Very funny, Monica," Lewis replied, as he rolled his eyes."

"Actually, that was very funny."

"Thanks Sammy, that will definitely be his new nickname for the next couple of months."

"Monica, that's perfect," Julio told her."

"I know, right? I'm so ready for Lewis to move back in with us."

"Me too, Monica."

Monica cracked her knuckles before saying, "Let the torture begin," and she high-fived Julio.

We all sat down on the ledge of the pool, and we just placed our feet in the water. When Michael and Arturo walked out onto the pool deck. Michael said, "Hello, everybody, we're back."

Carmen and Daphne jumped up from where they were sitting and ran over to Michael and Arturo and they were each greeted with a big hug. I walked over to them, with Julio and Greg. They each gave me a hug and high-fived Julio and Greg. They followed us over to the pool and they took off their loafers and placed their feet in the water.

"So, did we miss anything?"

"Michael, that question is such an understatement. I will try to catch you up on everything; but first, when are you going to start doing our makeup and hair?"

"Soon! Daphne don't worry. Your mom, Arturo and I worked out a plan before we came up here today to make everybody handsome and beautiful.

"Right after each one of you ladies take a shower, I will begin doing makeup and some hair. Your mom will also help us with ladies' hair. Arturo will work on gel back for the guys' hair. Oh, and he is on tie and lint brush duty. We will have everyone looking clean and pristine.

"Okay Michael, we're going to go and take a shower now. Do you and Arturo want to see our bedroom? There is a sitting area, as well as a dressing/makeup area in our room. That way Sammy and I can catch you guys up on everything."

"Oh! now that sounds good to me. Come on, Arturo. Let's go!" Michael was looking at the parents' table as he lowered his voice and told Daphne, "I need to know everything."

"And you will Michael."

Arturo rolled his eyes as he stood up. He followed Michael and Daphne into our bedroom through the sliding glass door. I turned to Julio and told him, "I have to go now." We both stood up and he walked me over to sliding glass door. He wrapped his arms around me and squeezed me.

When he released me, he said, "Samantha, I just remembered I didn't ask you…"

"You didn't ask me what, Julio?"

"I didn't ask you to be my date to the wedding."

Julio took my hand, and he looked into my eyes and asked, "Would you be my date to the wedding?"

"Our wedding or your uncle's wedding? I'm sorry, I'm confused," I informed him smiling.

Julio smiled and answered, "Both, Samantha," and he winked at me.

"I can only say yes to one of your invitations at this time. I'm sorry but I'm only a minor and I'm not legally allowed to agree to any weddings that involve me until I'm at least 18." I heard Michael and Daphne laughing from inside my room.

Julio looked away from me and I saw him smiling. Then he turned his head back toward me and asked, "So, will you be my date to the wedding taking place today for my Uncle and Julie?"

"Yes, I would love to be your date to your uncle's wedding today, Julio." I heard clapping from inside the room, Julio and I shook our heads smiling.

Julio leaned over and whispered, "You'll be more than my date someday, Mi Corazón. You will one day be my wife, and my date at our wedding." He kissed me on the cheek and when he pulled away, I just stood there lost in his big brown eyes. I was so caught up in the moment that I stood up on my tiptoes and quickly pop kissed him on the lips. I saw a spark in his eyes and that's when I ran into my bedroom and slid the door shut.

I ran past Arturo and Michael and plopped down on my bed. "Well, what happened Sammy?"

"Daphne, you should have seen Julio's face. I just pop kissed him right now on the pool deck in front of our bedroom door. I took him completely by surprise."

"Wait? Sammy, I'm confused. I thought you have kissed Julio, on the lips before today."

"Michael, I have! but I don't ever kiss him on the lips in public."

"I did this time and I saw his eyes light up. He had a huge smile on his face and that's how I left him when I ran inside. It was so amazing, and I loved surprising him like that."

"That's great, Sammy. I'm so happy for you, but you need to get in the shower now."

"Daphne, can I have a second to rest?"

"No, get in the shower Sammy."

Michael and Arturo were sitting on the two overstuffed chairs by the fireplace. Michael turned to me and said, "You and Julio are just too cute for words. We heard everything and who knows? Maybe one day, you will marry him, Sammy."

I stood up and ran over to Michael and hugged him. "Maybe, but it's like I said before. I'm a minor right now, so marriage is not even a possibility."

"Sammy, you have to tell me about Guillermo and your mom. Like, has anything happened?"

I sat down on the ottoman in front of Michael. "Sure, basically he has a huge crush on my mom. He asked Tommy and I if we will mind if he takes her out on a date."

"What? When did this happen?"

"When we were at the park yesterday, Daphne."

"Sammy, you never told me that?"

"I'm sorry, I forgot to tell you Daphne but so much happened yesterday."

"Daphne sat down beside me on the ottoman. "Your right Sammy, so tell us now what happened."

"Okay, we told Guillermo that we didn't have a problem with him asking my mom out on a date. Then we found out Guillermo hasn't been able to get my mom alone long enough to ask her out."

"So, what could you do about that?"

"Michael, once Tommy and I found that out, we came up with a plan immediately."

"What plan?"

"Daphne, yesterday we told everyone to jump in the limo when we left the park. That way Guillermo could drive my mom home in the car and he actually took her out on their first date yesterday."

"Oh, I thought that was Alex pranking Guillermo. I had no idea it was you, Sammy."

"Nope, that was mine and Tommy's plane. I only told Alex two things."

"What two things?"

"I told Alex we needed to ride in the limo, and he needed to give Guillermo the car keys."

"Now I know why you said you would tell me later, Sammy."

"Exactly, and now you know everything Daphne."

"Okay, but where did they go on their date?"

"I'm not totally sure Michael. Guillermo did say he wanted to take my mom to an Italian restaurant in Santa Monica. That's a casual place with great food and a variety of wines from Napa. Oh, and I know for certain he hasn't kissed her yet."

"How do you know that for sure Sammy?"

"Tommy and I spoke with Guillermo this morning and we asked him how the date went with my mom. That's when he mentioned he hasn't kissed my mom yet."

"Sammy, tell them about the balcony."

"Oh, yeah, the balcony. Daphne you tell them that story."

"No, you tell them it's your mom."

"Fine, I will. Yesterday Greg, Daphne, Julio, and I were out on the pool deck watching the sunrise. My mom and Guillermo were up on the balcony above us watching the sunrise together. Now I'm going to take a shower. Daphne, feel free to tell them the rest of the story and about the cabana boy."

Daphne started cracking up laughing. "I can't believe you're calling him The Cabana Boy."

"That's the best name ever."

"Wait, you have a cabana boy here?"

"Michael, we do, and his real name is Lewis."

We both broke out laughing again. Michael said, "Oh, this is going to be good. Tell me everything and start from the beginning Daphne."

Daphne, began to tell the story about Lewis, the cabana boy, while I headed into the bathroom to take a shower. I came out wrapped in a robe and my head wrapped in towel. Michael and Daphne were waiting for me in the dressing area with the vanity chair already pulled out.

Michael waved his hand and bent forward, and I sat down. Daphne started parting my hair into clips. Michael told me," I always thought that Lewis and Julio were the same age."

"Lewis is older by six months and they are only in the same grade because Lewis flunked the ninth grade. Some people think he flunked on purpose so he could stay another year in Miami."

"So, is your mom into Guillermo?"

"I think so. She smiles constantly and laughs more than I ever remember."

"I saw your mom when we first walked up to the limo. The minute she shook hands with Guillermo, she was smiling with big blue eyes. It was like she was mesmerized by his touch or something. I looked at the mirror and saw Arturo's reflection. He was standing behind us.

"You're right, Arturo. My mom still has those big eyes and smile every minute of the day since we arrived here."

Arturo placed his hands in his pockets as he leaned up against the wall and looked over at me. I looked back at him in the mirror and smiled. "Sammy, why do you look so worried?"

My eyes watered up as I stared back at Arturo in the mirror. "Long-distant relationships never work out. We leave here tomorrow, and my mom won't smile like that anymore. She will only leave here with the memories and not Guillermo. I've never seen her like this before and I enjoy seeing my mom happy."

Arturo, Michael, and Daphne all took turns hugging me. Then Michael raised my chin up and he handed me a washcloth. "Stop it, Sammy. Your eyes are going to get pink and swollen. I am your fairy godmother today and I can do miracles, but I hate having to do extra work."

I took the washcloth and wiped my face. I saw Daphne look at Michael, through the mirror. She was thanking Michael for calming me down. They both smiled and looked down at the back of my head.

Michael blow-dried my hair in sections. Then he applied some mousse and blow-dried some more. He had used the curling iron to make my curls stronger and tighter. When my hair was finished, it was beautiful. The sides of my hair were pulled into a beautiful gold barrette that was in the shape of a bow. Below the barrette my hair was flowing in long beautiful curls. My bangs were lying flat with loose curls on the side.

"So, what do you think, Sammy?"

"Michael, my hair looks beautiful."

"Well, when you said you were leaving here with the memories and not the boy; as your fairy godmother, it's my job to make sure you look undeniably gorgeous. Leaving him with such memories of you is my job."

I continued to look at Michael from the reflection in the mirror. "You are the best fairy godmother ever." I turned around and stood up to give him a hug.

"Yes, and don't I know it," he replied with a bright smile. "Now go and have a seat over there beside Arturo and remain in your bathrobe. I don't want your dress getting all wrinkled."

"Wait. What about Sammy's makeup?"

"Yes, I almost forgot! After I do your hair Daphne and makeup, I will do Sammy's. By that time, you girls can hang out for around 30 minutes before you need to get dressed. Arturo and I will head upstairs and start working on the moms."

"That sounds good to me, Michael. Thank you for everything."

"You're welcome Sammy."

"Michael, wait! When do I have to start working on the gel backs?"

"Arturo, you know how guys are. They won't take a shower until the last minute. We will both work on wrestling them all up and getting their hair done together."

Arturo smiled and said," I like that better."

"What do you like?"

"I like that we're going to be working together."

Michael stopped what he was doing and walked out of the vanity area and up to Arturo, who was sitting on the chair beside me. Michael bent over the chair and hugged Arturo. "You just made me feel magnificent Arturo."

Michael started blow drying Daphne's hair, and Arturo yelled out, "That's because you are magnificent!"

Michael turned off the hair dryer and walked back down the hall and over to Arturo. "That's only because you make me feel that way. Arturo smiled and Michael turned and walked back over to Daphne.

I walked up to Daphne as she was patiently waiting for Michael to start working on her hair again. "Daphne, tell them about Enrique."

"Sammy, I don't know if anything is actually going on between Enrique and my mom."

Michael turned around and looked over at Arturo. That's when Arturo stood up and he joined us in the dressing area again. Arturo looked over at me with a serious expression on his face and said, "Spill it, Sammy."

"Okay, so Enrique is Pilar's nephew. He is originally from Colombia and his parents moved to the United States in his late teens. He had been living in Texas until a year ago when he got a divorce and moved to California. He works for Guillermo."

"So, what does that have to do with my mom?"

"Arturo, they just spend a lot of time with one another laughing and enjoying each other's company. Basically, he makes your mom happy and they are really cute together."

"I see, and does my mom like him?"

"I don't know Arturo. I think so."

"Sammy, what makes you think so?"

"Arturo, your mom is constantly smiling and laughing every minute of the day.

"So, just like your mom."

"Exactly, Arturo."

We even have a nickname for all the parents when they hang out. We call it 'The Parents' Table.'"

"Daphne, what kind of name is that?"

"Michael, It's the perfect name trust me."

Oh, please explain this nickname to me Daphne.

"Okay, I will. When we first arrived, we had the luncheon and the parents all sat at one table and rest of us sat at the other table. Since that day it has been the same way every day. When they come to the pool, they all sit together at the table making it 'the parents' table.' In the kitchen we sit at the counter and they all sit at 'the parents' table.' Now do you get it?"

"The parents hang out everywhere in this house together. Whether it be the living room, dining room, or pool. They stick together all six of them, so wherever they sit, we call it —"

Michael and Arturo answered, "'The Parents Table.' Got it."

"Greg told us the parents came home Thursday night and they were dancing and drinking champagne until after midnight. We missed everything because Sammy and I fell asleep. When Greg told us what we missed, Sammy and I agreed to stay up and keep an eye on the parents."

"Did you keep an eye on them, Daphne?"

"No, Arturo because that whole thing went down at the cabana with Lewis. We took off with Eddie and Heather instead."

"Daphne, how are things between you and Lewis now?"

"Truthfully, Michael, he was not happy this morning. Lewis and Tommy got into an argument at breakfast. I'm just trying to stay away from the cabana boy until he calms down."

"Okay, well, let me start on Sammy's makeup now. Time to switch seats."

Daphne got up and walked over to Arturo and she looked beautiful. Her jet-black hair was all up in a big bun with several curls hanging down on the sides. Her bangs were straight lying like tassels just above her eyes. This made you focus in on her bright eyes. Her eyelids were done in brown and tan eyeshadow, brown eyeliner, and mascara. Her lips were in light peach lip gloss. "Michael, I don't know how you do it. Daphne's looks incredible."

"Yes, well! All I'm doing is highlighting your natural beauty with a touch of color. Come sit down." Michael patted the cushion on the chair. "You're my next canvas, Sammy."

I sat down and Michael said, "I want to make your blue eyes light up. Do you mind if I use black eyeliner and mascara? I won't apply the eyeliner too liberally; I will just apply a very thin line that should blend in with your upper and lower eyelashes."

"Okay, Michael. Do it! I believe in you fairy godmother."

When Michael was done, I couldn't believe it. My eyes looked as if like they were glowing; they were that bright. You couldn't even tell I was wearing black eyeliner; it was blended in so well with the black mascara. For my lips he applied a light mauve lip gloss.

I hugged Michael and Daphne, and Arturo walked over to the vanity area. "Your fairy godmother does great work.

"Thank you, Arturo."

"Although we've enjoyed spending time with you girls, we have to go and help the boys."

"We understand Arturo," Daphne said with a hint of disappointment in her voice. We each gave Michael and Arturo a hug, before they left.

Chapter 7 Kissing and Dancing

Daphne and I were relaxing in our room with our feet up on the ottoman. We were still dressed in our bathrobes and talking about Greg and Julio. Until Daphne's beeper started buzzing and she saw the time. That's when she jumped up and started yelling, "Sammy, we need to hurry or we're going to be late. "We both ran down the hall and grabbed our garment bags from out of the closets.

I took off with my bag in my hand and ran towards the bathroom. Daphne was already in there with the door locked by the time I arrived. I walked back to my bed and tossed the garment bag on top. I decided to wait and see Daphne dressed up first.

Daphne walked out wearing a tan sleeveless cotton dress; it was beautiful with a thick halter strap around the neck and a crisscross wrap over her chest. She's had on a thick white cotton belt with tan stripes around her waist. The length of the dress ran just past her knees. She finished off her outfit with nude colored panty hose and tan heels.

I started clapping with excitement when I saw her. "Okay, Sammy. So, it's your turn to get dressed. What are you waiting for?"

"I just wanted to see you all put together. You look terrific, Daphne."

"Thanks, Sammy. Now it's your turn."

I grabbed the garment bag and headed into the walk-in closet. I turned on the light and decided there was plenty of room in here for me to get dressed.

I put on the nude sheer hose first; then I stepped into the dress. I couldn't zip up the back of it, so I walked out of the closet and asked Daphne to help me. Once I was zipped up and turned around, I looked at myself in the full-length mirror. Now I could finally see how the dress fit. The color of it is light pink and sleeveless. The top of the dress is sheer, so I decided to wear a stretchy white lace blouse on top. The skirt of the dress was my favorite. It's pink satin in the shape of a bell.

"Daphne, do you know I loved this dress the minute I saw it at the mall? I kept thinking it was affordable, but I had nowhere to go that I could wear this type of dress. I placed it back on the rack and left the store. When we were invited to the wedding, I went back to the mall to get this dress. I never tried it on. I don't know why. I just looked for my size and bought the dress."

"So, wait. This is the first time you are seeing yourself in this dress?" I nodded my head yes. "What if it didn't fit, Sammy? What were you going to do?"

I walked back into the closet and grabbed my other garment bag. I pulled out another dress and showed it to Daphne. "What's this dress for Sammy?"

"This was the dress I would have worn if the pink one didn't work out."

"That's a pretty dress too but I still prefer the one you're wearing now. It all just works well together with the pink eye shadow, and lip gloss. You want to look perfect for Julio, so he can remember you after we leave."

I nodded my head yes, and realized I was starting to feel a bit emotional now. I closed my eyes and took in a deep breath and let it out slowly. "Sammy, relax. You look great and we're going to have so much fun at the reception."

"You know something? You're right!"

"Of course, I am."

"Thanks, Daphne."

There was a knock at the door and Daphne answered it. It was Michael and Arturo. They both walked in and sat down in the chairs.

"Well, we did it, girls. The moms' makeup is all done with. Carmen did all of the moms' hair. I did Carmen's hair and the gel back on Alex. Oh, and Guillermo, I didn't have to do his hair really. He already had his hair and beard all done. Arturo wrestled up the rest of the boys down here. He tied ties, gel backed hair, and we're bringing the lint brush."

Daphne and I started clapping and Arturo high-fived Michael. "Michael, we make a great team. Everyone looks fantastic."

"Yes, we do. I'm just glad it's done now and that's actually why we're here. The boys have a secret weapon: some cologne they intend to wear tonight. Greg and Julio were discussing it in front of us. Julio mentioned that it drives you crazy, Sammy."

Suddenly, I felt my cheeks warming up and I quickly turned my head away from Michael. He was smiling and waiting for me to say something. "Michael, he's right."

"He is?"

"Yes, Michael."

"Great, I have a plan Sammy. As your fairy godmother, I have brought you girls a weapon of your own." Daphne and I looked at one another and we were both smiling. "It's a perfume that smells amazing and it comes to you from Pilar's perfume collection. Now the trick is to only apply it to the key areas of the body."

The purpose tonight girls is not to overwhelm everybody with your scent. Instead, you want to surprise your boyfriends. Now you're probably thinking, 'Gee, Michael. How do we do that?' Well that is what I am going to teach you now."

We followed Michael into the dressing area. Once we were there, he pulled out a bottle of men's cologne and a bottle of perfume from his pocket. "Girls just copy what I do. Step- by-step."

"Okay, Michael," Daphne and I replied in unison.

"Start off by spraying a spot of fragrance to your index finger. Rub your two index fingers together and now tap each of your wrists with your index fingers." Michael watched us and when we were done, Michael said, "Very good. Now spray your prominent index finger again and tap one spot behind each ear." We did that and Michael told us to spray our index finger one last time. We both looked up at him and he told us, "Girls you have to trust me. Now I want you to tap three times going down your neck right below your earlobe."

"Okay, girls. Great job. Wash your hands, and let's go."

"Michael, I have a question."

"Sure, ask away Daphne."

"Why didn't we just spray all those spots?"

Michael laughed before he answered, "If you spray those areas, Daphne, you will give away the element of surprise."

"I need that Daphne."

"Need what Sammy?"

"The element of surprise to level out the playing field with Julio. His cologne drives me insane."

I reached up and hugged Michael, and told him, "Thank you."

Daphne reached over the sink and turned on the faucet. I yelled, "Wait, let's smell our hands first."

We did and I could smell a hint of jasmine. The perfume had such a clean fresh smell. It wasn't overwhelming and I thought it could work. I was thrilled with the idea that I might actually surprise Julio.

Daphne and I leaned over the sink to wash our hands. When I leaned back, I looked in the mirror over at Daphne and told her, "I know which cologne the boys will be wearing."

"Which one?"

"It's the cologne they both wore at your birthday party."

"That one? Are you sure? I love that smell."

"Yes, it's definitely that one."

"How do you know that for sure Sammy?"

"Daphne, that smell drives me crazy and Julio is totally aware of the effect it has on me."

"Maybe this time Julio intends to wear a different cologne and it won't have the same impact on you Sammy."

"Julio has already worn the cologne once since we've been here. I had to force myself to try to stay away from his neck all night. I had visions of tearing off Julio's shirt and touching his chest while inhaling that scent."

"Wow, Sammy," Daphne said laughing. "You told me all about your cause and effect cases with Julio before, but this is the best one yet."

"Well, now I'm looking for pay back and I think this perfume might do the trick. He always nuzzles my neck with the tip of his nose.

"When? I've never seen Julio do that to you Sammy!"

"Every time he whispers in my ear or places his head on my shoulder. It gives me goosebumps and he loves that. I'm hoping the smell of this perfume will surprise him and perhaps drive him a little crazy for a change."

There was a knock on the door and Alex said, "Come on, girls. It's time to go."

Michael and Arturo ran to the door and answered, "We're coming, Alex" in a high-pitched attempt at a girl's voice. When they opened the door Alex was laughing, "You two are something else. Can you please inform Daphne and Sammy that it's time to go?"

Michael opened the door the rest of the way.

"Hi Sammy."

Daphne walked out from the dressing area and waved to Alex." Whoa, you girls look stunning. My little brother and Greg are not ready for the two of you."

"Thank you, Alex." Michael was gleaming with pride for all the work he had done paid off.

"Okay, so you girls will be riding in the black Lincoln town car. It will be the five of us. Enrique, and Michael will be riding with the parents."

"Alex, wait up! I need to put my shoes on." I slid my feet into a pair of white heels and quickly caught up to Alex. Daphne was right beside me.

I couldn't wait to see Julio all dressed up. I loved it when he had his hair gelled back. I was starting to feel a bit excited. When we reached the front door and I was standing in front of Julio, I could feel his eyes on me as he looked me over, up and down, and up again. He was completely silent, and his eyes were big and bright. He took my hand in his and faced the door.

Alex laughed and asked, "Julio, aren't you going to say anything to Sammy?"

Julio nodded his head yes, and he turned around and faced me again.

Guillermo walked up behind Julio. He patted him on the shoulder and announced, "You all look wonderful and we're going to have a great time tonight."

"A wedding, then dinner and dancing. What else could a girl want?"

Guillermo started to laugh at Daphne's comment as Enrique walked past him over to the staircase with Chris. Guillermo joined them and the three of them stood there looking up.

It was Pilar coming down the stairs. She was wearing a peach colored evening gown. The top of her dress was sheer with sequins and the rest of it was satin. Her hair was pulled back into a twist with loose curls hanging down her back. Her eyeshadow matched her dress in tan and brown. Her lips were peach, and Pilar wore the definition of elegance. We all clapped as she made her way over to Chris.

Carmen came down next wearing a strapless gray satin evening gown. Her hair was held up by a gray and black oval shaped barrette with lots of curls hanging out the back of the barrette. Her eyeshadow was gray and white with an accent of black eyeliner and mascara. She was wearing a light shade of wine-colored lipstick. Enrique met her at the foot of the staircase, and he took her hand. We all clapped, and she was smiling uncontrollably. She wore the definition of content.

I looked over at Guillermo and he was still looking up. His mouth dropped open and his eyes lit up as my mom walked down the stairs. She was wearing a blue satin evening gown with spaghetti straps. The sides of her hair were pulled up into a twist with tons of curls hanging down her back. The eyeshadow she had on was blue and silver with a hint of black eyeliner. Her eyes were definitely bright, and her lips were in a shade of tomato red lipstick.

Guillermo walked up to my mom as she was on the last step. He looked as though he was in a trance or something. He took her hand and told her, "Your stunning!"

She smiled up at him and replied, "So are you."

Guillermo leaned in and my mom closed her eyes as he kissed her. She placed her hands onto his shoulders and when she opened her eyes, she looked radiant. Like, she was actually glowing.

Everyone's mouth dropped open and we all started clapping.

Then Tommy yelled out, "Finally!"

My mom was still wrapped in Guillermo's arms when she turned her head and smiled at Tommy. Then Guillermo still looking at my mom with such admiration said, "Finally, I have met the woman of my dreams."

Pilar whispered, "Yes, finally he has fallen in love." We all started to giggle, and Alex was frowning at us.

"That's great mom, it really is. Now everybody, let's get going."

"Alex!"

Mom we're going to be late to your other brothers wedding. Pilar rushed everyone out the door after Alex said that. The four of us followed Alex to the car. He tossed the car keys to Julio and told him, "You drive. I'll sit in the back seat. I don't want you and Sammy getting all wrinkled up before the wedding."

Julio unlocked the passenger's door first and pressed the button to unlock the rest of the doors. Julio held the door open for me and he shut the door behind me once I was seated.

When everyone was in the car, Julio put on his seat belt and we were off to the church.

Julio asked Alex, "Where is the church?"

"I don't know. I planned on following the limo, the driver should know where to go."

"Alex, are you serious? I need to drive back to the house and follow the limo?"

"Yes, Julio. You better hurry up and go now before they leave the house."

"Alright, Alex. I'm going back to the house now." He made a U-turn and headed back and when we arrived at the house, everybody was already gone.

Julio pulled into the driveway and got out of the car. He walked to the back and leaned against the trunk. I climbed out of the car and walked over to him. Julio had his right arm around his waist and his left hand pressed up against forehead. He was clearly upset, and I wished I could fix everything.

When I walked up to Julio, he wrapped his arms around me. He pulled me in closer and I felt him rest his head on my shoulder. "Julio, you look very handsome with your hair gelled back and I can smell it. You're wearing my favorite cologne." Julio lifted his head up from my shoulder and looked at me. He smiled and kissed me on the lips. I had instant chills; I pulled away from him as Alex walked up.

"So, what's the plan, Hermano?"

"I screwed up, Alex. I guess I can go in the house and beep Mom or Enrique or somebody. We'll just have to wait by the phone and hope someone calls us right back."

"Yes, we could do that or give me a second," Alex said. He ran back to the car and when he walked back over to Julio, he handed him a card. "Go ahead. Open it." Julio opened the card and it was the wedding invitation with the address and directions on the back.

Julio smiled as Alex laughed really deep and loud. Greg climbed out of the car and asked, "What's going on?"

Julio held up the wedding invitation and Greg walked over and read it out loud. He shook his head and handed the card back to Julio before climbing back in the car.

"Sorry, Julio. I just had to pull at least one prank on you before I leave here tomorrow." Alex hugged Julio, then said, "Kiss her one more time, Hermano. After all, you are the kissing bandits and she looks gorgeous." Julio was smiling as Alex took off and climbed back in the car.

"Samantha, Alex is right. You're gorgeous and you took my breath away when I first saw you tonight." Julio wrapped his arms around me before kissing me gently on my lips again.

My heart was beginning to sing, and Daphne yelled, "Hello! When are we leaving? We have a wedding to attend, remember?"

Julio and I quickly pulled apart and we were smiling at one another. "She's right Julio. We better get going."

We jumped in the car and pulled out of the driveway. "Alex, I thought you were in such a rush to leave the house. Now we might miss the wedding."

"No, will make it Julio. I planned for this to happen and that's why I was rushing everyone out of the house. I needed time to pull this prank on you little brother." Alex leaned over and rubbed the top of Julio's head.

"Alex, don't touch his hair."

"Sorry, Sammy. He removed his hand as he slowly leaned back in his seat.

Julio gave me a surprised look. "What? I like your hair like this."

Alex was right and we made it to the church on time. Seats were saved for us right behind the parents. When the wedding was over and we were leaving the church, the moms told all five of us to wait outside for them.

Julio was driving so he had to explain what happened to us. The moms seemed satisfied with the explanation, but we still had to follow the limo to the reception. We pulled up to the valet stand behind the limo and climbed out of the car. Julio handed Alex the keys and took my hand as we walked inside the hotel.

The banquet room was decorated so beautifully starting with the ceiling that had great big white and silver bells that were lit up. They were illuminating the room hanging down low from the ceiling. There was a DJ setting up beside the dance floor. At the front of the room was a stage with a band still setting up. All of the tables were covered in white lace with a shimmering silver skirt. There was an elegant bouquet of pink and white roses in the center surrounded by two glass swans. The swans were glowing from a lit candle hidden on the back of each swan. There was plenty of champagne being chilled beside each table in a silver bucket.

When we sat down at our table, Greg rubbed his hands together. The table was set with three forks to the left and two knives and a spoon to the right. Greg said, "With all this silverware on the table, we are really eating good tonight."

Julio turned his head and looked over at me and I looked back at him. We were both trying not to laugh. Then suddenly Julio leaned over and kissed me right on the lips. I was shocked! It wasn't something we did in public. Then the smell of his cologne hit me, and I had instant butterflies.

Julio leaned over to whisper in my ear. That's when I heard and felt him sniffing my neck and it tickled. Julio pulled his head away and he looked back at me with an astonished look. Then in a very low tone of voice he asked, "Are you trying to distract me the whole night, Mi Corazón?"

I laughed and answered, "Yes, that's definitely my intention."

Julio sucked in his lower lip. Then he released it. "I see, Samantha," and he squeezed my hand and smiled at me with a devilish grin.

"I'm glad that you're aware of my intentions."

Julio leaned in close to my ear and whispered, "Why do you want to torture me?"

I smiled and stared back at him as I spoke in a low tone of voice, "I should ask you the same question."

Julio was still leaning over my shoulder and whispered, "Are you trying to falsely accuse me of something?"

"No, of course not Julio. There is nothing false in that statement. You already took me by surprise with that kiss. I have butterflies now and if you do it again, I will become pointy and I don't wish for that to happen."

Julio smiled and whispered, "I'm already pointy after seeing you in this dress and smelling that perfume."

I smiled and whispered, "Poor baby. You deserve to be pointy wearing that cologne."

"Samantha, I know your weak points and you know all of mine. Are you sure you want to challenge me tonight?"

"Tonight, is my last night here with you in California. So yeah, I'm ready for a challenge. Are you, Soccer Player?" Julio sat back in his chair and he covered his mouth. He was trying to conceal his laughter.

Then all of a sudden, he leaned over and whispered, "Challenge accepted," and kissed me behind the ear. I looked down at my chest, and I was becoming pointy. I looked over at Julio and he looked down at my chest, then into my eyes and just smiled.

"Fine, now we're both pointy Julio, but you were pointy first." I looked into his eyes as I smiled and took a sip of my water.

Alex, Arturo, and Michael joined us at the table. "Finally, we made it upstairs," Alex said, "The parents were talking to everyone starting with the valet."

"Why? What happened?"

"Julio, Uncle Gio kept stopping and talking to everybody. Then he would introduce all of the parents to everyone."

"Alex, look at the bright side."

"What bright side, Julio?"

"The parents will show up here one day."

The DJ started off by playing 'Modern Love.' Michael and Arturo jumped to their feet and ran around the table. Arturo took my hand, and Michael grabbed hold of Daphne's. The four of us rushed out to the dance floor."

When the third song came on Eddie and Heather joined us on the dance floor. Heather was looking beautiful wearing a yellow satin dress and her hair was down. She was constantly smiling and kept her eyes on Eddie the whole time. Eddie looked very nice as well. He was wearing a black tuxedo since he was one of the groomsmen in the wedding.

I leaned over and whispered to Arturo, "They make a nice couple, what do you think?" He smiled and nodded his head yes. Then I saw Julio waiting by the dance floor beside Greg. I asked Arturo if he would mind terribly if I danced with Julio after this song.

Arturo answered, "Not at all. I only expected to dance with you for one song, and we danced to three." When the song was over, Arturo signaled Michael, and they both walked off the dance floor.

I walked over to Julio, and he met me halfway. 'Some like it Hot' started to play, and I smiled at him. We started to move slowly to the beat of the song. Julio looked down and smiled at me and slowly placed both of his arms around my waist. As the song played on and we danced, he kissed me behind my ear. Then whispered, "The perfect song don't you think for this challenge?" He pulled his head away smiling and waiting for a reaction or look on my face.

I pop kissed him and told him, "Your right, this is the perfect song and your challenge has been accepted." Julio bit down on his lower lip and he blinked a few times and shook his head. "Julio, is something wrong?"

He started to laugh and replied, "Your boldness tonight is enlightening." When the song ended, everybody began to clap. We turned around to see the married couple walking into the room. Julio took my hand and he walked me back over to our seats at the table.

The married couple was handed a microphone. Mr. Sanchez spoke first and thanked everyone for coming. He handed the mic over to Julie, and she said, "We have one more thing we would like to share with all of you tonight." Suddenly I felt eyes focusing in on our table. I began to look around the room to see where it was coming from. That's when I noticed Pilar and Guillermo staring directly at Lewis. He was sitting down at our table directly across from me.

I became nervous and wanted to protect Lewis from whatever was about to be said. Julie was beaming and smiling so bright. When she started to speak, my heart raced, and I squeezed Julio's hand. He looked over at me with a concerned look on his face. I looked back at Julio then nodded once in the direction of his mom and Guillermo.

Julie said she was so happy to announce that she was expecting. She was now two months along. Everyone began to clap and cheer for the married couple. Julio took in a deep breath and he looked over at Lewis then Alex. I looked over at Alex and he was watching Lewis. Eddie shouted, "Dad, I'm so proud of you. I thought you were too old. I hope it's at least a girl this time." The whole room erupted into laughter.

Julie and Mr. Sanchez were still laughing when I looked back at them. Mr. Sanchez leaned over to Julie and she held up the mic. Mr. Sanchez said, "For everybody who doesn't know, that beautiful comment came from eldest son Eduardo, the shy one." Everyone laughed even harder, and Eddie stood up and took a bow. Everyone clapped, and Julie handed the DJ back his mic.

The DJ announced the bride and groom would now have their first dance. 'The Search is Over' began to play and we all watched as the couple lit up the room with their smiles. They were so happy; you could see the love and pride Juan Sanchez was feeling at the moment for his bride Julie.

When the song ended, the DJ announced it was time for Julie's parents and the rest of the bridal party to join the wedding couple on the dance floor. Eddie and Lewis stood up along with Guillermo and they headed out onto the floor, followed by two of Julie's sisters and her best friend, the maid of honor. 'Hold Me' was playing and everyone was dancing.

Pilar walked up to our table and spoke with Alex first. Then she walked over to Julio, and said, "You know Lewis, this is going to upset him and I'm asking you to please be there for him. Try to prevent him from making a scene and destroying this night for his father and Julie."

"I will keep an eye on him, Mom."

When the song was over, everyone clapped. Lewis was the first one to arrive back at the table. Pilar hugged Lewis and told him how handsome he looked. Then she walked back over to the parents' table.

The waiters all came out to each of the tables to get the drink orders. Champagne was being poured at every table. The music was lowered, and Guillermo stood up. He gave his speech as best man and at the end of his speech he asked everyone to raise his or her glass up. He wanted to give a toast to the bride and groom. Everyone at our table had a champagne flute filled and raised in the air. After I took a tiny sip, I realized it tasted like apple juice.

I whispered to Julio, "It tastes just like apple juice."

He laughed and told me, "Because it is." Julio pulled it out of the ice bucket, and I read the bottle which said sparkling apple cider. "The parents wanted us to be able to participate in each toast and not the alcohol."

"That was smart and very nice. You know, Daphne loves apple juice, but usually with pancakes."

"Oh, I remember that, eating waffles and drinking apple juice when we all slept over your house in Tommy's room."

"Speaking of Tommy where is he at and where's Monica?"

"That's a great question." Julio stood up and began searching the room for them. He came back to the table with his hand held out to me. "Let's go use the bathroom." We walked out of the reception and over to the payphones. "I'm calling the house."

"Julio, there's no point in doing that. The ringers are all turned off. Call Monica's beeper and leave the phone number to the payphone."

"You're right, I will beep her now. Do you mind waiting out here with me to see if she calls back?"

"Of course not. I want to be wherever you are, especially tonight. You look gorgeous, and I'm not leaving you alone for a minute."

"Don't forget I smell good too."

"Oh, believe me Julio, I haven't been able to forget about that scent on you and it's most likely on your chest too." Julio had a mischievous look on his face after I said that.

"You know something Samantha?"

"What Julio?"

"There's only one way to find out if it's on my chest?"

I turned my back to him as I started to blush. I couldn't look at him and keep it together. He wrapped his arms around me from behind. "Hey, don't be shy, Sammy. It's me, Julio. Remember the guys whose shirt you want to rip open."

"Yeah, I think I remember you. I'm just still having a problem discussing the whole cause and effect thing with you. I want to open up; believe me I do."

"Mi Corazón, how are you going to win this challenge if you can't talk to me?"

"Julio, how is admitting I'm turned on really going to help me?"

"I'm turning you on?"

"Yes, Julio that's the effect you're having on me."

"That's great, because your having the same effect on me. I can tell you right now, I am completely turned on. It's not a bad thing to admit and I want to be honest with you. I'm unable to keep it to myself anymore. I want you to know the effect you have on me too. I just have to come out and say it. You made them turn blue on the dance floor."

"What? How did that happen? We were out on the dance floor, Julio?"

"Are you serious? How could it not happen? You were dancing and singing the lyrics to that song and you had your arms on my shoulders. I could smell your perfume and it happened. By the time the song was over, I could barely walk off the dance floor."

I just laughed and said, "Since we're out here, perhaps you should call Monica."

"Oh, that's right I completely forgot." Julio picked up the receiver and dialed her beeper number. He left the phone number to the payphone. We stood off to the corner out of sight from everyone to talk. We were still close enough that we could hear the pay phone when it rings.

"I hope your sister calls back soon. I want to get back inside and dance with you again."

"Do you want to dance with me or torture me Samantha?"

"A little bit of both truthfully, because you're torturing me right now with the smell of your cologne."

"Why? How does it make you feel?"

I looked down at the floor and began squeezing and pulling on my bottom lip. Julio lifted my chin up and I looked up into his eyes and released my lower lip. "Tell me the truth, Samantha."

I pulled my chin away and looked down at the floor again. When I finally felt like I had the courage, I spoke up and answered, "That cologne makes me want to rip off your shirt and feel your bare chest."

Julio hadn't said a word and I finally looked up from the floor at him. His mouth was slightly open, and his eyes blinked slowly a couple of times. He just stood there staring at me with a look of disbelief on his face. I swallowed once, and said, "So, this is extremely awkward."

"Julio swallowed before responding, "Yeah, well I want you to do that too. When do you want to touch my chest?"

I couldn't help it I started to laugh before saying, "I don't know. I have never really touched your chest before, Julio,"

"Yes, you have whenever we are in the pool and I give you a turtle ride. You touch my back, and that's why I always offer to give you a ride." He took my hand and placed it on his chest over his tie. He looked up into my eyes and he was biting on his lower lip.

"Julio, I don't think now is the appropriate time."

"I know, it's just that I've actually, had dreams about it."

"What have you had dreams about Julio?"

"You wanting to feel my chest, Samantha."

"Is that why you're always lifting weights?"

"Yes, that's when I started lifting weights.

"Really?"

"Yes, I wanted to impress you."

I slid my hand up from his tie to his left shoulder and gave it a squeeze.

Julio smiled and leaned in to kiss me. When the phone rang, he groaned and rolled his eyes. "Perfect timing, Monica," and he walked over to the payphone and answered it. When Julio hung up the phone, he said, "Monica and Tommy are together at home. The Nanny is not feeling well, and she went to the hospital, to get checked out. They are spending the night with Erika."

"Okay, then let's get back inside. Everybody is probably wondering where we went."

"Sammy, I want to kiss you again. Can we go back to the corner over there?" He pointed to the spot where we were just standing, before the phone rang.

"Julio, there is nothing I would rather do more than kiss you, but we need to get back inside. Our parents are going to send Alex to look for us any minute now."

"Too late," Julio pointed behind me. I turned around and saw Alex standing in front of the banquet doors with his hands on his hips and his eyebrows were arched up as he spotted us.

We walked back over to Alex and he asked, "Why are you guys out here? The waiter and everyone at our table has been waiting for the two of you."

"Waiting for us, why?"

"To eat, Julio."

"I'm sorry, Alex. We just came out here to call Monica. I noticed she wasn't here, and neither was Tommy and we were worried about them."

"You should have asked me. Mom already told me that she was at home taking care of Erika, and Tommy's with her."

"Why didn't you tell me this before, Alex?"

"Julio, you didn't ask."

They both started laughing and Alex put his arm around Julio. "Man, I miss you so much little brother. Now let's go eat. I'm hungry."

Alex grabbed the door and held it open for us. All three of us walked back to our table.

"Dude, finally, you're back. I'm so hungry. What was taking so long?"

"Sorry Greg, I was calling to check on my sister and Tommy."

"Yes, and, where are they?" Daphne asked.

"They are at the house with the baby. The nanny's sick and she went to the hospital to get checked out."

Michael replied, "Oh, I'm sorry to hear that Julio. I was looking forward to hanging out with your sister tonight."

The waiter came over to the table with a tray of food. He sat the tray down on a cart that had been wheeled out by another waiter behind him.

When he removed the covers off each plate you could see the steam rising. When the plate was placed in front of me, I could smell the vegetable medley and the stuffed chicken breast. It was making my mouth water, but I waited until everyone had their plate.

Julio asked everyone to bow their heads and he said grace. Dinner was wonderful and everything was delicious.

When we were halfway through our meal the waiter headed back over to our table and he filled everyone's champagne flute with more sparkling apple cider. A couple of minutes later, there was a speech from the bride's parents and then her best friend. Pilar was the last one to stand up and make her speech. At the end of her speech she said, now everybody, "Dance!"

The live band was on stage now and they started playing, 'Staying Alive' and the parents all headed onto the dance floor.

They were all out there dancing until 'Waiting for a Girl Like You' came on. Everyone cleared the floor except for the bridal couple and my mom and Guillermo. My mom had her arms around Guillermo, and he had his arms wrapped around her. My mom and Guillermo looked as though they were in their own little bubble together.

Then I saw Pilar walk over to the band. The next song they played was 'How Deep Is Your Love.' My mom's face lit up and Guillermo had that twinkle in his eye again along with a huge smile on his face. They were the only ones on the dance floor now. Everyone was watching them sing to one another, smiling at each other, while dancing in each other's arms.

"They really make a handsome couple."

"Yes, they do Michael."

Daphne, Michael, and Arturo watched them closely with great big smiles on their face.

"They really make each other happy Julio.

Julio squeezed my hand and said, "You make me happy, Samantha," and he kissed the top of my hand.

I smiled at Julio and turned my eyes away for a moment. That's when everyone started clapping.

Michael asked, "Did you see that Sammy?"

"See what?"

"Your Mom and Guillermo just kissed out on the dance floor."

I stood up and Julio stood up as I ran out the door. "Wait, Sammy, where are you going?"

"I have to use the bathroom."

Once I was inside the bathroom, the tears started coming. I tried to stop them, but I couldn't. I went over to the sink and I looked at my face in the mirror. Crap, I took in a deep breath and let it out to the count of ten. Then I noticed the mascara running down both corners of my eyes. I grabbed a few tissues and wiped gently under them.

When I walked out of the bathroom, Julio was leaning up against the wall waiting for me. He had a concerned look on his face when he saw me. I reached for his hand and he pulled me tight into his arms. "What is it? What's wrong?" I shook my head no, indicating that I didn't feel like talking about it now. "Please tell me Samantha. Tell me what's upsetting you."

I looked up into those big brown eyes of Julio's and gave in. "My mom is falling for your uncle. I know she is. I haven't ever seen my mom laugh and smile so much in my life. She kissed him twice now on the lips and she looks at him like nobody else exists. I know that feeling Julio, because that's how I feel when I'm with you."

"How is that a bad thing, Samantha?"

"It's bad because now we will both leave here tomorrow night and all that we are taking back with us are the memories. You and your uncle are staying here in Anaheim."

"Once I'm back home the loneliness will return, and my mom doesn't need to feel that pain. It's sort of freaking me out. It still hurts being so far away from you Julio, because I'm in love with you. I can't see you everyday anymore and there's nothing I can do about it. Now my mom is going to endure the same pain, that feeling of longing for someone who lives so far away. I won't ever see her smile and laugh like this again. Just knowing that breaks my heart."

Julio closed his eyes, and told me, "You're right, Samantha. The heartbreak I feel when we're apart is horrible." Then he opened his eyes and looked into mine and said, "But the love I feel when we're together makes it all worth it."

He leaned down and kissed me gently on the lips. Suddenly, my sadness was gone, and I was smiling, and I truly felt happy. "You're amazing, Julio! You said something that I needed to hear."

"What's that?

"You told me that the love you feel when we are together is what makes it worth it. I needed to hear that, Soccer Player."

Julio smiled and leaned in and he kissed me again. When he pulled away, he looked me in the eyes and asked, "Does that mean the challenge is back on?"

"Definitely."

We walked back inside. Everyone from our table was now on the dance floor. Daphne and Greg smiled at us and waved us over. We joined them out on the floor and danced to the song 'Something about You.' The band was on break and the DJ was playing song after song that kept us out there dancing. I noticed none of the parents were dancing. They were all back at the parents' table, laughing and having a good time.

Julio caught me looking at the table and whispered, "She's good, Samantha. She's happy."

I smiled and whispered, "So am I." That's when I placed my arms over his shoulders and pop kissed him. I pulled my head away quickly to see that smile I love and those eyes I adore. We danced to 'I Feel For You.' When the song ended, the DJ announced, "All of you single ladies please join us on the dance floor. It's time for the bride to throw her bouquet."

All of the guys left the dance floor and Daphne and I waved bye to Julio and Greg. They just moved to the side of the dance floor to watch the toss. Michael, Arturo, and Eddie joined them and soon followed all of the moms onto the dance floor. All of the guys and married ladies were watching the toss from the sidelines.

Julie walked up on stage with her mom and husband Juan. She yelled out, "Is everybody ready?" When everyone shouted "Yes," she turned around and threw the bouquet.

Carmen caught it and everyone went to clapping. I looked over at Enrique; he had a nervous grin on his face. I saw Guillermo and Alex pat Enrique on the back, and they were all laughing.

Julio and Greg walked up to us and Julio said, "Better luck next time."

I shrugged my shoulders and replied, "I'm still not of legal age."

Daphne turned to Julio and asked, "Next time? What wedding am I attending next, Julio?"

Greg and Julio broke out laughing and Greg answered, "Well, your mom's wedding of course she caught the bouquet."

I couldn't help it. I broke down and started laughing. Daphne appeared to be angry, "That's not funny, Greg."

"Baby, I was only joking." Daphne took off and we followed behind her. She walked up to her mom and congratulated her for catching the bouquet.

Daphne was about to walk away and stopped again. "Mom, I hope you're not getting married anytime soon. Or should I inform your boyfriend, Enrique?" Daphne turned and started to walk away. We all stood there shocked by what Daphne said. None of us could move.

Then Carmen said, "Come back here, kid." Daphne turned around and walked back over to her mom. Carmen reached out and hugged Daphne. They were both laughing, and I felt so relieved.

"Daphne, do you always have to say what's on your mind?"

"Yes, I learned that from you mom."

Carmen smiled and replied, "At least I don't have to guess what's going on in your head. Now you just assume Enrique is my boyfriend?"

"Well, isn't he, Mom?"

"No, he's not my boyfriend. However, that could change later on, but right now we're just friends."

The band was back on the stage. They started playing 'Give It Up,' and all of the parents were headed for the dance floor.

Daphne kissed her mom on the cheek, and told her, "Have a blast. We only live once." She grabbed Greg's hand and we followed Daphne out to the dance floor. We danced beside the parents for two more songs until it was time to cut the cake.

After the cake was passed out to everyone. I noticed the DJ was all packed up and the band announced this would be their last song tonight. The song was 'More Than a Woman.' Julio and Greg stood up as the band began to play. They walked us out to the dance floor where all the parents were dancing. Mom and Guillermo were the center of attention with their dynamic chemistry.

When the song ended, everyone was clapping, and Guillermo walked over to the band. He shook everyone's hand and thanked each of them for coming on such short notice. Guillermo walked over to the DJ and I saw him shaking his hand and speaking with him to.

My mom walked up to me and Julio was holding my hand. She asked Julio if she could speak to me for a moment alone. He released my hand and said, "Of course, Ms. Harris."

I walked outside with my mom and she told me, "We're not going back to the house tonight. All of us have arrangements, to sleep here at the hotel. We will join you kids back at the house tomorrow afternoon.

"How do you feel about this, Sam?"

"I don't know, Mom. How should I feel about it?"

"Are you okay with me spending the night here at the Hotel?"

"Does he make you happy, Mom?"

"Yes, he does."

"You only live once, Mom."

"I have my own room, Sam."

"Even better, I said with a smile."

My mom smiled too, and she wrapped her arms around me.

When I came back to the table, Julio stood up and whispered, "Is everything alright?" I nodded my head yes and he took my hand as he kissed me once on the temple.

Alex stood up and clapped his hands together. He announced, "It's time to go everybody. We are all riding back in the limo." Everyone stood up and Eddie ran over to Alex with Heather behind him.

Eddie asked if he could still have the car tonight. Alex told him it shouldn't be a problem. Since we're all getting dropped off at the house by limo. Alex told Eddie the keys are with the valet. I hugged Heather and Eddie before I followed Alex out of the hotel.

When we arrived outside, the limo driver was already waiting for us with the door open, to climb inside. Michael was already seated inside, and I noticed he was biting on his thumbnail. "Michael, what's wrong?"

"It's Arturo. I don't know where he is Sammy."

I whispered to Daphne, "We need to find your brother."

She looked over at Michael and then she looked up at Greg. Daphne tugged on the sleeve of Greg's shirt and told him, "I'll be right back."

Julio grabbed my hand, as I was climbing out of the car behind Daphne. "Julio, we have to find Arturo." Julio's face changed to a look of understanding and he released my hand. I ran back inside the hotel with Daphne and Michael.

When we reached the second floor, we spotted Carmen and Arturo. They were standing in front of the bathrooms. We ran over to them. Arturo was visibly upset, and Carmen appeared to be angry.

"Hey, Arturo, we have to go now." Arturo didn't answer daphne and kept staring at his mom."

"Arturo, I'm your mother, not the other way around. Now I will be back at the house tomorrow afternoon. I appreciate you caring about me, but I can make my own decisions. Now give me a hug and go." Carmen wrapped her arms around Arturo. She hugged him and planted a kiss on top of his head.

Michael walked up, and he was chewing on his index finger. Daphne looked over at Michael, then back at Arturo. She asked, "Can we just go now? Before Michael chews his hand off."

"Okay, Daphne, let's go," Arturo answered in a harsh tone. He was glaring at his mom before he turned around and walked past us and Michael.

The three of us were shocked, we just stood there looking at Carmen, not knowing what to say. "You three give me a hug and get going." We each gave Carmen a hug and we left.

Once we reached the limo, I was holding my breath hoping to find Arturo inside. We climbed in and he was sitting down beside Greg and Julio. The three of us sat down beside one another on the backseat. Alex told the driver we could go now.

As we pulled away from the hotel, Alex told us, "Tonight the parents are staying at the hotel. They have plans to have cocktails with Julie's friends and family. I have the phone number and room number for each of you. If you need anything, I can help you or if you need to call your mom or just want the number, I can give it to you."

"What if I want to call Enrique? Does he have his own room?"

"Yes, of course, he has his own room, Arturo. Everyone has their own room, and if you want his room number, I have it," Alex answered.

"Is that what's bothering you, Arturo? You're worried that Mom and Enrique are going to shack up tonight?"

"Daphne, shut up."

"Arturo, you know what? Mom deserves to fall in love and be happy. We all know she hasn't had love or happiness in a long time. If she wants to shack up, let her. She's old enough and she knows what she's doing. You don't have to protect her anymore. You just need to love and respect her."

Michael had his thumb in his mouth. He finally took it out, and said, "You know, Daphne's right, Arturo."

Arturo moaned and rolled his eyes. "I know she's right Michael, and I know my mom deserves all that and more. It's just a little surprising, to see her with someone other than my Dad, and I don't even like my Dad." We all broke out laughing, and Arturo hugged Daphne.

We arrived at the house and walked inside. Everyone went to their rooms to undress. When Daphne and I arrived back at our room, we quickly changed into shorts and a T-shirt. We headed into the family room where Julio and Greg were already playing foosball.

Greg was the first one to notice us walk in. He quit playing and walked up to Daphne. Greg told us, "We will catch up with you guys later. Daphne and I need to speak with Arturo and Michael." They walked out the sliding glass doors to the pool deck.

Julio shrugged his shoulders, then looked back at me and smiled. "Do you want to play foosball with me, Sammy?"

"No."

"Do you want to go down to the cabana?"

"No."

"Do you want to go to the theatre room?"

I smiled and nodded my head yes. We headed down the stairs and into the theatre room. Julio pushed the door open and allowed me to walk in first as he followed me inside.

"What movie do you want to watch, Samantha?"

"You can choose the movie, Julio."

I took a seat on the couch and grabbed a throw blanket. When the movie started playing, Julio turned off the lights. He grabbed a pillow and joined me on the couch.

"Sammy, sit up so I can place the pillow under your head."

I sat up and raised my hands up over my head. "Julio, can you take off my shirt?"

Julio swallowed once, and he looked down at me with an extremely scared expression. I put my arms back down, and said, "Aw, too late."

Julio instantly smiled. "I know what you're doing Mi Corazón."

"Yeah, what am I doing, Soccer Player?"

"You're trying to get me to take my shirt off, because you're dying to feel my chest."

"Oh, I am definitely not leaving California without touching your chest at least once." Julio's eyes were huge, and I know he was pointy now. Which meant, I was totally winning.

"Too bad you don't want to touch me."

"Samantha, I want to touch you very much. I just haven't or won't even try that until you tell me that you're ready for me to do that, okay?"

"Good, because I can honestly say that I'm not ready for that."

"Samantha."

"Yes, Julio."

"Will you help me take my shirt off?"

"Yeah of course." I stood up as he remained sitting down on the couch. He raised his arms up above his head. He watched me with his big brown eyes, and he looked as nervous as I felt.

I reached down and grabbed the hem of his shirt. I was about to pull it up, when Julio yelled, "Aw, too late, Samantha" and he put his arms back down.

I looked down at him, and I shook my head smiling. "Come here" and he took my hand and pulled me over to him. He wrapped his arms around my waist and laid his head down on my tummy.

After a minute he asked, "Are you still hungry? Your tummy is making a lot of noise."

"No, that's not hunger noise. That's just my nerves."

Julio stood up and he pulled me back over to the door and said, "Look, we don't have to be in here. We can just leave, Samantha. Wait right here a second," and he walked over to the VCR and turned off the movie. Then he walked back over to me and opened the door and turned off the lights. I turned to him and kissed him. He released the door as he kissed me softly at first then long and deep until I was totally weak.

He lifted me up and carried me back to the couch. I felt him pull away from my lips and he kissed me gently several times going down my neck.

I felt him sniffing my neck and he groaned. I freaked out and placed my hand over his zipper. "Don't get the wrong idea Soccer Player. We're only kissing. I'm not ready for anything else."

"Samantha, kissing you is more than enough for me. In fact, it's a dream come true."

Chapter 8 Second Chance

We woke up in each other's arms to the sound of knocking on the theatre room door. Julio ran and opened the door, it was Alex. "I had to knock. You had the door locked." Alex said this as more of a question. He had a look of concern on his face.

"Sorry, Alex, it was Sammy's last night here and we just wanted to be left alone."

"Julio, I only believe you because it's Sammy. Now we're all getting ready to watch the sunrise; if you want to join us, out on the pool deck."

I ran up to Julio and took his hand. "Let's go." We followed Alex out of the theatre room and up the stairs into the main house. We went through the kitchen and grabbed some water on our way out.

All of the lounge chairs from around the pool area were all lined up together at the edge of the deck. Daphne and Greg were curled up in a lounge chair together. Michael and Arturo were sitting side by side. Julio and I shared the empty lawn chair beside Michael.

Michael was wearing his sunglasses and it was still dark outside. He leaned over and pulled his sunglasses up to rest on top of his head. Then he smiled at us and said, "Well, good morning, you two." A giggle escaped me, and Michael asked, "What have you two been doing?"

Julio and I looked at one another and we started to smile. I looked back at Michael and answered, "Snuggling." That's when I felt Julio slide his arms around me. Michael and I both looked up at Julio and he was wearing a huge smile.

Michael was still looking over at Julio and replied, "Right, snuggling." He slid his sunglasses back down to cover his eyes. Then he sat back in his chair smiling at us with his arms crossed over his chest.

Alex jumped up out of his chair and asked, "Do you guys mind if three more people join us?"

We all sat up and turned around to see. Tommy, Monica, and baby Erika coming over.

Tommy and Monica sat down beside us in Alex's chair. Monica was holding Erika in her lap. Alex walked over to Monica and asked if he could hold her. Monica handed Erika to Alex and he walked back in the house with Erika in his arms. Monica just laughed before saying, "I obviously have a full-time nanny when I come to Miami." Tommy just looked over at me with a forlorn look on his face.

"Oh, you guys are going to love the show."

"What show, Michael?"

"The sunrise, Daphne. Many people call it God's show. It's his best performance."

"Oh, I didn't get that. I'm still half asleep."

Tommy sat up and finally spoke, "Dude, you're right. We have front row seats to the show." That's when we all broke out laughing and I was glad the tension had been lifted.

Monica and Tommy curled up together on their lounge chair, and the eight of us all sat there watching our last sunrise together.

We all remained in the lounge chairs talking for over an hour until Greg started to complain that he was hungry.

That's when I stood up and said, "Come on girls." The three of us walked in the house to start on breakfast. I asked Monica to wash some blueberries and strawberries. I asked Daphne to find some bowls. I was in the middle of making the pancake batter when Tommy ran into the kitchen. He shouted, "It's a cook-off. I have been waiting for this challenge since I stepped foot into this kitchen. Now what are you making, Sam?"

"What does it look like I'm making, Tommy?"

"Mom's home style pancakes. I'm totally going to beat you with my bonging waffles." Daphne smiled at Tommy with her sly grin and sprayed him in the face with a can of whipped cream.

Tommy ran to the sink and turned on the faucet. He grabbed the sprayer attempting to spray Daphne, but when he squeezed the trigger nothing came out. I looked over at the sink and noticed the faucet was turned off. Monica was smiling and said, "Sorry, Tommy," and he looked over at the sink and realized the faucet was off.

"Oh, you teamed up on me! I'll be right back." Tommy ran out of the kitchen and we went back to preparing breakfast.

Tommy came back inside a few minutes later and he brought all of the boys with him. I just smiled and told him, "Perfect timing, Tommy. Breakfast is almost ready."

"Great, I need to eat something before I pass out."

"Greg, have a seat at the table and your food will be coming out in a minute."

"Thanks, Daphne."

Greg sat down first, then all the boys followed and joined him at the table.

"I'm sorry, Sam. I didn't mean to leave all of the cooking up to you. I really wanted to have a cook-off, but we got to talking and I lost track of the time."

"Tommy, it's fine. I love cooking plus I had help from Monica and Daphne." I grabbed the pancakes and Monica grabbed the butter and syrup. We set everything down on the table.

Daphne headed out to the table after us with a gallon of apple juice and took a seat. Monica came back to the table with the plate of sausage.

Julio asked, "What about Alex? He needs to eat."

Monica smiled before saying, "He already had breakfast. We fed him first. We played with Erika while he ate. He's back in the family room watching cartoons with Erika. Now let's all hold hands and bow our heads and thank our creator for everything."

"Yeah, like, for that incredible sunrise this morning." Julio and I looked over at one another and smiled. I think Greg surprised us both with that statement.

Greg finished his stack of pancakes first. He promised to wait for everyone to finish eating, before he starts on a second plate."

"So, I take it you enjoyed the pancakes Greg."

"Sammy, they were delicious."

"Oh wait, I wanted to ask you Julio, what was up with the live band last night?"

"What do you mean, Greg?"

"Are they a cover band?"

"I'm sure they are," Michael replied. "There's a lot of cover bands here and in LA."

"I'm only asking because I noticed they mainly played The Bee Gees, so I'm thinking they are really a Bee Gees cover band."

Tommy and I looked over at one another from across the table. I started coughing to cover up the laugh that escaped me. Tommy was still staring at me with his hand over his mouth. He was having a hard time playing it cool too.

Julio scowled at me and Tommy before saying, "Well, my uncles are both fans of The Bee Gees. My uncles have all their albums and cassettes."

"Wait a minute. Isn't your mom a big fan of The Bee Gees? I remember your mom playing this song from them. Like every single day, right after your mom and dad first split up. What was the name of that song?"

"Tragedy," Tommy and I said at the same time.

"Yeah, that's it. I know that song word for word from spending weekends over at Sammy's house."

"I remember that too Daphne."

"Sorry, I didn't mean to bring up your Parents divorce Sammy."

"It's fine Daphne, it was a long time ago." Julio reached over and squeezed my hand. I looked back at him and he had a ridiculous grin on his face now.

Michael leaned over and rubbed his chin with his thumb and index finger. He replied, "That's very interesting." Michael and Arturo smiled at one another then looked back at Tommy and me.

"What's interesting Michael?"

"Well, we all know the band was invited last minute by your uncle Guillermo, because we heard him thanking the band for coming on short notice. The question is, did he invite the cover band to play for his brother, who is a fan or for Lori the woman he is infatuated with?"

Julio sat up in his chair and faced me with his elbow on the table and his hand pressed up under his chin. Then I noticed everyone was staring at me. I looked over at Tommy and he sucked in his lips with his eyebrows raised up.

"Just spill it, Sammy."

I sat up in my chair and said okay Daphne, gosh. "Guillermo was informed that my mom loves Italian food, and her favorite music is from ABBA, The Beatles, and The Bee Gees. He was so excited when he was told my mom likes The Bee Gees. He said he had all of their albums and could play her favorite songs."

"Well, he did that! In the form of a cover band last night."

"Arturo, there is nothing wrong with that. It's actually pretty awesome. It was like a two for one gift. He made Ms. Harris happy and his brother at the same time."

"I agree with Greg, mystery solved."

"Okay, Julio, but did you notice the parents only danced when the band was playing?"

"Yes, I'm pretty sure Tio hired the DJ for us."

"Yeah, I'm glad they hired the DJ and a band. Both were a hit with the parents and us. It was such a great night. It actually seemed like everyone had a lot of fun, even when you weren't dancing, and were just watching the parents dance, especially Ms. Harris and Guillermo. I couldn't keep my eyes off them."

"Oh Michael, neither could I. That kiss on the dance floor was so romantic and it was while they were dancing to The Bee Gees. What song was that, Sammy?"

"'How Deep Is Your Love,' Daphne."

"That's it, thank you Sammy."

"Mom and Guillermo kissed again Sam?"

"Yes, Tommy, they did. Mom really appears to be happy with Guillermo. I don't know what's going to happen when we leave here today. I only know that it's great to see Mom this happy for a change."

"It sounds like you guys had a lot of fun last night."

"We did Monica, and I'm sorry that you and Tommy missed out on it."

Tommy placed his arm around Monica. Then said, "Sam, I had a great night too. I spent my evening with Monica and Erika." Monica smiled at Tommy and he leaned over her with his arm still resting on her shoulders and kissed her on the side of her temple.

They were both smiling at one another. That's when Michael stood up and asked Monica to come outside with him. Michael slid open the sliding glass door, and they both headed out the door to the pool deck, with Arturo behind them.

Daphne and I grabbed the plates and took them over to the sink. When I came back to the table, I grabbed the syrup and Julio caught my hand. I turned around to face him and he told me, "You cooked. We're going to clean up."

Tommy stood up and added, "You girls can leave the rest to us." I kissed Julio on the cheek and told him thank you."

Daphne placed the pitcher of apple juice in the refrigerator and she walked with me into the family room. Where Alex was passed out on the couch. We walked over to the bassinet and Erika was sound asleep. I covered Alex with a throw blanket, and we left the family room.

Monica walked back inside, and she saw us sitting down in the living room. We told her Erika was asleep in her bassinet and Alex was sleeping on the couch in the family room. She sat down with us on the couch in the living room and pulled out a photo album. Inside the album were pictures of her family. The first photo was a black and white photograph of her mom when she was just a baby. "Can you see how much Erika looks like my mom?"

"Daphne smiled and said, "Your daughter definitely takes after your mother."

Monica showed us pictures of her uncles. They must have been around the ages of twelve and thirteen. "Do you see it?" Monica asked.

Daphne smiled before asking, "Is that Guillermo? Monica nodded her head yes. "That's incredible. Lewis looks just like him."

Monica pointed to another picture and told us, "This is Uncle Juan." Then she looked over at me and smiled. After viewing the photo, I was in shock. I pulled my head back and Monica had an even bigger smile on her face. "

"Wow, Julio is going to be gorgeous when he gets older."

I frowned at Daphne and asked, "What do you mean? He's gorgeous now."

"Yeah, but not like Juan Sanchez. He's like really gorgeous. Don't worry, Sammy. Clearly, Julio takes after him. He is going to look just like Mr. Sanchez, when he gets older."

I just looked over at Monica and rolled my eyes. Monica broke out laughing before saying, "You two haven't changed much," and she wrapped her arms around us. When she released us, she sat back on the couch and said, "I'm going to miss you both when you leave. I'm really sorry for all of the things I said and did before I left. I was so crazy back then and I really missed out on a lot because of it."

We hugged Monica and told her we forgave her and will miss her too. When we pulled apart the three of us had tears in our eyes.

"Well, I'm honestly happy to see you again and meet baby Erika."

"Me too, Sammy. I really have calmed down, and I'm back on track. My mom and I have become so close since my daughter was born. I've come to realize and appreciate how much my mom has done for all of us.

"For my mom it's always been what would make her kids happy. What will make them study harder and focus on their future?"

"She came here to America for three reasons. 1. She didn't want my uncle Juan to come on his own. 2. My mom wanted the family to stay together. 3. She wanted all of us to have the opportunity to become whatever we wanted. She knew that the possibility of opportunities would be endless if we came here. It would be all up to us and what we decide to pursue.

"My mom — was a widow, she just lost her sister-in-law, who was her best friend. Then she suffered the loss of her mother — left everything she ever knew to come here to America with five children and her brother. That took so much courage. I can only imagine how scared she must have been. My mom is incredibly strong and brave. I look up to her now, knowing she has so much strength and courage inside her.

"Unfortunately, these are the only photos my family has left from Colombia. We had more but they seem to have been lost or misplaced. My mom collected all the pictures that she could find; then put them all in this album. This album has been around since we came here to the United States," Monica concluded.

We sat back on the couch with Monica, as she showed us more pictures, now of her grandparents. She showed us pictures of her father, who Alex takes after. We saw pictures of Enrique, and of his parents, when he was little boy. When we finished looking at the photo album, Monica said, "I think it's time we check on the boys." We walked into the kitchen, and everything was clean in there, but no boys.

We walked into the family room, but the boys weren't there either. Daphne slid open the sliding glass doors and we followed her out onto the pool deck. Arturo and Michael were sunbathing, but the boys were nowhere in sight.

Michael called out, "Daphne, if you're looking for Greg, he's down there," and he pointed to the second yard.

"Thanks, Michael." The three of us headed down the stairs. We started to walk over to the cabana, and we stopped when we heard a kissing sound. Daphne's eyes popped open wide and she stomped her foot. Monica and I reached over, and we grabbed Daphne. Monica whispered, "Don't say anything. Just listen."

Suddenly, we heard Julio, in a high-pitched voice say, "Oh yes, Lewis you're so handsome." Greg replied, "I know but can you tell me again?"

"Oh Lewis, you have such big strong muscles and your head is so big. How does your neck and shoulders hold that big head of yours?"

We could hear all three boys laughing, and we couldn't help it; we started laughing too.

The boys' laughter suddenly stopped, and I whispered, "Crap, they heard us." The three of us took off running in separate directions. I started running around the side of the house. I was almost to the side door of the garage when my feet were no longer touching the ground. I was thrown over Julio's shoulder watching the door get farther and farther, away.

"I don't know why you do it."

"Why I do what?" Julio.

"Why do you continue to try to outrun a soccer player?"

"I know it's impossible, but it's a lot of fun trying."

Julio stopped walking and set me down. He looked into my eyes and told me, "I'm going to miss you, Samantha."

"I'm going to miss you too, Soccer Player." We wrapped our arms around one another, and we just stood there holding each other for a few minutes. I could hear his heart beating and still smell his cologne lingering on him from last night.

After a couple of minutes, we heard Greg and Daphne calling out for us. Julio and I looked at one another and he quickly kissed my lips. Then took my hand and we walked back over to the cabana.

"Look who I found," Julio said, as he raised our hands up that were held together.

Greg smiled and replied, "Look, I found someone too," and he raised his hand up. Which was locked in Daphne's death grip.

The four of us walked into the cabana together. Monica was behind the bar and Tommy was sitting on the sofa. Something about Tommy's expression made me think he was busted for misbehaving.

I smiled at Tommy and I looked back at Monica. She had a great big grin on her face as she was staring at Tommy.

The four of us all sat down, and Daphne asked, "What the heck was going on in here? I mean you guys have a fondness for Lewis obviously."

We all started laughing and Monica replied, "No, it's not them who has a fondness for Lewis. It's her."

She threw something over the bar and when it landed on the floor, Daphne and I shouted, "Tracy!"

We all turned to Tommy; he had his head down with his hand cupping his forehead.

"Dude, you're so busted, when Mom finds out you brought Tracy here. She is going to kick your butt."

"Come on, Sammy. You can't tell Mom. I only brought her so I could show her to Julio. I had told him all about her during some of our phone calls."

"Okay, I won't tell her, Tommy, but you owe me big time."

"Fine, what do you want, Sam?"

"In exchange for my silence, I want you to carry my suitcase upstairs when we get home. Plus, you have to walk Daisy every night until you leave back to school."

"That's only five days Sam. I leave on Saturday."

"That's fine. Do we have a deal, Tommy?"

"Yes."

Tommy and I shook on it, and he grabbed Tracy off the floor. He walked over to the bar and grabbed hold of Monica's hand. They walked out of the cabana and we followed behind them.

Daphne was saying, "Look at your brother. He's walking up the stairs with Tracy on one arm and Monica on the other."

"Greg replied, "That Dude's a Casanova."

"We all stopped walking and started laughing until we heard Michael squeal. Then we ran up the stairs just in time to hear him ask, "Is that a blow-up doll?"

Tommy nodded his head yes and Michael snapped his fingers and said, "Hand her to me."

Then Michael stood up and announced, "I'm going in the pool with her."

"Michael, I thought you were going to get a tan."

"I was Arturo, until miss thing showed up. Now get in the pool with us."

Arturo walked over to the pool shaking his head, and Michael was right behind him, carrying Tracy. Down the stairs and into the pool they went. I couldn't control my laughter. It was all so funny watching this interaction everyone was having with Tracy.

Michael was now using Tracy as a lounge chair in the pool. He yelled, "I guess it's true what they say. Blonds are a lot of fun."

We played a ton of pool games, Marco Polo, Minnows Cross the River, and Red Light, Green Light. Tracey played along with us in every game. The boys just had a chicken fight and Tracy won the last fight.

Michael was mad and said, "Arturo thinks he's fooling me, but I know he let Tracy win." We all broke out laughing.

Until my mom asked, "Is that what I think it is?" We all turned around, and my mom, Carmen and Pilar were all standing there at the edge of the pool looking at us. Julio still had Tracy on his shoulders from the last chicken fight.

Guillermo and Enrique ran out of the house and up to my mom. Guillermo took my mom's hand and asked, "Is everything okay, Lori?"

My mom looked over at Tommy as she faked a smile. "Yes, everything is fine Guillermo." Julio was about to take Tracy down off his shoulders, as Guillermo turned around. Julio had his hand on Tracy and quickly dropped his hand.

Guillermo's eyes grew wider when he looked over at Julio. Guillermo asked, "Is that Tracy?" Julio nodded his head yes, slowly. Guillermo walked over to Julio and reached out his hand. Julio bent his head down as he pulled Tracy off his shoulders and handed her over to Guillermo.

Guillermo carried her over to Enrique. He said, "This was the girl I told you about from the bachelor party."

"Oh, she is much better looking than you told me, Tio."

They were both laughing, and Guillermo said, "Thank you, Tommy, for bringing her. She was one of the best events at the party. I have told everybody how we all tried to get a date with Tracy."

"Oh, you're welcome," Tommy responded with a smile.

Guillermo, Enrique, and the moms took a seat at the parents' table and Tracy sat with them in a chair soaking wet in my sundress. Guillermo began to tell our moms all about Tracy and the bachelor party.

The moms were all laughing even my mom. That's when Alex slid open the sliding glass door and walked out carrying Erika. "Hey Monica, I think she's wet. Where do you keep her diapers?"

Monica climbed out of the pool and wrapped herself in a towel. She told Alex, "Hand her to me."

Alex turned around and he took a step back and asked, "Oh hey, it's Tracy, when did she get here?" Everyone started laughing.

Monica leaned in close to Alex and said, "I hate to be the one to tell you this, but her heart is already spoken for. Apparently, she has an extreme fondness for Lewis now."

Greg looked over at Daphne and me. Then he yelled, "You guys were eavesdropping?" Daphne and I just nodded our heads yes. "So, what? We were just playing."

"Yeah with dolls, Greg."

"Monica, you know what I think?"

"No, what do you think Greg?"

"I think you girls are just mad because Tracy beat Arturo on the last chicken fight."

Carmen asked, "How does that even happen?"

"Well, like I've been saying, I know that your son let that promiscuous girl win." That's when parents started laughing.

"Michael, go easy on Arturo. It's not his fault, he's just not a fighter. Right, Arturo? You lost a fight with a blow-up doll named Tracy. Hey, it happens. You win some and you lose some. Momma's still proud of you for trying."

Arturo was turning bright pink in the cheeks with visible embarrassment. He shook his head and smiled at Michael, then looked over at the parents' table and said, "Thanks, Mom."

"Oh, you're welcome. That's what mothers do. We encourage our kids, so they don't feel defeated in life. Oh, and don't worry Greg, your secret is safe with me."

"Carmen, it was only one doll. Come on; I won't make it a habit."

"You promise, Greg?"

"I do...

The parents were laughing, and Julio was giving Greg a goofy grin.

"What dude?"

"Wow Greg, you just lost some of your masculinity."

Greg splashed water at Julio's face then replied, "Whatever, dude. You were the last one with Tracy up on your shoulders, so you play with dolls too."

Guillermo stood up and clapped his hands together, "Hey guys, we don't want to rush you. However, I have an activity planned for us today. Then will have lunch, and after that, will come back here to allow everyone plenty of time to shower and get packed."

I looked over at my mom and she faked a smile. She looked as though she was uncomfortable with her shoulders tilted in forward. Her smile looked more like she just bit into something sour.

When we arrived back at our room, Daphne asked, "What are we going to do with all of these wet clothes?"

"We need to take them off and throw them in the Jacuzzi. Like we always do."

"Sammy, we already have wet clothes in the Jacuzzi plus the wet clothes we're wearing now. We need to pack these clothes into our suitcase later. Remember we're flying back to Miami tonight."

"Oh crap, you're right. We need a washing machine. Let's find Julio and ask him where it's at. Actually, forget it. I remember where it is. Hurry up; let's grab all of our wet clothes. We have to be fast about it."

We ran into the bathroom, grabbed our wet clothes from inside the Jacuzzi and put them in a pile. I quickly took off all my wet clothes and threw them on top of the pile. I jumped into the shower. When I came out, I put on my undergarments and wrapped myself in a robe.

Daphne was waiting in the dressing area wrapped in a towel. She walked into the bathroom and threw her wet clothes on top of the pile. She stepped into the shower and I grabbed the pile off the floor.

I carried the wet clothes down the stairs and into the garage. I placed the wet clothes on top of the dryer so I could have a free hand to open the lid on the washing machine. I opened the lid and looked on the shelf beside the machines. I found the detergent and tossed a cap of it into the machine. I placed the clothes inside, turned the machine on, and shut the lid.

I went back to the door and it was locked. Crap, I was going to have to walk around. I looked down and realized I was only wearing my underclothes a robe and clogs. I thought to myself: the side door it is.

As I was walking along the side of the house, I gave myself a lecture on taking a moment and getting dressed before leaving my room. That really would have helped at a time like this. At least checking the doorknob to make sure it was unlocked before pulling the door shut behind me, would have been helpful.

I finally made it to the pool deck, and I was walking over to the sliding glass door. When I heard, "What are you doing out here in your bathrobe?" I turned around, and it was my mom. She was standing there waiting for an answer. The rest of the parents were sitting at the parents' table further away.

"Mom, I just took a shower and put my robe on. I had to hurry up and take all of our wet clothes to the washing machine, which is in the garage. That's when I managed to lock myself out of the house. I had no choice but to walk around the side of the house to get back in my room."

"Okay fine, hurry up and put on a pair of jeans. Be sure to tell Daphne to wear jeans too.""

"Right, Mom, I will," and I knocked on the sliding glass door. Daphne opened the door and looked rather confused.

As I walked inside Daphne asked, "What were you doing outside in your bathrobe?"

"I'll explain that to you later. Just get dressed, and you need to wear jeans." We both were dressed in ten minutes, wearing blue jeans and sweatshirts with the sleeves, hemline, and necklines cut off them. We were also wearing a tank top underneath. We put on our high-top sneakers.

When we were dressed, Daphne braided my hair in the vanity area. We walked to the pool and met up with the moms at the parents table.

"Well, you two look cute.

"Yes, they do Carmen."

"In fact, they are dressed like twins with the same outfits only in different colors, Lori."

Daphne whispered, "Mom, our shoulders are sunburned, and we can't wear a bra, so this is the best way to conceal them."

"Oh, I think that's very smart," Pilar replied. "I couldn't even tell."

"Well, I'm glad none of the guys are out here. That would have been totally embarrassing."

"Sorry, Sammy. I didn't mean to embarrass you in front of your mother-in-law." I slapped Daphne on her shoulder, and she yelled ouch.

We took a seat with the moms. Guillermo and the boys all came outside a couple of minutes later. "Is everyone ready to go? We only have 20 minutes to get there, so we should leave now."

"Gio, we were just waiting for you." Guillermo smiled at Pilar and mentioned he had an emergency, but it has all been solved now.

"Wait, stop walking Gio, and tell me what happened."

"Pilar it was nothing, don't worry. Monica wasn't going to come with us at first. She wanted to stay here with her daughter. I told her what I had planned for today and I told her that I wanted her to come with us. She wanted to go, but she didn't want to leave the baby with the nanny."

"Alex doesn't want to go. He asked us to bring him back some lunch. He wants to stay behind and take care of his niece. Monica showed Alex where everything is now, and she wrote him a list of some sort. She is now inside the house putting on a pair of jeans.

Alex is watching cartoons in the family room and playing with Erika. Truthfully, I think your son just enjoys all of the nap times in between feedings."

"Oh yes, nobody likes to take a nap more than my Alex."

When we walked out the front door, Chris was speaking to the limousine driver. "You're here, Chris! I didn't think you could make it." Pilar walked up to Chris and he was smiling down at her. He said something about leaving everything until tomorrow and he opened the door on the limo.

They climbed inside, and we followed them in and took a seat. When the limo was full and there were no more seats with six people left outside, Guillermo said, "Lori and I will take the town car. Who wants to ride with us?" Carmen and Enrique followed them to the town car. Tommy climbed into the passenger's seat beside the driver. I sat on Julio's lap and Monica sat in my seat.

Pilar said, "If everybody moves over a little bit and Greg, you close your legs, there will be enough room for Sammy to sit down here." Everyone moved over and there was more than enough room. I sat down beside Julio.

We arrived at what appeared to be a ranch. We saw people everywhere walking around with cowboy hats. Some people were riding horses, others were walking horses around, and there was a big red barn. Then we all spotted a horse's pen with two horses inside prancing around in a circle. We parked and walked up closer to the barn. I was able to see it wasn't a barn, but a large stable filled with horses.

Guillermo walked up behind us and asked, "What do you all think? We're going horseback riding."

"We are?" Daphne and I asked in unison.

"Yes girls, isn't that exciting?"

"Guillermo, I haven't been horseback riding since I rode the carousel at the fair years ago."

"That's my daughter a true cowgirl from the carousel of the Dade County Fair."

Monica walked out from the stables with a horse. She told me, "This is Blaze. He is a very gentle and loving horse. Samantha, you should ride him. I walked up to the horse and the handler handed me a carrot to feed Blaze.

Monica came out again with another horse. He was beautiful with a shiny jet-black coat. Monica told us, "His name is Midnight, and he is very tame and a wonderful horse for the first-time riders. Daphne should ride him. Daphne walked up slowly to the horse and she was clearly nervous.

A few minutes later, everyone was standing beside a horse and it was time to ride them. We each took turns mounting our horse. We would walk up these three steps, place our left foot into the stirrup and swing our right leg over. Monica and a handler helped us onto the horse.

Monica, Guillermo, and Pilar were like expert riders. They knew all of the commands; they were comfortable on a horse. Michael was extremely nervous. In fact, Arturo and Carmen had to calm him down before approaching the horse.

It turns out Michael was afraid of horses and horseback riding wasn't something he ever intended to do in his life. Monica knew exactly what he needed to calm down. She introduced Michael to a horse named Blondie. She was brown with a gold mane. She had one white stripe from her forehead to her nose. For Michael, it was love at first sight. Monica gave him a brush and showed him how to brush her. He gently brushed her mane.

After a few minutes, she gave Michael a carrot and he fed Blondie the carrot. The handler asked, "Would you like to sit on her?"

Michael's response was unexpected. He asked, "Can I?"

"Of course, Michael. Blondie would love that. Especially if she gets the chance to go out on the trails with all her friends." The handler helped Michael mount the horse. When Michael was finally seated on top of Blondie, he had a huge smile on his face.

Now we were all in a line, traveling along a path with one horse behind the other. It was still so hard for me to believe that we were doing this. I was actually sitting on the back of this beautiful horse.

I loved the sound of the horse's hoofs on the ground. Guillermo, Pilar, and Monica were riding beside all of us. Joe our tour guide would point out different spots to us, trees, and birds. I just kept trying to take everything in. Nobody spoke the whole ride. Everyone paid attention to Joe and the beauty surrounding us. I would look around the wooded trail, but my attention was always on Blaze. When we arrived back at the ranch, I bent over and hugged Blaze and thanked him for the ride.

Julio climbed off his horse and handed the reins over to a handler. He walked beside Blaze, and he put his arms up to me. The handler was already holding the reins, and I slid down into Julio's arms. He kissed me once and set me down.

Guillermo said, "Oh, you are going to outdo me, sobrino." Then he walked up to my mom's horse and the handler was there to help my mom down. Guillermo said something to the handler. My mom reached out her hand to Guillermo. He kissed her hand and put his foot in the stirrup. He swung his leg over and sat behind her on the horse. He took hold of the reins with his left hand and wrapped his right arm around my mom. He smiled down at Julio before the horse, my mom, and Guillermo left the stable.

Julio wrapped his arms around me from behind. He whispered, "My uncle Gio was looking for any excuse to take off with your mom."

"Yeah, I think you're right."

Monica and Pilar called us over. They showed us how to brush the horses. We gave each of the horses an apple afterward. When my mom and Guillermo returned, she was laying her head back against his shoulder and my mom was looking up at him smiling. Guillermo was smiling so much that his eyes were twinkling.

A handler came over to the horse they were on, and Guillermo gave him the reins. He climbed down off the horse and helped my mom down. He wrapped his arms around her and just held her.

Pilar walked out of one of the stables with Chris and Carmen. "Gio, I'm hungry and we're going to be late for lunch."

"Pilar, I forgot about lunch. Will go now."

Greg walked up behind Pilar and told her, "I'm starving, these carrots are not a cure for my appetite."

Pilar looked up at Greg and answered, "I know you are, Greg, we're going to eat lunch now. Stop eating the carrots. They are meant for the horses, not you."

"Pilar, it was a fair exchange. I gave him my apple, so I ate his carrot." Guillermo and Pilar looked at one another and started laughing.

Once everyone was rounded up, we headed out to have lunch.

When we arrived at the restaurant, Guillermo walked up to the hostess stand and said, "I know we're late. We are the Sanchez party of 20. Do you still have the room saved for us?"

"Yes, Mr. Sanchez. Four members of your party have already arrived."

We walked to the back of the dining room. The area had two long tables set up, one behind the other. One table was set up for eight people, and the other table was set up for 12 people.

The newlywed couple was already sitting down at the table for eight. I thought to myself, that must be the parents' table.

Eddie and Heather were already seated at the table for 12. We each took turns hugging Julie and Juan Sanchez and congratulating them. Then we headed over to our table. Eddie and Heather stood up, and we took turns giving them each a hug.

When we all took our seats, Monica said, "Tio, I thought you would be on your honeymoon."

"Our flight leaves in four hours."

"Where are you guys off to for your honeymoon?"

"Lori, we are going to my second home, in Spain. I want to show my wife where I went to school, and we have a beautiful house there that she has never seen. We are also going to spend some time in Portugal and Morocco."

"That sounds amazing. I have never been to any of those places."

Guillermo leaned over and spoke in a low voice, "Maybe one day you will allow me to take you to those places."

"Maybe."

A little giggle escaped me. At that very moment, I realized where I get my nonchalant attitude from.

Julio leaned over and whispered, "It's not nice to eavesdrop on other people's conversations."

I giggled again and whispered, "You're doing it too, and that's why you knew why I laughed."

Julio smiled at me and said, "Touché, Mi Corazón," as he took a sip of his water.

I smiled back at him, and he whispered, "We're still the cuter couple."

"Yes, I think we are too, Soccer Player. Gee, my poor mom won't ever be able to run away now."

"Why would she need to do that?"

"It's not about her needing to that. It's about her not being able to do that."

"I don't get what you're saying, Samantha."

"Julio, you know better than anybody. You can't outrun a soccer player."

Julio laughed and yelled out, "I love you, Samantha. You are the best. " He reached over and hugged me and kissed the top of my head at least three times.

Guillermo turned around and said, "Whoa, Soccer Player, calm down." Then we both turned around and saw Guillermo and my mom smiling back at us.

"Guys, we're sitting right behind the two of you and we can eavesdrop on your conversation too."

"Mom, seriously."

"Seriously, Sam."

"Yes, and we are the cuter couple," Guillermo replied, then he stuck his tongue out at us before he turned around in his chair. Julio and I started to laugh, and I could hear my mom and Guillermo laughing too.

The waiter came around and took down everyone's drink order. That's when Lewis walked in, holding Amy's hand. He walked up to his father and Julie first. Then he came over to our table. I stood up and Lewis gave me a hug and a kiss on the cheek.

I suddenly felt Amy's glare, so I said, "Hi Amy," she smiled but didn't say anything. Julio waved to the both of them, and she rolled her eyes. Greg, Daphne, Arturo, and Michael stood up to greet Lewis and Amy. They eventually had a seat at the end of the table beside Arturo and Michael. The waiter came back with the drinks and was ready to take everyone's order.

That's when I realized I never even opened the menu. Of course, I was also the first person the waiter started with. He asked, "What would you like to have?"

"I'll just have a cheeseburger."

Everyone broke out laughing, and my mom leaned over and whispered, "Sorry, eavesdropping again. Sam, this is a Chinese restaurant. They don't have cheeseburgers here. Is there something else you would like to have?"

I closed my eyes and tried to conceal my embarrassment. When I finally opened my eyes and looked up at the waiter. I smiled and told him, "I will have the honey chicken, please."

"Very good, ma'am. Which kind of rice do you want with it?"

"Stir-fried,"

"Yes, ma'am, but which kind of stir-fried rice? Pork, shrimp, or vegetable?"

This is when I began to feel a bit anxious and lots of regret for not reading the menu. "Vegetable is fine."

"Very good, ma'am, and what kind of soup would you like?"

"Oh, I would like wonton soup."

"Excellent choice, and do you want the tea?"

"Tea?"

"Yes, ma'am, the hot tea cleans your pallet and assists with digestion."

"Sure, then I'll have some tea."

After he took my order, he left the table. Eddie asked, "What happened, Sammy? All you had to do was look at the menu. Then you order something from that menu. Now you scared him away. Sorry, Greg."

"Everyone laughed but Greg."

Julio looked over at Greg and asked, "Do you need a hug, dude?" Then Julio and Tommy jumped up out of their chairs and ran over to Greg and hugged him. Julio kept stroking Greg's head like a puppy dog while saying, "It's going to be alright. You'll eat again soon."

When the waiter came back, Greg jumped up out of his chair and said, "Welcome back, dude. We missed you, man." The waiter looked scared, and he backed away from the table.

Then he spoke to us from a distance, "I'm sorry. My wife called me into the kitchen. I just had to go help her for a second."

"No man, you don't need to apologize for anything. I'm just glad you came back."

Greg sat down and you could see the relief on the waiter's face. He walked up to our table again and took down everyone's order. Then he went over to the parents' table. I could hear Pilar and my mom apologizing to the waiter for Greg scaring him and for me, trying to order a cheeseburger. I heard Carmen say, "Yes we're really sorry, Sir. It's the first time the kids have been to a restaurant. They'll know how to handle it better next time."

Julio and I laughed and my mom said, "Some people are so noisy." I turned around and looked at my mom. She was already facing me, smiling. I cracked a smile back at her, and we both started laughing.

During lunch, Heather and Amy got into a bit of fight. Amy was upset because Heather refused to come to her house to pick her up. When the food arrived, we were all eating quietly until Amy and Heather got into it again. I don't know everything that was said through the course of the conversation. However, we all know now. That Amy is considered promiscuous even by her own parents. That's why Amy is not allowed out of her house without a chaperone. Which is usually one of her two cousins.

We were also informed that Amy is presently babysitting Erika. Or at least that's what she told her parents.

Monica's mouth dropped open and she was staring Lewis down with daggers in her eyes. Lewis tried his best to change the subject, but Amy wouldn't allow it. By the time lunch was finished, we also learned a little about Heather.

She is a frigid virgin with no sex drive and Eddie would have better luck dating a nun.

Guillermo stood up and announced, "I would like to give a toast to my brother, Juan, and his lovely wife, Julie. Congratulations again, guys." We all stood up and toasted our glasses and took a sip from our water glass and sat back down. Guillermo told us, "I'm not done yet," and he was smiling. We all stood up again and Guillermo went on to say, "I would also like to thank Carmen and Lori for making the trip up here. It has been such a magnificent week, one of the best in my life. When we were about to take another sip Guillermo said, "Wait, I'm still not done yet," and we all let out a little chuckle. "Most importantly, I would just like to say it has been a real pleasure getting to know all of you." Then Guillermo looked over at Amy and Heather. He held his glass up toward them and said, "Well, maybe we didn't need to know that much about some of you." Everyone laughed and Carmen choked on her water.

We all sat back down at the table and Heather was beaming with a smile. Amy looked like she was turning fuchsia. I turned around in my chair and said in a low voice, "Thank you for lunch Guillermo, it has definitely been a memorable experience.

Guillermo replied, "I bet." Then he laughed so hard that his cheeks turned pink. When we all finally settled down, Guillermo announced, "It's time to go."

We said our goodbyes and climbed back into the limo. The newlyweds waved bye to us as we pulled away. Pilar sat back in her seat and looked over at Julio and me. She said, "Wow, those girls are really something," and she rolled her eyes.

We both laughed, and Julio asked, "Mom, is Amy the new nanny for Erika?"

Pilar's mouth dropped open and she placed both her hands on her lap as she leaned over to get a good look at Julio and asked, "Are you crazy?"

We all started laughing and Monica was shaking her head. "Mom, that girl is nothing but trouble." Pilar nodded her head yes in agreement. "Oh, and I can't believe Alex missed the show at lunch today."

"Are you kidding, Monica? I can't believe we had front row seats. It was insane. I think we should make it our duty to tell Alex everything he missed when we get back to the house."

"You have a deal, Michael," and they shook on it.

When we arrived back at the house, Julio and I were the last ones to exit the limo.

He took my hand and asked, "Would you come with me for a second?"

"Of course, where are we going?"

"I need to take you somewhere. It's not far from my house." We climbed into the golf cart and drove past his house. We pulled into a park, and he took my hand and said, "Come on."

We walked up to the swings and I started to giggle. "Sit down." I did, and he kissed me on the cheek. Then he pulled the swing all the way back and set me free. I started soaring up toward the sky. He pushed me in the swing for a few minutes, until eventually it slowed down and came to a complete stop. I looked up at Julio, and he was staring up into the sky. I knew that he had something on his mind. That's when Julio looked down at me and realized my swing had stopped. I was just looking up at him. "Hopefully, you'll come here again, and I will push for as long as you want, Samantha."

I stood up and told him thank you. He sucked in his bottom lip and his eyes were watering up. I wrapped him in my arms and inhaled his scent. I don't know exactly how long we stood there holding one another. I only know it wasn't long enough.

We walked back to the golf cart and he drove us to Guillermo's house. When we walked inside there was nobody around. I released Julio's hand and told him, "I have to go and get packed now."

He placed his hand over his mouth and looked down at the floor. "Julio, I'll meet you back in the family room when I'm done." He nodded his head, yes, and remained in the foyer by the front door. I felt his eyes on me as I left the room.

When I walked into the bedroom, Daphne was in the dressing area packing up all her cosmetics. Michael and Arturo were sitting down in the two overstuffed chairs. They were talking to Monica and she was sitting on the ottoman.

"Where have you been, Sammy?" Daphne asked.

"We went to the park down the street from here. Julio pushed me in a swing for a few minutes."

"Oh, that's sweet, Sammy. Now you need to pack."

"Yes, I know that Daphne. Thank you."

Monica walked over to the dressing area and she had a sad expression on her face now. "Do you need any help packing, Sammy?"

"No, I got it, Monica. Thank you."

I grabbed my suitcase out of the closet and set it down on the bed. I grabbed everything out of the closet and drawers. Then tossed them all into the suitcase. That's when I realized a whole section of my suitcase was still empty. I yelled, "Oh crap, Daphne, I still have the wet clothes in the washing machine, and they need to be placed into the dryer."

"I can do that for you Sammy."

"Monica, that would be great."

"No problem, I will be back in a couple of minutes."

"Can I come with you, Monica?"

"Of course, Michael. Let's go."

Monica and Michael left the room. Arturo stood up and said, "Here, let me help you, Sammy." He grabbed all my shoes off the floor, and he helped me roll them up into my jeans.

I zipped closed that section in my suitcase. Arturo asked, "Is there anything else you need to pack?"

"At the moment, only the clothes that are going into the dryer now. Oh, and the garment bags!" I ran back into the closet, and pulled out the garment bags, I tossed them up on the bed beside the suitcase.

"Have you written a letter to leave behind with Julio?"

"No, and I'm not going to, Arturo. I don't want to be pen pals. I want to give us a second chance and ask him to be my boyfriend again."

"Sammy, you know that means you will be in a long-distant relationship."

"Yes, and it's going to be hard, but I love him."

Arturo smiled and replied, "It will be tough, but you can handle it, Sammy."

"I hope so, this is my second chance to do it right this time." Arturo hugged me and Daphne came running over to hug the both of us.

When we finished packing, I went out to the family room to look for Julio.

He was in there with Greg and Tommy, playing foosball. Alex was in there taking a nap. "Hey, where's Erika?"

Julio pulled his head up from the foosball table when he heard my voice. He smiled and answered, "She's upstairs with the moms."

"Oh, that's good."

"Yeah, as long as she's not with Amy," Tommy said with a snicker.

A few minutes later, the moms headed downstairs. Pilar told me, "Your mom and I are going to make sandwiches for all of you to eat on the plane. Can you ask the others to come into the kitchen please?"

"Of course, I will let them know right now." I told everyone in my bedroom to go and speak with the moms in the kitchen.

I walked downstairs and went into the garage to check on the clothes. They were still damp, so I set the dryer for another 20 minutes. I walked over to the staircase and was suddenly picked up off the ground.

Julio carried me into the theatre room. Once inside, Julio set me down and locked the door. He dimmed the lights and wrapped his arms around me. "I'm going to miss you so much, Samantha. I feel like my heart is broken again and you haven't even left yet."

"Julio, I'm feeling the same way. I was wrong, and I was scared when you moved away. I don't want to be pen pals anymore."

"No?"

"No, I want you to be my boyfriend again, Julio."

"Are you asking me out, Samantha?"

"Yes, I'm asking for a second chance?"

Julio picked me up and I wrapped my arms and legs around him. He leaned my back up against the wall as he kissed me slowly repeatedly. He carried me over to the couch and I looked up into his eyes and asked, "Will you be my boyfriend, Julio?"

He reached out and placed his thumb on my chin. He looked into my eyes and said, "Just until…" he paused, and turned his eyes away from me. I suddenly felt my heart racing.

I was starting to feel nervous and asked, "Just until, Julio?" I took in a deep breath and tried to prepare myself for his answer. He leaned in and closed his eyes and I pulled away from him. He stood up and paced the floor in front of me. He had me completely freaked out. I knew something was wrong.

He finally stopped pacing and was looking down at floor. "Samantha, I have been dreaming about you giving us another chance ever since I moved here."

Then he looked up into my eyes and said, "We can do this Samantha; I know we can." He sat back down on the couch and wrapped his arms around me.

I pushed his arms away from me and stood up. "All I know Julio, is that your keeping something from me." I pulled the door open to leave.

"Samantha, you're leaving here today with my heart."

Julio when I leave here today, I will only take back the memories. I was caught up in the moment when I asked you for a second chance.

"Samantha, please, we deserve a second chance. You are more than just a memory to me." Julio was visibly upset now with his eyes red and nose running.

I turned my back and closed my eyes as I told him, "It just feels natural for me to be with you Julio. What doesn't feel natural is the distance and the amount of time we would spend apart. "I opened my eyes and had tears running down my face. I heard the buzzer go off on the dryer and said, "I'm sorry, but I have to go now." I ran out of the theatre room and into the garage.

Julio was waiting for me beside the stairs when I walked back inside. He walked up to me and grabbed the clothes from me. He carried them upstairs and followed me to my room.

I walked inside and over to my suitcase that was sitting on my bed. I started to unzip the case and thought to myself, where's Julio. That's when I looked behind me and saw him still standing at the door. He had his arms filled with my clothes. I waved him over and told him, "Just drop my clothes on the bed."

Julio walked in and dropped the load of clothes into my suitcase instead. I just zipped up my case and placed it on the floor.

I heard my mom yell, "Sam, let's go."

Julio and I froze in place and looked at one another.

I had to close my eyes to prevent the tears from forming. I felt Julio take my hands as he kissed me frantically on my cheek, forehead, other cheek, nose, and chin. Then he lifted up my chin and I opened my eyes. I knew at that moment he was seeking permission to kiss me on my lips. I just stared back at him and nodded my head yes. He kissed me once gently on the lips and I opened my eyes as he pulled away from me slowly. He had a frantic look on his face, but the hesitation when I asked him for a second chance was still pondering me. I wanted to leave here as his girlfriend, but I have to go with my instinct.

"I really do love you Julio and I'm leaving here with some amazing memories." He bit down on his bottom lip and didn't say another word. I grabbed my garment bag off the bed, and he grabbed my suitcase.

We both walked into the kitchen, and Pilar smiled. She handed me a zip lock bag and said, "Here's your sandwich for your flight Sammy."

I hugged Pilar and told her, "I'm going to miss you so much." She wrapped her arms around me and held me. I could hear her trying to suck in her tears.

Guillermo walked into the kitchen. His smile was gone, and he looked as though his heart had been crushed.

He was standing beside Julio and I noticed they both had the same gloomy facial expression. My mom looked up at Guillermo and she laughed through watery eyes and told him, "I can't believe you put that suit and cap back on."

"Lori, it's my last chance to be your driver. I will drive you back to the airport tonight. Tomorrow I will bring everything back to my car service."

My mom covered her mouth with the palm of her hand. Guillermo walked over to my mom and he wrapped his arms around her. She was looking up into Guillermo's eyes as he said, "Lori, you have opened my eyes and changed how I see and feel about everything."

That's when Tommy barged into the kitchen and said, "Mom, I'm ready to go when you are.

My mom and Guillermo pulled apart. Guillermo grabbed his keys off the counter. My mom wiped under her eyes and put on her fake smile. She looked up at me, then my brother and told us, "Let's get going, guys. We don't want to miss our flight."

Pillar walked with us to the front door. She gave each of us a hug before we walked outside. Alex was the last one out the door. Pilar gave him a hug.

Her lips were trembling and there were tears in her eyes when she said, "I'm going to miss you, mi hijo." Alex used the hem of his shirt to wipe away her tears. He hugged her once more before walking out the door.

When Alex reached the car, he replied, "I will miss you too mom." I turned around to look over at Pilar and ran right into Julio's chest. I just put on an awkward smile and looked over his shoulder at Pilar. She was no longer crying, instead she had the biggest smile on her face. Then I noticed what made her smile. Standing two feet away from us was Enrique with his arms wrapped around Carmen.

That's when I heard Guillermo say, "Julio, Enrique, if you two want to take a ride with me to the airport, get in." Julio shoved something into his back pocket, and he climbed into the limo. Enrique, Carmen, and I followed him inside.

Once we arrived at the airport Julio climbed out of the car behind me. He hugged me and lifted up my chin; he looked into my eyes and said, "Te amo, Mi Corazón." He kissed me on the cheek, then handed me an envelope.

I looked down at the envelope in my hand and asked, "What is this Julio? I looked up at him and he had a somber expression on his face.

Julio took in a deep breath before saying, "Don't read it until your home Samantha." He had tears in his eyes as he turned and walked back to the car.

He left me standing on the curb by myself, feeling extremely upset, and totally confused.

Then I looked back at the limo and saw my mom and Guillermo. They were holding one another, and he pulled away, just far enough to lean down and kiss my mom for the last time.

Chapter 9 Back to Reality

We walked inside the airport and my mom headed straight for the bathroom. She blew her nose and wiped away the mascara from under her eyes that was running. When she looked up to view her reflection in the mirror, she noticed that I was standing behind her, and asked: "Where's Tommy?"

"I think he's with Carmen and everybody else. All I know is that everyone was gone by the time I climbed out of the limo, except for you, Mom."

"Okay, then we need to hurry up and get down to the gate Sam." We left the bathroom and started walking at a fast pace. When we finally arrived at the gate, everyone was looking at us with soulful eyes.

Tommy stood up and wrapped his arms around my mom. "Mom, I love you, and thank you for this amazing trip. I had so much fun, and I'm sorry I brought Tracy."

My mom placed the palm her hand to her forehead and said, "Tommy, not now. I just need to sit down."

"Yes, of course, Mom. Come sit down here beside me."

Carmen looked up at my mom and asked, "How are you doing?"

My mom smiled and sat down, "I guess it's better to have loved and lost, then not to have loved at all, right? Isn't that how the old saying goes?"

Carmen wrapped her arms around my mom and told her, "It will all work out one day. Everyone comes into our lives with a purpose. Besides, you have us, your sisters, to lean on. Pilar is a phone call away, and I'm ready when you are with a mimosa in the morning and a margarita in the evening."

"Oh, that sounds fantastic, Carmen. Your plan is for us to become raging alcoholics."

Carmen smiled at my mom and replied, "Just for a little while." They both looked at one another with a serious face, then broke out laughing.

My mom was settling down and asked, "Did you know that he's never been in love?"

"Who?

"Guillermo!"

"Lori, I don't think that's the case anymore."

Michael walked over to me and sat down. "Sammy, do you want to sit beside Daphne and Greg, or me and Arturo?"

I thought about it and realized the last thing I wanted to hear or see right now was Greg and Daphne being all lovey-dovey. So, I answered, "Definitely you and Arturo."

"Great, Tommy will sit beside Greg and Daphne. I will be right back. I just need to tell Daphne to sit by the window. Greg will need to sit in the middle, and Tommy can sit in the aisle seat. That way when Daphne falls asleep, Greg and Tommy can speak to one another."

"Sounds good, Michael. Thank you." He smiled at me and I forced a smile back. After Michael walked away my mind went back to that letter. I just couldn't stop thinking about it. I wanted to read it so bad; will the letter tell me what's wrong with Julio? Or is he just telling me goodbye?

That's when I felt my mom take my hand and I looked down at our hands held together. My mom whispered to herself, 'How did the time go by so fast?' I looked back at my mom and she was staring at the floor. I realized that I had bigger things to worry about. That letter from Julio should be the least of my concerns right now. My mom had clearly fallen for Guillermo and now she was leaving here with a broken heart. My mom started to speak to Carmen, so I remained quiet as she held my hand.

My mom said, "All of these years I have always put Tommy and Sam first. Dating wasn't something that I was ever interested in you know that, Carmen."

Carmen laughed and replied, "I know."

My mom stayed quiet for a moment then she squeezed my hand. My mom took in a deep breath, released it slowly, and began to speak. "From the moment I saw Guillermo I was vastly intrigued with him." She looked up from the floor and smiled at Carmen.

"Yes, I saw it in your eyes Lori."

Oh, Carmen when I saw his piercing brown eyes and gorgeous smile. It was too late! I was a goner! I knew I was in trouble. I had been swept right off my feet and he hadn't even said a word to me yet."

Carmen laughed again and hugged my mom, "Yes, everyone could see there was an instant attraction."

My mom sat up in her seat and whispered, "Carmen was it that obvious to everyone that I was smitten?"

Carmen leaned over and answered, "I would say that it was pretty obvious you both were smitten with one another?"

My mom sat back in her seat before saying, "It was an incredible trip. I'm so happy we went on this trip together. "

"Lori, I couldn't agree with you more. We all had a great time."

My mom released my hand and covered her mouth for second. She was deep in thought looking down at the floor when she said, "Can you believe that I forgot how it feels to be attracted to someone?"

"Lori, maybe Guillermo is Mr. Right. After all! he did manage to sweep you off your feet."

"Carmen he lives in Anaheim and I live in Miami."

Carmen was about to say something when their names were called over the intercom. My mom and Carmen stood up and walked over to the counter. I watched from my seat as they were handed out boarding passes.

My mom and Carmen headed back over to us and we all stood up. We followed my mom and Carmen over to the door. The woman at the entrance asked us for our boarding passes. Once she had all of them, she tore a slip off each one and handed the stubs back to us. She said that would be our seat assignment and we could go ahead and board the plane now. She wished us all a safe trip as we all headed down the sky bridge to the plane.

My mom showed the flight attendant her seat stub when we entered the plane . We followed the flight attendant to the first-class cabin.

Carmen looked over at my mom and told her, "We're having a drink on this flight, Lori."

"Guillermo shouldn't have done this, Carmen."

"Have a seat Lori, I'm ordering you a mimosa."

Carmen looked back at the rest of us. We were all still standing behind them looking around the cabin. "Come on guys, let's get in our seats." We each looked at our stub and found our assigned seat and sat down. I was now sitting beside Alex and noticed there were only two seats side by side instead of three. My mom and Carmen were siting in front of us, Arturo and Michael sat down behind us. Then directly beside us was Greg sitting alone. Daphne and Tommy sat behind him.

Once the door was closed on the plane, I asked Greg why he was sitting alone. He told me that he needed to get some sleep before he starts his double shift Monday morning.

A flight attendant came around taking drink orders and another passed out blankets and pillows. Alex and I talked about his uncle's surprise of upgrading our tickets. Then Alex mentioned he flew first-class on the way up here to. I thought to myself mystery solved; that's why we didn't notice Alex boarding or exiting the plane. They loaded and unloaded the plane from the first-class cabin.

The lights were dimmed after taking off and we reclined our seats back to take a nap.

We were both awakened by a flight attendant who simply asked us to prepare for landing by moving our chairs back into the upright position. I looked over at Alex, and he looked just as surprised as I was. I moved my chair back up and Alex was smiling. He was looking out the window now and said, "I can't wait to see Maria."

"Yes, I'm sure she can't wait to see you either."

When we exited the plane, Maria was outside the gate waiting for Alex. The minute she saw him her eyes lit up and she ran over to him. He picked her up and she wrapped her arms around him, and he kissed her.

We headed down to baggage claim, grabbed our bags and were off to the garage. Tommy carried my suitcase to the garage. Alex and Maria stopped on the second floor. We hugged them as they got out. We stopped on the third floor and hugged everyone before we got off the elevator. Greg asked, "Can I ride back to your house? My cousin needs to pick me up."

"Sure, Greg, come on."

"Great, Ms. Harris." He walked off the elevator and Daphne stepped off the elevator behind him.

"Oh, no you don't young lady. You're going home to unpack and get some rest. You can see Greg later." Daphne walked back into the elevator and waved bye to us as the door closed.

"That Daphne!" Tommy said, and he laughed the entire way to the car.

When we pulled into the complex at home, my mom pulled up to Tonya's building first. She told me, "Go and get Daisy. It's time for her to come home."

I climbed out of the car and walked upstairs. When I reached Tonya's door, I was about to knock when she opened the door, she screamed from being startled. Then, she wrapped her arms around me and told me, "I missed you, Muñeca." Daisy ran out from behind her and jumped up on her hind legs whimpering and licking my face. Then she suddenly stopped and began to frantically sniff my hair and my clothes. Then she dropped to all fours and howled. Tonya looked down at Daisy and asked, "What's wrong with her?"

"Nothing, she's fine."

"Muñeca, she sounds like she's in agony."

I could feel the emotions just building up inside me. I sniffed once to hold back the tears that I could feel on the verge of falling. When I finally felt able to speak without becoming a total mess, I told her, "Daisy can smell Julio's scent on me."

Tonya let out a big sigh of relief and replied, "Well, I'm guessing that your emotions are a little too high now to talk about your trip."

I nodded my head yes and said, "My mom, Tommy, and Greg are in the car waiting for me downstairs. I just came by to pick up Daisy. I haven't actually been home yet. "

"I didn't realize that. I'm just so happy to see you Muñeca."

I wrapped my arms around Tonya and told her, "I missed you too, Cuban Booty and we definitely should talk about my trip to Anaheim. A lot happened.

I mean huge, wow, no way, kind of things happened. So, if you want to come over later, after I get unpacked." Tonya was frowning at me and Daisy was pulling me towards the stairs.

"Or just come now Tonya, if you're not doing anything."

Tonya walked back inside, grabbed the keys off the wall, and said, "Let's go now," as she quickly shut the door behind her. Tonya and I walked down the stairs with Daisy. By the time we reached the first floor, Daisy pulled us straight over to the grass.

"I can't believe she made it down five flights of stairs. You know she hasn't been outside until now. I was just heading out to take her for a walk when you arrived. I'm just glad she didn't pee while she was walking down the stairs."

"Oh, poor Daisy. I kneeled down when Daisy was finished and said, "I'm sorry, girl." Daisy licked my cheek several times.

When we walked around the building and headed into the parking lot, my mom and everybody was gone. "I guess they got tired of waiting Tonya. We're walking back to my place."

"Well, that works out nicely, doesn't it, Daisy? You will be able to get your walk in and Muñeca will get some exercise." Tonya rubbed the top of Daisy's head and Daisy licked her hand.

"Tonya, before I left for Anaheim, I saw you get picked up by some guy. He drove like a show-off, you know, fast and peeling out."

"What about him?"

"Who is that? Is he your boyfriend?"

"No, he is just some guy that I have been sort of seeing over the summer. It's nothing serious; besides, he leaves in a week back to school."

"Back to school? Wow, where does he go to school?"

"He's in college, at one of the universities up in the panhandle. So, you see it's not serious. He will be gone in another week just like Lewis."

I realized at that moment Tonya was not totally over Lewis. Now I started to think that telling her about the cabana boy might not be such a good idea.

Tonya started talking about how we had just two weeks left of summer; then it would be off to school again as sophomores. I was zoning out as Tonya kept on talking. I was thinking about Julio and wondering if he would be awake yet, and if he was, would he watch the sunrise and think of me?

"Muñeca, are you even listening to me?"

I instantly quit daydreaming about Julio and answered, "Yes, of course, Tonya. I'm just as excited as you are and kind of nervous to be attending high school."

When we arrived at my front door, Tommy was outside on the cordless phone talking to someone.

Tonya waved hi to him before we walked inside. As the door shut, I heard someone yell, "Sammy."

I opened the screen door and walked back outside. I saw Mig. He was downstairs in his van. He was waving up to me, so I waved back. "Welcome back, Sammy. Can you tell my cousin to come downstairs please?"

"Of course, Mig. I will tell him right now."

"Sounds good! Oh, and it's good to see you again, Sammy." I just smiled and walked back inside.

Greg was asleep on the couch in the living room. I shook him awake and told him, "Mig is downstairs waiting for you."

Greg sat up and rubbed his eyes, "Already? What time is it?"

I walked into the kitchen and looked to see what time it was on the stove. I walked back out to the living room and told him, "It's half past nine."

"Okay, then I have to get up and go. Tell Daphne I love her and I'm going to work now." He stood up and walked over to the bathroom.

I ran outside and told Mig, " Your cousin should be downstairs in a couple of minutes."

"Samantha, are you going to the Bonfire on Friday? We're playing this weekend. If you decide you want to come, you can ride with us."

"Oh, I don't think I can do that right now Mig."

"Boyfriend?"

"No, we didn't get back together."

"So, you're not going out on weekends anymore."

"No, not right now."

"Wow, sounds rough."

"Yes, it sort of is."

"Well, the invitation still stands if you change your mind."

Greg walked outside and said, "Bye, guys." I waved bye to Greg, and Tommy turned around and waved bye to Greg as he was still talking to someone on the cordless phone.

Greg ran down the stairs and he climbed into Mig's van. "It was great to see you again, Sammy, and good luck." Mig backed out of the parking space and pulled away.

I walked back inside and went straight to my room. Tonya was sitting on the end of my bed beside the stereo. "Hey Muñeca, I'm making a really awesome mix tape right now. I can't wait for you to hear it."

Tonya was flipping through the stations and I heard Peter Gabriel. "Wait . Go back, Tonya." She flipped through the channels. "Stop."

"Do you want me to record that song for you?"

"Tonya, that would be great."

"You got it, Muñeca. I am making us a cassette tape of all the songs we listened to this summer."

"That's cool. I hope you have enough room for the Bee Gees."

"Oh no, what happened?" Tonya ran over to me and sat down on the floor in front of me.

"It's not 'Tragedy' again, is it? I mean every time I hear that song; I still remember how hard the divorce was on your mom."

"Yeah, it was pretty rough on everyone and my mom wasn't even in love with my dad anymore. That's why I'm so worried about my mom now. I mean, she really fell in love with this guy."

"What guy?"

I began to tell Tonya all about the limo driver at the airport and who Guillermo turned out to be. Then how he was singing and dancing all by himself on the balcony to 'In Your Eyes.'

"I bet the lyrics have something to do with how he feels about your mom." Tonya pressed the rewind button on the tape player. Then she turned her head to look over at me. "Are you ready?" I nodded my head yes, and she pressed play on the tape player.

My mom walked into my bedroom right as the song began to play.

"Oh, hi, Tonya."

"Ms. Harris." Tonya stood up and ran over to my mom and hugged her.

"How have you been?"

"Good, I missed you guys."

"We missed you too, Tonya. How was Daisy?"

"I loved having her at my house. Whenever you go out of town again, I hope you will let me watch her. We had so much fun and she even went jogging with me. I can't even get your daughter to do that."

Well, I will let you girls get back to whatever you were doing. My mom turned to leave and suddenly stopped. She turned around and asked, "What song is that?"

"The song is called 'In Your Eyes.' It's by Peter Gabriel. If you like it, I can make you a copy."

"Tonya, I would love a copy."

"Coming right up, Ms. Harris." Tonya smiled at me before she took out a blank tape and placed it in the second cassette player. My mom stayed in my room listening to the song while it was recording. When the song was over, Tonya asked my mom if there were any more songs she would like to have on the tape.

"Yes, no, I have those songs on records already."

"Even better, Ms. Harris. If you have the record albums I can record them onto this cassette for you, so you can play the songs in your car."

"I would like that, Tonya. Give me two minutes to bring you the records with the songs. Can you record all of them on the same tape?"

"Yes, I believe so." My mom stood up and left my room. She was back with a couple of records and a list of songs she wanted Tonya to record.

Tonya looked down at the records and asked, "Do you have the Foreigner album?"

"No, I don't, but I would like to have that song."

"What song, Mom?"

"Waiting for a Girl Like You.'"

"I have that song on my Foreigner cassette. Tonya will be able to record that song for you mom."

She smiled and clapped twice before saying, "Great, I really appreciate it girls." Then she stood up and left my room.

Tonya faced me and said, "You better tell me everything. I haven't ever seen your mom smile like that."

"Okay, but first let me read the list." Tonya handed me the list. I read the list out loud. "'How Deep Is Your Love, More Than a Woman.' Those two songs are from The Bee Gees, and then, of course, 'Waiting for a Girl Like You,' by Foreigner. Oh wow, Tonya, these are the songs that my mom and Guillermo danced to at the wedding reception."

Tonya sat back down on the floor facing me and replied, "Finish telling me everything." I sat down beside Tonya on the floor in my room facing her. We sat there until I told her everything about Guillermo and my mom from the beginning to the end.

"Do they plan to stay in touch?"

"I don't know, but I'm worried about my mom."

Tonya wrapped her arms around me, and I sighed. "We'll get her through this together. Don't worry, Muñeca. Speaking of heartache, tell me what happened with you and Julio."

I started off by telling her about the luncheon. How everything was going great until my instincts kicked in on the second day.

"What do you mean, Muñeca?"

Well, I kept feeling like there was something Julio wasn't telling me. I tried to ignore this feeling, but a little voice in my head was telling me to watch out. Something was not right here. That's when I asked Julio my first question.

"What was your first question?"

"I asked him if he had a girlfriend or if he was dating someone else."

"What did Julio say?"

"He said something about 'how he understands why I would ask that question. That I've been pushing him away since he left Miami.' Then he said, 'he understood the whole breaking up thing until we live in the same city.'"

"That's was Julio's answer?"

"Yes, then he looked me right in the eyes and said, 'If and when we are ever in the same place at the same time, he will drop everything to be with me even if it's just for mere seconds.'"

"I don't believe you."

"Tonya, I'm telling you exactly what he said. I just sat there waiting for him to answer my question."

"How long did you wait Muñeca?"

"I don't know it seemed like forever. Julio eventually whispered in my ear, 'No, there is no one else.'

"Do you know why he whispered that in my ear?"

"No, tell me why you think he did that."

"Julio couldn't say those words aloud and look me in the eyes. I would know he was lying to me, so he leaned over and whispered in my ear."

"You might be right Muñeca, what did you do?"

"Tonya, I just laughed and played it off because I wanted to believe him. We didn't speak about it again and everything seemed fine."

"Seemed fine?"

"Yes, until he left me at the airport with this letter."

"What did the letter say?"

I held up the letter and told her, "I don't know yet."

"You haven't read it?"

"No, Julio told me not to read it until I was home."

"Now, I'm afraid to read it."

"Muñeca, why?"

"Once I do, my dream will be over, and I will know the truth."

"What truth?"

"That Julio has moved on and I'm just a girl from his past. "

Tonya wrapped her arms around me and held me. I told her how we spent like every minute of the day together. I told her how wonderful and exciting it felt just to be held in his arms again. How I opened up about my feelings for him. I even told her about feeling his bare chest which was a huge step for me. That I have avoided and fought that temptation off for so long until last Saturday night.

"Oh, I know Julio enjoyed that. He would lift weights, like every single morning, just in case you ever wanted to touch his chest.

"Who told you that?"

"Lewis of course. Were you impressed? Was he really ripped?"

"Yes, and yes."

"I love everything about Julio and that's the problem. Tonya, I completely forgot about our conversation on the second day. So, on the last day I asked Julio to be my boyfriend and he hesitated. It was so painful the silent rejection. That's when I knew there's someone else. I tried to save some part of my dignity and told him I was just caught up in the moment. Mentally, I was shocked and so disappointed. Then he was the one trying to convince me that we should give it a second chance."

"Do you feel better now, Muñeca?"

"No, not really."

"Good!"

"How is that good Tonya?"

"You need answers open that letter from Julio now."

"I know, Tonya," I took in deep breath and began to read the letter out loud.

Dear Samantha,

I know when you read this, you will be back in Miami and my heart will have gone back with you. Since the day I left Miami I was unable to speak to you for almost a month. I was even told that you no longer want me to call you. That's when I went out on a double date with Lewis, Amy and her chaperone cousin Megan. That night I made a huge mistake and slept with Megan. We are not in a relationship or boyfriend and girlfriend. I was convinced if I slept with her, I would be able to forget about you. That was the biggest lie I ever told myself. Now I'm living in fear that you won't ever speak to me again. That's why I didn't tell you about this while you were here. It would have ruined everything. Now it's day five and I have just spent the most wonderful five days of my life with you. I can honestly say now that I'm glad that I waited to tell you like this. I'm becoming a man and I'm owning up to my mistake. I know that I messed up bad and I will always regret it. I love you so much Samantha and I hope that you will forgive me. Please call me after you've read this letter.

Te Amo, Mi Corazón,

Julio Sánchez

"Well, the good news is he didn't lie to you, Muñeca. He isn't with anybody else and he still loves you."

"Tonya, he slept with somebody else. I feel so stupid right now because I thought wow what a big step for me. I finally allowed myself to feel his chest, his bare-naked chest. He has gone all the way. What I did, basically, was a big deal only to me."

"Muñeca, you are only 15 years old. Are you honestly ready to have sex with him?

"No, that's not what I'm saying. I don't know how to explain it, except that for me that was a big deal, and Julio pretended that it was a big deal for him too, and I feel ridiculous now."

"What makes you think that wasn't a big deal for Julio?"

"Tonya, how can it be? If he has already had sex? Come on, think about it."

"Muñeca, he had sex and called it a mistake. You are the big deal! He loves you and he regrets what he did. He obviously doesn't have any feelings for this other girl. Just him being in the same room with you makes him feel alive. Hello, you wanting to feel his chest means the world to him. He would lift weights every day just hoping you would want to feel his chest someday. You're all that matters to him."

"Tonya, it doesn't matter now."

"What do you mean?"

"This happened when we were broken up and we're going to remain this way."

"Hey, I know Julio let you down-"

"No, not really."

Tonya rolled her eyes before saying, "Well he let himself down, not only you. I have to admit Muñeca, I'm impressed with your instincts and how well you know Julio. "

I sat down on my bed and replied, "Julio had sex and although we're not together it's disappointing. I know this might sound a little bizarre, but I feel angry, upset, disappointed, and confused all at the same time."

"The feelings you have right now are completely understandable and I am honestly feeling a bit disappointed with Julio myself."

"Can we change the subject, please?"

"Tell me about Lewis, Muñeca ."

"Are you sure?"

 "Yes, I want to know about his girlfriend Amy."

"How do you-"

"Julio mentioned Lewis and his girlfriend in the letter."

"Oh, that's right. I guess that means I need to tell you about the cabana boy."

"I'm ready to hear everything. Tell me, Muñeca."

I told her all about the cabana boy incident, and the lovely lunch we shared on our last day in Anaheim.

Tonya was laughing and said, "Now you know that Heather is not a liar."

We both laughed and when we finally stopped, I replied, "Of course she's not a liar, she's a nun."

 Tonya and I spoke for so long that I had to stand up and stretch. "What are you doing Muñeca?"

She caught me looking out the window at Julio's apartment. Well it use to be his apartment before he moved to Anaheim. "It's already dark outside Tonya." I pulled my head away from the window and asked, "Do you want to stay for dinner?"

"Hmmm, I don't know. What are you having?"

I walked into my mom's room and asked: "Do you want me to cook dinner?"

"Sam, there are no groceries to cook with, honey. I just ordered a pizza. We can go grocery shopping tomorrow."

"Is there enough for Tonya to eat too?"

"Of course, I even ordered a pepperoni pizza for you girls."

"Oh, that's our favorite."

"I know," my mom answered, smiling.

"Thanks, Mom."

"Now go tell Tonya and I will let you know when the pizza gets here."

I headed back into my room and told Tonya, "We're having pizza, and it's pepperoni."

Tonya smiled and asked if she could sleep over. "Yeah, of course, but why are you asking?"

"Well, I'm not really sure how upset you are over the whole Julio thing. Apparently, Tommy thinks you're in bad shape because he just took Daisy for a walk."

"Oh, no, that was over Tracy."

"The blow-up doll?"

"Yeah, it's a long story."

"Great, because I'm staying the night, so tell me the story."

I told Tonya about Tracy in the cabana, then about Tracy in the pool. I seemed to have forgotten to tell Tonya about Monica and Tommy hooking up. Tonya freaked out and told me to tell her everything about Tommy and Monica.

"Monica is actually Tommy's ex-girlfriend; you know the one that broke his heart. Things are different now and they hung out together the entire trip.

Monica is actually the one who told me everything about her and Tommy. She's totally back to normal and doing great. Monica's an awesome mom. Her daughter Erika is so beautiful. Pilar and Monica have become super close and Erika is loved and adored by everyone in the family.

My brother came back in the house with Daisy from her walk. Tonya and I called out, "Daisy!" She came running into my room giving us kisses. Then she ran back out to the kitchen for her bisquit.

Once the pizza arrived, my mom let us know the pizza arrived. We walked into the kitchen and we each grabbed two slices. We sat down at the table to eat with my mom and Tommy. My mom asked us how her cassette tape was coming along. Tonya said, "Oh, we are still working on that." My mom smiled and thanked Tonya.

When we finished eating, we headed back into my room. Tonya worked on my mom's tape as I told her about Enrique and Carmen. By the time I was finished, Tonya asked if we were on the Dating game. I told her that it all has something to do with Carmen's cherub earrings. Tonya laughed and mentioned that she needed to speak to Carmen right away.

We both fell asleep around midnight. I was woken up by Tommy an hour later when he walked in my room and shook me awake.

When I opened my eyes, he whispered, "Sam, get up and get the phone."

I walked out to the kitchen and picked up the phone. "Hello."

"It's me Julio. Why haven't you returned any of my calls?"

"What calls Julio? This is the first call I have received from you."

"Samantha, I beeped you at least 20 times today."

"Well, I haven't turned my beeper on. I read your letter by the way."

"I figured that and that's why I'm calling. I was worried you wouldn't speak to me anymore and that you were avoiding my calls."

"Julio after reading your letter…" I stopped talking mid sentence when I felt a piercing sharp pain in my ear. I lost all train of thought for a second.

"Samantha, are you still there?"

"Yes, after reading your letter I'm just glad I didn't give you a second chance. Thank you for checking on me. I can assure you that I'm fine. I have to go now Julio." I hung up the phone and went back to bed.

I was woken up again later on by Tonya jumping up and down on the bed yelling, "Get up, Muñeca. Let's go jogging with Daisy."

I hugged my pillow and told her, "No, you and Daisy go. I'm staying right here in bed with my pillow where I'm comfy."

An hour later, I was woken up by Daphne and Tonya. "Get up, Sammy. Greg is keeping his promise and he's taking us to the pool."

"No, I've spent enough time at the pool. I have a sunburn on my shoulders, remember, Daphne?"

"Oh yeah, I forgot. So, what do you want to do today, Sammy?"

"Nothing, Daphne, I want to remain in this bed for the entire day."

"Muñeca, you can't stay in this bed all day. I know why you're trying to stay bed. I won't let you do this again." Tonya reached over and grabbed the comforter off me, and she snatched the pillow under my head.

I sat up and yelled, "Tonya, give me back my blanket and pillow."

"No Muñeca, you're not staying in that bed with a broken heart again. You want to get even! Get showered and dressed and let's go someplace and do something."

"No, I don't need to get even. I'm not interested in sleeping with anyone."

"What are you talking about, Muñeca? You can't get even by making the same mistake he made. Everybody knows that. Even Julio regrets what he did and knows that now."

"Then how do you get even?"

Tonya sat down on my bed and she put her arms around me. "You hang out with us, your friends. We will listen to music and dance at the beach, pool, or even in an arcade room. I won't let you waste another second of your life alone in this room feeling depressed."

Then Daphne sat down on the bean bag. She looked up at me and asked, "Can I read the letter now, Sammy? Tonya told me about the letter Julio gave you."

I stood up from my bed and grabbed the letter out from the drawer in my nightstand and I handed it over to Daphne. She sat back in the bean bag and began reading. When she was done, she said, "I can't believe it, they had sex on the first date. Heather was right. Megan is a bigger slut than Amy."

Tonya stood up, crossed her arms over her chest and asked, "Is that cabana boys, Amy?"

Daphne and I broke out laughing. Daphne answered, "Why, yes, it is, Tonya. Just how much did Sammy tell you?"

"Oh, I told her pretty much everything, Daphne."

"Really, Sammy, like how we caught them naked in the cabana and the fight with her cousin at lunch?"

I nodded my head yes, and Tonya replied, "We talked about like the whole trip since the minute she arrived at my house at eight in the morning until midnight last night."

"Oh, and there is one more thing I need to tell you both. Julio called me last night after we went to bed."

"No way, Muñeca, and did you speak with him?"

"Yes."

"What did you say?"

"I told him that I read the letter and that I'm glad I didn't give him a second chance."

"And what did Julio say?"

"Nothing, I didn't give him a chance to. I told him I had to go and hung up.

"That means we have to get ready now. Today is tomorrow. You can't be here when Julio calls back. He needs to know that you are out having fun and not sulking in your room over something he did, Muñeca."

"What makes you think he's going to call me back?"

"Muñeca, he will call you every day unless he is told not to call you anymore."

"She's right Sammy."

"I know she is Daphne." Tonya faced me and started tapping me on my shoulders and back.

"What are you doing? Why do you keep tapping me?"

"Does it hurt, Muñeca?"

"No, it doesn't hurt. Does it hurt you?" I reached over and started tapping on Tonya.

"Stop it, I just wanted to see if your shoulders still hurt from your sunburn."

"In that case, no! My shoulders don't hurt anymore."

"Great, go get ready Muñeca. I'm going to the kitchen to get us some breakfast."

"Sammy, I can call Greg back and tell him to pick us up. He really wanted to take us to that pool in the Gables today."

"Fine, Daphne, call him. That sounds perfect. Give me like ten minutes to get ready and find some sunscreen."

Daphne left my room and I began to get ready. I walked into the kitchen as Tommy was making waffles. "Hey, Sam, you're finally up. Good, now take a seat at the counter. I have a bonging waffle ready for you."

"Thanks, Tommy," I took a seat at the counter and he just stared at me while I began to eat.

"Hey, Sam, are you going to tell me about this letter Julio gave you? According to Tonya, Julio is a horny toad and not a prince after all.

"Where's Tonya?

"I'm not sure, she came into the kitchen and told me to make you and Daphne a waffle."

"Did she tell you anything else, Tommy?"

"Just that we all need to be dressed and ready to leave here in 20 minutes. Greg is coming by to pick us up."

"About that, we're going to the pool, so I need to find the sunscreen. Do you remember where we put it?"

Tommy opened the cabinet in the kitchen above the counter and handed me the bottle of sunscreen. "I don't get it, Sam. If we're going to the pool, why would Greg pick us up? I mean the pool is about a hundred yards from our doorstep."

"We're not going to our pool. We're going to some historic pool in Coral Gables."

"No way, I love that place. I would go there all the time when I was in high school. We would jump off the cliff and hang out in the cave. I'll be right back, Sam."

"Wait, where are you going, Tommy?"

"To my room to call Monica. Never mind, I'll call her later, when we get back. It's only six in the morning where she's at."

"If I let you read the letter, Tommy, do you promise not to tell Mom?"

"Of course, Sam. It must be pretty bad if you don't want Mom to know."

"Well, I just don't want Mom to think bad of Julio. I shouldn't care about that right now, but I still do. I think that a lot of what happened had to do with the lies my brother told him in the first place."

"Get me the letter Sam and let me read it in front of you then."

I walked back into my room and grabbed the letter off the beanbag chair. Daphne was on my bed surfing the channels on my stereo for a song. "Hey, when are you going to get ready, Sammy?"

"In like five more minutes, Daphne, I promise."

"You better. They will be here to pick us up by then."

"They?"

"Yes, they! Greg and Mig."

"Daphne, I can't see Mig, not right now."

"Oh yes you can, he will be here in like five minutes or sooner, so you really need to get ready."

"Daphne, you don't understand. I don't want to see Mig, not today. I'm trying my best right now to keep it together and not feel overly upset."

Daphne looked down at my hand and I could see she zeroed in on the letter I was holding. "Sammy, what have you got there?

"Julio's signed confession."

"Please tell me you're not going to read it again."

"No, I'm going to let Tommy read it. Reading this once was enough for me."

"Yeah, I think once is enough for anybody, Sammy. You better hurry up and let Tommy read that letter now before we go. Then hopefully, the two of you can get dressed."

"Okay, Daphne, I'll be right back."

"Sure, I heard that already from Tonya ten minutes ago and she's still not back yet."

"Where's Tonya?"

"She left to go see your mom with some tape she made her."

"Okay, then I'll be right back. "Daphne rolled her eyes and went back to surfing channels on the stereo.

I walked back out into the kitchen. Tommy was at the sink rinsing the last dish. He looked over at me and saw the envelope in my hand. He asked, "Is that it?"

"Yes, of course, Tommy. How many letters do you think I have?"

He dried his hands on a dishtowel and walked over to the kitchen counter. He took a seat in one of the stools and I sat down beside him. He put out his hand and I handed him the letter. I felt so nervous that I had to look away as he read it.

"Oh man," Tommy said. I turned around to face him as he was shaking his head while continuing to read the letter. When he was finished, he folded the letter back up and handed it back over to me inside the envelope.

"Monica was right. She said that my actions could have pushed her brother too far. I told her that she needs to stop exaggerating and her brother would be just fine. I only want the best for you, Sam. You're my little sister and I'm only trying to protect you." Tommy began to chew on his lower lip. He turned his eyes away from me after he said that. Which left me feeling like there was something he wasn't telling me. When I stood up to walk away, he asked, "Do you blame me Sam, for what he did?"

I sat back down and let out a long sigh and answered, "No. I don't know if I can blame anyone other than Julio for his own actions. Did you know about this, Tommy?"

"No, of course not Sam."

"Why do I think your lying to me?"

"Look Sam, I won't tell Mom about this, not to protect Julio, but to protect Pilar."

"Well, were not together anymore so it doesn't really matter. Just learn from this Tommy and don't ever do this to me again."

"I'm sorry, Sam. I mean of course after all that I said, Julio should just go on a date and have sex with some other girl the first chance he gets just to spite you. That's called revenge sex, Sammy. Usually the revenge always ends up on the one person seeking revenge."

"Yeah, I call that karma."

Tommy smiled at me and when I didn't smile back, he became serious. He placed his arm up on the counter and leaned in closer towards me. He looked me in the eyes and asked in a low voice, "Did he try to take things further than you wanted to go? Did he try to sleep with you, Sam?"

I started to laugh and told him, "No, Tommy. He hasn't ever been that way with me. He always understood that I'm not ready for anything even close to that. We're only 15." That's when I stopped talking and thought, Julio felt the same way once or at least I thought he did.

"Just so you know Sam, I'm sort of mad at Julio."

"Believe me Tommy, I am too."

"Oh, and I'm sorry for asking you such personal questions Sam. I just freaked out a little after reading that letter. Actually, I started to panic and thought, did he try to take advantage of my little sister?"

"Yeah, I get that Tommy. I'm sorry that I accused you of lying to me. Julio didn't try to tempt me into anything. In fact, it was the other way around, I was the one being touchy feely not him."

Tommy covered his ears and declared, "You are my innocent little sister and I don't ever want to hear that again." I nodded my head okay and Tommy removed his hands from his ears.

"Sorry, that was a bit awkward for me to Tommy. I just wanted you to know the truth. Julio has always been very respectful and protective of me.

"So basically, a prince."

"Yeah, exactly!"

"I don't know how Julio behaves with other girls and I really don't want to know. I'm totally turned off knowing what he has done on a first date with this other girl."

Tommy smiled and said, "Sex is bad, Sammy. In fact, it's disgusting, and you shouldn't ever do it."

"Well maybe one day after I'm married."

He leaned in over the counter and told me, "Even then Sam, you don't have to do it. It's not a requirement."

"You can't be serious Tommy."

"Well, maybe after your married it won't be that disgusting." We were both laughing, and my mom walked into the kitchen.

"I thought you kids were going to the pool?"

That's when I noticed the clock on the stove and jumped off the stool. "We are mom and we have to get dressed right now." I kissed her on the cheek and ran into my room.

Chapter 10 Day Two

I dove into my dresser drawer and pulled out my bikini, shorts, and a tank top. I walked into my closet to get dressed in there.

When I came out, Daphne and Tonya started clapping.

"Okay, Sammy's dressed. Let's go."

Daphne, I just need a second to speak to my mom. I ran into my mom's room so I could let her know that we're finally leaving.

"Sam, what should I tell Julio if he calls looking for you?"

"The truth mom, it doesn't matter we are not together anymore. Besides, I'm just going out with my friends." I gave her a quick hug and left.

I met up with Tommy and Daphne in the kitchen. "Where's Tonya?"

"Sam, she's in your brother's room on the phone like usual."

The front door was open, and we could see Mig pulling up through the screen door. Daphne called out, "Tonya, they're here. Let's go."

"I'm coming now," Tonya came running through the kitchen and out the backdoor. The three of us followed behind her.

We walked down the stairs and over to the van. When Mig saw us, he climbed out of the driver's seat, walked around the van, and met us on the other side. He slid open the side door and Tommy climbed inside first. Then he helped Tonya, Daphne, and me into the van. Once we were all inside, Mig climbed in behind us and slid the door shut. He welcomed us all aboard as he climbed over the center console to the driver's seat.

Greg put in a tape of AC/DC as Mig pulled out of the parking space. The boys were all headbanging and playing air guitars and drums. Tonya, Daphne, and I just watched them. It was actually quite entertaining. We finally arrived at the pool in Gables.

We were walking toward the entrance and this tall guy wearing Bermuda shorts, a Hawaiian shirt, and sunglasses walked up to Tonya.

He grabbed hold of her hand rather possessively and asked, "Who are those guys?"

Tonya just laughed and told him, "They are just my friends. He was staring down my brother and Mig. We all just stood there staring back at Tonya until she said, "Everybody, this is Rick." The boys all shook hands with him. While Daphne and I just said hi and continued walking again toward the entrance.

Greg and Mig walked past us up to the booth. I turned around and noticed Tonya and Tommy were still in the parking lot speaking to Rick. By the time I turned back around, Greg and Mig were already leaving the line.

"Sammy, come stand over here. We already paid for you girls to get in." Daphne and I moved out of the line and stood off to the side beside the booth to wait for Tonya, Rick, and Tommy.

"Greg, I know that you're already short a days pay on your check. Why did you pay for me to get in?"

"Sammy, I didn't pay for you."

"You didn't?"

"No, Mig did."

"Why would you let your cousin do that?" Daphne was smiling at someone behind me. That's when I realized Mig was standing behind me. He must have overheard my conversation with Greg.

I swallowed once, faced Mig and said: "Thank you."

He just kept smiling, "You're welcome, Sammy."

Tommy bellowed, "Alright, time to go babe watching. Where's the beach?"

We all followed Tommy up to the entrance. The boys allowed us to walk in through the gate first. We found the bathroom to undress and a locker to keep our clothes in. We walked out to a little beach area. There were several people sprawled out on the sand lying down on their towels getting a tan.

The boys walked up behind us and Greg asked, "Who's going in the water first?"

"Wait," Daphne said, "First show me where the cave is."

Greg and Mig pointed to the cave.

"If you want to go into the cave, you will have to get in the pool."

Daphne replied, "Greg, that's why I'm here, to go in the pool."

Tommy snorted before saying, "Someone sounds nervous. Are you nervous girls?"

Tommy, Greg, and Mig were smiling at us and Daphne asked, "What's so funny?"

"Daphne, nobody laughed," Greg answered.

"Yes, but you're all grinning. What's wrong with the pool?"

"Nothing's wrong with the pool, Daphne. It's awesome. The water is the best part. It's actual spring water. Now let's get in," Tommy said, with a wicked smile.

Daphne looked back at us and tossed her towel onto the beach. "Come on, girls. Let's go."

Tonya and I tossed our towels beside Daphne's and we followed her out to the pool. Daphne whispered, "Let the guys go in first."

We all nodded our heads in agreement. We watched all the boys enter the pool and none of them showed any type of reaction. That's when Daphne told us, "Look, it's fine. We're freaking out over nothing."

We followed Daphne to a ladder on the side of the pool. When she placed her foot in the water, she screamed and snapped her foot out of the water. Tonya and I jumped back away from the pool and asked, "What happened?"

That's when the boys started laughing. "It's spring water, girls, so the temperature's freezing. But once you're inside the pool for a while your body will adjust to it. You'll be fine, Daphne. Come on, get in the pool already."

Daphne just stood there looking fearful and did not say a word back to Greg. Tonya and I stood off to the side facing the pool, watching everyone swimming around and jumping off the cliff. Tonya finally asked, "How bad could it be, Muñeca?"

"I don't know, Tonya."

"Tommy, I want to go to the cave. I need to get out of the sun; my shoulders are sunburned already."

"Sammy, the only way to the cave is to swim to it. Which means you need to suck it up and get in the water."

I looked back at Tonya and Daphne and whispered, "We're going to get pointy."

Tonya stood back from the water and asked, "What is that, Muñeca?"

I yelled out, "Your boobs, Tonya, are going to freeze up and become pointy in the cold water."

The four boys broke out laughing and Tonya's mouth dropped open. She was shooting daggers at me with her eyes.

I closed my eyes and took in a deep breath trying not to laugh and told her, "I'm so sorry, Tonya."

"Oh no, Muñeca, I'm sorry that you have to be the first one to jump in the pool."

Greg smiled and said, "Actually, you're not allowed to jump into the pool unless you are jumping off that cliff over there." He pointed to the coral rock behind him. People were jumping off a platform that was on top of this coral rock into the pool. "Maybe you should just gradually get in the water girls, but don't jump in." Greg looked as though he was trying his best not to laugh.

Tonya placed her hands on her hips and replied, "Whatever, Greg." Then she told me, "You're jumping off the cliff first then, Muñeca."

"Fine, whatever Tonya, let's get in." The three of us took turns going down the ladder into the pool. It was the coldest pool I have ever been inside. We decided to swim around to warm up and check out the pool.

The architecture was Mediterranean and everything appeared to be made of coral rock. There were two towers and a bridge. Then there was the sandy beach and lots of tropical foliage complete with palm trees. Making you feel like you were on a tropical island instead of just a pool.

"It's so beautiful here Muñeca. What do you think Daphne?"

"I think Greg was right! After a few minutes your body adjusts to the temperature and it actually feels invigorating. Do you girls want to swim up to the cave."

"No, not yet."

"Why not Tonya?"

Daphne, "the boys are getting ready to jump from the cliff and I want to watch them do it."

Tommy swam over to me and asked, "Do you want to jump off the cliff with your big brother Sam?" I thought about it for a second and was about to say no. Then I noticed how excited Tommy was to do this with me. I nodded my head yes and we swam over to the other side of the pool. We climbed out and stood in line on the coral rock stairs. We were standing behind Mig and Rick when Greg came up behind us with Daphne.

"Hey guys, let the girls go first."

Mig turned around with a look of surprise to see us standing behind him. "Sure, you can go ahead of us girls. Mig moved to stand behind me and he was checking me out from head to toe. "You better hold onto your bikini top when you jump Sammy. Some girls have been known to lose theirs."

"Thank you for the heads up, Mig."

Two people jumped off the cliff and I heard the splash into the pool. My heart started pounding. Mig smiled and said, "You're up, Sammy." I swallowed once and took two steps toward the edge of the platform. I looked over at the stairs behind me and spotted Daphne with a death grip on Greg's hand.

Tommy was nowhere in sight. I shook my head feeling aggravated and took one more step forward. I was now standing at the edge of the platform about to look down.

Mig whispered, "Don't look down, Sammy." I took one step back and looked over at Mig.

"Can you tell me if it's all clear below?"

Mig smiled at me and said, "It's all clear."

I took one step forward and I was once again standing at the edge of the platform. I took a deep breath and Mig grabbed hold of my hand and yelled, "Jump."

We jumped off the cliff together and when I landed in the water, he released my hand. It felt like such an adrenaline rush with the water being so cold.

"How do you feel, Sammy?"

"Really, good."

"Sammy, do you want to swim over to the cave now?"

I looked over at the cliff and saw my brother standing off to the side. He was talking to some girl. I thought to myself, I can't believe I did this for Tommy, and he didn't even bother to watch me jump.

"Mig, that would be awesome."

There were two openings to the cave, and it was all made out of coral rock. I had never been inside a cave before, so I didn't really know what to expect. I noticed immediately the water in the cave was much colder and I suddenly had goosebumps everywhere.

The cave was awesome with a couple of archways. One of the paths has a beautiful waterfall on the side of the wall. The sound of the waterfall was echoing throughout the cave; helping me to feel calm and relaxed. The cave was becoming darker the further we swam down the path. Which I thought was a bit mysterious and scary.

I swam all the way around the cave until I came up to the waterfall again toward the entrance. That's when I placed my head under the waterfall and it felt wonderful. I remained under the waterfall until I noticed someone was staring at me. It turned out to be Mig and I instantly felt relieved. He was leaning against the wall of the cave in front of me.

I was about to swim past him and out of the cave, but Mig caught my hand, and he pulled me over to him. I was now face to face with Mig. He was staring into my eyes and said, "I think you're a fan of the cave, Sammy."

I leaned my head back and replied, "It's nice." I leaned my head back even further until I could feel the waterfall pouring down over my head. Mig was still holding my hand, and truthfully, I didn't mind at the moment. I was a little bit fearful of being in the cave alone.

After a couple of minutes of having my head under the waterfall, Mig pulled me back over to him. I was again standing face to face in front of Mig. I felt him release my hand and he wrapped his arms around me. He looked into my eyes and told me, "I want to kiss you, Sammy. How do you feel about that? Do you want me to kiss me?"

I just stood there staring back at Mig, hoping the feeling would pass. I was kind of feeling it too. It was the cave and I was angry with Julio. Everything was affecting me. Then out of nowhere I realized I was courageous today and challenged my fear. "What's that look about Sammy?"

"Mig, it's silly but I'm sort of proud of myself."

"Nothings silly, tell me about it."

"Well, I've never jumped off a diving board before. I have always been too afraid, so jumping off that cliff was a big moment for me."

"That's a big deal. How did you overcome your fear Sammy?"

"You ran up to me, held my hand, and said jump. I had this adrenaline rush and jumped or maybe it was revenge."

Mig laughed, and then saw the look on my face and said, "Whoa, are you serious?"

"Yes," I was beaming with a huge smile. "The cave is like a bonus because it's also new to me.

"Do you like the cave, Sammy?"

"I'm enjoying how peaceful it is in here and I love the waterfall." Mig moved closer to me and I was leaning against the wall. I swallowed once and he leaned in even closer to me. "You don't want to kiss me Mig, not today. It will only be a revenge kiss and will never mean anything more to me than that."

Mig looked astonished for a moment with his mouth gapping open and his back pressed up against the wall of the cave. He swallowed once before saying, "I can tell you're hurt, Sammy. I think right now you just need a friend. I'm a great listener, if you want to talk about it."

"You know something, Mig? I really appreciate your ability to be so understanding. However, I think we should just leave here now."

"Yeah, I think you're right Sammy." He planted a kiss on my cheek and swam out of the cave. Once he was gone, I touched my cheek and thought that could have gone incredibly wrong. I decided to wait inside the cave another minute. I laid my head back under the waterfall.

Daphne and Tonya swam into the cave less than a minute later. Tonya asked me what I was doing in here all alone. I told her I was in here with Mig. Daphne's eyes grew wide after hearing that and she began to ask me if anything happened. I told her of course not and that Mig just left the cave to go find everyone. Then I noticed Rick and Greg swim into the cave through the other entrance. "Girls, I need to go look for Tommy. They both nodded there heads okay with a stunned expression still on their face. "Nothing happened, so can you girls stop looking at me like that?" I swam out of the cave feeling completely annoyed now.

When I found Tommy, he was on the beach talking to some girl. I didn't want to intrude, so I just walked over to my towel and laid it out on the sand and sat down. I saw when Greg and Daphne came out of the cave. Greg was holding Daphne's hand as she was floating in front of him on her back. A few minutes later, Rick swam out of the cave with Tonya on his back.

That's when Mig joined me on the beach and asked, "Do you want to tell me about this whole revenge thing or is it to personal?"

I replied, "It's personal."

"Got it."

"Yeah, right."

"Look, I don't know what happened while you were gone, Sammy. I do remember us having a great time hanging out at my house before you left for California."

"Mig, I remember that too."

"Well, I would still like us to be friends."

My eyes had become watery and my nose was starting to run. He put his arm around me, and I placed my head on his shoulder and I broke down and began to cry. I just couldn't hold it inside anymore. Mig was stroking my hair back and trying to calm me down. "What's wrong Sammy?" I couldn't speak. I just shook my head no and looked down at the sand.

It was just all too much for me. I missed Julio; we had such a great time. Now it was over. The trip, everything was over. I read the letter and now I know truth. I'm so broken up and confused; I just don't really know what to do. My mind keeps telling me, it's over now, move on. He's polluted. My heart keeps saying, "No, don't give up."

Sitting here watching how happy Daphne and Tonya are right now. I couldn't help but think that was me just a couple of days ago. Happy, laughing and smiling. Now I am completely miserable, and I miss being happy and the feeling of being in love.

Mig held me in his arms and rocked me back and forth. He even asked me if I wanted to go back to the cave. That caught my attention and I pulled my head away giving him a dirty look. Mig laughed and said, "I only mentioned the cave because you seemed so happy and relaxed in there."

"Okay, let's go back in the cave, but no flirting, Mig."

"Sammy, I can't be held responsible for what you do. I am irresistible, and you have a hard time controlling yourself whenever your around me. So, before we go in that cave, I am going to ask you to please control yourself and no flirting."

He got me to smile and I told him, "Mig, I will try my very best to control myself."

"And, what else, Sammy?"

"And, I won't flirt with you."

"Well, okay, then. Let's get back in the pool and swim over to that cave."

"Don't take it personally, I just don't want people to think that the finest girl at the pool has a thing for me. It's not good for my reputation."

I started to laugh and told him, "You're silly, Mig."

"Okay, there it is, and you are finally smiling again, Sammy. Now let's go to the cave before they turn off the waterfall."

"Do they actually turn it off, Mig?"

"I hope not, Sammy. Let's go find out."

Mig, and I, went back inside the pool, and we swam over to the cave. Once we were inside, I took hold of Mig's hand and I placed my head back under the waterfall. This time Mig joined me and he placed his head under the waterfall too.

We swam to the back of the cave and leaned against the corners of the walls. We stayed in there talking. I thanked Mig for literally lending me his shoulder to cry on. I also told him how I was scared to be in the cave alone and that's why I wanted to hold his hand. When I saw a frown appear on his face; I admitted that I was not in a relationship anymore. Mig smiled and admitted that he was not really sorry to hear that.

We climbed out of the pool and Daphne ran up to us. "You two need to hurry up. We're all ready to go now."

Daphne, Tonya, and I walked over to our locker and we grabbed out all of our clothes. We took a second in the bathroom to change out of our wet bathing suits and put on dry clothes. We met up with the boys at the exit.

Tonya hugged me, then Daphne. She told us, "I'll come by and see you girls later. I'm leaving with Rick now. Oh, and Muñeca, Tommy is coming with us.

Rick wants to introduce your brother to some girl." That's when I shrugged my shoulders and waved bye to Tommy. The three of them hopped into Rick's Z28 and he peeled out with the tires squealing as he drove away.

Mig shook his head and I heard Greg say idiot under his breath.

Mig asked, "Who's up for pizza?" We all raised our hands as we walked over to his van.

When the side door was unlocked, Greg slid it open and climbed in the back behind Daphne. "Sammy, maybe you should ride in the passenger's seat beside me?" Greg and Daphne were already snuggled up together on the back seat.

"Yeah, I think you're right." Mig smiled and slid the side door shut. He opened the passenger door for me. I climbed inside and reached over the steering wheel to unlock the door for him. When I sat down, he was still holding the passenger door open.

"Thank you for unlocking the door for me. I have never had a date unlock the door for me."

"You're welcome Mig, and we're not on a date."

"Not yet," he replied with a smile and shut the passenger's door.

After Mig was finally seated behind the steering wheel. He turned to me and said, "Oh and don't worry, Sammy, it's not romantic up here. We're sitting in these captain's chairs. Or at least not as romantic as the back seat. "Then he pointed to Greg and Daphne, who were in the back kissing.

"Now what would you like to eat, Sammy?"

"Pizza is fine, Mig. Actually, it's perfect."

"Great, I also have a new release from the video store. I can pick up a pie, and we can go back to my place and watch a movie." Before I could give him an answer, he announced were here. There was no response from the backseat. "Do you want to come inside with me Sammy?"

I looked in the backseat and saw Daphne and Greg still all lovey-dovey. They didn't look like they were coming up for air anytime soon. "Sure, I can go with you." He smiled and we climbed out of the van to head inside the pizza place.

He ordered what I call the garbage pizza, because it has everything. Plus, a pepperoni pizza, for Daphne and me. Mig and I took a seat on a love seat sofa by the door. While we waited for our pizza. "How are you feeling now, Sammy?"

"I'm feeling a little bit better, but my mind is just running full speed ahead. I've been through so many emotion in the past week. The last 48 hours have been the roughest. I'm so sorry for falling apart at the pool earlier. Thank you for staying with me Mig."

"Sammy, I was happy to be there for you."

Our food was finally ready, the hostess came over and handed us each a box of pizza. We left and walked back to the van. When we climbed inside, Daphne asked, "Where have you two been?"

"Daphne, look," and I held up the pizza box.

"Oh, I didn't even realize we were stopped. I just noticed you guys weren't here when the door opened, and you climbed back in."

"Yeah, well you and Greg have been busy."

"Hey guys, I've got an idea. Let's go back to Mig's house and eat. Then we can hang out and play Monopoly."

"Seriously, Greg, I had that same idea as —" I looked over at Mig and placed my index finger to my lips. Mig stopped speaking midsentence.

While smiling at Mig I said, "That sounds like a great idea, Greg. Would you like to watch a movie instead?"

"Yes, Sammy, that sounds even better. Let's go." Mig was smiling and shaking his head as he backed out of the parking space.

We arrived at Mig's house and his parents were outside. Mig turned around in his seat to face me. "I've got a question for you."

"What is it?"

"Are you up for meeting my parents, Sammy?"

"Sure."

That's when I stood up and walked over to Greg and Daphne in the back seat. I handed them each a pizza box. They both looked confused until I explained that I just needed them to hold on to the pies for me while I'm outside meeting Mig's parents."

As I was about to walk back to the front of the van, I heard the side door slide open and for some reason my heart went to racing. Mig popped his head inside and he offered me his hand. I took hold of it and he helped me down from the van.

I walked with him over to his parents. They were both standing beside another car in the driveway. Mig said, "This is Samantha." His mom greeted me with a kiss on the cheek and a beautiful smile. She smelled amazing.

His dad said, "Hello, Samantha," and he shook my hand and smiled at Mig.

"Guys, it's been great, but I just picked up some pizza, so we're going to eat and watch a movie." His parents had a very concerned look on their face once he said that; until Greg slid open the van door and he climbed out with Daphne.

He waved to his uncle and aunt while he walked over to the gate on the side of the house. All I can say is I saw happy smiles, fear, then finally relief on his parents' face all in less than ten seconds.

Mig's dad said, "Don't let us keep you. Go and eat before my nephew eats everything."

"Tell your cousin I have not forgiven him yet for eating the flan. That was for everyone to have after dinner last night. Not for him to snack on. I wouldn't be so mad if he had saved me a little piece."

I couldn't help it. I started laughing. Mig's mom just shook her head and told me, "Greg is a walking garbage disposal."

"Yes, he is, and that's why we need to get going Mom."

Mig's father looked back at us and asked, "Does Greg have the pizza?" We both nodded our heads yes. "Oh, no, you better get that pizza away from Greg before there is nothing left." We all started to laugh, and his father told us, "I'm serious."

"Mig took my hand and we walked through the gate on the side of the house.

Once the gate was shut, I grabbed my hand back and asked, "Mig what was that all about?"

"Greg stayed over my house last night when he got off work. He was hungry and instead of waiting for dinner he ate the dessert my mom made."

"Oh, sorry to hear that Mig, but I'm talking about you holding my hand."

"I didn't even realize I was holding your hand Sammy until you pulled it away. I didn't think nothing of it since we already held hands in the cave.

"Mig, you know why I held your hand in the cave."

"Well, maybe, you used the cave as an excuse to hold my hand." Mig was smiling and his dimple appeared on his cheek. "Sammy, feel free to hold my hand anytime you want."

Look Mig, I'm in a really bad place right now. If you want to be friends, I'm cool with that. However, if you are expecting something more than that. I have to tell you now; I'm not your girl. Believe me; I'm not anyone's girl right now." A tear slid down my cheek and Mig grabbed the hem of his T-shirt and wiped it away.

"I'm really sorry, Sammy. I can be just friends with you. I don't know what's going on in your life at the moment. Obviously, it's a lot. I won't flirt with you anymore, seriously. Just remember if you need to talk, I'm here for you, okay?"

I sniffed back the tears, and I was sucking on my lower lip. Finally, I answered, "Maybe one day we can talk about it, but not today. I'm to caught up in all of these emotions and it's making me crazy."

"It doesn't have to be today. One day is good enough for me, Sammy."

Mig opened the door and we walked inside. Daphne and Greg were in the kitchen sitting at the bistro table eating. I followed Mig into the kitchen area. Mig, looked over at Greg before he opened the pizza box. "Dude, is there any more pizza left?"

Greg looked up at Mig and then pointed to the counter where another box of pizza was sitting. I walked over to the counter and stood in front of the second box of pizza. I knew without opening the lid it was the pepperoni pizza. When Mig opened the box, sure enough, pepperoni pizza.

"Do you mind if I have a slice of your pizza?"

"Mig, you paid for both pizzas, which means I should be asking you if I can have a slice of your pizza."

"I bought it for you, Sammy."

"In that case, would you like to share a pizza with me, Mig?"

"Yes, I would like that very much. Mig reached up into the cabinet above the sink and handed me a paper plate. "I have the good stuff, nothing but the finest china for our first lunch together."

"Here." I handed Mig his plate with two slices of pizza. We ate standing up at the kitchen counter.

When everyone was finished eating, we headed into the living room and watched a movie. We decided not to watch the new release. It was a drama and I had enough of that at the moment. We decide to watch a comedy and it was so funny, I laughed from beginning to end. All I can say is I don't think wearing a bra on your head is a good look for anybody.

When the movie was over, I thanked Mig for having me over, and I let him know that I needed to get back home now.

He suddenly had a frown on his face, as he grabbed his keys off the coffee table. Daphne and Greg stood up, and thanked Mig for the pizza and the movie. Then we all headed outside to the van. Mig drove me home first, and I said bye to everyone before I walked upstairs. When I reached my door, I looked down at Mig. He was still downstairs inside the van with the window down. I opened my door and walked inside. When I turned around to shut the door behind me, I saw Mig, backing out of the parking space.

I just shut the door, and my mom called out, "Sammy, Julio called you. He asked me to tell you to call his beeper. When you arrive home."

I shook my head and said out loud to myself, "Call his beeper? I don't think that's a good idea at the moment."

"Thank you, Mom." I walked into my bedroom and sat down in my bean bag chair beside the window. I saw Mig's van drive away down the boulevard. My mom knocked on my bedroom door before she walked inside.

She took a seat down on the edge of my bed, "Is everything alright between you and Julio?" I shook my head no and could feel my eyes watering up.

"Do you want to talk about it, Sam?"

"No, Mom. I will be okay. I just have to get back into my routine and remember Julio is no longer a part of my routine."

"Sam, he called you today. He sounded very disappointed that he wasn't able to speak to you. His voice dropped a whole octave when I told him you were out with your friends."

"Mom, don't worry about it. Julio goes out with Lewis all the time on double dates and everything. He will find someone else to speak to other than me. He found someone else only a month after he left Miami."

"Does this mean you're not dating Julio anymore?"

"No, were not together anymore. I have my memories and Julio has his. I live in Miami and he lives in Anaheim now. How can I date somebody that lives so far away?"

That's when I felt a tear betray me as it slid down my cheek. "I don't know Sam, but love can overcome many things including distance. You are starting high school in a couple of weeks. I think that will be enough for you to deal with at the moment."

"Thanks, Mom. I appreciate you coming in here to talk to me." I stood up and hugged her.

She wrapped her arms around me and squeezed me. "I love you, Sam. I even love Julio, but I want what's best for my girl."

"Can I ask you a question Mom?"

"Of course, what is it?"

"Have you spoken to Guillermo since you've been back?"

My mom sat back down on the edge of my bed. She took in a deep breath and let it out; then she looked up at me and shook her head no. "Mom, we had the most amazing trip and those memories will remain even after we're old and gray."

She laughed and replied, "I hope we're not old and gray for a very long time, Sam."

"Well, Mom, when we do get old and gray, there's always Carmen's Salon and Michael is a makeup wizard." That made my mom laugh again, and it felt good to hear my mom just laugh. I was so worried that my mom would find it hard to laugh after heartache. It turns out I was wrong. I think she is going to be fine.

"Hey, Sam, do you want to order a pizza and watch a movie?"

"Mom, I just did that earlier with Daphne. What I really would like to do is play backgammon." My mom had the biggest smile on her face once I said backgammon.

"Really, Sam?" I nodded my head yes. My mom stood up and said, "Give me two seconds and I will be right back."

She came back to my bedroom door within seconds. My mom was carrying a little designer style briefcase, and I followed her into the living room. "Do you mind if we sit on the floor?" I shook my head no, and we sat down on the floor. She placed her briefcase on the coffee table. When she opened the case, it was the coolest backgammon board I had ever seen yet. The board was black leather with silver glitter and gold glitter strips. The cups were wrapped in black leather and you had your choice of gold or silver dice.

"Mom, when did you get this board?"

"Guillermo bought it for me after we went to the park. We sat in this little Italian restaurant and had dinner and talked for hours. During one of our conversations, he asked me if I knew how to play chess. I told him no, but I love to play backgammon."

"The next day was the wedding, and that evening we all had our own hotel room. When I walked in my room, there it was in a big red box with a big gold bow on top, just sitting on my bed. Along with a card that read, "Would you teach me how to play, Lori?" It had his room number just below his signature."

"I called Guillermo's room, and he met up with me downstairs in the lobby bar. We sat at one of the round booths at the bar away from everyone. It was fantastic. We played even after the bar was closed. We sipped on hot chocolate and I taught him how to play backgammon. It really was a lot of fun. He is a great man and I'm glad to have met him. Even if it was only for five days, he made every day so enjoyable.

Now that we have the board set up, it's time to play, Sam."

"Wait, Mom, you forgot to tell me one thing."

"What's that, Sam?"

"Who beat who?"

"Sam, I have to tell you Guillermo was a quick learner and he beat me after a couple of games, but I won a couple of games too." My mom had a huge smile on her face as she spoke about Guillermo.

Tommy walked in through the back door in the kitchen two hours later. He saw Mom and me in the living room playing backgammon. He waved at us and he grabbed Daisy's leash.

When Daisy heard her leash jingle, she came running down the hall from my mom's room. Tommy yelled out, "Hey, I will be back in a few minutes. I just need to take Daisy out for a walk."

My mom replied, "Okay," and she waited until the door was shut to ask me the question that had been on her mind for a couple of days now.

"So, why is Tommy taking Daisy out for her walks and he carried your suitcase when we left the airport? What dirt do you have on him this time, little sister?"

"It's all over Tracy. When I saw her in Anaheim, Tommy told me he would walk Daisy until he left for school and carry my suitcase, if I didn't tell you he brought her."

"I already know he brought her, so why is he still walking Daisy?"

I shook my head and the dice in my cup at the same time, and answered, "I don't know, Mom."

She turned and looked back at the kitchen door as Tommy walked inside. When the kitchen door was shut and the leash was off Daisy, my mom asked Tommy to join us in the living room.

Tommy walked into the living room and he spotted the board. "Nice backgammon board, pretty girly."

"Would you like to play the next game, Tommy?"

"Sure, Mom. Who's been winning so far?"

"That would be Mom. She has already beaten me three out of five games. I have to warn you, Tommy. All of her moves are very calculated."

"Why is that, Sam?"

"Mom has been playing against a chess player."

My mom just looked over at me and she sucked in her lower lip and smiled. Then, with her next move, she beat me again. I stood up and told her, "Great game, Mom."

My brother sat down in my spot and he picked up the cup of dice. "You can go first, Tommy."

"Thanks mom."

He took his turn and my mom began to shake her cup of dice. She was looking at Tommy when she finally asked, "Why are you walking Daisy?" Tommy didn't say anything and just looked over at me.

Finally, he looked down at the board and answered, "I can't tell you that, Mom. I would betray Sam and hurt her at the same time." I shook my head confused by his answer.

Then I asked Tommy, trying not to laugh, "What are you talking about?"

He gave me a look, like oh crap, with apologetic eyes. That's when I realized he wasn't kidding and I told him, "Spill it."

Tommy turned his eyes down toward the floor and replied, "I just didn't want to be the one to tell you."

"Tell me what Tommy? You haven't told me anything."

"Sam, because it was like on day two in Anaheim."

"What happened on day two?"

Tommy stood up and turned his back on me. He was facing my mom and said, "Lewis called me over to him, and I followed him out to the garage. Lewis asked me if I wanted to go out on a double date with his girlfriend's cousin, Megan. I said, 'no way, dude. I'm totally not interested.' I turned and left the garage. Lewis followed me back inside the house. He told me, 'Come on man; you would be doing me a huge favor. I can't see my girl unless her cousin comes along with us.' Then he told me something about her being a lot of fun."

"What kind of fun, Tommy?" My mom asked with a harsh tone to her voice . I took in a deep breath and hoped it wasn't going to be too upsetting.

That's when Tommy faced me, and swallowed once before answering, "Lewis told me Megan was a lot of fun because Julio slept with her on their first date. I was shocked and I asked if Julio was currently dating this girl. Lewis said, 'No, definitely not while Sammy's in town.'"

"So, what does that mean? When I'm not in town anymore, he will just go back to dating this Megan girl?"

I closed my eyes when tears started to form. My mind went back to the whole conversation Julio and I had where he told me, 'he would drop everything to spend mere seconds with me' and it was on day two. I didn't want my mom to ever know about this. Now I couldn't care less.

What's really bothering me is that my own brother knew Julio had sex with some girl and he didn't bother to tell me. Plus, he lied to me when I asked him if he knew anything about this. I sniffed back the tears as I stood in front of Tommy. "Did you ever plan on telling me about this?"

Tommy looked up at me with remorseful eyes. He swallowed once and said, "I thought Lewis was exaggerating and trying to change my mind. Sam, I didn't believe Lewis. I thought he was full of crap, until I confronted Julio myself."

"You did?"

"Yes, I had to Sam. It was eating me up inside."

"What did he say, Tommy?"

"Sam, all he said was that it was a mistake, and it shouldn't have happened."

"Why didn't you tell me about this?"

"Julio asked me not to tell you."

"And you just agreed not to tell me?"

"Yes, because we both agreed it would be better if it came from him."

"Tommy, he told me in the form of a letter."

"Sam, we didn't discuss the way he was going to tell you. He only promised to tell you and if he didn't, I would have. No matter what, you were going to know the truth. I preferred it came from Julio.

"Even Monica was really mad about it, and she wanted to tell you herself."

"So, what? Everyone in his family knows what he did with this other girl?"

"Apparently, Sam."

I turned my head away from Tommy and that's when I noticed my mom was crying. She had her head down and tears streaming down her face. I walked over to my mom and hugged her. Tommy stood up and grabbed some napkins from the dining room table. He handed them to my mom, and she wiped her eyes.

She shook her head and said, "I'm so sorry, honey. I can only imagine what you must be feeling right now."

"Truthfully, Mom, I feel betrayed. Even though we were not together, and I don't know if I have the right to feel this way. He loved me so much, that when it was over, he slept with the first girl he went out on a date with. How is that love?"

"Sam, what your feeling is completely normal, and you have every right to feel that way."

"Mom, we hadn't even come close to that. Now he's gone all the way. Why should he wait around for me? I'm not ready to go all the way. That hasn't even crossed my mind. That is something I wanted to do when I get married. I feel like now; he will expect more than I'm willing to offer him. The fact that I live over two thousand miles away changed our situation and makes me realize that he obviously didn't wait for me, and with us so far apart, why should I wait for him?"

"Sam, I agree with you."

"I think now, more than ever before, Tommy was right, Mom. I just need to take the memories, enjoy them, but I can't expect more. It will only lead to disappointment and a broken heart."

"I'm here for you, Sam, and I am very proud of you. You're right for thinking and feeling the way you do."

My mom hugged me and Tommy. "I'm so proud of the both of you."

"Well, I think I'm going to go to bed now."

"Good night Sam." I waved to them both as I walked down the hall to my room.

Tommy came into my room hours later. I was in a deep sleep and he shook me awake. When I opened my eyes, he said, "Phone, Sam. It's Julio again."

I dragged myself out of bed. When I reached the kitchen, I looked at the stove to see what time it was, the clock read two o'clock.

I picked up the phone in the kitchen. Tommy hung up the phone in his room when I said hello.

"Hi, Samantha. I'm sorry that Tommy had to wake you up."

"Why are you calling my house so late, Julio?"

"Actually, I didn't call your house. My sister was on the phone with your brother when I walked in the door. I asked her if it was Tommy she was speaking to. When she said yes, I asked if I could speak to your brother. Monica handed me the phone and I asked your brother if I could speak to you."

"So, you're just coming home now?"

"Yes, it's only eleven o'clock here. I called you earlier and spoke with your mom. She told me you went out with Daphne and Tonya."

"Yes, I did, but I was back home by six."

"I spoke to Greg and he told me he picked you up with his cousin, Mig."

"Julio, they picked up Daphne and Tonya too."

"Oh, so it wasn't just the four of you hanging out at the pool in Coral Gables?"

"No, and Tonya invited this guy, Rick, to meet us at the pool. Why does that even matter to you?"

"Everything you do matters to me."

"I'm not dating Mig if that's what your so worried about."

"Samantha, just for a moment I want you to hear me out."

"Speak, no one's stopping you."

"I'm upset Samantha."

"Why are you upset?"

"I'm feeling a bit betrayed."

"Betrayed," I giggled after repeating those words back to Julio.

"Is that funny to Samantha?"

"Yes, because that's exactly how I felt after reading your letter Julio? Are you even entitled to feel that way anymore? Am I?"

"Maybe not but let me ask you a question."

"Go ahead."

"If Daphne's hanging out with Greg and Tonya's with some guy. That leaves me to wonder, who were you left to hang out with?"

"Is that your question?"

"Yes."

"I hung out with my brother, and Mig."

"Greg didn't mention Tommy was there."

"Yeah, my brother went with us. We had a lot of fun. I jumped off a cliff, and I got the chance to go inside an actual cave. It was cool and speaking of cool, the water was freezing."

"Yeah, I remember. I have been there a few times. Did you like it?"

"Yes, I did."

"What did you do after the pool?"

"We picked up some pizza and went back to Mig's house."

"Did everybody go back to Mig's house? I mean, it's a small place."

"Julio, were not together anymore, so stop worrying about what I do. I intend to live my life and it no longer includes you."

"Fine, lets change the subject Samantha."

"Great, you mentioned that you just got home yourself. Where were you?"

Julio was quiet for a moment before he mumbled, "I was out with Eddie and Lewis."

"Oh yeah, was Amy, Heather, and Megan with you?" He remained silent again.

"It's alright Julio, I already know the answer to that question."

"I was only doing a favor for my cousin. Lewis can't see his girlfriend, unless her cousin goes as a chaperone."

"That's nice, Julio. I hope you had a good time tonight. Truthfully it doesn't matter to me what you do or who you're with. It's none of my business."

"Samantha, nothing happened it was a mistake that only happened once."

"Julio, I don't care so there is no need for you to explain anything to me."

"I think your just saying that and you really do care Samantha."

"Fine, so let me get this straight Julio. You are a great Samaritan, who sacrificed his evening to be Megan's date tonight. Amy was out of the house free and clear, with the help of Heather and Megan as her chaperones. Her dad is none the wiser, and you did a good deed for your cousin Lewis. Did I get that right?"

"No, you didn't because Heather refused to go to Amy's house. She was still mad at her cousin since the argument at the restaurant. You remember the argument they had on your last day here."

"Julio, your story has a lot of holes. If Eddie and Heather agreed to go out with Amy, then why would she refuse to be her chaperone? I want you to know what I think is really happening here. I think that Megan is actually your girlfriend and while I was up there in Anaheim you blew her off for a week to spend those five days with me."

"No, absolutely not Samantha. She is not my girlfriend and I regret what happened."

"Yeah, whatever Julio. If you're holding onto that much regret how could you agree to go out with her again tonight?"

"I told you already Samantha, I did it for Lewis."

"That's such a horrible excuse, you couldn't come up with something better?"

"Samantha, I don't have to come up with anything because I'm telling you the truth."

"The truth is your wasting my time Julio. It really doesn't matter if something or nothing happened tonight. You already had sex with Megan. I'm glad you told me the truth, but I'm not into you anymore. Have a great night and don't ever call me again."

I heard him say, 'wait, Samantha,' but I just hung up the phone and went back to bed.

The next few days I spent the mornings with Tommy and Tonya. I even went jogging with Tonya twice. The first day that I went for a jog was sort of rough. My frustration was pumping my adrenaline and I jogged one mile past my house. Then the exhaustion kicked in and I walked one mile back. I woke up the following day stiff and stayed in bed until Tonya came back from jogging with Daisy. On the third day we went jogging again. Afterwards, we had breakfast and went back to school shopping with Abuela, and my mom.

It was difficult to find a parking space at the mall. There were clothes thrown around everywhere inside the department stores. My mom made me try on every outfit she saw. Waiting in line to use the dressing room was lots of fun.

The only part that I looked forward to was having lunch. We were finally having lunch at my mom's favorite restaurant. Tonya headed for the salad bar and that's when Abuela spoke to my mom about Tonya. She noticed some bruises on her arms recently and she was worried about her. Tonya arrived back at the table and Abuela quickly changed the subject. She talked about Tonya's new summer fling Rick. Abuela does not like him or trust him, and she told Tonya to stop seeing him. That quickly escalated into an argument between Tonya and Abuela. Which ended when Abuela stood up from the table and walked outside. We quickly followed her out and my mom drove us all home.

Rick was already in the parking lot standing next to his IROC Z28. When we dropped Tonya and Abuela off in front of their building. An hour later Tommy walked in through the backdoor with Daisy.

"How was your walk with Daisy?"

"It was fine. I saw Tonya leave with that jerk, Rick."

"What?" I got up off the couch and followed Tommy into his room. "Hey, why did you call him a jerk?"

Tommy was frowning and shaking his head. I sat down on the edge of his bed while he was bent over taking off his shoe. "He's a total scumbag and he beats on Tonya. He belittles her and flirts with other girls in front of her, like she's not even there."

"What do you mean he beats on her?" I bent down and untied Tommy's other shoelace that he was having trouble with.

"Thanks."

"Your welcome, now what do you mean he beats on her?"

"That guy Rick beats on Tonya. I saw it with my own eyes, Sam. Tonya yelled at Rick for flirting with another girl at the table beside us. Rick just raised his hand and slapped Tonya across the face. He told her to keep her mouth shut. I jumped up and got in his face. I told him don't ever touch her again. Tonya told me to stay out of it. That's when I called Alex, he came and picked me up from the Grove. Which reminds me, I need to call Monica."

Daphne, Arturo, and Michael came over an hour later. We wanted to go to the Grove, and we invited Tommy. He declined and said he had enough of the Grove after being there last night with Tonya and her sidekick, Rick.

When we arrived within five blocks of the Grove, it was already congested. Everybody was cruising with their music blaring. Michael was clearly unhappy that we had reached the Grove with the top up. He kept saying things like, "We need to be seen. We're in the Grove with the convertible top up and you call this cruising?" Arturo put the top down and Michael was all smiles for the next five blocks. He waved to all the girls, who flirted and waved to him and Arturo. All of the cute guys were pointed out to me and then rated on a one-ten scale by both Arturo and Michael.

Finally, we pulled into a parking garage, and there was plenty of parking. Michael said, "We only found parking because it's still early. In another hour you can forget about the garage. It will be packed and people will be lucky to find parking in the street."

We walked over to my favorite burger place. Placed our order and went straight to the game room. A couple of minutes later Daphne's beeper went off and she blurted out, "They're here."

I looked over at Michael and Arturo, and asked, "Who's here?"

Arturo smiled and said, "You know."

"Please tell me she didn't invite Mig tonight."

"Sammy, honey, after the phone call you had with Julio last night and that letter, we all told her to call Mig."

I frowned and told him, "Thanks! Michael."

"Come on, Sammy. He likes you and you know there was some sort of connection. I saw it and you felt it. I know you did." Arturo was smiling and he sounded so excited that I couldn't remain mad at him or anyone.

"Okay, thank you. I appreciate your concern. I really do, guys. I just wish you would have told me he was coming."

"Why? If we did that, you wouldn't have come out with us and you need to get out of the house and have some sort of fun."

I knew Arturo was right and I nodded my head yes in agreement.

"It's Friday night, time to party." Michael was saying this as he was dancing around me in a circle and shaking his hips. He had me laughing and that's when Daphne came back to the game room with Greg.

Michael stopped dancing and he stood perfectly still. "Hello Greg, how was work today?" Arturo and I tried not to laugh. Michael went from party boy, get your groove on in less than a minute, to a proper distinguished gentleman in the next.

"Oh, it was good. Lots of movies to watch and R&R."

"That's sounds fantastic. Everyone needs a little R&R," Michael replied with a wink.

"Michael, R&R means rewind and restocking shelves."

"Sorry, I didn't realize that Daphne."

"Oh Greg, you worked the shelves today. You must be tired, and your feet must be hurting," .

"Nope, they're just fine Daphne. That's a typical day at the video store."

"That's cool," Arturo said with his I'm-totally-not-interested voice. Then he asked, "Where is your cousin?"

"I'm right here. Mig walked in behind us and we turned around to face him. "I just put in our order while Daphne and Greg joined you in the game room."

"Well, we're going to find a table. Why don't you guys just hang out in here? We'll meet up with you in a few minutes at the pick-up counter."

"That sounds good Arturo."

Michael smiled at Mig and said, "Nice to finally meet you." He put out his hand and Arturo started shoving Michael past Mig out the doorway. Michael kept on talking and told Mig, "We can talk again later." He waved bye to Mig with Arturo behind him. Two seconds later, Arturo leaned his head into the game room. He tugged on the back of Daphne's shirt. When she finally noticed, she turned around and left with Arturo. Greg followed her out.

Mig turned his head back to me and he was smiling. "Sammy, you look beautiful tonight. Did you get all dressed up for me?"

"Mig, I didn't even know you would be joining us tonight."

"Then you must always look beautiful, and I thought tonight it was just for me."

"Do those lines of yours really work, Mig?"

"I don't know what you're referring to, Samantha. I'm just constantly saying what I think. Right now, I think you look great in that dress."

"Since you're so honest with me, then I want to tell you that I have enjoyed hanging out with you. I mean, after all, you let me cry on your shoulder."

He walked up to me and looked me in the eyes and asked, "Can we be friends now, Sammy?"

I stared back at him and answered, "Yes, we can be friends."

I noticed him looking at my lips and then back into my eyes. He leaned in towards me and I tensed up. He kissed me on the cheek and slowly pulled away as he said, "Friends, I really like that." Then he leaned back the rest of the way and smiled at me.

Our names were called over the intercom. "Time to go."

Mig backed away from the entrance and replied, "After you."

I walked past him and Mig followed me over to the pick-up counter. My tray was sitting up there alone. Then one more tray was tossed up onto the counter. It was a burger topped with mushrooms and onions. Mig smiled and grabbed the tray. He headed over to the veggie station with me and then the cheese station. When we didn't see anyone in the main dining room.

We both looked over at one another and said, "They're outside." We walked through the doors and saw them all seated at the very same table we sat at last time.

As we walked over to the table, I could feel the nervous knots beginning to build up in my belly from the memory of our last time here. Now, I was about to sit directly in front of Mig. It instantly brought back this intense curiosity; I was feeling sort of drawn to him again. We placed our trays down on the table and I grabbed my cup. "I'm going back inside to get a drink. Does anyone want anything?"

"Yes, I would like two shots of tequila."

"Michael, is there anything else that I can get for you? That does not require me to be the minimum age of 21?"

"Well, now that you said all that, I guess not Sammy." Michael put his cup back down on the table with a fake frown on his face.

Mig followed me inside to the drink station. "Sammy, I noticed you will be sitting in front of me at the table this time."

"Yes, I will be."

"Are you okay with that?"

"Yes, why did you ask me that?"

Mig turned his eyes away from me and answered, "I don't know."

"Yes, you do, and I want you to tell me."

"Alright, I was just remembering the first time we were here and...

"And what?"

"And I was starting to feel a bit nervous." He let out a nervous laugh and told me, "Forget what I said it's stupid."

"No, it's not and I really appreciate the honesty and...

"And what Sammy?"

"I sort of felt the same way."

Once our cups were filled, we headed back outside to our table. It wasn't until after I sat down that I realized how things were changed around. We were on the far-left end of the table. It was a table for two, pushed up against the table for four or at least it was when we left our trays on the table. Now it has been pushed away from the other table. Arturo and Michael were looking over at me smiling. I was aggravated by the change and wanted to say something.

That was until Mig sat down in his chair in front of me. He was smiling and said, "Now I have something beautiful to look at while I enjoy my meal."

"Mig, give me the chance to get to know you for real. I appreciate all of your flattering comments; however, it's now become a bit excessive and no longer sounds genuine. It's just making me feel very uncomfortable. So, can you, like, stop? You have been extremely nice to me. I know that you like me, and you don't have to constantly compliment me. Just be yourself."

"I'm sorry, Sammy, I don't ever wish to make you feel uncomfortable around me. I'm just so into you. I have wanted this chance to get to know you since the first time I saw you."

"Oh really, when was that?"

"Back when I still played soccer. I saw you outside walking your dog. Greg was beside me and I pointed to you and asked, 'Who's that?' Julio popped up behind us, and blurted out, 'That's my neighbor, Sammy.'"

"So, what happened? Why didn't you speak to me?"

"Well, I think that I was lacking confidence at the time. A few months later, my cousin, told me you were dating Julio."

"Why did you quit playing soccer?"

"Between work and band practice, I just wanted a day to kick back and relax at home with my family. Plus, Sunday is usually the day that all my family gets together."

"That sounds nice, Mig, it must be nice to have such a close family."

"It is, and my parents are really cool. Greg's dad, my uncle, is a great guy too. That's why I do make time to spend with my family. Even if it's just attending Sunday dinners."

"Sammy, enough about me. How are you doing?"

"I'm doing okay."

"Feel free to ask me anything or tell me anything and I promise to keep it to myself. As you must already know firsthand, I am a great listener."

"That sounds perfect, Mig. Right now, I just want to get to know you, the real you." I leaned in closer to him across the table and looked up into his eyes, "I find you attractive to and very interesting." He smiled as I leaned back in my chair. "I also have to admit, my interest doesn't last long after hearing all of those excessive compliments; I don't get it, Mig. What changed since the first time we hung out at your place?"

"The truth is, when you left Sammy for California, I thought you would get back with Julio. I felt like I lost my chance again, on getting to know you."

"What do you mean by again?"

"I was disappointed for not approaching you the first time I saw you. When I found out you were dating Julio a few months later, I thought that could have been me, if only I would have found the courage to approach you months earlier when I first saw you.

"Greg knows how I feel about you and he's not happy about it."

"Why do you think that is?"

"Actually, I know why. When you started going out with Greg's best friend. He was constantly worried about me trying to steal you away from Julio."

"Wow, I can't believe Greg thought you were capable of that Mig."

"He knows me very well Sammy."

"Yeah, but I guess Greg doesn't really know me. When Julio lived in Miami things were completely different and nobody could have stolen me away from him. Not even you."

"How do you know that for sure when I never even tried?"

"Julio had my heart and I was totally in love with him."

"And now?"

"He shattered my heart into a thousand pieces and I'm no longer speaking to him."

"Sammy, I didn't even know that." Mig had a serious look on his face.

"You didn't know what?"

"That you fell in love with Julio and he broke your heart. I could tell by the look in your eyes that you meant it."

"Enough about Julio. How is Greg feeling about us becoming friends?"

"Well, this time when we met up again, a couple of weeks ago, I no longer had to hide my feelings for you. Greg was still unhappy about it. You know, the idea of his cousin talking to his best friend's ex." A nervous giggle escaped me, and I covered my mouth with the palm of my hand. I sat up and Mig leaned in closer and whispered, "My cousin can't stop the inevitable, can he?"

He sat back in his chair and continued to say, "I mean the truth is, you're attracted to me and I'm obviously attracted to you, Sammy."

Michael gasped and I looked across the tables over at him; he was pretending not to have heard a word Mig just said. Arturo is not an actor, and he was smiling trying not to look at me. Daphne and Greg were seated far enough away that they didn't hear our conversation.

I turned my attention back to Mig and thought to myself: oh, Boy! He has no problem with his confidence now. As I paid closer attention to Mig, I noticed he has light brown eyes. When he smiles, a dimple appears in his left cheek. He has long brown hair that goes right past his shoulders. He's wearing acid wash blue jeans, a white T-shirt, and a tan and blue print cotton vest. He's a rocker and I'm not into rockers, but again, this guy is smart, motivated, and has a compassionate side.

"You're suddenly quiet Sammy. Is everything okay?"

"Yes, I'm just enjoying my burger."

"Really, because it looks as though you haven't touched it."

I looked down at my plate and noticed I only took one bite of my burger. I smiled and replied, "I like to eat the fries first, while they're still hot." I picked up my burger and took a bite.

Greg walked up to our side of the table. "Hey man, I don't want to rush you, but we need to go soon." Then he walked back over to his side of the table and sat back down.

"You have to go now?"

Mig frowned before answering, "Yes, I do. We're playing tonight and we need time to set up everything."

"That's cool, where are you playing?"

He placed his arm on the table and leaned over toward me. "We're playing at the Bonfire. I invited you to go on Monday, but you shot me down and told me you couldn't go anywhere. Or maybe it was just anywhere with me. Have things changed? Obviously you have been out with me twice since Monday. Should I invite you again, to come out with us to the Bonfire?"

"A lot of things have changed since Monday." He smiled and his dimple appeared on his cheek. I couldn't help smiling back at him when I saw it; he was so cute.

"Does that mean you don't have a boyfriend, or a long distant thing happening in another state?"

"No, I don't have a boyfriend and I don't do the long distant thing."

That's when Mig's smile became broader. "Maybe I should invite you to the bonfire again."

I shrugged my shoulders before saying, "Maybe you should."

Mig was smiling so much that his eyes were gleaming. "Sammy, would you like to go with me to the bonfire? There's plenty of room for you and Daphne in the van."

"Mig, I would love to go to the bonfire, and watch you play. I don't know about the ride in your van. If we go, I want Michael and Arturo to drive us there." That's when I looked over at Michael and Arturo. They were both smiling at me.

Arturo told us, "Hold on, we should speak to my sister first."

"Hey Daphne," she didn't respond, and Arturo called her name a couple of times. Eventually, he just sat back in his chair with his arms crossed over his chest. That's when Michael started waving his hands back and forth in the air, yelling 'Daphne' until she finally responded to him.

She was in the middle of a conversation with Greg and she finally stopped talking long enough to ask, "What is it, Michael?"

"Go ahead, Arturo. I have her attention now." Michael sat back in his chair with his arms crossed over his chest.

"Daphne, I just wanted to know if you would like to go to the bonfire tonight?"

"Of course, I would like to go Arturo, but I can't because I'm staying at Sammy's house."

Michael shook his head and tried not to laugh before saying, "Maybe you should ask her, Sammy."

I stood up and called out to Daphne. When she turned and faced me, I asked, "Will you go to the bonfire with me tonight?"

Daphne stopped talking to Greg midsentence. She just stood there smiling at me with a look of disbelief on her face. When she didn't say anything, Greg asked her, "Baby, what do you say?"

She jumped up out of her seat, and started chanting, "Yes, yes, yes, I want to go." She ran over to me and gave me a hug. "I can't believe it. We're actually going to the bonfire, finally."

Greg stood up from the table and turned to Arturo, "We need to get going now. Do you guys want to ride in the van or follow us over there?"

Arturo looked over at Michael before answering, "Actually, we're going to follow you."

"Great, let's get going then." Greg took Daphne's hand and he opened the door that leads back into the main dining room. We all followed Greg into the restaurant. We walked to the exit, down the stairs, and out to the parking lot.

Mig's van was parked in the second parking space. Arturo turned around and said, "Why don't you girls ride in the van with Mig and Greg; since I'm parked in the garage and his van is right here?"

"Wait, Arturo. I thought you needed to follow us to the bonfire."

"No, don't worry about it, Greg. I know how to get there."

"Arturo, can we drive you over to the garage?"

"No, we don't need a ride. We need to get some exercise. Especially after eating that burger but thank you for offering, Greg."

"No problem, we can take the girls and meet up with you at the bonfire."

"That sounds good," Arturo replied, as he waved bye to all of us. Michael was pouting as he hugged Daphne and then me.

Chapter 11 The Bonfire

When we walked up to the van, Mig opened the passenger's door. He climbed inside and slid open the side door. Greg held Daphne's hand and helped her inside. Mig jumped back out and took my hand as he led me over to the passenger's door. "You can be the DJ for us, Sammy." I climbed in and unlocked the door for Mig.

We were stopped at a red light and I noticed Alvaro walking by. He was hanging out with two friends. As they crossed the street in front of us, I waved to Alvaro. He came up to the window and asked, "Where are you off to Mig?"

"We're headed to the bonfire down south," he answered.

"Oh yeah, I think that's where we're going too. Can we catch a ride with you?"

Mig looked over at me, and asked, "Do you mind if they ride with us?"

"No, of course not."

Greg opened the side door and told them to get in. Alvaro climbed inside along with his two friends. Once they were inside, the light turned green, and we moved two whole inches right past the light. Alvaro told Mig to make a right on the next block, and he would show him a side street to take without traffic.

We took the side street and Alvaro guided Mig until we reached Miller. Before I knew it, we were way down south in the middle of nowhere. Mig turned onto a dirt road which made for a super bumpy ride. We pulled into this open area and the first thing I noticed was the lake. Lots of people were gathered together on the right side of the lake. Mig pointed to them and told us they are making a fire pit before it gets dark.

"Why do they build a fire pit?"

"Daphne, after the sun goes down it becomes extremely dark out here. The bonfire keeps the light on for us and keeps the bugs away."

"That's cool, thanks Mig."

Greg added, "That's all true but the main reason is to prevent people from accidentally walking into the lake. That's why the pit is always set up beside the lake and no one hangs out by the lake after dark."

"Now that's smart and makes total sense."

"Yeah, I think so to Sammy."

Mig pulled into a spot and Alvaro slid open the side door. He waved bye to everyone and hopped out of the van with his two friends.

Mig and Greg opened the two back doors of the van and started unloading. They had two throw rugs, Mig's drums, a couple of amps and a generator that made the van smell like gasoline.

Once they were all set up, they placed the generator back in the van along with one of the throw rugs. They carried a cooler out from the back of the van, slid the side door open and placed the cooler inside there.

Then Mig told us, "That's for easy access if you girls get thirsty. There's plenty of drinks in the cooler."

Greg replied, "The girls don't drink soda. We should have picked something up on the way here."

Mig frowned and told me, "I'm sorry. I should have asked you before we got here. Sammy, do you drink coffee?" I shook my head no, "I didn't think so."

"Why, what's in the cooler Mig?"

"Sodas and some other stuff that belongs to Vince."

"What's the other stuff?"

"Wine coolers."

"Mig, why do you have wine coolers?"

"They belong to Vince."

"Come on let's go for a walk."

We walked up to Daphne and Greg and they joined us. We followed Mig and Greg around the bonfire. There were so many people here and it was starting to get dark outside. More and more cars were pulling into the bonfire. There were already three rows of cars parked out here. Each row had about 15 cars and we spotted Alvaro on the first row. He was hanging out with two girls behind a truck with a loud system playing 2 Live Crew. We waved to him as we walked by and Alvaro asked, "Do you guys want something to drink?"

"No, we're good." Greg answered, "But thanks, man."

"Sammy, we have your favorite apple juice." Daphne and I both turned around and ran back over to Alvaro. He handed us each an apple juice.

"Thank you, Alvaro."

"No, thank you Sammy. Now we have room for some real drinks."

One of the girls came around the truck and she wrapped her arms possessively around Alvaro. I could tell by the look on her face that she didn't like us talking to him. I waved bye to Alvaro, and we ran back over to Mig and Greg.

Alvaro, yelled out, "Hey, I'll be by to watch you guys play later."

Greg yelled back, "Sounds good, dude. We're just waiting on Vinnie."

We walked down to the next row of cars and saw another truck. It had a couple of guys and two girls sitting down in the back.

One of the guys started playing "Home Sweet Home" on an acoustic guitar. While everyone was singing along with him. Greg and Mig walked up to the truck and joined in on the singing.

Everyone kept singing, especially this one guy who eventually stood up to hit the high note of the song. He sounded like Vince Neil. When he finished singing, Greg said, "Hey girls, this is Vincent. We call him Vinnie, but he likes it when the girls call him Vince.

Greg and Mig went to laughing and he leaned over the side of the truck. "Hi girls, I'm the lead singer in our band." He extended his hand out to us and we introduced ourselves to Vinnie. This guy over here playing on the acoustic is our part-time bass player, Carlos.

Carlos stood up and shook my hand and then Daphne's. "It's nice to finally meet you, Daphne. Vinnie says I'm part time because I work full time and go to school." Greg told them everything was all set beside the van.

"Is the cooler inside the van? I'm expecting some girls from school."

"Yes, it's in the van. Just stick with the soda before we play Vinnie."

"Yeah, I'll be there in about an hour Greg."

"Okay, catch you later guys." We waved bye as we headed down the next row of cars.

"Mig, why is Vinnie giving girls wine coolers? Do you do that too?"

"No, I don't do that. Vinnie's in College and he's also 21."

"Sorry, Vinnie doesn't look 21 so I…

"Had the wrong idea."

"Exactly."

I turned my head away from Mig and spotted Tonya. She was standing by herself behind Ricks Camaro. I noticed Rick was busy talking to a few guys in front of his car. I walked up behind Tonya and covered her eyes. She started to laugh and said, "I have no idea who this could be." I removed my hands and she yelled, "Muñeca" as she hugged me; then she noticed Daphne was beside me and she hugged her too.

"What are you guys doing here?"

Daphne pointed to Greg and told her, "We're here to see him play tonight."

"That sounds great, lets go." As we walked past Rick, Tonya waved and told him she'll be back. Rick gave her a nasty look, but he didn't say anything. He was busy talking to his friends.

The five of us walked back to the van. The fire pit beside the lake was burning bright and really lit up the area. Greg looked over at the fire pit and said, "Now it's a bonfire."

Vinnie and Carlos walked up to the van with two girls. Carlos introduced the girls to us. The first one was named Lupe; she was around our age. The next girl was older around 18 and her name was Dayana. She was engaged to Carlos. The five of us girls hung out on a throw rug that we sat on beside the van. The boys brought out the generator and another throw rug for the amps to rest on.

Tonya suddenly stood up saying, "Well, I better get going. It was nice to meet you Lupe and Dayana."

"Where are you going Tonya?"

"Daphne, I need to check on Rick.

"Can't you wait to do that? I mean Greg and his band are about to play now."

"I'll be back in a little bit to watch them play."

"You promise?"

"I promise Daphne." She hugged Daphne and smiled at me shaking her head before she left. The boys conducted a test of the mics and the amps. A crowd started to form around them. That's when they began to play 'Still of the Night.'

I was so impressed and I felt an adrenaline rush from the sound of the guitars and the sticks hitting those drums. It was exciting and I couldn't believe how much I enjoyed it. We all stood up on the rug and started moving to the music. I couldn't keep still. I started moving my head and my hips back and forth to the music. I loved it so much and I don't even listen to rock music.

Vinnie was singing, he had a deep scratchy voice at times and at other times he just had a deep masculine tone of voice. It all depended on the song he was singing. He really has a great vocal range. Vinnie has long blond hair and big blue eyes. It seemed like he had every girl out here screaming his name. He totally looked the part of a rock star. Wearing blue jeans with tears in them, a white vest, and no shirt underneath. He would move around the area as if he were on stage and performing in front of a huge crowd. He was not shy. Just full of confidence.

Girls were going crazy for Vinnie, like he was an actual rock star. They were all trying to hug him, squeeze him and feel on his chest. Vinnie was all smiles. He appeared to enjoy every minute of it. When they began to play the beat to "Don't You Forget About Me' by Simple Minds. It was like everyone at the bonfire came running over. It became really exciting to watch such a large crowd of people sing along with the band.

Vinnie hit every note perfectly and he turned the mic out to the crowd; the crowd would yell out the lyrics to parts of the song. They went on to play three more songs. When they finished everyone was chanting, "One more song!"

Vinnie said, "Alright, but this will be our last song for the night." Mig kicked off the beat to the next song and everyone's face lit up. Mig had a huge smile when Greg came in with the guitar. Vinnie started to sing, and the crowd went crazy. There were girls dancing everywhere and the majority of the guys were just watching the girls and singing along to 'Girls, Girls, Girls' by Motely Crue.

When the song was over a girl pulled up in a Nissan 300zx. She put down the window and called out to Vinnie. He handed the mic over to Greg and climbed into the passenger seat. He waved bye to everyone as they drove away.

Greg and Carlos climbed inside the van and grabbed a soda from the ice chest. Mig grabbed a thermos from the front seat. He poured the contents of the thermos into a green cup and took a large sip. I walked up to Mig as he was standing beside the driver's door. He leaned inside the van, and I asked, "What's that you're drinking?"

He pulled his head back, saw it was me and smiled. "This?" He raised his little green cup above his head. I nodded my head yes and walked up closer to him. He tried to hand me the cup, but I wouldn't take it. "Sammy, it has no alcohol." He took the secured lid off his thermos and poured a little bit more into the green cup. "Try it if you want or pour it out." I took the cup and smiled as I raised the cup to my lips. Then I heard Tonya scream at the top of her lungs! I threw the cup down and went running.

I yelled Daphne and she came running toward me. "It's Tonya! I just heard her scream. We have to go find her. Something's wrong." I ran through the row of cars frantic to find her. Daphne was beside me. Then I heard her scream again and I ran even faster. I spotted Alvaro and yelled out, "Help me find Tonya. She's in trouble." Alvaro and his friends came running up the aisle beside us looking for Tonya.

Then I heard Greg holler from behind us. "That's his car right there," and he pointed to the IROC Z28 parked halfway up the row. We ran over to the car. Tonya and Rick were inside the Camaro. Rick had his hands around Tonya's throat. He was choking her, and she was red in the face. I tried pulling on the handle of the passenger's door, but it was locked. Greg was pulling on the driver's handle. The same thing, locked. We all banged on the windows and windshield while shouting at him to stop.

Alvaro yelled, "Move," and he smashed the driver's side window open with a crowbar. Rick let go of Tonya's neck instantly. Alvaro reached his arm inside the car and opened the door. Rick was belligerent and tried to reach for Tonya again; Alvaro's friends yanked the door open wider and pulled Rick out of the car. I heard Alvaro yell, "Move again and I will smash your head in with this crowbar."

While Alvaro and his friends were dealing with the super intoxicated Rick.

Mig pressed the door locks button and unlocked the passenger door. I yanked the door open and Greg reached in and grabbed Tonya. She was coughing bad with her neck and face red. Greg yelled, "We should take her to the hospital." Greg walked off at a fast pace carrying Tonya and we had to run to catch up to him.

"Greg, hand her to me, and go get the van." Greg stopped walking long enough to hand Tonya over to Alvaro and he took off running with Daphne.

Greg pulled up and Mig slid open the side door on the van. He climbed inside and Alvaro handed Tonya over to Mig. The rest of us climbed inside afterward.

Mig set Tonya down on Alvaro's lap and climbed into the driver's seat. As we were pulling away Alvaro's friends ran up to the van and beat on the side door. He stopped the van. The door slid open and the two of them climbed inside. One of them locked the door and asked, "How is she?"

Greg told him, "Grab a seat man. We're headed to the hospital now to get her checked out."

Alvaro just held Tonya, and kept saying, "You're going to be fine. "I was sitting on the same bench seat with Alvaro and Tonya was holding my hand. She looked scared and now the handprints had turned into bruises all over her neck. Her face was still red but not as dark as it was before. I had to hold in the tears I felt burning my eyes. Tonya was looking at me and she tried to speak, but her throat was sore. Alvaro said, "Shhh, don't try to speak." She looked at him with tears in her eyes.

When we arrived at the hospital, we had to take her to the ER. She was taken to a room where a nurse told us she needed to contact her parents. I gave her the phone number to Abuela. We were also told that only two people at a time will be allowed in the room with Tonya. Alvaro made her feel safe. That left Daphne and I to take turns in the room.

When I walked out to the waiting area. Mig, Greg, and Alvaro's two friends appeared to be bored and exhausted. Mig let me know that it was after midnight. He knew that my curfew was eleven o'clock. He reached over and handed me a quarter for the payphone. When I didn't take the quarter he asked, "Why aren't you calling your mom?"

"I'm just wondering how much I should tell her. It's super late past my curfew. I have to tell my mom something. Or else she will freak out."

"Just tell her the truth but don't get too detailed."

That's when Daphne came back out to the waiting room. "It's your turn Sammy."

I walked back into Tonya's room. Alvaro was now sitting down in a chair beside Tonya's bed. Tonya was holding onto his hand and they were just staring at one another.

A few minutes later Tonya's grandparents walked into the room. When they saw Tonya, they immediately ran over to her and hugged her. Abuelo shook hands with Alvaro and Abuela hugged him.

The nurse came back in the room and told Alvaro and me we had to leave now. I hugged Tonya one more time. Alvaro released Tonya's hand; she sat up and wrapped her arms around him. Tonya started to cry, and she refused to let him go. I told the nurse, "He may have saved her life tonight. She's scared and he makes her feel safe."

She looked over at Alvaro and Tonya, then back at me. "Okay, he can stay for now."

That's when I tried my best to smile and said, "Thank you." Before I walked out the door, I looked back at Tonya one more time and she still had her arms tightly wrapped around Alvaro. She had a look of sheer panic on her face. Alvaro held a look of contentment as he stood there in Tonya's arms. I waved bye to everyone and left the room.

Walking back into the waiting area, I noticed everyone was asleep. Mig was the only one still awake sitting up in a chair watching TV. I noticed Mig had his green thermos beside him on the table. Smiling, I walked up to Mig and took a seat beside him. I reached over and grabbed the thermos from the table. I took off the little green cup and handed Mig the rest of the thermos and said, "Now, where were we?" Mig sat up and smiled at me as he removed the top from his thermos and poured the content of it into the cup I was holding.

Finally, I took a sip and said, "Mystery solved, it's American coffee."

He smiled and replied, "I'm guessing we should wake the others and get going,"

"What's my second option?"

"Well, we can curl up in these chairs beside one another and watch some TV or we could get really crazy and just talk to one another Sammy."

"Mig, I think I will go with option three."

We talked about the bonfire and I told him how I felt like I was at an actual concert. 'He said that's what they were trying to do. That the whole reason they play at the bonfire is to get used to playing in front of a live crowd. Their goal is to get paid for playing at local hot spots in the Grove.'

At some point we both fell asleep. We were woken up by Abuela. It had to be at least two hours later. They were waiting on the X-rays and if everything was good, then Tonya would most likely go home. She hugged me and told me to go home and get some sleep. Then it dawned on me, I never called my mom. I hugged Abuela and told her I was going home now.

Mig dropped us girls off first to my place. It was so late that we tiptoed through the kitchen over to my bedroom. As we opened my bedroom door it made a loud squeak, I just pushed the door open quickly. We both ran inside, and I quickly shut the door.

The next morning, I woke up to the smell of waffles. I walked into the kitchen and poured myself a glass of apple juice.

"Mom is going to be surprised to see you home."

"Tommy, how much trouble am I in?"

"None yet. I told her you were sleeping over at Daphne's house or maybe it was Tonya's? I can't remember which house I said, but one of them."

"It was after midnight, so she couldn't call either house to check on you."

"Why did you cover for me?"

"Well, I kept calling your beeper and you left it in Arturo's car. He passed by to drop it off and told me you went to the bonfire."

"Yeah, I did."

"It's easy to lose track of time out there." He tossed my beeper up on the counter.

"Thanks, I owe you big time." I grabbed my beeper off the counter and turned to jump down from the stool.

"Oh, and Sam." I turned back around and faced Tommy dreading whatever he was about to ask for in return.

"What is it?"

"Julio called a bunch of times last night."

"Tommy, what did you tell him?"

"Sam, I told him you were out with your friends and he didn't believe me."

"How do you know that he didn't believe you?"

"Julio called here for like three straight hours."

"Tommy, that's because I told him not to call me anymore. I guess he thinks you're blocking his calls for me."

"When Julio called the last time, Guillermo answered the phone. He hasn't called back since."

"Wait, Guillermo answered the phone?"

"Yes."

"Guillermo's here in Miami?"

"Yeah, Guillermo came knocking on the door shortly after you left last night. He surprised Mom and took her out to dinner. She arrived home after midnight and asked if you were home yet."

"That's when I 'Your big brother' covered for you, Sam."

"Tommy, I think I should tell you what happened last night."

"Sam, I think you should tell me too, but first let me grab this waffle." He brought two plates over to the counter each one loaded with a waffle and a sausage link on top.

"Are any of your friends here?"

"Yes, Daphne."

Tommy snorted with laughter and waved his hands back and forth. "Sorry, it's just that I knew it was her. We all know Tonya can't stay up past ten o'clock."

I took in a deep breath and jumped down from the stool. "Let me go get Daphne."

When I walked into my room, Daphne was just waking up. I told her to join us in the kitchen for breakfast and that we have apple juice.

Daphne followed me into the kitchen and poured herself a glass of apple juice. She joined us at the kitchen counter, and I shared my waffle with her.

"We have to tell Tommy what happened last night." Tommy was distraught after learning what happened to Tonya. He told Daphne about what happened the night he went out with Rick and Tonya.

Daphne snickered and said, "Well if the cops want to find Rick, they should check the bonfire. There's a good chance he's still out there stranded."

"How do you know that?"

Alvaro's friends took Rick's car keys out of the ignition. They didn't want him to be able to follow us, so they threw them in the lake at the hospital."

We all laughed when we heard that part. I told Daphne, "I didn't even know they did that."

"Yeah, one of Alvaro's friends pulled out a set of keys from his pocket. He held them up and asked, 'Who wants to go for a walk and checkout the lake?' We all said 'It's nighttime! You can't really see anything.' Then he shook the keys and told us, 'These keys belong to that prick guy. I took them out of the ignition of his car.' I'm not kidding, we all stood up at the same time and the five of us walked over to the lake. We all yelled 'Prick' at the same time, and he threw the keys into the lake."

Tommy and I started to howl with laughter. "I can't explain it guys, but we all felt good after that. It was like we just needed that release of aggression. It was such a simple thing and we all felt better afterward. When we walked back inside the waiting room, we went to asleep."

"Do you know how Tonya is doing now?"

"No, Tommy. We really don't know anything but I'm sure she must be resting up after being at the hospital until who knows what time."

"Okay, just call me Sam to let me know how she's doing?"

"Why? Where are you going, Tommy?"

"Daphne, I'm going back to school today. Summer break is over for me."

"How does the tray look? It's the last bonging waffle for my Mom."

"It looks perfect. Oh, wait a minute." Daphne jumped off the stool and ran into the kitchen. She poured a cup of coffee into a mug and a glass of apple juice. She set them down on the tray and said, "Now, it's perfect." Tommy smiled and thanked Daphne. He picked up the tray and headed for my mom's room.

We jumped down from the counter and walked into the kitchen. Daphne helped me clean up the kitchen from breakfast. I told Daphne she needed to take a shower first. I let her know that we would need to be ready to leave here in a little bit, so we could go with my mom to take Tommy to the airport.

She was already dressed, and her hair was braided by the time I came out of the shower. She wanted to braid my hair as soon as I walked back into my room. She was also talking as fast as she was braiding. "Look Sammy, I don't think it's a good idea for you to tell your mom what happened last night." I turned my head to the left and gave Daphne a bewildered look. Daphne tied the elastic to the end of my braid before she sat down beside me to explain.

"Okay, here's the thing Sam. I know your mom becomes depressed every time Tommy goes back to school. I'm not saying you shouldn't tell her. What I'm trying to say is maybe you should wait and until tomorrow or something."

"You're right Daphne, I should wait a couple of days."

There was a knock on the front door. Daisy started barking and whimpering like crazy. I wasn't able to open the door fast enough for her. I knew it had to be Tonya if Daisy was acting like that. I took in a deep breath and braced my emotions ready to see Tonya.

When I opened the door, it was Eddie and Guillermo. I couldn't believe how happy I was to see them. Eddie started laughing and asked, "What happened to you, Sammy? You look like you saw a ghost." They both went to laughing and I hugged them.

Daphne, "Come out here." She walked out into the living room and took off running to Eddie and gave him a hug, then Guillermo. Tommy came out and high-fived Eddie, and he asked Guillermo if he was ready for today. Guillermo gave him a thumbs up and followed Tommy over to the counter. They were talking about some plans Guillermo has for my mom.

All I heard was, 'Good! my mom will love that.' Then Tommy walked up the hall and Guillermo sat down on the couch beside Eddie. Daisy sat down in front of Guillermo and placed her two front paws up on his lap. He reached over to pet her, and she gave him kisses on the palm of his hand. Daisy stood up and backed away slowly from the sofa.

Guillermo told her to stay and she stopped. He told her to sit, lie down, and roll over. She followed every command he gave her. Then she sat down in front of him again. He reached into his pocket and pulled out a ziplock bag. I watched as he opened the bag and grabbed a toothpick out with a beef chunk on the end of it. My mouth must have dropped open. Guillermo looked over at me and said, "I know not too many beef chunks. My nephew and my sister already told me the most I can give her are three a day." He gave Daisy the beef chunk and told her that it was from Julio.

I was stunned. "Please thank Julio and Pilar for me when you see them."

"You know, I got up early this morning to cook these for her."

"Oh Daisy, you are spoiled. I heard Guillermo doesn't like mornings."

"Who told you that, Sammy?"

"Julio, of course, when we saw you dancing on your balcony one morning to Peter Gabriel."

"Oh yes, that is my favorite song. I can't stop thinking of your mother every time I hear that song."

"How often do you listen to that song Guillermo?"

"Truthfully, I have the CD to listen to in my house and the cassette I listen to everywhere. I listen to it whenever I miss your mom."

"Which is all the time," Eddie added.

"What's the name of the song?"

"In Your Eyes," Eddie, Guillermo and I said at the same time.

Eddie told Daphne, "He plays that song constantly. I think he has a big crush on Sammy's mom."

Guillermo replied, "I have to admit just a little bit." He had a twinkle in his eyes along with a huge smile on his face when he said that. Guillermo stood up and that's when I saw my mom walking down the hall.

She had that big and bright familiar smile back on her face. "Good morning, Eddie and Guillermo. I wasn't expecting to see you so early."

"Lori, I want to enjoy every moment I have with you. Your son invited me to go with you to take him to the airport today. I hope that's alright."

My mom smiled and looked over at Tommy. "Isn't that great, Mom? He agreed to ride with us. I thought we could all hang out for a few minutes, before I have to go."

"Tommy, what do you want to do? We have to be at the airport in less than two hours."

"Yes, I know, Mom. Can we just sit down at the table together and look at some pictures from our trip to Anaheim?"

"Guillermo, do you have the pictures already?"

"Yes, Lori, I have some of the pictures. You know the ones we took with the disposable cameras? Would you like to take a look at the pictures now? I mean, do we have enough time before we have to drop Tommy off?"

My mom had the biggest smile on her face. "Yes, we do. Let's all have a seat at the table and have a look at these pictures." Daphne and I looked at one another with a shocked expression. We never thought we would have the chance to see these photos.

Eddie came to the table with a box and took out two albums. We saw the photos that were taken at the luncheon. It was on the first day we arrived in Anaheim. We all met up with one another in the banquet room at the hotel. I can still remember how nervous I was to see Julio again.

There was even a photo of Julio and me which was taken the first time we hugged one another outside of the banquet room. I can still remember that look in his eyes. I loved and hated this photo all at the same time. I just kept thinking, Alex really captured a moment and a feeling I won't ever have again.

There were some beautiful pictures of my mom. In every photo she was smiling. I didn't know my mom could ever be that happy. The next several pages were photos taken on our second day at the pool. That's also the day Greg arrived. My favorite picture was of Greg carrying Daphne back into the house. Someone was able to capture the surprised look on my mom and Carmen's face. Daphne was all smiles in all of the photos from that day forward.

We viewed photos taken from the formal dinner. My favorite photo from that evening was a photo taken of Pilar and Chris puckered up, eyes closed about to kiss. When I turned to the next page in the album, the very next photo blew me away. My mom took the words right out of mouth. "Now that's a fantastic picture."

It was a picture taken at the park. We were all on the lake in our separate pedal boats. We were all captured in a kiss at the same time. Julio and I were right smack in the middle of the lake, lips locked in a pop kiss. I looked up at my mom and Guillermo, and I felt a little bit embarrassed.

"I turned to Tommy and asked, "Did Monica take that picture."

"Yes, that's what we saw when we drove into the park. I have to tell her I saw the photo when I speak to her tonight."

My mom was smiling at Tommy. "That's a really great picture. Monica really captured a moment. Maybe she should go into photography. I know Pilar must love this photo."

"Lori, you're right. My sister loves this photograph. I wish you could have been there when Julio and Lewis first saw the picture on the coffee table."

"Julio spotted the picture first and he picked it up. He looked at the photograph and asked his mom, 'What is this?' She smiled and told him, 'Young love.' He looked at the photo again and Lewis was looking at the photo over his shoulder. They both turned red and Monica started teasing them."

"Sadly, the picture has not returned to the coffee table. I had to find the negative to have copies made of this photo."

"Yes, and Tia Pilar said that she's going to make coffee cups and dinner plates with that picture. It's going to be on everything in the house."

"Eddie, she wouldn't do that! Would she?"

"No, but it was funny to see that type of fear in your eyes Sammy. Eddie high-fived Tommy and they went to laughing."

The next photo showed Lewis and Julio popping open the trunk on the limo. They looked surprised to see all of their soccer gear in the trunk. There were more of these really great moments captured of Eddie and Lewis with their father. My favorite photo was of Mr. Sanchez walking into the gazebo for the first time. The photo captured the moment Lewis and Eddie first saw their father.

The second album held all of the photos from when we went horseback riding. There were photos of my mom and Guillermo when they rode off on the horse together. These pictures were so romantic. I looked up at my mom and Guillermo, and they had their eyes locked on one another.

Daphne turned the page on the album. The rest of the photos were of when we were following the tour guide down the trail. There was one photo that caught my attention. It was of me sitting on top of my horse, Blaze. I was very focused on where we were going. Julio was right behind me on his horse; his eyes were on me and he was smiling. I felt like I needed to see that picture. It made me think that maybe he was into me and the distance was the real problem for him to.

All I know for sure is that he really made me happy until I arrived at the airport. He left me just standing there all confused until I read that awful letter. Then I started to think about how his smile always made my heart sing and now it's broken. That magical feeling is all gone now, and I need to move on with my life.

The last picture in the album was of my mom and Guillermo. They were holding one another at the airport. You could see me in the corner turned sideways. I was waiting for my mom and looking the other way. That picture took me back to that moment. I remember feeling so happy until he handed me that letter.

"Julio has a copy of this picture in his room, Sammy. He said that's how he saw you for the last time before you walked inside the airport."

Between that picture and what Eddie said, its kind of all hit me like a ton of bricks. "Sammy are you alright? I smiled at Eddie and nodded my head yes and stood up."

Daphne told him, "She's fine. She'll be right back Eddie."

That's when I ran into the bathroom and threw water on my face. I blew my nose and looked at myself in the mirror. Standing there looking at my reflection I decided to give myself a lecture. 'You can't shed another tear or waste one more moment. What's done is done, and it's over, so now it's time to get it together.' When I came back out to the living room, the photo albums were nowhere in sight. Michael and Arturo were here now sitting down in the living room. They were on the sofa sitting opposite of Guillermo and Eddie.

Arturo stood up for a hug, and I reached over and gave him hug. I bent over and hugged Michael before sitting down beside him. "What happened to the two of you last night?"

"Sammy, to make a long story short, we went to the Spot on Miami beach."

"Michael, isn't that a club?"

"No. Well sort of, I guess."

"Sammy, it's actually a restaurant and it has a dance floor."

"Thank you, Arturo. Now can you explain why you stood us up last night?"

Michael released a long-exaggerated sigh. Arturo looked over at Michael and shook his head. "Yes, I owe you an explanation Sammy. To tell you the truth, we didn't ever intend to go to the bonfire with you. We just said that so you would go with Mig."

"Wow, thank you Arturo."

"Sammy, did you have fun?"

I looked over at Eddie and Guillermo and answered, "Oh yeah, tons Michael. We can talk about it later."

Tommy called me over. He was standing in the hallway. I quickly stood up and followed him into his room. He shut the door behind me. "I called Carmen. She sent Arturo and Michael over here to pick up Daphne."

"Why would you do that?"

"Just listen. After you drop me off at the airport, Guillermo is taking the four of you out to this really amazing place for an early dinner."

"What place?"

"That's a surprise, but you and mom are going to love it. Just make sure you dress nice, and make sure mom does the same."

"Okay, Tommy, but why are you doing all of this?"

"Do you really have to ask me that? I'm doing it for mom. This is her second chance to fall in love and find true happiness. I mean isn't that what you told me Sam?"

"Yes, it is Tommy."

"I see what you see Sam. Guillermo is the one that makes mom happy. You're right, we've never seen mom this happy before and I'm going back to school. Before you know it, you will be leaving for college and mom will be alone."

"Tell me one thing. Did you know that Guillermo was coming here to see mom?"

"Yes, of course. Monica and I planned this together a few days ago."

"Monica is in on this too?"

"Listen, she was tired of seeing her uncle Guillermo unable to sleep, eat, or do anything since mom left Anaheim. That guy has been completely miserable without mom. He's in love with her and she's in love with him."

"Really? Then why hasn't he called mom since she left?"

"Guillermo was waiting by the phone for mom to call him. You have to remember; he hasn't ever been in a serious relationship before. I'm telling you, Sam, this guy is really into mom. Forget the phone call. He showed up here in person on the fifth day."

I couldn't help it, I laughed as I thought of how cute this all was. Tommy and Monica are playing matchmakers. I hugged Tommy and told him, "In that case, I better go get mom ready. Wish me luck."

"Good luck! Remember, it's a surprise, so don't tell mom that you're going out to dinner after dropping me off."

"Okay, I got it." I left Tommy in his room and walked into my mom's room.

When I saw what my mom was wearing, I asked her if that was what she intended to wear to the airport. At first, she just looked at me with a confused expression on her face. She was wearing jeans and a T-shirt. "Guillermo's here, and I just thought you would wear something nice, like a casual dress, or just something more memorable that he hasn't seen on you before."

"Sam, do you think I should? I don't want to look over dressed when I drop Tommy off at the airport."

"Yes, I definitely think you should." I walked inside her closet and came out with a white cotton dress. It had navy blue piping, a tailored collar, and short sleeves. It was definitely perfect for a dinner date and not too casual.

"Mom, what do you think of this dress?" I held up the dress as I walked out of her closet. She told me it was perfect and to pick out a pair of shoes. I picked out her white, open toed sandals with a 2-inch heel. I left my mom in her room to get dressed.

I headed back into my room. Daphne was in there on the phone. Then I noticed she was holding a phone to her ear that I hadn't seen before. "Where did that phone come from?"

"Sammy, I don't know, but it's plugged into your wall. So, I guess it's your phone."

"Yeah, that's makes" I walked back into my mom's room.

"Mom."

"Yes, Sam."

"Where did the mauve colored phone in my room come from?"

My mom was smiling at me. "Do you like it? Tommy and I picked it out for you yesterday when we went out to dinner with Guillermo, and Eddie."

"You didn't go out to dinner alone with Guillermo?"

"No, but after dinner we went over to Carmen's house. We had drinks and dessert with Carmen and Enrique."

"Enrique is here too?"

My mom smiled and nodded her head yes. "Sam, he really likes Carmen and I think she really likes Enrique too. She's just afraid to let her guard down."

"Well, thank you for the phone, Mom. I really needed one."

"You should be thanking your brother, Sam. I didn't even know you needed a new phone until Tommy mentioned it."

"I will thank him right now, Mom. I appreciate you both for thinking of me."

My mom was facing the mirror smiling as she applied her makeup. "You're welcome, honey. We know you love that color pink."

"Mom, its not pink. It's called mauve because it's a combination of purple and pink. My mom rolled her eyes and said, "Whatever," mimicking me and I laughed.

"Either way your right mom. Mauve is my favorite color and I love my new phone." I left my mom's room and walked back into my room.

Daphne was sitting beside the window in the bean bag. "Daphne, help me. I need to pick out a sensible outfit for an early dinner tonight."

"Wait, what are you talking about, Sammy?" I told Daphne about the surprise dinner for my mom. Daphne was laughing and said, "Who knew Tommy was actually Cupid?"

I walked into my closet and picked out my favorite skirt. Daphne matched it with a white, stretchy lace top, and my favorite baby pink tank top to wear underneath. I shut the closet door and began to get dressed inside. When I was finished, I grabbed my white net sandals off the floor and left the closet.

"You look great, Sammy. I just need to fix your bangs and apply a little makeup, then you will be ready to go." Daphne already braided my hair earlier, so she styled my bangs, applied some mascara and lip gloss to my face and I was ready. We both went into my mom's room to help her get ready. She was already dressed, and her makeup was perfect. Her hair was already up in a twist with curls hanging down the back. We knew that Michael styled my mom's hair; that was his signature hairstyle.

When we walked back out to the living room, Michael, Arturo, and Daphne waved bye to the five of us and left. Guillermo was smiling at my mom and told her, "Lori, you look beautiful." My mom started to blush and thanked him. That's when Tommy stood up and announced it was time to go.

Eddie smiled and asked Tommy, "Did you remember to pack Tracy?"

"Oh yeah, she was the first thing I packed." We all laughed, and Tommy had this ridiculous smile on his face.

"In that case, we're ready to go then."

"Great, open the door for us Eddie."

Eddie opened the door and Tommy grabbed his suitcase. Eddie grabbed the duffel bag, and we headed out the door.

My mom and Guillermo were still in the house together when I heard the door shut. The three of us were standing downstairs waiting, but no one came down the stairs. A couple of minutes went by, and I heard the door open and shut again. My mom and Guillermo finally walked down the stairs holding hands. Guillermo was now wearing my mom's pink lipstick and he tossed Eddie the car keys.

Eddie pulled up to the building in a black Lincoln town car less than a minute later. He climbed out to unlock the trunk.

I asked Guillermo, "Did you drive here?"

He laughed before saying, "Oh no, this is a rental car."

Eddie grabbed the duffel bag and tossed it into the trunk. Tommy picked up his suitcase and placed it inside and shut the trunk. We all climbed into the car and Eddie drove us to the airport. When we pulled up to the terminal, Guillermo climbed out first.

He handed the skycap some money and helped him remove the bags from the trunk. The skycap opened his hand and he had a huge smile on his face. He ran back over to Guillermo with a cart and loaded everything up. Tommy handed the skycap his driver's license and his ticket. He walked over to his podium with the luggage cart. In less than a minute later he returned with Tommy's boarding pass and license. We all climbed out of the car and Tommy gave each of us a hug, even Eddie. He thanked Guillermo for everything before he walked inside the airport.

My mom sniffed once softly, and her eyes were watery. Guillermo handed my mom a handkerchief. My mom wiped her eyes and she lightly wiped her nose. Guillermo wrapped his arms around my mom. Eddie and I climbed back into the car; except this time, Eddie joined me in the backseat. When Guillermo and my mom climbed back in the car, Guillermo reached over and held my mom's hand. She looked down at their hands and the sniffling stopped.

Guillermo turned on the radio and my mom's favorite song was playing 'Mamma Mia.' My mom went from the verge of crying to singing ABBA. I couldn't believe it.

"Lori, I would like to take you and Sammy to a restaurant I heard about. Would you like to go with me?"

"Yes, I would love to go with you. What is the name of the restaurant?"

"Tio, what restaurant? I'm hungry." Right after Eddie said that his stomach started growling.

I snapped my head around and stared at Eddie. "Well, it's not like I'm going to eat you Sammy."

"Are you sure about that Eddie?"

"No, not really Sammy."

"Guillermo, I would like to go with you and make sure the alien gets fed."

That's when my mom turned her head around and she gave me a strange look. Until Eddie's stomach growled again. "Mom, don't be scared. That's just the alien in Eddie's stomach. As long as it's fed no one gets hurt." The three of us started laughing.

"Eddie, I didn't mean to laugh. I just had no idea what my daughter was talking about until your tummy began to growl."

"That's okay, Ms. Harris. The growling is actually starting to scare me too. I'm just hoping the alien doesn't get anxious and eat Sammy."

Guillermo covered his mouth and my mom laughed even harder. We all did.

One time, the growling was so loud that Eddie yelled, "Sammy, run."

"Where am I going to go, Eddie? We're in a moving car."

"I don't know, Sammy, but you need a plan B."

As we walked inside the restaurant, my mom's mouth dropped open and I couldn't believe my eyes. It was an actual Luau restaurant complete with a Polynesian show. My mom would tell me bedtime stories when I was a little girl. One of the stories was about her night in Hawaii spent at a Luau. Ever since then, I have always wanted to go to a Luau.

Being here at this place was like a dream come true, not only for me but for my mom too. She often said she wanted to attend a Luau again. I told her when she goes, I want to go with her. My mom would always say, hopefully one day. Now look! We're here together. I even had a non-alcohol Pina Colada served to me in a real pineapple.

A photographer came over to our table and took several pictures of the four of us. Then he took a couple of pictures of just my mom and Guillermo. Eddie told us that he had a bowl of cereal for breakfast and apparently, he can't drink milk anymore. That lately whenever he drinks milk the alien noise begins. I told Eddie I hope that he's full and the alien is satisfied.

Eddie whispered, "Will soon find out and he did the creepy laugh."

"Mom, do you think I can take a cab home?"

"What?"

I looked back at Eddie and told her, "Mom, I don't want to become desert for the alien."

"Sam, Eddie is just lactose intolerant you'll be fine."

"Eddie winked at me and whispered, "All we can do is hope that she's right." Then he sucked down his virgin Pina colada.

Before we left the restaurant, the photographer came back to our table. He asked if we were ready to view the photographs taken earlier. Guillermo told him, yes, and we viewed all five of the photos. The photographer asked if we made up our minds on which photo we'd like to have. "Oh no, we can't just pick one. We must have all of them." The photographer smiled and he left the table with all of the photographs. He came back to the table a few minutes later with each of the photos in a cardboard picture frame.

The whole ride back home my mom and I thanked Guillermo for taking us to the Luau. My mom told him how it was like a dream come true for us. He was smiling and just kept saying, "It was all Tommy's idea."

Chapter 12 Making It Official

When we arrived home, the phone was ringing. I ran into the kitchen to answer it. When I picked up the phone, I was about to say hello, but I froze up. I thought what if it's Julio? What would I say? I just hung up the phone and walked back into my room.

My mom followed me into my room. "What was that?"

"You saw that, mom?"

"Yes, I did, Sam," and my mom's eyebrows were arched up. She was staring at me with her arms crossed over her chest. I turned my eyes down toward the floor feeling completely ridiculous. I was trying to find a way to explain what was going on in my head.

"Sam, I'm waiting for an answer."

"Mom, I totally panicked."

"Panicked? Why did you panic, Sam?"

"Mom, when I answered the phone, I thought, what if it's Julio?"

"Oh, I see, but what if it was Tommy just wanting to let me know he was back at school or somebody else?"

"You're right mom and I'm sorry. It's just that if it was Julio, I'm not ready to speak to him yet. I just don't know what to say to him right now."

"Sam, I understand what happened. However, next time you feel that way just let the answering machine get the phone. Don't answer the phone and hang up. You don't know who or why somebody is calling."

"Oh, and Sam, you better figure out what you intend to say to Julio. He will be here tomorrow with Lewis."

"What? Why?"

"Alex is giving Eddie the van on his birthday. The three boys will be driving the van back to Anaheim on Tuesday. That is, unless Guillermo can convince the boys to allow the van to be shipped back to California. If he is able to do that, the boys will stay here for the rest of the week until Saturday and they will take a plane back to Anaheim."

"Mom, you have to be kidding me. I'm not ready to see Julio tomorrow, I don't even know what to say to him over the phone."

"Sorry, you will need to figure that out Sam. Julio has been invited over to our house tomorrow night."

"You've got to be kidding me. Why would you do that?"

"I'm cooking my homemade spaghetti and meatball dinner for the Sanchez family."

"Monday we're having a surprise birthday party at the club house for Eddie. You should let Daphne and everybody else know. I'll be in my room if you need me."

That's when I picked up the phone and called Tonya. She didn't answer, so I left her a message on her answering machine to call me ASAP.

I called Denise and told her that Eddie was in town. I then told her about the birthday party for him on Monday. She told me she would love to go, that Eddie and she have remained friends. In fact, they talk all the time, and she would like to meet Heather. I told her Heather's not here, and the birthday party is a surprise. Denise was excited about the party and she was bringing her new boyfriend. I told her that sounds great, see you both on Monday.

Daphne was the next person I called. Arturo answered the phone. The first thing he asked was how dinner went with my mom and Guillermo. I told him that it was fantastic; however, Julio and Lewis arrive in Miami tomorrow. Then I told him about the dinner at my house tomorrow night with the Sanchez boys. Then, of course, we talked about Eddie's surprise birthday party on Monday.

Arturo just broke out into laughter and I just patiently waited for him to stop laughing. Finally, he said, "Sammy, it's like the Sanchez boys are invading Miami. We even have one at our house, Enrique. What you need is your fairy godmother, Michael. He can make sure no matter what happens, at least you will look devastatingly gorgeous when Julio sees you again. That's the best revenge. Look your best and show him what he lost."

I asked where Daphne was, and Arturo said she was out having dinner with his mom, Enrique, and Greg. He said that he would be sure to tell her to call me once she gets back from dinner. He also told me if I needed to talk, he was always available day or night. I was about to say bye and hang up. Then he mentioned Daphne told him everything about last night. I heard the phone beep and he was receiving another call. He told me he had to get the other line and he'll call me back.

When I hung up the phone with Arturo, my phone rang. It was Maria. She asked me how Tonya was doing. I told her that I hadn't spoken to her since I left the hospital. She told me her brother, Alvaro, told her everything that happened. The hospital was keeping her one more night. I told her I didn't even know that she was still in the hospital. Maria said she wanted to go to the hospital, and I told her I want to go to. We hung up because she thought it was Alex calling on the other line.

Arturo called me back and I told him Tonya was still in the hospital for observation. Arturo told me if that's the case he was going to visit her.

Denise was the next person I called back. I told her about what happened to Tonya. Then I told her she was still in the hospital. She said she's taking a shower now and heading to the hospital.

Just as I hung up the phone, there was a knock at the door. I left my bedroom and answered the back door. It was Maria, she said, "Come on. Let's go see Tonya."

"Oh, Hello Maria." I turned around and saw my mom standing behind me. Before Maria could respond, I asked if I could go out for a little bit. "Yes, just be home by curfew." I headed for my room to grab my shoes. As I was walked out the door my mom asked, "Do you have your beeper Sam?"

I turned around and walked back inside. "No, I almost forgot it. Thanks mom." I walked back into my room and grabbed my purse with my beeper off the nightstand. Finally, I was out the door with Maria beside me. When we arrived downstairs, she told me to follow her. We ran down the parking lot and over past two buildings until we reached the black town car. I opened the door and climbed inside.

Alex was in the driver's seat and Eddie was in the passenger's seat. "I'm sorry, girls, that I couldn't park closer to the house. It's sort of like were on a secret mission right now. My uncle Gio just arrived home and let me borrow the car to visit Maria for an hour."

Eddie snickered before saying, "I had to tell Tio I was going out with friends in order to get out of the house."

"Well, I haven't told my mom about Tonya yet. I had planned on telling her tomorrow but now I'm not even sure about that. I was just waiting to find a good time to tell her."

"You don't have to worry about your mom. Tio has so many plans to keep your mom busy Sammy. In fact, I know he wants to take your mom out on another date tonight. I had to warn Alex when he called me that Tio wanted the car back."

"Sammy, the problem is that this car is our only transportation to the hospital. My van is getting fixed at the mechanics."

"That's not a problem, Alex. You don't have to explain anything to me. I'm just glad you guys included me on your mission to see Tonya."

"Alex just told me that Tonya is in the hospital. What happened to her? Why is she in there?" I told Eddie the whole story and at the end he just wanted to know where he could find this coward, Rick. He was so angry that any man would raise a hand to a lady.

"Truthfully, I don't know if Rick went back to school or if he was picked up by the police."

Alex pulled into a parking space at the hospital. He turned around in his seat and asked, "Did you just say this guy's name is Rick?"

I nodded my head yes.

"Eddie, do you think it could be the same one?"

"It could be Alex. He's dating a girl that's about to attend high school and he's going back to college. He drives an IROC Z28, and his name is Rick. There is a lot of the same things happening here."

I listened to Eddie and Alex when I realized what they were discussing. "Do you think this Rick is Erika's father?"

Eddie turned around in his seat and replied, "It could be. When Erika was first born, Pilar insisted Rick knew she was here. That Pilar just feels it's morally right to let him know as he is the father. When Monica finally agreed and called his beeper, it was no longer in service. She called the university to try to get his address. That was no longer an option because the university informed her, he was no longer a student there."

"Oh, that's totally bizarre, and I wish you the best of luck with that mystery. Just do me a huge favor and don't ask Tonya anything about Rick. She has really been through a lot and she's in fear for her life because of that guy; so, don't even mention his name."

"Alex."

"Yes, Maria."

"I agree with Sammy. Don't you dare ask her anything about Rick."

Alex and Eddie both said they knew better than to ask her about him. They just want to see Tonya and be there for her. We walked into the hospital and went to the information counter. That's where we ran into Denise. She already had Tonya's room number. We followed Denise to the elevator and walked over to Tonya's room together.

When the five of us walked inside, Tonya was asleep. Alvaro was holding her hand, sound asleep in the chair beside her bed. A nurse walked into the room and looked over at Tonya. Then she waved her hand for us to follow her out of the room. She held the door open until the last person walked out, then she quietly shut the door.

We followed the nurse over to the nurses' station located in the center of the wing. She said, "I know that you all have come to check on my patient, Tonya. I'm going to be the villain now and ask that you all leave. I don't want her to be disturbed. She did not sleep at all last night. Now, I know that my patient would want to know that you were all here. That's why I am going to give you each a pen and a piece of paper. You can each write a note to her and I will make sure she gets them as soon as she wakes up."

We each wrote a note to Tonya and left them behind with her nurse. When we reached the parking lot, Denise gave everyone a hug. Eddie walked Denise back to her car. The three of us were sitting in the car waiting for Eddie to return. Alex turned to me and said, "My brother will be here tomorrow, Sammy. Julio called me today and told me he didn't know if you would speak to him anymore."

I was able to remain calm and conceal how I truly feel. "Alex, we're not together anymore. Which means I don't care what he does or who he's with. Julio is very aware of how I feel. I don't think there is anything left for us to say."

Eddie climbed back in the car right after I spoke to Alex.

"Sammy, If you need to talk you can always talk to me." I hugged Maria and thanked her.

"Maria, do you want to spend the night at my house tomorrow?" If you decide to sleep over, I have to warn you, my mom is making her homemade spaghetti and meatballs for dinner. Pretty much all of the Sanchez boys will be there. It will be like some sort of Sanchez boy invasion."

"Oh yeah, we're back Sammy, and more of us will be here tomorrow." Maria and I laughed, and Eddie continued saying, "And we're not missing that dinner. I'm sure Julio and Sammy will sneak off to walk Daisy. Maybe not right away, maybe they will wait until after dinner, but for sure at some point during the evening. While Julio is in town, Daisy will be going out on plenty of walks. That's for sure! Right Alex?"

Everyone stopped smiling and looked over at me. Even Alex looked back at me through the rear-view mirror. I just turned my head and stared out the window.

"What happened? What did I say? Why is everyone suddenly so quiet?"

"Eddie, Sammy and Julio are not together anymore."

"What? When did this happen Alex?" The rest of the car ride was silent, not even the radio was turned on.

When I arrived home, I forgot my house keys and knocked on the door. My mom answered, "Sam, you have perfect timing. How do I look?"

"You look beautiful, mom. Where are you going?"

"Out on a date with Guillermo. Just the two of us. Alex has the rental car and the van is already at the shop being painted. He has scheduled a car service to pick us up in about 30 minutes."

My mom was smiling as she was spinning around in a circle. I just watched as her bell-bottom red dress twirled around. She was so happy. I really enjoyed seeing her like this. I only wished her happiness could last forever.

There was a knock on the front door. When I answered, it was Guillermo smiling just as big and bright as my mom. "Hi Sammy, I'm here to pick up your mom. My mom walked up behind me, and she kissed me on the cheek as she walked past me out the door.

I waved bye to them both, and they both waved back to me before they walked down the stairs holding hands. I just thought to myself, I could totally get used to seeing my Mom like that as I shut the door.

I heard the phone ring, and I ran into my room to answer the phone. It was Daphne. I told her that we went to the hospital to visit Tonya and what occurred. Then I told her Julio was going to be here tomorrow with Lewis. She already knew about the Sanchez invasion. Enrique talked about it over dinner tonight, and she wanted to know if I needed her to come over and spend the night tonight. I told her yes, and she said she would be over in an hour.

When Daphne arrived, she hugged me as soon as I answered the door. Then she told me that she came with Mig and Greg. She tossed her duffel bag into my room. Then she continued to tell me that Greg wanted to hang out with her after she returned home from dinner. Greg would be sleeping over at Mig's house tonight and Mig wanted to see me again.

I put Daisy on her leash and the three of us girls walked over to the picnic tables beside the pool. Greg was talking non-stop about Julio being in town tomorrow. He was definitely excited to see Julio and he had plans on convincing him to stay until Saturday.

I asked Greg what type of plans. Greg mentioned a soccer game and he wanted Guillermo to play to. I told him that everyday has been planned out already for Julio until Tuesday. A soccer game could only happen if they don't leave on Tuesday.

"What type plans does Julio have?" I told Greg about the dinner at my house tomorrow night. Eddie's surprise birthday party on Monday night. The big reveal gift on Monday or Tuesday morning. That still depends on the body shop.

"That's it! You have convinced me, Sammy. With Guillermo having every day planned out already, I have no choice but to convince the guys to have the van shipped. That way they can stay in Miami until Saturday."

He turned to Daphne and told her, "Let's go for a walk."

"We will be right back, Sammy."

"Okay, see you in a little bit Daphne."

When they left Mig turned his chair around to face me.

"So, I take it my cousin has no idea how bad Julio has hurt you."

"I guess Daphne doesn't tell Greg everything after all."

Mig smiled, "That's a good thing to know about your friend."

"Yes, it comes in handy during times like these."

"Have things changed between us again, Sammy?"

"What?"

"You said we could be friends."

"I told you we are friends Mig and I meant that."

"So, I take it you haven't spoken to Julio yet."

"No, I said everything that needed to be said the last time we spoke on the phone. Why would that have any effect on our friendship though?"

Mig looked away for a second and then he looked back at me. "Julio knows that I have a thing for you, Sammy. He won't be happy when he finds out that we've been hanging out.

"Too late Mig. He already knows, and I don't care."

"Sammy, we haven't really discussed what caused you to be so unhappy. I just know that it has to do with Julio."

"Your right Mig, and I have no intention of discussing that with you."

"I've enjoyed the times we have been able to hang out together Sammy. I'm just concerned that when Julio comes back tomorrow, you won't be allowed to associate with me anymore."

"Look, I understand why you feel that way Mig. On Monday I turned your invite down to the bonfire. But a lot has happened since Monday, Mig."

"Yeah, Like what?"

"Tuesday and Friday, Mig." He didn't look convinced.

"Tuesday my bubble popped, and I cried on your shoulder. You just held me and comforted me and managed to keep that whole incident between us."

"Friday night you helped me rescue my best friend. You rushed her to the hospital and waited for me in the ER. You even stayed awake after everyone else fell asleep just to talk to me and make sure I was alright."

"So, like I said, Mig. A lot has changed since Monday."

"Do you think I should go to Eddie's birthday party? Greg wants me to go. He told me I should go because I'm friends with Eddie. Then he mentioned if anything has happened between us, he doesn't want me to go out of respect for Julio."

"Mig, you can tell Greg something has happened between us. It's called building trust and forming a friendship. Neither one of those things should prevent you from attending the party."

"What is the actual situation between you and Julio now?"

"Truthfully Mig, it's a mess. We're still broken up and filled with lots of hurt feelings: a feeling of betrayal and tons of regret, supposedly."

Mig sat back in his chair and placed his hand over his mouth. He turned his head away from me. When he turned his head back to face me, he said, "I can't believe Julio would be that stupid."

"What do you mean, Mig?"

"Well obviously, you're the one feeling betrayed and that's the reason for the breakdown Tuesday at the pool. Julio is undoubtedly the one filled with regret after losing you. Most likely he hooked up with some chick that wasn't worth a cup of coffee."

"Mig, I'm impressed. You really do pay attention."

"Yeah, so I guess there is only one question left unanswered now."

"What's that?"

"Does Julio know that it's over yet?"

"That's the funny part. We were no longer together when it happened and were not together now."

"Has Julio accepted that it's over between the two of you?"

"Mig, how are you doing this?"

"I told you already, I pay attention. I noticed you weren't excited to see Julio tomorrow. You didn't look mad or even upset that he was coming. Instead you just appeared distant. Which leads me to believe there is still some unfinished business between you two."

I placed my elbow on the table and my hand to my forehead. I looked down at the table and said, "Mig, that is exactly what's going on."

"Do you want to talk about what you're feeling, Sammy? It might help to unravel all of the confusion. It might even bring you some clarity."

"Okay, if I tell you, Mig, it has to stay between us."

"That goes without saying, Sammy. I'm still working on building trust and forming a friendship with you."

"Okay, here it goes Julio called me the other night. I made it clear that I would not accept anymore calls from him; That's very easy to say and do when he's in California. Now I'm just afraid I won't be as strong when I see him face to face. I've made up my mind to put my walls up. My fear now is that he can tear them down with a simple smile or explanation. Julio has a completely different affect on me in person. I honestly don't know how strong I am or how much I can stand. My weakness and feelings for Julio could end up hurting me again."

"I know you're stronger than you realize, Sammy."

"Yeah, I thought you would say that. But I'm not so sure, Mig."

When Daphne arrived back at the table with Greg, I told her I was going upstairs now. I explained to everyone that I just needed to get to bed early tonight. I knew for sure tomorrow would be a very long day for me.

When I stood up Daphne told me she would be upstairs in a little bit. Mig walked me back to my door and thanked me for trusting him enough to be so honest and open with him. He kissed me on the cheek and told me, "I will see you Monday at the party." Then he jogged back down the stairs.

I walked inside and went straight to bed. I woke up very early the next morning and went straight into the kitchen to make breakfast. Daphne got up out of bed a few minutes after me, and she joined me in the kitchen. While I made three omelets, Daphne made a pot of coffee.

We set my mom's tray up with an omelet, coffee, and juice. I carried the tray, and Daphne turned the doorknob to my mom's room for me. I walked inside and set the tray down on my mom's coffee table. Daphne tapped me on the shoulder and when I turned around, Daphne pointed to my mom's bed. The bed was empty and already made up.

My mouth dropped open. Daphne's eyes were popping out of her head. I turned around and picked up the tray from the coffee table. Daphne didn't say a word, she just followed me out of her room. She remembered to shut the door behind us on the way out.

"Oh wow! She's up early today," I placed the tray down on the kitchen counter.

Daphne didn't have to say a word, I knew what she was thinking because I was thinking it too. We sat down at the counter and had our breakfast in silence. After we finished eating, we cleaned up the kitchen and took Daisy out for a walk.

My mom and Guillermo walked in the back door an hour later. Eddie and Alex walked in behind them and they were each carrying a couple of chairs. My mom showed them where to set them down. Then she asked me to set up the folding table and chairs she just bought. She headed back out the door again with Guillermo.

"Where are they off to now?"

Alex put up his index finger and said, "Hold on Sammy, I will tell you right now." He was bent over trying to catch his breath. He finally took a seat on the couch beside me and took a sip of water.

'They are headed to the grocery store."

"What happened to you, Alex? Why are you so exhausted?"

"Tio doesn't sleep anymore, Sammy. He came into my room at six o'clock in the morning. He told me to get up were going to breakfast. I told him, let me sleep, Tio. I'm working. He told me, that's okay, no problem. Eddie heard that and jumped off the bed beside mine."

"What did you do?"

"Me, I remained in bed and went back to sleep. Then he poured a glass of water over my head while I was in bed sleeping. I could hear Eddie laughing, and Tio saying, 'Alex, you are not working today. It's Sunday. We're going to breakfast. Get up.'"

"I sat up and said 'Tio, I told you I was working on my sleep.' Sammy, it was like the man couldn't even hear me. He just said, 'Alex, meet me downstairs in ten minutes with the car. I will be waiting for you in front of Lori's building.'"

"Then what happened?"

"Nothing, Tio left to go get your mom."

Daphne and I looked at one another and we said, "That's okay, no problem." in our best Guillermo accent. All four of us broke out laughing.

"When your Uncle says, 'that's okay, no problem,' you were just given a warning shot in the air. You better run."

"That's for sure! Daphne, I ran out of that room so fast when Tio said that. I knew it was too late for Alex. There was only enough time to save myself."

"Wow, Eddie I'm your cousin."

"Yes, you are Alex until Tio gets like that; then it becomes every man for himself!" Daphne and I were laughing so hard until we had tears in our eyes.

We got to work on the tables and chairs. Once everything was all set up in the dining room area, we had a seat in the living room. We were watching a movie until there was a knock at the door. When I answered the door, I felt really nervous. Luckily, it was Tonya, Alvaro, and Maria. I wrapped my arms around Tonya feeling relieved to see her. Everyone came inside. When Alex saw Maria his face completely lit up.

Everyone took turns hugging Tonya. Eventually we all sat back down in the living room. Tonya talked about what happened and what caused Rick to become so angry with her. Apparently, she wanted to walk back over to us and watch the band play. They got into a verbal dispute when she tried to leave the car. As soon as she opened the door, Rick slapped her and reached across her lap to pull the door shut. She tried to climb out of the car again; that's when he lost it and began to choke Tonya.

Everyone just stood there looking stunned; it was so quiet that you could hear a pin drop. Finally, Tonya said, "Thank you, guys, for showing up to the hospital last night. I received your notes from my nurse this morning before I was released."

"How are you feeling now, Tonya?"

"Alex, my esophagus wasn't crushed or damaged. The bruises on my neck will go away eventually. I feel safe as long as I hold onto Alvaro." That's when I noticed how tight she was holding onto Alvaro's hand. I also noticed the huge smile on his face.

Tonya looked back at the dinning room area and asked, "What's going on here with the additional table and chairs?" I told her about Julio and Lewis coming over for dinner tonight.

Tonya grabbed my hand, "Excuse me, everyone. We will be right back."

We walked into my bedroom and I told her about everything. The dinner tonight, the birthday party Monday, and of course the walls I built to keep Julio away.

I told her I was afraid of my weakness and how it's going to be hard, if not impossible, to remain strong when I see him in person.

"Muñeca, this is like totally crazy. Do you want me to stay here for dinner tonight?"

I nodded my head yes and she said, "Fine, I will be here with you. Together we can keep your walls up and they will be strong. You'll see."

Tonya released my hand and I asked, "Are you okay now?"

"Yes, I feel safe in your house, so I don't need to hold anyone's hand while I'm here."

"That's good." Tonya smiled and we walked back out to the living room. At the same time, my mom and Guillermo walked in through the kitchen door. Guillermo asked Alex and Eddie to grab the groceries from the car. Tonya and I followed them into the kitchen. She hugged my mom and said hi to Guillermo. We walked out the backdoor and left the door open.

As we reached the stairs, we overheard my mom telling Guillermo, "That's Tonya." My mom went on to say, "Your nephew Lewis was her boyfriend until he moved to California."

"I heard about Tonya from my sister Pilar. Now I understand the comparison to Amy looking a lot like Tonya, the first girlfriend." Tonya and I looked at one another and we both tried not to laugh as we jogged down the stairs.

We walked to over to the car and the trunk was popped open. There were still four grocery bags left. "Come on Muñeca, two each." We bent over and reached inside the trunk.

That's when I heard, "Hello, Samantha."

I froze in place. Tonya looked over at me and squeezed my hand. Luckily, I was still facing the inside of the trunk, so I had just a couple of seconds to get a hold of myself. Then I heard, "Hi, Tonya."

I looked over at Tonya. She had her eyes closed and she took a deep breath. When she opened her eyes, she arched her eyebrows up at me and released my hand.

We each pulled only one bag from the trunk leaving the other two bags inside.

When we turned around, I said, "Hello, Julio."

Tonya smiled before saying, "Hi, Lewis. There are still two grocery bags left in the trunk that need to be brought inside." We both smiled as we walked past them up the stairs. I was doing everything I could to play it cool and not show the panic I was actually feeling.

As we walked back inside my mom took the bags from us. "Where's Julio and Lewis?"

Tonya told her they should be upstairs any minute now with two more bags. As soon as Tonya said that, they walked in through the kitchen door. I looked back at Julio, and his eyes were already glued to me.

My mom, Tonya, and Guillermo were watching us. Julio handed my mom the bag of groceries and asked if he could see Daisy now. "Of course, Daisy will be so excited to see you Julio."

Then she told me to go get Daisy from her room for Julio. I reminded my mom that Daisy gets anxiety when there's a lot of people in the house. That's when my mom told me to bring Julio to my room and to bring Daisy to him right now.

I found Daisy curled up asleep in her bed. I woke her up and asked her if she wanted to see Julio. She sat right up and licked my face over and over again. Then she jumped up out of bed and ran to my mom's bedroom door. I placed Daisy on her leash and walked her over to my room.

Julio was waiting for us in front of my door. When Daisy saw Julio, she went crazy barking, whimpering, and wagging her tail. I opened my bedroom door and Daisy jumped up on her hind legs. She managed to knock Julio into the door frame. I started laughing and he was laughing too. Julio was barely in my room. When she jumped up and knocked him over again. She stood over him and licked his face. He wrapped his arms around her, and she started to whimper and smell him from head to toe.

After a while, with all three of us in my room with the bedroom door shut. I walked over to my stereo and put in a cassette tape. I turned up my stereo, playing the song 'Cuts Like a Knife' by Bryan Adams. I had a seat on the floor in my bean bag chair and I just stared out the window.

I looked away from the window for a second. That's when I noticed Julio was on his knees in front of me. I felt Julio's arms wrap around me, and he pulled me closer to him. As he leaned in to kiss me. I said, "Julio, stop! Remove your hands from around my waist." I was looking him straight in the eyes and he was looking back into mine.

"Samantha, please don't do this. You need to forgive me. It was just a mistake and we weren't even together anymore."

"Yes, of course! your big mistake. I read it all in your letter. Julio, please let go of me." He slowly removed his arms and I stood up.

"Samantha, we need to talk about this."

"Fine, we can talk about this if you really want to Julio. I sat back down in the bean bag. "Julio, you led me to believe that you were still single and in love with me for those 5 straight days that I was in California. Maybe I deserved it for breaking up with you before you got on the plane for Anaheim. I was only trying to protect myself from the pain of being without you. It didn't work! I was miserable after you left. I couldn't eat and I had trouble sleeping for close to 3 weeks. I will admit that when I read your letter I was devastated, but not surprised. You have changed and you're becoming a man as you stated to me in that letter. Well! if lying, cheating and having sex is making you a man; I can tell you now that I made the right decision to end things with you."

"That's not what happened Samantha."

"Julio, a relationship is all about trust. We don't have that anymore. It's gone now. How much do you really love me, and how devastating was that phone conversation with my brother Tommy? Really?"

"Sammy, it tore a hole in me. When I hung up the phone; I felt like the wind had been knocked out me."

"Let me try to understand what you're telling me. You are heartbroken and devastated after you hung up the phone with my brother. Then you go out on blind date that same night and go all the way with some girl you just met. Now that's romantic. I'm touched, Julio."

I stood up and walked out of the room. I left my stereo on playing a cassette tape of my favorite breakup songs. When I shut the bedroom door, I went straight to the bathroom. I felt like I was burning up. I had to throw some cold water on my face. Feeling better, I walked back into my room. Julio stood up and said, "I listened to what you had to say and how you feel, Samantha. Now it's only fair that you listen to what I think and how I feel."

"Fine, I'll listen."

"Samantha, I did everything I could to be with you until I was told I couldn't be with you anymore. I needed closure. I called your house every day. Even after I was told you didn't want me to call your house anymore, I called again because I had to hear those words from you. I had no idea that your brother made all that stuff up. All I knew was that I was happy to finally hear your voice again. That's because I love you more than anything else in this world. I will always love you but you're right a relationship is not possible without trust and it's not possible without respect. I will have to work on regaining both your trust and respect back. Until then I have a song for you to listen to."

He walked up to me and I looked up into his eyes.

He had a look of despair on his face.

"You have no idea how much I regret losing you Samantha."

"What about keeping the truth from me for five days Julio?"

"That I wont ever regret Samantha. Those were the best five days of my life and I didn't even realize that until you were gone." He turned his back to me and walked over to my stereo. "This song is for you. He pressed play on my stereo and walked out of my room.

'That Was Yesterday' by Foreigner started to play on my stereo. As I listened to the lyrics with tears streaming down my face. I realized this song was Julio's way of telling me that he has accepted that it's over between us.

Daisy was jumping up on her hind legs, pawing at me, trying to get my attention. I sat down on the edge of my bed. Daisy jumped up and licked my face. She successfully licked away all my tears and made me laugh. I left my bedroom and walked straight into the bathroom and washed my face. I put the leash on Daisy and walked out the kitchen door.

I made my way to the sidewalk, when I heard, "Wait up." I knew by the sound of his voice who it was. I stopped walking and let him catch up. "Thank you for waiting, Sammy."

"No problem, I'm guessing you need some fresh air. That's why you are out here with me and Daisy."

"No, Sammy. I'm here because I wanted to know if you're okay. If you want to talk, not about what's going on, but just talk about anything."

"Yes, I would like that. I have a question for you."

"Okay, go ahead ask me."

"Guillermo, what are your intentions with my mom? I mean, what's the plan? Why are you here?"

"Sammy, I haven't felt like this ever in my life. I am over 40 years old. I haven't ever been married or in love. That all changed the minute I looked into your mother's eyes and I saw her smile. This is the first time in my life that I know without a doubt she is the one for me." I stopped walking and stood there on the sidewalk looking at Guillermo in total shock.

Guillermo started walking and talking. "I just know that I want to be with your mom. I can't stop thinking about her every minute of the day. I want to know her opinions and thoughts on everything. To me, what she thinks, and how she feels means everything. I want to look into her eyes and see her smile every day. I can't wait to wake up and see your mom. Basically, what I'm saying is that I plan to ask your mother to be my girlfriend."

"Wow, that sounds serious, Guillermo. Are you sure you're ready for such a commitment?"

Guillermo stopped walking and he faced me. "I am definitely ready."

"That's cool, when are you going to make it official and ask my mom to be your girlfriend?"

"I'm planning on asking her tonight after dinner. I want everyone to be there."

"You have my blessing, Guillermo. I wish you good luck tonight. Thank you for going on the walk with me and Daisy."

"I enjoyed it, Sammy." He opened the kitchen door and allowed Daisy and I to walk in first.

Once we were back inside, I saw that Tonya, Daphne, and my mom were in the kitchen preparing the meatballs for dinner. Mom's sauce was already simmering in a pot on the stove.

"Sammy, I'm glad you're back. Would you please assist the girls? I need you to all start making golf ball-sized meatballs."

"Mom, let me just wash my hands first."

Guillermo stood at the counter smiling at my mom. "Your nephews have all gone back to apartment. If you want to leave and head over there, you can. I will call you when dinner is ready." Then I saw her reach into her apron and pull something out. "Or, you can have this remote control to the cable box." Guillermo smiled and put out his hand. My mom handed him the remote. Guillermo leaned in and kissed my mom before he walked over to the living room. My mom was smiling as she watched Guillermo have a seat on the sofa.

We finished preparing the meatballs, and my mom thanked us for helping her. She asked us to come back in an hour to set the tables.

"No problem, mom. We're just going to my room to listen to music until then."

An hour later we walked out to the linen closet. I grabbed the tablecloths and Daphne helped me cover the tables. Tonya went into the kitchen and covered the kitchen counter that the stools were up against with another tablecloth. We grabbed the silverware and napkins, and everything was ready for dinner.

"Thank you, girls!"

"You're welcome Mom."

"Do you need us to do anything else Ms. Harris?

"No, not at the moment Tonya. We are just waiting for the boys to return."

"What about Carmen and Enrique?"

"I'm right here Sammy."

Daphne took off running towards the living and gave her mom a big hug. We all walked over to the living room and saw Carmen and Enrique sitting together at the end of the couch. That's why we didn't see them from the kitchen.

We spoke to them for a few minutes and that's when the boys walked in. My mom said, "Alright, everyone have a seat at the tables."

The three of us girls followed my mom into the kitchen. We helped her prepare three baskets filled with garlic bread. We set out the butter and parmesan cheese on each of the tables.

Then Daphne took drink orders and brought Greg his drink first. Then she handed me a piece of paper with everyone else's drink written down. While she headed for the cabinet and grabbed glasses down, Tonya grabbed the ice from the freezer and began to fill up the glasses. I balled up the list from Daphne and tossed it in the trash. I placed a 2-liter bottle of soda on top of each table along with a pitcher of homemade sweet tea. Tonya handed everyone a glass filled with ice.

Then we headed back into the kitchen. I grabbed the plates down from the cabinet and my mom began loading up each plate. Tonya and Daphne took the plates to the tables. They were moving fast taking two plates at a time to the dining room.

Once everyone had their plates, my mom finally took her seat at the parents table. Alex and Maria were also seated at the parents table tonight. My mom noticed Tonya and I were still standing up. That's when she said, "You girls walk over to the boys table so we can say grace, please."

Daphne basically got up from the counter and ran over to their table. Tonya and I looked over at one another with our eyebrows raised at each other. The boys all stood up. Julio and Lewis were looking across the table at one another. This moment really felt uncomfortable.

My mom said, "Okay, everyone, hold hands, and let's say grace."

Tonya grabbed Eddie's left hand and I grabbed his right hand. Then I reached beside me to grab Greg's hand. Somehow, I ended up holding Julio's hand instead. All I can say is that the minute I felt his hand holding mine, I was trembling from head to toe.

Guillermo said grace and I raised my head up. I looked across table and saw Tonya holding hands with Lewis. We both looked over at Daphne. She was just smiling looking down at the table. Julio rubbed the top of my hand with his thumb twice before releasing it. Tonya and I walked back over to the counter, and Daphne eventually joined us. We kept the seat between us for Daphne.

When Daphne arrived at the counter, she wouldn't look at either one of us. She just sat down and said, "That wasn't my fault. I had nothing to do with that, girls. I even tried to take your hand Sammy, really, I did. Greg pulled my hand away and placed Julio's hand in yours, Sammy."

"What about me, Daphne? I ended up holding hands with Lewis."

"Tonya, Lewis placed his own hand over yours."

"Who did you hold hands with, Daphne?"

"Greg."

"Who did Greg hold hands with?"

"Me?"

"Who held your other hand?"

"No one, Sammy," and she laughed.

"If Alvaro would have just stayed for dinner tonight that wouldn't have happened to me."

"Why didn't he stay, Tonya? I invited him."

"I know you did, Muñeca. But he wanted to go home and have dinner with his mom and spend time with her."

After we finished eating, the three of us took our plates into the kitchen. I set out a towel on the counter beside the sink. I grabbed two more dish towels from the linen closet. Tonya began to wash the dishes, Daphne dried them, and I put them away.

The boys all came into the kitchen with their plates. We all had our hands full of dishes from the parents table. Lewis didn't appear to realize that, and he handed Tonya his dirty plate. She took the plate with a smile from Lewis. He leaned over and kissed Tonya on her cheek. "Thank you for dinner."

"Here, Sammy," I looked behind me and Julio was handing me his dirty plate. I took the plate from him and said with loads of attitude, "Mr. Sanchez, I hope you enjoyed your dinner with us tonight."

He kissed me on the cheek and pulled away looking into my eyes saying, "Now I have," with a grin as he walked out of the kitchen.

Eddie and Greg just sat there listening and watching everything going on. "Ladies, those two are *pénibles*, and they are crazy in love with the two of you. It's torture for them to see what they have lost." We both hugged Eddie and thanked him for the compliment. Then he left the kitchen and joined the others back at the table.

Daphne and I walked over to the tables and removed the bread baskets, butter, and parmesan cheese. When we walked back into the kitchen, my mom asked me to take out the German chocolate cake from the refrigerator. She asked me to set it out on the counter. Guillermo came into the kitchen and made four white Russians. When he arrived back at the table, he asked, "Is anybody driving home?"

Carmen answered, "No."

"Okay, then you can have one." Guillermo handed out the white Russians to Carmen and Enrique. Guillermo reached over and handed my mom her white Russian. Then I looked over at the dining room table again when I heard everybody getting excited. I walked out of the kitchen and saw Guillermo. He was down on one knee in front of my mom. Everyone's eyes were about to pop out of their heads. Carmen's mouth dropped open. Daphne, Maria, and Tonya were covering their mouths. Then I felt someone looking at me and I turned my head to the right. That's when I saw Julio staring at me. I'm pretty sure he was wondering how I was handling this moment. Little did he know, Guillermo already told me about this. He took my mother's hand and all the girls gasped and swallowed.

"Lori, I have not ever felt like this about anyone before. I doubt there is anyone else in this entire world that can make me feel the way you do. I have to ask you —" Guillermo paused midsentence and swallowed once.

I kept thinking, yeah, I know that feeling nerves.

My mom was smiling, with tear-filled eyes and said, "Of course, Guillermo, I'll marry you."

Guillermo's face lit up like a neon sign in Vegas. "You'll marry me, Lori?"

My mom just nodded her head yes. Guillermo stood up and wrapped his arms around her. He gave her a big kiss. Then he turned to face everyone and said, "She's going to marry me," and he kissed my mom again.

Everyone was clapping, and the boys were all yelling, "Congratulations, Tio."

I just stood there in the kitchen thinking how in the world does this even happen. I mean, how is this going to work? We live in Miami. He lives in Anaheim. My head was starting to hurt. I needed some fresh air.

I walked into my bedroom and put Daisy on her leash. I headed outside with Daisy through the back door. It was dark outside, but I didn't care right now. I wanted to head out to the golf course and clear my head. I took the leash off Daisy once we were deep into the golf course. I yelled, "Come on, girl." I started to run as fast as I could. I needed to release this anxious energy that was stirred up with confusion.

Daisy was running beside me when she suddenly stopped. Then I stopped running and Daisy ran to stand in front of me. She began to bark like crazy and backed up to me, shielding me from something. I was starting to feel really nervous; I couldn't see anything. It was too dark. Then I heard a loud whistle and Daisy took off running. I exhaled with relief the minute I saw Julio's form from a distance. Daisy was running beside him headed in my direction.

"Julio, what are you doing out here?"

"I just wanted to make sure you were alright, Samantha."

"I'm fine, Julio."

"A lot just happened upstairs, and you went for a run on the golf course at night. Yeah, sure, everything's fine."

"You don't have to worry about me anymore."

"Samantha, you don't ever stop worrying about those you love. I will always love you and worry about you. Now, I'm not leaving you out here alone. It's not safe."

"I'm not alone, I have Daisy."

Julio had both of his hands on his hips and luckily, I still couldn't see his face clearly. I could tell he had something more to say, but he was holding back. I turned around and took a deep breath to calm myself.

Julio walked up behind me and placed both of his hands on my shoulders. I turned my head to the side, and I looked up at him. Now with him standing this close to me, I could clearly see his face. Now, that wasn't going to be good for me.

"Samantha, do you want to go for a walk by the lake and talk about it? Or we can walk over to the tire swing?"

"No, I really don't feel like talking about anything right now, Julio."

"Sammy, don't be so stubborn. You will feel better if you talk about it."

"I don't agree with you, Julio. I said everything that I needed to say to you over the phone and just a few minutes ago in my room."

"Look, I meant with how your feeling about Tio and your mom. The whole thing with Megan is just stupid. I shouldn't have ever gone out with her. I know that and I regret it."

"Julio, I don't care about your regret. In fact, I don't care about you or what you do anymore."

"That's not true Samantha, you care about me and what I do. The same way I care about you."

"Julio, your polluted."

"Wow, is this really how it's going to end between us?"

"Of course, this is how it ends between us. What did you think was going to happen? You live in Anaheim and I live in Miami. It's over now! We move on with our lives and perhaps one day we can become friends."

"Friends, that's what your hoping will become of us? Samantha, you can't be serious."

"Come on. At this point, Julio, it's pretty clear to me that you are with Megan. Whether you want to admit it to me or not, it doesn't matter. You can't mess with me just because you're in town for a few days and go running back to her after you leave. That's not right and I didn't think you were capable of being so deceitful.

"You're still accusing me of being in a relationship with Megan?"

"Look, I don't hold it against you Julio. You had to move on and start over."

"Samantha, I've told you the truth over and over again. Now you're just calling me a liar. Go ahead and believe whatever you want."

"Julio, I don't know what to believe anymore."

"You should believe me."

"Why would I believe you?"

"I have never lied to you Samantha."

I began to laugh and replied, "I asked you a question on my second day in Anaheim."

"Yes, and I told you the truth. I don't have a girlfriend and I'm not in a relationship."

"No, you just had sex with someone and delayed telling me until after I left."

"Let's change the subject. What did you do on Friday night Samantha? Who were you out with?"

"Why? Did you hear something, Julio?"

"Yes, I heard you were at the bonfire with Mig."

"Your source is correct."

"I was also told you had dinner with Mig at your favorite burger place. You and Mig even sat together at your own table. Oh, and your date with Mig must have been going well. I heard that after the whole incident that happened with Tonya; the two of you were found snuggled up with one another in the waiting room at the hospital."

"Julio, you don't really know all the details about Friday night."

"Okay, then let's talk about Tuesday. When you went to the pool in Coral Gables and jumped off the cliff holding hands with Mig. Then the two of you spent the rest of your time inside the cave together until you left."

"It wasn't like that, Julio. I closed my eyes and took in a deep breath. I just couldn't believe we were having this conversation now.

"Oh no, then what was it like?"

I opened my eyes and released a heavy sigh. "Mig tried to calm me down after I cried on his shoulder."

"Why were you crying Samantha? What happened?"

"I read your letter Julio, and it tore me up inside. Mig has been there for me and he's my friend."

"Why is it you're allowed to have male friends and go out with them, and I shouldn't question it? Knowing very well that Mig would like to be a lot more than just friends with you Samantha."

"It's not your business anymore what I do or who I spend my time with. I've read your letter and it's over."

"But I want you to explain something to me."

"Explain what to you Julio?

"What is the difference between you going out with friends and me going out with my cousins?" I was smiling and shaking my head. He stood there in front of me with a smirk on his face.

"Brace yourself Julio."

He crossed his arms over his chest and smiled.

"You're the only guy I have ever kissed and I'm still a virgin after going out with my friends. Can you say the same thing?" I stood in front of Julio and I searched his eyes back and forth. He was no longer smiling and staring back at me with a look of horror. I turned my back on him and was about to walk away.

"No, I can't. I messed up Samantha." I spun around and faced him. I looked into his eyes that were now filled with sadness.

"Julio, what are you so upset about? You already went all the way with some girl. I'm sure you want more of that and I don't blame you. It's definitely more than I'm willing to give you. Either way, you have moved on and I need to do the same. I wish you all the happiness in world, because sadness sucks."

I took off running deeper into the golf course. I just had to release this frustration I was feeling; it was continuing to build up inside me. As I was running midway down the grass, I could no longer feel the ground beneath me. Julio caught up to me and lifted me up off the ground. I didn't even bother to pull away or fight him off. I just gave up and laid my head back and looked up at all those stars above.

"You run pretty fast nowadays, Samantha."

"Yes, I have had a lot of practice trying to run away from you."

Julio stopped walking and he kissed the left side of my cheek. He set me back down on the ground and the three of us walked back to my building in silence.

When we walked inside everything was cleaned up from dinner and nobody was in the living room. Things were really not what I had expected. My mom and Carmen were having a sleepover. They were in their PJ's sitting on the sofa in my mom's room talking. Carmen was sleeping over again which has been a monthly occurrence since her divorce.

I noticed the door open and a light on in my brother's room. I walked by the door and saw Guillermo and Enrique tucked in the bunk beds. I guess they were sleeping over tonight too. They actually reminded me of Tommy when he was a teenager with his friends over. They were both lying down in the bunk beds talking about girls. Actually, talking about my mom and Carmen. Whatever, its still boys talking about girls.

I walked into my room, and nobody was in there. Which meant Daphne and Tonya were hanging out by the pool. I really wasn't up for hanging out right now. I decided it would be better if I hung out here for the rest of the night. I bent over and took the leash off Daisy.

I walked back into the kitchen to put her leash up. That's when I noticed Julio was still here. He was standing in the kitchen staring back at me. Talk about feeling overwhelmed by everything tonight. I completely forgot Julio walked inside with me. I walked over to him and was about to explain, when he asked, "What are you going to do now, Samantha?"

"I'm tired. It has been a long day Julio. I just want to go to bed."

"Okay, I will see you tomorrow." Julio leaned over and kissed me on the lips. He searched my eyes as he slowly pulled away. I sucked in my bottom lip and stared back at him until he turned and walked out the backdoor.

He left me completely speechless. Walking back to my room, I reminded myself that Julio was polluted. I turned on my stereo and fought off the urge to look out the window to catch a glimpse of him.

Chapter 13 Today We Celebrate Eddie

As soon as I woke up, I headed for the kitchen to start making breakfast. I ran into Carmen and Enrique. They waved bye to me as they walked out the back door. My mom walked into the kitchen a couple of minutes later. She poured herself a cup of coffee and asked where's Daphne. I told her she's still asleep in my room. My mom walked over to the dinning room table and asked me to join her.

"A lot happened last night, Sam, and I want to know how you're feeling."

"Mom, I think you found your soulmate. I want to see you happy and he makes you happy. Plus, I like Guillermo. He's a great guy. I'm just worried about one thing."

"What's that Sam?" I swallowed once and looked down at the table.

"Sam, what are you worried about?"

"It's just that, I don't want to leave Miami."

"Sam, I have no intention of moving anywhere while you're in high school."

"Really, Mom?"

"Really, Sam," I jumped up from the table and hugged my mom. That's when Guillermo walked into the kitchen whistling a happy tune. We pulled apart and glanced back at him.

"I'm sorry, I didn't mean to interrupt you girls," and he turned to walk out of the kitchen.

"Oh Guillermo," He turned around with a sorrowful look on his face.

"Yes, Lori?"

"You're not interrupting. I was just telling Sam that we have no intention of leaving Miami anytime soon."

Guillermo suddenly had a smile on his face. He asked if he could join us. My mom was smiling and nodding her head yes. He practically ran over to the table and sat down.

"Sammy, I love this place."

"Guillermo, do you love Miami enough to stay here for three more years?"

"Yes, I do. In fact, I have some big plans that involves buying up some houses and remodeling them. It's all very exciting and I can tell you more about it at a later time."

My mom stood up from the table and grabbed her coffee, "Yes, a later time would be better."

"Where are you guys going today, Mom?"

"We are going to visit the paint and body shop. Guillermo would like to take a look at the van."

A couple of hours later, Daphne and I watched a movie. My mom and Guillermo walked in the door as it finished.

"Can you girls decorate the clubhouse for the party tonight?"

"We sure can Ms. Harris."

"Great, this is everything you will need." My mom handed Daphne four bags filled with birthday decorations. I called Tonya and asked for her to help us. She showed up at the clubhouse 20 minutes later with Alvaro. We hung up streamers and a banner that said Happy Birthday.

When we were cleaning up Carmen and Enrique walked in the clubhouse. Alex came in behind them with Maria and they brought up a bundle of inflated balloons.

"Carmen, where do you want them?"

"Alex, separate the balloons and let them float up to the ceiling. Just be sure to keep them all in that area," she pointed to the space over by the stereo.

Enrique gave Carmen a strange look. "Trust me Enrique, that area is used as the dance floor."

"Oh, I get it now. That will look fantastic with everyone dancing underneath the balloons."

"Exactly," Carmen answered.

I was suddenly picturing myself dancing beneath all of these balloons with the curled ribbons cascading down from the ceiling. That was until Tonya disturbed me.

"Muñeca, what are doing over there?"

Before I could answer, Daphne answered for me. "It's obvious Tonya; Sammy only smiles like that when she's dreaming of Julio."

Alex laughed and said, "Well, Julio does a lot of dreaming about Sammy too." As he walked over to the sectional sofa with Enrique. Carmen instructed them to move the sectional to the back of the room. Leaving only one sofa in front of the dance floor.

Alex walked back over to me. He had his hands on his hips and he was smiling. "Now you and Julio will have plenty of room to dance tonight Sammy."

"Thank you so much Alex," I told him with a smirk on my face and a touch of sarcasm.

"Anything for the-" I gave Alex a serious look and crossed my arms in front of me. He stopped speaking midsentence.

Carmen walked up to Alex and Enrique. "Where is the van now?"

Alex started laughing before saying, "It's right downstairs Carmen." The best part is that the van is packed with balloons inside.

"How come?"

"Carmen, when Eddie goes to climb in the van, He will be smacked in the face with tons of balloons. I just can't wait for his reaction; it's going to be so funny."

"Alex, when are you giving the van to Eddie?"

"Hopefully soon Sammy," Carmen answered. "She was rolling her eyes and shaking her head at Alex.

We all left the club house and headed downstairs. Julio, Greg, and Lewis were at the pool. "Mom, give me one second."

Daphne, where are you going now?"

"I just need to say something to Greg."

"Carmen, we need to grab something from the van."

"That's fine Alex." Maria, Alvaro, and Alex headed for the parking lot.

"Maybe, we should just have a seat here and wait for everyone to return."

"Tonya, I think that's a great idea.

"Thank you, Carmen, I do too. Carmen chuckled and shook her head at Tonya's comment. The three of us sat down at a picnic table.

I watched Daphne walk over to the pool. That's when I spotted Julio again, he was in the water. He had both of his hands on the ledge of the pool. His arms flexed with all these muscles as he pushed himself up and out of the pool. I couldn't pull my eyes away. He was wearing blue and green Bermuda shorts. They were clinging to his legs, and I was in complete awe.

Carmen laughed and said, "Sammy, close your mouth honey."

Tonya turned around in her chair and faced me. "Muñeca, I don't think you can give all that up."

"Tonya," I blurted out in shock by her honesty in front of Carmen.

Carmen leaned over smiling at me. "Sammy, he has turned into such a handsome young man." She sat back in her chair and told me, "Don't let him go honey."

"Well, at least he put on his sunglasses. Now his eyes won't torture me anymore." Carmen snorted with laughter and Tonya was cracking up. I just had another glimpse of Julio and released a long sigh.

"I think Julio is torturing you on purpose, Muñeca."

"Tonya, I think you're right and he does it effortlessly."

Finally, Daphne came back over to the table, and we walked back to my place. My mom and Guillermo had all the food ready for the party. I was handed a tray filled with empanadas and arepas. Daphne was given a tray filled with shredded pork and Tanya was carrying a tray filled with rice. Carmen was right behind us carrying a box with the birthday cake inside. Together the four of us headed out the backdoor for the Clubhouse. My mom and Guillermo weren't far behind us with two bottles of wine and goblets.

Alex and Alvaro were in the club house when we arrived. They were setting up two coolers with ice for soft drinks. "The cart is over there, Sammy. It's turned on now. You can place all the food inside."

"Alex, what is that cart for?"

"Tonya, it keeps the food warm until you're ready to eat. My mom used it when she was doing catering,"

"Oh, so that's Pilar's secret.

"What secret Tonya?"

Muñeca, I always wondered how Pilar kept the food warm. At every party or gathering she would have for us; her food was always warm. Especially on Sundays, she would make like two trays of arroz con pollo." I nodded my head yes and we both smiled remembering soccer Sundays.

The three of us grabbed the trays and slid them inside the little cart. "This cart is neat. We totally need one of these for our parties."

"Yeah, I think that's not ever gonna happen Tonya.

"Why, Muñeca?"

"That thing, is like totally expensive."

"Well, if you want to have a really nice party with warm food, then we have to get one Muñeca ."

"Okay, whatever you say," and I started to laugh.

Enrique walked out from the back room. "Tio, I just turned on the air conditioner. The room will need about an hour to cool down."

Guillermo clapped his hands together and said, "That's perfect. Alex! Go get Eddie! We can give him his birthday present now."

When I arrived downstairs with Tonya and Daphne. I spotted Guillermo and my mom standing beside the pool. They were talking to Julio and Lewis. I felt Julio's eyes on me as I walked over to the picnic tables. I remained standing and everyone else had a seat.

Alex came back a couple of minutes later with Eddie. The van was now painted black and parked in front of the picnic tables in the first parking space. The minute Eddie saw the van his face lit up. Everyone walked over to the van and Eddie was telling Alex, "She's beautiful, man. I love the new paint job you gave her."

Alex replied, "Open the door and take a look inside." Eddie grabbed the chrome handle and pushed the button inward on the handle with his thumb. He pulled the door open and Alex reached inside to open the adjacent door.

We all yelled, "Surprise!" Just in time before all the balloons flowed out of the van.

Alex handed Eddie the keys and we all sung Happy Birthday. Eddie was in shock with his hand over his mouth. He slowly pulled his hand away and said, "No way, I don't believe it. Alex, are you really giving her to me? She's mine?"

"Yes, Happy Birthday Primo. She's all yours, and she has the Miami Vice stripes airbrushed on the other side." We all walked around to the other side of the van. From the driver's side door to the porthole window there are two stripes in teal blue and florescent pink.

"I can't believe what you have done with her. Can we go for a drive now, Alex?"

"Alex, go. Let Eddie drive his van, but make sure you're back in an hour."

"Eddie was beaming when he said, "Okay, no problem Tio, we'll be back in an hour."

Everyone started to laugh except for Guillermo. He was looking perplexed by everyone laughing and he asked Enrique what's so funny?"

"Tio, I will tell you later."

My mom took Guillermo's hand and he smiled at her with that twinkle in his eyes. He clapped his hands together and made an announcement. "Everyone, you have one hour to get ready for the party. Then we all need to go upstairs to surprise Eddie."

Michael and Arturo arrived at my place 30 minutes later. We were dressed and ready to go to the party in less than an hour.

Daphne left my hair down with all of its natural curls. She styled my bangs and had them cascading around my face. Michael did my makeup, along with my mom's, and Carmen's.

Daphne, Tonya, and I decided to wear something fun, since Eddie is so lively and fun to be around. I wore a white layered, tutu skirt with a red tank top, and a white jean jacket. I put on my red and white slouch socks and wore soft white leather ankle boots. Tonya was also wearing a tutu skirt in black, with a black sweatshirt that had the sleeves, neckline, and hem cut off. She had on black slouch socks, with boots that had a 3-inch heel. Daphne wore a triple layered ruffled skirt in black, a shimmering gold tank top and gold colored pumps. We all put on our long dangle necklaces that hung down to our waist. My necklace was in silver and had a big cross on the end. Tonya's was a gold necklace with a round medallion that had a star in the middle. Daphne chose to wear her two long pearl necklaces with one tied into a knot.

Michael saw us and said, "Oh no, girls! Daphne and Tonya need to swap necklaces." Michael was totally right. The gold necklace matched what Daphne was wearing, and let's face it, Daphne is a star.

My mom came out of her room with Carmen. Their hair was down with just the sides picked up and held in place with a barrette. They both had on blue jeans. My mom and Carmen were also wearing matching Miami Vice T-shirts.

"You ladies look so pretty and I love the twins look."

"Thank you, Tonya. Is everybody ready to go? We only have 10 minutes to get back to the clubhouse. Or we are going to have to explain why we're late? It's going to be an 'okay, no problem' situation."

"Wait, which one will be telling us that? Eddie or Guillermo?" Carmen laughed and told Tonya she enjoyed her boldness.

On the way up the stairs to the club house, my mom and Carmen told Michael and Arturo about the van and Eddie's reaction. When my mom and Carmen were done. Arturo and Michael said, "Okay, no problem," and we laughed.

When we walked inside the clubhouse, the first person I saw was Julio. He stood there looking at me with his big brown eyes and gorgeous smile. That was until Greg walked up behind him and he turned around to speak with him.

Then, I noticed Guillermo's face light up as soon as he saw my mom. He walked right up to her and kissed her hand before he held it. That's when I saw my mom smile and by the look in her eyes, I was reassured he was the only one for my mom. I suddenly remembered when my mom would talk about finding real love one day. When she talked about it, she made it sound like falling in love was mythical at least for her. Now look at her. I thought Guillermo must be my mom's unicorn.

The stereo was turned on, and 'Alive and Kicking' by Simple Minds was playing. I walked over to the dance floor with Tonya, and Daphne. Michael and Arturo soon joined us. The five of us were dancing together under all of these balloons.

When the next song came on, it was 'We Don't Have to Take Our Clothes Off' by Jermaine Stewart. All four of them stopped dancing and just stood there looking at me, until I started to laugh.

The truth is I called Julio's house a few times. When he answered the phone, I would put this song on full blast and place the phone against the speaker. It made me feel better until one-time Lewis answered the phone. I thought it was Julio and placed the phone against the speaker. When the song was over, I hung up. He called me back and said, 'Julio's not here right now, but I will let him know you crank called him again.' I found out they have *69 and I haven't called his house since. Of course, everyone knows about this thanks to Greg.

"Sammy, we're definitely dancing to this song."

That's when I felt Julio's eyes on me. I turned my head to look, and he was staring me down. I suddenly felt embarrassed and quickly turned my head back around. "Michael, I can't do this." He pulled me into the circle, and everyone was already dancing. I turned to the side and Julio was still staring at me. He was biting on his lower lip and just watching me. I wanted to sing the main verse of the song and point to him, but I didn't do it. I just danced to the song with Michael.

Denise walked into the Clubhouse with her boyfriend right when the song ended. We all ran over to them. She introduced us to her boyfriend Mike. He seemed very nice. We spoke to them for a few minutes until Alvaro walked in with his sister, Maria.

Tonya ran over to Alvaro and took hold of his hand. I walked up to Maria and asked, "When is Alex coming?"

Maria whispered, "I don't know, Sammy. They passed by my house and picked us up. Eddie said something about wanting to see some girl named Elena."

"Wow, she was his first girlfriend. Why does he want to see her all of a sudden? I mean he has Heather now, and I thought he was happy with her."

"I don't know, Sammy. I just heard Alex tell him 'It's your birthday Eddie. We can go wherever you want, but you better do it fast.' That's when I told Eddie to drop us off first."

"So, they just dropped you and Alvaro off and now they are going over to her house?" Maria just nodded her head yes. A couple of minutes later, Mig walked in the door. I walked up to him and leaned over to kiss him on the cheek as I greeted him. We joined Michael and Arturo over by the stereo.

While we were speaking with them. Alvaro walked up to Mig. "Hey man, I didn't know you were coming here tonight." Alvaro high-fived Mig, while he jokingly said, "Long time no see." Tonya hugged Mig and thanked him for everything. Then she released him and pulled all three of us into a group hug. This suddenly made me feel nervous to be in the same room with Julio and Mig. I could feel Julio's eyes on me, and I don't want him to get the wrong idea.

I smiled at Tonya and pulled myself away from the group. That's when Eddie and Alex walked into the Clubhouse and we all yelled out, "Happy Birthday, Eddie."

"Again? Guys, I thought we already celebrated my birthday." Everyone was laughing, and Eddie said, "Thank you Alex and Tio for the van. You both know how much I love her, and I named her Miami. I even have this awesome keychain for her keys." He held up the keychain; it was black with Miami written in teal letters.

"Your welcome Sobrino, I hope you enjoy it."

"Tio, I will. Now turn up the Música, and girls let's dance." Arturo turned up the stereo, and 'Rock the Casbah' by the Clash was playing. Tonya, Daphne, Denise, Maria, and I, were dancing in a circle around Eddie. He was in the middle dancing under the balloons. Then he began to pull the balloons down from ceiling and tie them to our hair. Once we each had a balloon, Eddie went back to dancing with his hands above his head.

While we were dancing, I noticed five more people walk into the club house, two girls and three guys. When the song was over, I pointed out the five people to Eddie. He thanked me before walking over to them. I noticed when Julio and Lewis joined them.

Greg took Daphne's hand and walked her out to the dance floor with Tonya and Alvaro.

"Sammy, which one of those girls is Elena?"

"I'm not sure Maria." I glanced over at the group again and of course my eyes went straight to Julio. He was standing in front of them with his back to me.

Mig walked up to me and asked, "Do you want to dance?"

I was instantly nervous and started to grin. I didn't know what I should say or do. I don't want to offend Mig by saying no. At the same time, I'm concerned with what Julio will make of it. He has been accusing me of having something with Mig.

I felt like a deer in headlights. I told him, "Maybe later, Mig. I was just in the middle of a conversation with Maria."

"Sammy, she just left when I approached you."

"What?" I turned my head to look for Maria, and he was right she was gone. I quickly scanned the room and that's when I spotted Maria walking over to Alex.

"How about that dance?" Mig had such a radiant smile on his face. That's when I took in a deep breath and nodded my head yes and we walked over to the dance floor.

Tonya was dancing with Alvaro to 'Come Go with Me' by Exposè. Thank goodness it was a fast song, I thought to myself. When the song ended, the next song to come on was, 'I Wanna Dance with Somebody' by Whitney Houston. We continued dancing and I began to pay attention to the lyrics and immediately thought, I have to get off this dance floor now.

I was leaning over Mig to tell him, let's go. Just as Eddie joined us on the dance floor. He introduced us to his friend Lupe. Mig smiled and said, "You're late Eddie, we already know each other."

"Oh yeah! you hang out at the bonfire, Lupe?"

"Yes, I do every Friday night, but that's not how we know each other Eddie."

Eddie looked surprised and raised his palms up. "Maybe, you should dance with Mig instead of me Lupe?"

Mig stated, "No, dude, it's nothing like that."

Lupe suddenly had this look of disappoint on her face. "He's right Eddie, we just work together." She sounded completely disappointed. Mig leaned across me to give Lupe a hug. I felt a bit awkward after realizing I was dancing with her crush. Until she said, "Hi, Sammy." I was completely startled; than she leaned over and gave me hug.

"You probably don't remember me. We met the other day at the bonfire."

I looked back at Mig, and he smiled. Then I suddenly remembered her. "Oh yeah, I do remember you. How are you, Lupe?"

"I'm good, but I heard what happened to your friend Tonya. How is she doing now?" I pointed to Tonya dancing beside us with Alvaro. "Wow, she looks great after what she's been through."

"Tonya's happy now, more importantly, she's safe. In fact, that's her new bodyguard." Mig smiled when I said that.

Then Eddie took my hand and asked, "Do you ever intend to dance with me, Sammy?" Before I could answer him. He told Mig, "Hey man, we're swapping partners." He walked me over to the other side of the dance floor. I looked back for Mig and saw Lupe's face instead. She was definitely thrilled to be dancing with Mig. She was looking up at Mig with adoring eyes. I thought Mig was so lucky to have someone so infatuated with him. I was happy Eddie removed me from the equation. 'Bizarre Love Triangle' by New Order was playing, when we started to dance. Daphne and Michael were dancing beside us. Before the song was over Tonya and Arturo joined us.

The next song came on and everyone was looking in my direction. It was 'Is This Love' by White Snake. Then I smelled his cologne before I felt his arms wrap around my waist from behind. I heard him say, "Sorry, Primo, but this is our song." Julio pulled me away slowly from his cousin.

Eddie was grinning and waving bye to me. Lewis was standing by the stereo smiling. Obviously, this was all cleverly planed out by the Sanchez boys. Julio suddenly stopped and leaned over me. I could smell his cologne and I felt his breath by my ear as he whispered, "Don't dance with him anymore, Samantha." He squeezed me and I turned around in his arms to face him.

He was looking intently into my eyes. I knew Julio was waiting for a response, but I found it hard to give him one. I just blinked once and tried to clear my head. My eyes went to his biceps as I slid my hands up over his arms and let them rest on his shoulders. Julio bit on his lower lip as he pulled me in closer to him. We danced to our song and when it was over, I began to pull away.

Julio caught my hand, "Samantha, please." I looked up into his pleading eyes. "Dance with me, for just one more song." I stood there quietly looking up at him. While my head was telling me no, walk away now. My heart has a mind of its own and I nodded my head yes, instead. He pulled me slowly back over to him while wearing this gorgeous grin. We danced together for the next two songs. When 'In Your Eyes' by Peter Gabriel came on. We smiled at one another and the memories of Anaheim were vivid in my mind. We danced beside my mom and Guillermo; they were dancing to their song now.

Fleetwood Mac 'Everywhere' came on next. Julio took my hand and he spun me around. My head landed on his chest and I heard his heart beating. That's when I lost all desire to walk away from him. Instead I closed my eyes and wanted to remain wrapped up in his arms. As we moved together to the beat of the song I began to sing along and for the first time I paid attention to the lyrics.

As I continued to sing, the song was striking a chord with me. I looked back at Arturo and he was watching us with a concerned look on his face. That's when I realized I have lost all control of reality.

Suddenly I heard Julio whisper, "I love you." I snapped my head back around and Julio lifted up my chin as he closed his eyes. I quickly pulled away from him before his lips could touch mine. His eyes popped open and he had a shattered look on his face.

Looking back into his eyes I began to feel my walls crumbling. So, I closed my eyes and said, "I will always love you, Julio." Then I opened my eyes and continued to say, "But it's over."

Julio released me that instant and walked away.

It took a lot out of me to say that and I instantly felt like the wind had just been knocked out of me. My legs grew heavy and my head was spinning. Tonya and Daphne ran over to me and asked what's wrong. I was sitting down on the sofa holding my head. I just shook my head and held back the tears.

We walked downstairs to the restrooms. Once I was inside, I blew my nose and wiped under my eyes. I told the girls my walls were crumbling and how it took all of my willpower not to kiss Julio. I told them what I said to him and how it felt like I stabbed myself in the heart. Now I'm left feeling emotionally and mentally exhausted. They both hugged me before we walked out of the bathroom.

When we opened the door, we were greeted by Alvaro, Greg, and Mig. Alvaro spoke first and asked, "Is everything okay Tonya?"

"Everything's fine. We just needed to use the bathroom. Now let's go back upstairs." The six of us walked up the stairs to the clubhouse. When we reached the entrance, Mig asked if he could speak to me for a moment. Alvaro heard that and slid the sliding glass door closed.

I walked over to Mig as he stood by the railing looking down at the pool.

"What's up, Mig?"

"Did I get you into trouble tonight with Julio?"

"No."

"Are you together Sammy?"

"No."

"I only ask because it really appeared that way when you two were together on the dance floor." He looked away from the pool and back at me.

I took in a really deep breath and let it out with a sigh. "The truth is I really do love him," and I shrugged my shoulders as a teardrop slipped from my right eye. "It just sucks."

"Well, I don't know all the details, Sammy, but if you need me, I'm here for you. Like I said before, I'm a great listener and whenever you feel up to talking about it, I'm ready to listen."

"Truthfully, I have said everything I want to say about this situation tonight. I said more than I intended to. Thank you, Mig, for being there for me. So far you have been a pretty good friend."

He leaned in to hug me and I put my hands up to stop him. "Sorry, I don't think you should hug me right now." Mig turned around to see what I was looking at. The entire clubhouse is nothing but sliding glass doors on this side of the building. Everyone from inside the clubhouse was staring at us.

Mig turned his head back around to face me. "I think I should leave now, Sammy. Please, tell everyone bye for me," and he jogged back down the stairs.

When he reached the bottom step, Mig looked up and said, "You look beautiful tonight, Sammy. Did you go through all that trouble for me?"

"Mig, I didn't even know you were going to be here."

"That's our line Sammy," and he waved bye.

When I walked back inside, everyone was sitting around two tables eating; except for Julio, he was standing by the sliding glass doors. Now he was wearing a stone-cold look on his face.

Julio walked up to me and asked, "Is he coming back?"

"No, Mig has gone home. Did you even say hi to him while he was here?"

"No, he didn't come to see me. He came to see you."

"Fine, I'm going home to get Daisy and take her out for a walk. You can come with me if you want." He didn't say anything. When I tried to look into his eyes, he turned his back on me. So, I turned around and left out the same sliding glass door.

I was angry. As soon as I reached the last step, I took off running to my building and I was at my doorstep within seconds. Once I was inside, I leaned up against the kitchen door to catch my breath. Suddenly I was startled by someone knocking on the reverse side of door. When I heard that I jumped away from the door and bumped the side of my head in the process.

By the time I opened the door, I was rubbing my head.

Mig frowned and said, "So, you're already getting a headache from all of this?"

Laughing I answered, "No, I was just surprised when I heard the knock on the door and managed to bump the side of my head. I thought you left Mig. What are you still doing here?"

"The truth is, I was pulling out of the parking lot when I noticed you running into your building. I pulled back into the parking space and walked up here to check on you. Can you see it from here? I parked my van over there in your guest parking spot." I looked out across the parking lot to where Mig was pointing to and saw his van.

"Oh, yeah, I can see your van from here. Thanks for checking on me Mig. Now, I need to take Daisy outside for a walk."

"That's cool, so I guess your alright then Sammy?"

"Yes, I'll be fine Mig." He gave me a fake smile, which indicated he didn't actually believe me. "Do you want to come with us Mig?"

"Sure, I'll go with you."

"Great, give me one second to put the leash on Daisy." I ran inside and found Daisy asleep on her bed. I shook her leash once, and she stood up.

We walked Daisy down the back staircase and over to the sidewalk. Mig asked what happened with Julio. I told him that Julio and I aren't actually on speaking terms at the moment. However, I did invite him to go with me to walk Daisy.

"Sammy, did you tell anyone besides Julio that you were leaving to take Daisy for a walk?"

It wasn't until he asked me that question that I realized I hadn't. "No, I just kind of left."

"You need to return to the clubhouse, Sammy. Everyone is going to become worried about you, and you could ruin the party for Eddie."

"Mig, you mean we, right?"

"Yes, if you agree to go back to the party, I will go back inside with you. That's what friends do for one another, don't they?"

"Yes, I suppose they do, Mig." We dropped Daisy back off at my place and we walked back over to the party. As soon as we entered the clubhouse Tonya and Alvaro came running over to us. Tonya wanted to know why we wandered off. She had been concerned and even went looking for us downstairs with Alvaro.

"Tonya, I had to take Daisy for a walk. I'm sorry, I should have mentioned it before I left."

"That's ok, Muñeca, I'm just glad you're back now." Tonya then squealed, "That's my song." She grabbed my arm and pulled me onto the dance floor. Mig and Alvaro joined us. Now the four of us were dancing together to her favorite song 'Into the Groove' by Madonna. I shook my head and whispered to Tonya, "I shouldn't be out here dancing with-"

"What are you talking about, Muñeca? It's a party. That's what you do at a party."

"Yeah, but not with Mig."

"Why not Mig?" I rolled my eyes and Tonya smiled at me as she pointed to Julio. He was standing across the room, with his back to us. I nodded my head yes and she frowned and shrugged her shoulders. Alvaro leaned over Tonya and kissed her on the cheek. I heard him ask, "What are you whispering about?"

I turned my back to them and continued to dance to the next song. It was 'Never Gonna Give You Up' by Rick Astley. Mig had a big smile on his face the minute the song came on. Even his dimple in his left cheek was showing. I knew the song but never really paid much attention to the lyrics before. A minute into the song, Mig began to point and sing the song to me. That's when I freaked out and tried to exit the dance floor. Tonya noticed and grabbed my hand to stop me from leaving. She whispered, "Don't do this! Not to Mig."

"Fine Tonya, but just until the song is over."

That's when someone yelled out. "It's time to cut the cake." I closed my eyes and thanked God for his perfect timing.

Shortly after Eddie blew out his candles, the cake was being served. Everyone said their goodbyes and left for the night. Only seven of us stayed behind to clean up the clubhouse: Daphne, Greg, Carmen, Guillermo, Enrique, my mom and me.

Julio came back inside with Alex around 30 minutes later. They grabbed Pilar's food warmer and the coolers filled with melted ice cubes. I watched them leave as I was cutting into the balloons with scissors to release the helium.

Daphne and I tossed all of the decorations and dead balloons into a trash bag until it was full. That's when Guillermo announced that he was taking out the garbage and going home.

My mom and Carmen walked over to the glass doors. They watched Guillermo and Enrique walk down the stairs. When they were out of sight Carmen sighed and turned to us. "Girls, it has been a long night and it's time to go."

"Mom, can we just stay a little longer to clean up the balloons?" There were deflated balloons all over the floor. Plus, around another twenty balloons that still needed to be deflated.

"That's alright with me since Alex should be back up here in a few minutes. When he comes back it's time to go. Got it?"

"Okay, Mom."

A few minutes later I was back to picking up the balloons off the floor. "Daphne, can you bring me another garbage bag from the storage closet?"

"Sure, I can do that for you in a minute. I just need to use the bathroom first." I was about to tell her let's just leave now, but she was already walking out the door. Greg was waiting for her on the other side.

Feeling a bit annoyed, I walked into the storage closet to get the bags myself. It was a large closet and I was having trouble finding the garbage bags. Then I heard the door open and saw Julio walk inside and shut the door. He had his back to me, and when he turned around, he was evidently surprised to see me standing there. I had my hands on my hips and I was once again looking at his stone-cold expression.

"I'm looking for the garbage bags Julio. Do you happen to know where they are?"

"Do you know how much it hurt me to watch you dance with another guy tonight?"

"I can beat that question Julio. Do you know how much it hurts me to know that you slept with someone else right after we broke up?"

Julio's eyes were squinting at me. His jaw was tight from his lips pressed together. He was definitely angry, and I was totally annoyed.

"Do you know where the garbage bags are or not?" He pointed to the counter beside me. I turned around and looked to my right, sure enough that's where they were.

"Thank you, Julio. Oh, and just for your information, I didn't dance with Mig. Tonya sort of dragged us all out onto the dance floor."

"That's not what I'm talking about, Samantha."

"Then what are you talking about Julio?"

He walked up closer to me and no longer had the stone-cold expression on his face. Instead, he now had hooded eyes, and pouty lips. "It hurt me to see you with Mig tonight. You were laughing, dancing and talking to him most of the night."

I had to turn my head away from Julio. I was starting to feel remorse for him, and he didn't deserve it. "Julio, maybe you should..."

"Maybe what Samantha?"

Just hearing the anguish tone in his voice was enough to tear me up inside. I looked down at the floor between us and said, "Look, I don't want you to be hurt, not by me Julio."

"Samantha, I know you didn't intentionally set out to hurt me, but honestly, seeing you with Mig really messed me up. I have no one else to blame but myself. I just can't believe I lost you and you no longer believe me. I love you and only you. I don't want anyone else."

"Well, just so you know, nothing happened between us. Mig is my friend and nothing else, so stop making more of it. He knows I'm still in love with you."

"How does he know that? When I don't even know that anymore, Samantha?" I remained quiet and just crossed my arms over my chest.

"Do you know why I ignored you earlier, Samantha?"

"Yes, because I was speaking to my friend Mig outside and you didn't like that."

"No, I ignored you because after you danced with me, you told me you loved me, but it's over. That's the moment I realized you're not willing to take me back and give us a second chance."

"Your right Julio, I'm not. You don't deserve a second chance."

"Samantha, I don't know how to deal with that." I mean, I'm having a hard time accepting that were over. He had tears running down his face. I grabbed the hem of my shirt and wiped under his eyes. Julio just stared at me and I felt his arms slide around my waist. I looked up at him and before I could speak, Julio covered my mouth with his. He pulled me in closer to him and continued to kiss me with everything he was feeling. It was a long deep kiss and when he pulled away; we were both out of breath.

I stood back against the built-in cabinet and placed my hands behind me for support. I could barely feel my legs, and my mind was completely blown away. "I honestly don't know how to live without you Julio. I just know that we can't be together anymore." I dropped my hands back down to my sides and walked past Julio out of the closet.

The lights were off now, and no one else was here. Julio followed me out of the closet and took my hand. He placed it to his lips and kissed my palm. I was looking up at him feeling really nervous. He has torn down all of my walls. He tilted his head to the side and asked, "Will you dance with me Samantha?"

I couldn't say no, and I just stood there nodding my head yes. We walked over to the stereo and Julio turned it on. He lowered the volume and turned the dial until he found a slow song. As we began to dance the song ended. The next song came on and it was 'Stay With Me Tonight' by Jeffrey Osborne. He released me from his embrace and danced with me to this song.

As I was starting to feel relieved and a bit more relaxed now. Julio stopped dancing and asked, "Will you?" He took my hand and kissed it.

"Will I what?"

"Stay with me until Alex comes back, Samantha." Before I could answer he already bent down and picked me up. He carried me over to the sofa. I had his shirt off and was feeling those biceps the minute, we reached the sofa. I had more courage with the lights off and so did Julio. That's why I felt it necessary to remind him that I had no intention of doing anything more than kissing.

We were snuggled up in each other's arms, lying down on the sofa, when the lights turned off outside. I pulled away from him and walked up to the sliding glass doors. Julio walked up behind me and wrapped his arms around me. We both just stood there and watched the sunrise over the pool. Shortly afterwards Alex and Eddie showed up. They were knocking on the locked glass door. We walked over to the door and Julio pulled out the key from his pocket.

"Julio, you had the key the whole time. What happened to stay with me until Alex comes back to lock up?"

He was smiling now and winked at me before saying, "Alex gave me the key and asked me to lock up. I waited until everyone left to walk back inside. I just happened to double check the storage closet and found you."

"Really?" I asked smiling.

"No, actually I watched everyone leave except for you and Daphne. I sent Greg up here to get Daphne and I walked back inside and locked the door. I turned off the lights and joined you in the closet. I just needed to be alone with you Samantha. Even if I leave here with you mad at me."

I wrapped my arms around Julio and kissed him. "I'm not mad at you."

"No?"

"No," I said smiling at him. He leaned in to kiss me and I grabbed the key from Julio's hand.

"I unlocked the glass door and said, "We both needed this for closure Julio."

Eddie pulled the door open and Alex said, "I'm sorry, guys, but it's time to go." I waved bye and took off running as fast as I could. Now I felt like a complete mess. I had tears pouring down my face and a runny nose. I was climbing up the stairs when Julio ran past me up the staircase. He stood on the top of the stairs waiting for me.

"Julio, what are you doing here?"

"I want to go for a walk with you and Daisy before I leave?"

"Great, she'll love that," I told him, and my voice cracked. He had a concerned look on his face as he jogged back down the stairs to me. He took off his shirt and wiped away my tears. My eyes went straight to his chiseled chest and tight abs. Now I wished the lights had been on earlier in the clubhouse.

We walked out to the golf course, and Daisy chased Julio around the lake for a bit. We eventually sat down under our tree. He wrapped his arms around me and said, "Samantha, I wish you could trust me enough to tell me honestly what you're feeling or what you want."

"The truth is that whenever I hear one of our songs, I want to dance with you. When I go out with my friends, I wish you were there with me to.

"Samantha, I know that feeling, because I feel the same way. "You still love me and would give me a second chance if I lived here again in Miami."

"I think your right Julio, but you don't. Every time were together it just feels natural for me to hold your hand and kiss you. What doesn't feel natural to me is the distance; the amount of time we have to spend apart. Truthfully, that's why we can't be together anymore."

Julio squeezed me and said, "I hope you enjoy your first year in high school."

That's when I pulled my head back and looked up into his piercing brown eyes and faked a smile. "I hope you will too, Julio." After that, I stood up and offered him my hand to help him up.

He took my hand and pulled me back down onto his lap. He kissed me once more and he was teary-eyed. "Don't forget about me, Samantha." I grabbed Daisy's leash and stood up.

"Julio, I can't. Believe me, I've tried." I took off running and ran the whole way back home with Daisy beside me. It was the only way I could release the pain I was feeling, knowing that my time with Julio was over once again.

The rest of the week went by so fast. Guillermo sort of moved in with Alex until Enrique got back in town. When my mom said she wasn't leaving Miami for at least three years, Guillermo just said, "Okay, no problem. I can't live without you. I will buy a house and live here." My mom just smiled and talked about how lucky she was to have such an understanding fiancé.

On my first day of school, I was a nervous wreck. I kept dropping everything I came into contact with prior to leaving my house. I took Daisy for a walk. When I came back inside, I grabbed my book bag off the counter. I was walking out the door when my mom said, "Wait for Guillermo. He would like to take you to school on your first day."

"Mom, I'm meeting up with Tonya at the bus stop."

"Guillermo can pick her up on the way to school, Sam."

"Fine mom." I took a seat on the stool at the kitchen counter. He came knocking on the door around five minutes later.

He was smiling and ready to go. "Come on, Sammy. You have to get there and check everything out before everyone else arrives." I followed him downstairs to the car. Once we were in the car, Guillermo asked, "Are you still grounded?"

"Yes, and I understand why. I had no right to spend the night at the clubhouse with Julio. It was selfish of me to make my mom worry like that."

"I know it was hard for Julio to leave you, Samantha. The two of you have feelings for one another that I have never felt until I met your mother. I know that love does not have a time limit, and one day you may find yourself back with Julio."

I released a loud exaggerated sigh and turned my head to look out the window. Guillermo pulled into a parking space and put the car into park. "I'm sorry Sammy."

"For what?"

"For bringing up you know who." I started to giggle after he said that and turned my head around to look at Guillermo.

"Why? I don't mind if you talk about Julio or mention his name."

"Are you sure about that Sammy?"

"Yes, I just...nevermind."

"Right now, you're starting high school Sammy, and you will be going to lots of parties and football games. You will meet lots of people; some you may form a friendship with. Others are placed in our lives to teach us valuable lessons. Whatever the case may be, you just need to remember to stay focused in class. The grades you earn now are your ticket into college."

"Thank you, Guillermo."

He smiled and asked, "For what?"

"For taking the time to talk to me. Oh, and before I forget, we need to pick up Tonya."

"Where's Tonya?"

"Oh, she should be at the bus stop already." As soon as we pulled out of the complex, Tonya was walking out onto the sidewalk.

We pulled up alongside her and Tonya climbed in. I decided now was a good time to ask about the cars. "Guillermo, whose minivan is this?"

"I got it for your mother."

"It's really nice, Guillermo."

"Yes, I think so too. This is the first car I gave to your mother."

"Does my mom like it?"

"No."

"Why? What's wrong with it?"

"Your mother said she doesn't need a new car."

Tonya and I went to laughing and he was shaking his head."

"Sorry Guillermo. Mom thinks if it's not broken, why replace it?"

"Whose black Mercedes is in the parking lot?"

"I bought it for Alex to replace the van. He wanted a Lincoln town car instead of the Mercedes. I bought him one in navy blue. I gave your mother the Mercedes. She said, no thank you, that's too fancy for her. She just wants her own car, and that's fine."

"That's fine, really it doesn't sound fine. Why is that? Is there something wrong with my mom's car. Is it unacceptable to be seen inside it or something? I mean this is Miami and I know it's not a Mercedes but it's what my mom can afford."

Guillermo laughed and asked, "Are you finished Sammy?" I nodded my head yes and Tonya was looking over at me with her eyebrows raised. "Good, now I will tell you the truth the whole truth and nothing but the truth. If that's alright with you Sammy?"

"Who cares what Muñeca thinks, tell me."

I turned my head towards the back seat and gave Tonya a dirty look.

Guillermo saw it and laughed again. "How about I tell you both. Tonya is that okay with you?"

"Go for it, Guillermo."

"Okay, so back to what I was saying before. The problem now is that my nephew Eddie was not paying attention when he drove your mom's car last week and he wrecked the whole front end of her car."

"How did he do that? Is the car able to be repaired?"

"Well, to tell you the truth he had Lewis in the car. Who knows exactly what happened? I only know that nobody was hurt, and he has not told your mother. The car appears to be a total loss and not worth the amount of money to repair the damages. Of course, I will pay whatever to fix her car. I just want your mother to be happy."

"Eddie never told my mom before he left?"

"No, he did not tell her. He is a coward. I was driving your mom around in the rental car all week. So, we didn't know anything. Eddie didn't tell me until an hour before he left on Tuesday. I told him to tell your mother, but she was not home before Eddie left."

"Now, before I show your mother her car, I want to make sure she has something she would be happy to drive in place of her car."

"Good luck, Guillermo."

"Yes, good luck," Tonya said. We both exited the van and waved bye to Guillermo.

We walked inside school through the main entrance. We ran into Michael first, and he hugged us and asked if we have seen Daphne and Arturo yet. We both said no, and he told us they should be here any minute.

Alvaro and Maria found us next. The minute Alvaro saw Tonya his eyes lit up. Tonya was just as excited to see Alvaro. Maria stood by Michael and me. We all asked what time everyone is scheduled to have lunch. "Finally," Tonya said as she squeezed me. "We have lunch together Muñeca."

The bell rang, and I headed to my homeroom. I found Greg, Arturo, and Daphne sitting all together in my first class. It was so exciting as Arturo and I shared a desk. Greg and Daphne shared another desk in front of us. We only have the one class together, but it's already my favorite. Plus, we all have lunch at the same time on second shift. When the bell rang and our computer class was over, I told everybody to save me seat at lunch.

It was the end of the day and Michael ran up to me and asked, "Where's your last class, Sammy?"

"Hi, Michael, I don't know," and I handed him my itinerary.

"Oh no way, that's perfect. It's with me, Sammy. I can't believe you chose Drama."

"How could I not, Michael? That's all you talked about last year: High School Drama class. I had to find out what all of the excitement was about."

"It's this way, and we need to hurry up. We don't want to be late." He was practically running down the hall to class.

When we walked inside, Mig was sitting down at one of the tables. Michael saw him and said, "Over here, Sammy, next to Mig."

That's when I saw Mig smile and wave us over.

"Hi Sammy."

"Mig, do you usually take drama?"

"No, this is my first year. I thought this could help me with my stage fright."

"So, it wasn't because I talked about checking out the drama class. It's because you have stage fright, Mig?"

"Maybe it was a little bit of both, Sammy."

I had my right elbow up on the desk with my hand under my chin smiling at him. When I asked, "Are you sure about that? I have to say there's a guy who looks just like you at the bonfire. I saw him play a couple of weeks ago. He played the drums in front of a crowd and had no stage fright whatsoever."

"That could have been me, who knows." I let out a giggle and he said, "Okay so it was definitely me. The thing of it was that I was only able to play with such confidence because of a certain girl. On that night when you saw me, she was there. Now I've had a crush on this girl for a while. Do you think she was impressed by my performance?"

"I can't really speak for someone else, but I was impressed."

Then Mig leaned over and spoke in a low voice, "It could also be that I found out there is only one drama class per school year. That made the chances of me having the same class with my high-School crush a hundred percent." A sort of laugh/cough escaped Michael just then. Honestly until that point I forget he was sitting beside me. We both turned around and faced Michael. He was smiling at the both of us.

Chapter 14 The Lie

It's been about a year now since I last saw Julio. I heard that he is doing really well in school and he is in an on-again, off-again relationship. We don't speak to one another, but we are pen pals and write to one another. He hasn't ever told me about his girlfriend, but my mom and Guillermo are always on the phone with Pilar.

I'm 16 now and it's the summer of '89. I've been spending most of my time at the pool or at the beach during the day with Arturo and the girls. I don't have a boyfriend and I don't want one. I go out on dates here and there, but nothing exciting.

Arturo says I'm single because I compare every guy to Julio. That's why everyone I date eventually ends up in the friend zone. I told him that's not it. I love my life the way it is now. I get to spend time hanging out with my friends. We cruise the Grove and go to the bonfire every Friday night. I don't have to deal with jealousy and heartache anymore. It's like I'm finally free from all that emotional stuff. I was in love once and that's enough for me.

Tonya is still dating Alvaro, and they have been official now for nine months as of yesterday. I can't believe it took Tonya almost two months to commit to Alvaro. I mean she obviously can't stand to be away from him. Michael and Arturo have their own theory on that subject. They think it has something to do with her unspoken feelings that still linger for Lewis.

My mom and Guillermo are still the cutest couple on earth. They continue to make each other so happy and it's like everyday they grow closer to one other. Carmen is also very content in her relationship with her boyfriend, Enrique. They are officially a couple and walk around beaming with a newfound joy of life that they are currently exploring together.

Enrique and Guillermo live in the building next door, or should I say Alex's old apartment. Guillermo knew Alex was at the age where he needed his own space. He also knew he enjoyed living close to my mom, so he did the next best thing and bought a house for Alex. Which happens to be down the street from his fiancé Maria.

That's right Alex and Maria are engaged to be married. Alex had a big dinner about a month ago and invited all of us to attend. He also invited his mother Pilar, and Maria's mom. It was at this dinner that Alex proposed to Maria. She screamed when she saw the ring. It wasn't until Alex removed the ring from the box and slid it onto her finger that she finally said yes. Maria was in shock and couldn't believe her dream to marry Alex was coming true. It was a great night. The parents were all together again and Alex made Maria the happiest girl on earth.

It was at this same dinner that Pilar told us how she couldn't wait until we were back in Anaheim. I looked across the table at my mom, she was smiling and talking about how the time has flown by. She can't believe Erika will already be a year old. Pilar reached into her purse and pulled out a little photo album full of the latest pictures of Erika.

Everyone was looking at the photos, when Pilar noticed I had drifted off somewhere else. She lowered her voice so only I could hear her and said, "Sammy, I know it would mean a lot to Monica for you to attend Erika's birthday party. Everyone misses you and besides your brother Tommy will be there." I told her of course, I would be there, and Pilar, hugged me.

"Hey, Sammy, are you going to eat your slice of pizza?"

"No, you can have it, Greg."

Daphne stood up from the table and walked over to me. I just sat down on the sofa to start watching a movie with Mig. "Sammy, I want to speak to you."

"Okay, Daphne, so talk."

"Sammy, I think we should speak in private."

"Daphne, don't be silly; I have nothing to hide. You can speak to me in front of Mig unless it has something to do with you. Does it have something to do with you?"

"No, it doesn't. So fine, I will just come out and say it. I have noticed that since you had dinner with Pilar, you don't eat very much unless it's a salad or a fruit bowl. I have also heard that you have taken up jogging with Tonya."

"Yes, that's all true. I have been thinking more than ever about getting fit. Now I have been watching what I eat, I'm taking aerobic classes and I'm feeling better about myself."

"Sammy, that's so great! I am truly happy for you, but why all of a sudden?"

I sat back down on the couch and rolled my eyes. "Listen, I need to look good and feel confident when I go back to Anaheim."

"Why? Is Erika really going to be that concerned with your appearance? She's only a year old. I don't think she cares Sammy."

"Very funny, Daphne. It's because her uncle will be there, and he is really into working out everyday and he lives at the gym. Plus, now he has a girlfriend, and I'm like totally single. I don't want him to think that I'm incapable of having a boyfriend. You know, like, if there is something wrong with me. I just thought, if I look good, and I'm confident, then Julio won't actually think something awful like that."

"What's the truth, Sammy?"

I looked down at the floor and then back up at Daphne. "The truth is that I'm nervous about seeing Julio again."

"Why? It's not like you can be together."

I stood up and said, "I know that, but what he thinks of me and his opinion of me matters to me. I have been waiting for these feelings to go away, but they don't Daphne." I plopped myself back down on the sofa and stared at the coffee table.

"So, what's the plan? What are you going to do?"

"Daphne, I don't have a plan and I don't intend to do anything. Maybe your brother is right and that's why I don't have a boyfriend and I will be single for the rest of my life."

"Oh, you have got to be kidding me," Greg yelled from the kitchen. "I thought you were the one that broke up with Julio."

"She was," Daphne shouted back to Greg.

"Actually, it was mutually decided before he ever moved to Anaheim."

"No, Sammy, that's not what I'm talking about. Julio told me you ended it again the last time he was here for Eddie's birthday. In fact, he had no intention of leaving on that Tuesday last time he was here. He already had his plane ticket and was planning on staying in Miami until Saturday. He only left because you wouldn't give him a second chance and he was heartbroken again."

"Look, Greg. I know that Julio is like a brother to you. I also know that you have his side no matter what. I am going to ask you not to mention one word of what I said here tonight to your friend Julio. Remember I am your friend too and I forgot you were in the room." I had tears in my eyes and needed a second to hold them in. Once I felt in control of my emotions again, I said, "My feelings for Julio need to remain in this room between the four of us."

"Sammy, I won't say a word, if you can keep a promise to me."

"What type of promise?"

"Don't break my friends' heart again." Greg put up his pinkie and we shook on it.

"Thank you, Greg, for being a friend to me too."

I turned my head to look over at Mig. He had been quiet, this whole time. "Mig, what's wrong? You haven't said a word. Are you okay?"

"Yeah, I just realized why I didn't have a chance with you from the beginning. Don't get me wrong. I treasure our friendship, but I always wondered why you wouldn't give me a chance. Tonight, is the first time I found out why, and I don't know. I guess you can say, I'm a little bit jealous of Julio right now."

"Oh, Mig, come on. Would it help if I told you that you're the only guy since Julio that I ever found attractive?"

"Really?" I nodded my head yes.

"That bit of information helps a lot. My ego has been restored. Thank you, Sammy, but you still won't let me take you out on a real date."

"No, I would rather stay single at the moment. Besides we're together all the time. We just had dinner. Mig, remember the pizza?"

"Come on, Sammy. You know that's not what I mean."

"No, what do you mean?"

"I want to take you out to a restaurant for dinner. I want to go to a movie with you just so I can casually rest my arm across the back of your chair. You know, a real date. I will even buy popcorn."

"Okay, Mig, you totally convinced me a real date with popcorn and everything. I have no choice I'm a sucker for popcorn."

"That sounds great guys. Now can we watch the movie?"

"Sure Greg, here you go." Mig handed Greg the VHS tape and he inserted it into the VCR. Then the four of us all gathered around the TV as we waited patiently for the for the VHS tape to rewind. It was from the video store and someone returned the tape without rewinding it first. We all fell asleep during the movie and I woke up to the sound of my beeper going off.

When I took a look at my beeper, I saw that I had nine minutes to get home. I quickly woke up Daphne and placed my index finger in front of my mouth indicating to be quiet. Then she looked over at Greg, he was passed out beside her on the floor. She gave me the pouty look like, isn't he adorable? I just nodded my head yes and waved come on. She finally stood up and we slowly tiptoed out of Mig's house. We locked the door behind us and ran to my mom's car and jumped in.

Daphne put on the radio, and 'That Was Yesterday' began to play. I haven't heard this song since Julio played it for me about a year ago. When the song ended, I had tons of emotions I hadn't felt in a long-time creeping in.

My brother was outside waving to us with Daisy beside him. Tommy walked over to the car smiling and I lowered the window.

"Why are you smiling, Tommy?"

"You should be asking me how much trouble you're going to be in for arriving home after curfew, especially when you borrowed mom's car?"

"Okay, fine. How much trouble am I in?"

"None, mom was already in bed around eleven o'clock. I called your beeper about 20 minutes ago and I grabbed Daisy's leash and headed outside for a walk. Now, if mom is awake when you walk inside, you can just say we were outside walking Daisy."

"Oh man, what do you want in exchange for this, Tommy?"

"Your window seat on the plane, Sam."

"Fine, Tommy, but I don't even know where I will be sitting on the plane."

"Mom said earlier tonight they purchased the plane tickets and we're riding first class."

"So, what, Tommy? That doesn't mean I have a window seat."

"Actually, mom also said in order to be fair, I have the window seat on the ride to Anaheim and you have it leaving."

"Fine, you can have my window seat Tommy. Now let me go park the car."

As I was walking upstairs Tommy began his interrogation. "So, where did you guys end up going tonight? I know you didn't go to the bonfire with it raining most of the night."

"No, that plan was cancelled. We decided to pick up a pizza and bring it over to Mig's house. We all just hung out and watched a movie, it was so good that we all fell asleep."

As we walked inside, Tommy yelled, "You slept over some guy's house?"

That's when I quickly walked back outside with Tommy and shut the door behind us, leaving Daphne and Daisy inside. "No, not like that. It wasn't on purpose, so don't yell at me. We all just fell asleep on the couch watching a movie. I must have slept maybe an hour, if that. It wasn't like I intentionally went over to Mig's house to spend the night, or something."

"Sam, if you're that tired, come home. You don't fall asleep at some guy's house. When you're asleep, you are vulnerable, and a lot of guys would take advantage of that opportunity."

"Mig is not like that, and Greg was there. Do you honestly think he would allow anyone to take advantage of me?"

"Sam, you didn't tell me Greg was there until now."

"Oh sorry, yeah, he was there, and it was just the four of us,"

"Okay, then I know you were safe not because of Mig, but because of Greg. Still remember what I said, if you're tired like that just come home. Don't nap at some guy's house."

"Okay, Tommy. You're right. If I feel sleepy in the future, I will go home."

Then Tommy hugged me and said, "I'm your big brother. It's my responsibility to watch over you."

"I know, Tommy, and I love you for it. I'm going back inside now. I need to get some sleep."

The next day we woke up early in the morning to the sound of knocking on my bedroom door. When I opened the door, my mom told me we needed to get up now. We have to be ready to leave here in less than an hour.

When I shut my bedroom door, Daphne pulled the comforter over her head. Then, she told me to wake her up when I was out of the shower. I just grabbed my bathrobe out of the closet and headed for the bathroom. When I came back into my room, Daphne already made my bed.

She hung up the phone and walked out of my room to take a shower. We were both dressed and ready to go in less than 30 minutes. We headed into the kitchen and I made us each a fruit salad for breakfast. We were eating at the counter when my mom walked in to check on us.

"Girls, it's going to be a long day today and I hope you both are ready for it. Oh, and please tell me you both have your bags packed."

"Yes, Mom. I packed my suitcase yesterday, and so did Tommy."

"What about you, Daphne?"

"Yes, I have almost all of my stuff packed. I only have one thing left to pack, and that's Greg. The problem is I haven't found a suitcase big enough to hold him."

My mom laughed and she hugged Daphne. "You will be alright without Greg. It's only four days. Besides, your brother, Sammy, and Tommy will be going up with you. When you get up there, the entire Sanchez family will be there and of course, Michael.

"I know, Ms. Harris. I just struggle with separation anxiety whenever I imagine being that far away from Greg."

I just looked over at Daphne and shook my head. "That's why I'm staying single."

Daphne whispered, "That's not why?"

I looked over at Daphne and I was panicking. "Don't bring that up again, especially when we're in Anaheim."

"Bring up what, Sam?"

"Oh, nothing, Mom."

"Okay, well you girls need to wash out your bowls and grab Daisy. We're leaving here in two minutes."

When my mom left the kitchen, Daphne said, "I was only teasing you. That's why I whispered. Man, I can't believe how upset you got over that, Sammy."

"I'm sorry, I'm just really nervous about this trip. I have a feeling it's going to be rough on me this time."

"Don't worry, Sammy. We're all going to be there with you. It will be fine, and I promise not to tease you anymore about what you said last night."

"Thank you, Daphne. Now let's go get Tommy before my mom comes back."

My mom wasn't wrong when she said it would be a long day. We dropped Daisy off at Tonya's house first, on our way out to Carmen's Hair Salon. We all must have our hair done according to my mom and Carmen. This was including the guys, except when they were finished, they all left. We had to stay behind to have our nails done too. When we were done at the salon, we headed back home, but only long enough to change clothes and pick up our bags. We stopped off at the deli to pick up some sandwiches for the flight. Finally, we were off to our last destination in Miami, the airport. We found out an hour later that the plane we were supposed to be on hadn't even arrived yet.

When we landed at LAX Airport, it was after midnight Pacific time. We still had another 45-minute drive to Guillermo's house. By the time we arrived at his house, we all just walked inside and went to bed.

I woke up the next morning and I was still dressed in my clothes from the day before. I looked around the room and that's when I remembered I was in Anaheim. Suddenly, I felt excited to be here again. I loved this bedroom. It was the same room we stayed in last time we were here.

I climbed out of bed and looked over at Daphne. She was still sound asleep in the bed beside mine. I put on my sneakers and walked out to the kitchen. Tommy and Alex were sitting at the counter eating a bowl of cereal. I grabbed a bowl down from the cabinet and sat down beside them.

"Good morning, Sammy."

"Good morning, Alex."

"Good Morning, Sam. Did you see who is outside by the pool already?"

"No, I haven't. I just woke up, Tommy." I was curious to see who was here. I couldn't see anyone from the counter, so I stood up and walked over to the sliding glass doors. I still didn't see anyone on the pool deck, so I walked back to the counter. Once I sat back down, I poured some cereal and milk into my bowl.

"Well, that's kind of rude, Sam. You're not even going to say hello to him."

"Very funny, Tommy. There's nobody out there."

"Sure, there is. Maybe he walked down to the cabana to take a nap."

"Alex, if he is in the cabana, I definitely have no business disturbing him. We all learned that lesson the last time we were here."

"Touché, Sammy," Alex said, as he held up his glass of orange juice to me.

"I was just thinking about all of the suitcases we need to bring in the house from the car . He could help us out. Four people would make the job easier."

"You're right, Tommy. So why don't you go down to the cabana and ask your mystery friend to help us?"

"Okay, I will." He stood up and walked out the sliding glass door. I watched him leave, then I went back to eating my cereal.

Daphne walked in the kitchen a minute later and asked, "Who is Tommy speaking to?"

I looked up from my bowl and out the sliding glass door. I realized it was Michael and jumped up from the counter to run outside, Daphne followed me.

We both ran over to Michael and hugged him. "You're here already? What time did your dad drop you off?"

"My dad didn't drive me here. Are you kidding? I wouldn't be here for at least another four hours. I drove here myself in my car."

"Your dad bought you another car?"

"No, Daphne, it's just a rental car for the summer. My dad thought it would be easier on both of us, if I had my own car to get around in to attend auditions and rehearsals. Oh, and Sammy, I signed up for summer acting classes."

Daphne yawned, indicating this conversation was boring. "I can tell you all about that later. What took you guys so long to get here? When I spoke to Alex and Tommy, they said it took forever."

"Michael, our flight was delayed three hours in Miami, we arrived after midnight, but we're here now."

"So, what's on the agenda today, girls?"

"Truthfully Michael, we still need to remove our luggage from the car. We were so exhausted when we arrived here last night that we just left our bags in the car and went to bed."

"Oh no, that's horrible, Sammy, we need to get the makeup out of the car before it all gets ruined by the heat."

"We don't need to worry about that, Michael. My mom and Ms. Harris placed all of their makeup into carry-ons. Those two cases were the only ones to make it into the house last night."

"Daphne, I should have known your mom wouldn't allow anything to happen to the makeup. It's a necessity to look fantastic all weekend. Especially with family photos at the birthday party. This weekend is going to be so much fun, girls."

"Michael, are you going to be our fairy godmother all weekend?"
"Aren't I always, Sammy?"

I wrapped my arms around him and said, "I'm so glad you're here with us, Michael. We already miss you, and you haven't been gone that long.

"Oh, stop it Sammy. You're going to make me cry."

The three of us were laughing when I heard, "Hello, Samantha."

Michael and Daphne both looked back at me. I squeezed Michael's shoulders once, before I removed my arms entirely from his shoulders. I turned around and faced Lewis and said, "Good morning."

I walked over to him and gave him a hug and a kiss on the cheek. I asked him if he would help us grab the luggage from the car.

"No problem, Sammy."

He walked over and shook hands with Michael. Then he hugged Daphne and kissed her on the cheek before walking back inside the house.

Once the sliding glass door was shut, Michael grabbed his chest and said, "I thought I was going to have a heart attack. I didn't know how your relationship was with Lewis anymore especially after the whole group dating scenario with his girlfriend's cousin."

"That's ridiculous, Lewis and I are fine. I don't blame him for what Julio did."

"Well Sammy, I wasn't really sure of that because you didn't speak to him at all during Eddie's party."

"Michael, he was hanging out with Julio during the party and you already know what happened between us that night."

He slapped his hand to his forehead and said, "Oh that's right, Mig was there."

"Yup, I guess all we have to worry about now is your interaction with Julio."

"Daphne," I exclaimed.

"Really, I'm kind of looking forward to that Daphne. I think it's going to get steamy, if you know what I mean."

"Stop it guys. He has a girlfriend now."

"Yeah, and she's not you, Sammy, so I'm sure it's just some girl he hangs out with to pass time. Either way, not to worry. Your fairy godmother is here. Whatever happens, you will always look stunning."

I huffed blowing out my cheeks in the process and decided to ignore their comments. I know they mean well but it's not helping my nerves. I hugged Michael again and told him, "Thank you so much for agreeing to stay with us the next four days. I feel so much better knowing you're here."

"Well of course, that's what friends are for. We stand together and give each other strength and courage. I know it will be rough, but you will get through this. Besides, you have nothing to worry about. Just remember your weakness and don't give into them."

"I remember, Michael. My weakness is Julio and I need to avoid eye contact with him. Hey, maybe I will get lucky, and he'll wear sunglasses the whole time I'm here."

"That's some really wishful thinking, Sammy."

When Arturo woke up, we had just finished bringing in the last piece of luggage. It was hot and we all decided to go to the pool. We told Arturo our plans and left him in the kitchen eating his cereal. While we all headed to our separate rooms to get dressed, Alex walked upstairs to wake up Maria and invite her to join us.

There was a knock on our bedroom door two minutes later. Daphne was in the bathroom getting changed. I quickly pulled my T-shirt on over my bathing suit and answered the door. It was my mom and she looked upset.

"Hi, mom."

"Sam, you guys can't go to the pool now. We're meeting up with Pilar and the rest of the family for brunch in another hour."

"Mom, we didn't know that. I'm sorry, we'll get dressed now. How do you want us to dress for brunch?"

Guillermo walked up behind my mom smiling. "Lori, it's fine. Let them all go to the pool and we can have everybody come over here instead."

"Guillermo, are you sure about this? What are we going to feed everyone?"

"Lori, baby, we can go to the grocery store now and pick up everything we need. We will have a barbeque, and everyone can come over here. Everything will be fine. I will call my sister and my brother, now."

My mom was smiling as she watched Guillermo walk away. Then my mom called out, "Carmen, wait, change of plans."

"What was that Lori?"

"Carmen, I will explain everything to you in a minute. Let the boys go to the pool."

My mom hugged me and said, "Have fun at the pool, Sam." Then she ran down the hall toward Carmen.

I shut the bedroom door and walked over to the bathroom door. I told Daphne to hurry up and get out here. When she walked out, she was wearing her black one-piece bathing suit.

"I'm ready to race Arturo and your brother. I can't believe they think they're faster than me. I know I'm faster than the two them put together and I'm going to prove it."

"Daphne, sit down. I need to talk to you."

She walked over to chair and sat down. "What happened now? I thought we were going to the pool."

"We are going to the pool, but my mom was just here, and things have changed."

"What changed?" I sat down in the ottoman in front of her.

"To make a long story short, Guillermo is calling Pilar and his brother and he's inviting everyone to come over here, like right now." Daphne stood up and declared that to be awesome.

"Why is that awesome?"

"Sammy, now we can totally take out Tommy and Arturo. I want Monica and Michael on our team. I only have one suggestion."

"What's that?"

"Change into your one-piece bathing suit."

I quickly changed into my one-piece, and we met up with Arturo and Michael at the pool. I told them the entire Sanchez family was coming over here now. Arturo and Michael hugged me. "It's going to be alright, Sammy. We're all here with you. Remember that."

"Thank you, Arturo."

"Hey Sammy, maybe you'll get your wish, and Julio will be wearing sunglasses. Now we only have to hope that he swims with his shirt on or you will be tortured by his bulging biceps." I rolled my eyes before thanking Michael for the reminder. Michael laughed and told Arturo we didn't plan for that type of torture.

That's when Tommy walked outside with Alex and Maria.

"What's so funny?"

"Oh, nothing, Tommy. Do you know that everyone is coming over here to join us at the pool, and we're having a barbeque?"

"No, I didn't know that. Who told you that, Daphne?"

"Your sister."

Alex smiled and told Maria, "I can't wait for you to finally see Erika. She is so beautiful and smart, just like her uncle Alex." Maria just smiled and shoved Alex into the pool. Daphne and I ran up to Maria and we pushed her into the pool to be with Alex. The two of them were laughing and telling all of us to get in.

Once everyone was in the pool, Daphne wanted to race. Alex suggested we wait for everyone and play Marco Polo. He volunteered to be Marco first. He started to yell Marco when Eddie, Lewis, and Julio came running toward the pool yelling Polo and jumped in. I had an instant feeling of elation the minute I saw Julio. My mind went blank for a second and Alex was headed in my direction. I was standing right beside him when he called out Marco. I had no choice, I had to yell out Polo, and he tagged me.

I was now Marco and swam over to the middle of the pool. I counted down from ten and yelled Marco. Everyone yelled out Polo, and I headed in the direction that I heard the calls from. I stopped swimming when I felt the wall beside me. I stood still and tried to catch any sound that I could. I was just about ready to call out Marco again when I picked up on a sound. I reached out my hand and quickly tagged the person in front of me. When I opened my eyes, it was Julio. He hugged me and kissed me on the cheek. "Welcome back to Anaheim, Sammy." I had instant butterflies, and he swam off to the middle of the pool and began counting. We stayed in the pool until Monica arrived with Erika.

The Sanchez boys hung out beside the barbeque grill. The rest of us hung out at the table with Monica and Erika. Lewis turned on his boombox and the parents all came outside together laughing and dancing. We had our lunch poolside. The parents went back in the house once everyone was finished eating. Monica had to take Erika home to have a nap, so Tommy and I went with her.

When Monica dropped us off at Guillermo's house two hours later. The parents were all in the living room and Guillermo called us over. He told us everyone's downstairs watching a movie.

We walked downstairs to the theatre room. The lights were turned off and a movie was playing. Everyone was spread out on different sofas. Daphne was the first person to notice us walk in the room. She sat up and called us over to sit with her on the U-shaped sectional. She whispered, "Great timing. Lewis just put the movie on, and I think it's supposed to be scary."

Julio walked up to me and handed me a blanket. "In case you get scared or disgusted, you can cover your eyes."

"Thank you, Julio," I reached for the blanket and grabbed Julio's hand instead. I quickly released it and said, "Sorry." He smiled and placed the blanket down on my lap. He took a seat on the opposite side of the sectional facing me.

The whole time the movie was playing, my mind kept drifting off, thinking about Julio. His smile, those eyes, and that chest of his. Wow, it was pure torture being in the pool with him today. He was taller now and his voice was much deeper and so masculine. The movie was awesome! Don't get me wrong, but it couldn't keep my attention off Julio.

Especially now that I'm in the same room with him and sitting on the same sofa. When the movie was over and the lights were on, I casually turned my eyes toward Julio. He was staring back at me. I quickly turned my head to the side and whispered, "Daphne, let's go."

We both stood up to leave, but we noticed Maria and Alex were locked in an embrace in front of the door. I was beginning to feel anxious as I noticed Julio was standing beside me. I turned my head around to look at Daphne and Eddie said, "Hey, your blocking the door and I need to go."

Alex and Maria pulled apart and took a seat on the couch beside the door. Daphne and I followed the boys out of the room. When the boys all began to walk up the stairs, I grabbed Daphne's hand and we walked past the stairs and out the garage door. We walked through the garage, out the side door, and along the side of the house to the backyard. When Daphne spotted the cabana, she headed straight for it and I followed her inside. "Now this right here brings back memories, doesn't it, Sammy?"

"Yes, everything here brings back memories, Daphne, including Julio. That's the problem. I just feel so happy, and it's because Julio is in the same room with me. I can't explain it. I just feel like I'm going to pop from so much happiness building up inside me." Daphne started to laugh, and then I heard footsteps outside. I looked over at Daphne and said, "Shhh."

Arturo and Michael came running inside the cabana. They sat down on the couch and Arturo asked, "Why did you two take off like that? What's going on?"

"Arturo, it's my fault. I am really trying my best to keep it together."

"Why? What happened? I really thought you two were getting along. At least it seemed that way when we were at the pool. What did I miss?"

"You didn't miss anything and you're right. We have been getting along. It's me. I'm just feeling overwhelmed with happiness. I can't explain it."

"I don't blame you one bit, Sammy. Did you see his biceps? They're even bigger now."

Arturo gave Michael a dirty look, and Michael said, "I'm sorry, I was just being sympathetic. I know it must be torturing, Sammy. I mean, he wasn't even wearing sunglasses."

"You know he's right, Arturo. It has been a day of torture for me. Having to be in the pool with him and not even able to drool. I mean, I was drooling on the inside, of course."

"Of course, you were, Sammy. You're only human."

"Thank you, Michael. Plus, I have this serious problem where I can't stop smiling." Everyone laughed, and I yelled out, "But I'm being serious. I need help. I really can't stop smiling."

"It's called euphoria, Sammy, and you're swimming in it. Or at least you were earlier today."

"Michael, you have to stop making me laugh."

"Daphne's right my cheeks are starting to hurt Michael."

"Sammy that's not from me making you laugh, that's from Julio making you smile."

That's when Julio and Lewis walked into the cabana. Lewis asked, "What do you guys want to do tonight?"

"I don't know. Did you ask Tommy?"

Monica just stopped over the house long enough to pick up your brother. So, it's safe to say Tommy has other plans tonight, Sammy."

"Okay, then what do you feel like doing, Lewis?"

"I wanted to see my girlfriend, but she's not allowed out tonight. You guys will get to see her tomorrow at the party."

"Now that really gives me something to look forward to, Lewis. Thank you. I can't wait to see her again."

We all turned around and just looked over at Michael. "Sorry, was that a bit much? I was trying to sound enthusiastic. I guess I need to work on that." Daphne and I couldn't help it. A giggle escaped each of us. Lewis gave us an angry look, and I covered my mouth with the palm of my hand trying to hold in the laughter.

"Lewis, I think we should just hang out here. I mean, we practically have an arcade here and tons of movies we haven't watched yet. We really don't have to go anywhere."

"Is that what you want to do, Arturo? Stay here?"

"Yes, Lewis. We don't need to go anywhere tonight."

"Arturo, I have an idea."

"What is it Julio?"

"Why don't we go sit by the pool, play some music and dominos like old times."

"Yeah, let's do that."

We all followed Julio and Lewis up the stairs to the pool deck and took a seat at the table. Julio walked inside long enough to grab two packs of dominos. Lewis turned on the radio, and Julio sat down in front of me at the table. We played a couple of games, but I was having a hard time paying attention. I couldn't remain focused and I looked up at Julio several times. He caught me and smiled every time. I couldn't take it anymore. I stood up from the table and walked over to a lounge chair on the other side of the pool.

Then one of my favorite songs came on the radio, Michael ran over to me. He pulled me out of my chair and back over to the radio. We danced to 'Take Me Home Tonight' by Eddie Money and Ronnie Spector. The next song came on and it was 'Pour Some Sugar on Me' by Def Leppard. Daphne jumped up out of her chair. Together, we did our little dance that we always do at the bonfire. When the song was finished, Lewis and Julio's eyes looked like they were going to pop out of their heads and their mouths were dropped open like a drawbridge.

Lewis said, "Damn, I need to buy that album. Do all the girls dance like that to Def Leppard?"

"They do at the bonfire, when Greg is playing," Daphne said, smiling.

Julio had an instant stone-cold look on his face as he looked over at me. I looked back at him smiling and I knew what he was thinking. I just thought to myself, oh fantastic; I can't wait for him to start asking me tons of Mig questions again.

'Fantasy Girl' by Johnny O was playing and Arturo walked up to me smiling. He said now this is my freestyle jam and we started dancing. Daphne was already dancing with Michael, and I could feel Julio watching me even with my back turned to him. I turned around once and saw him staring at me. So, I winked at him and he instantly bit down on his lower lip. I turned my head back around to Arturo and continued dancing. When the song was over, I walked inside to get something to drink.

Carmen was in the kitchen and she asked if we're going to join them for dinner. The parents are going to an Italian restaurant, but before I could answer, Julio said, "No. We can just order a pizza or pick up something later."

I turned around when Carmen left the kitchen. "I didn't know you were standing behind me."

"Well, I followed you inside, Sammy."

"You're following me around and you're calling me Sammy?"

"I always follow you. I always watch you. I'm in love with you and you're aware of this." Julio leaned in closer to me, and I backed up against the counter. "I even followed you earlier today, when you left after the movie."

I pulled away from him and focused my attention on the countertop. After I felt like I was in control of my nervous laughter, I looked up at Julio and asked, "How much did you hear me say?"

"I know that I make you feel happy, Sammy." I looked down at the counter again and felt extremely vulnerable now. I knew he heard everything, and I really wasn't prepared for him to know all of that. Then I thought, so what if he knows?

The parents all said bye to us as they walked past the kitchen and out the front door. When the door closed, my heart started pounding and I could feel the beating of it in my throat.

"Julio, I didn't intend for you to know anything, since I'm aware you have a girlfriend."

He looked as though he was repulsed by what I said. "Well, I've said enough. I think I should go back outside now."

When I turned around to walk out of the kitchen Julio said, "No."

That's when I stopped walking and turned around to face him again. I crossed my arms over my chest and looked up at him. Then he looked down into my eyes and said, "No, I don't have a girlfriend. I haven't had a girlfriend since you. I don't know who told you that, but they're wrong."

"Your mom told my mom about your girlfriend."

"My mom's wrong Sammy and I have told my mom I don't have a girlfriend. Besides, even if I did, she doesn't have my heart. You do." Julio leaned in closer to me, and I was now pressed up against the counter again.

"Julio, what are you doing besides making me feel uncomfortable?" Julio raised his hands up as he backed away from me.

"I just want to talk to you, Sammy. We haven't spoken since the last time I was in Miami." Julio pulled out a stool for me, and I sat down. He grabbed a stool and moved it to the other side of the counter. With Julio now sitting directly in front of me, I had to look up into his eyes. I just kept thinking, don't crumble now.

"So, Sammy, you go to the bonfire now. Is it a regular thing?"

"Yes, I go to the bonfire every Friday night and watch Greg and his band play. Why?"

"Daphne mentioned it, and I'm sure Mig must be happy to see you there watching him play at the bonfire."

"Yes, Mig is very happy when I watch him play at the bonfire. In fact, we are very close."

"How close, Sammy?"

"Very close, Julio."

"Is he your boyfriend now, or are you just dating him?"

"I don't have a boyfriend now, Julio, and I'm not dating anyone."

The interrogation was more enjoyable than usual. I knew by the look on Julio's face that he was still jealous of Mig; it reminded me of how I felt about Megan. I stood up and walked over to the cabinet. When I reached up for a glass, Julio walked up behind me. He grabbed a glass out of the cabinet and handed it down to me. When I looked up to say thank you, Julio leaned over and kissed me on the cheek. "I will see you outside, Sammy," and he left.

I poured myself some water and headed back outside. I noticed my reflection on the sliding glass door, I had a huge smile. I just told myself, I'll take smiling over crying any day. The radio was still on and the boys were all playing dominos. I noticed Daphne sitting by herself on a lounge chair just watching the sun go down. I walked over to Daphne and took a seat in the lounge chair beside her. "What's up? Are you okay?"

"Yeah, I'm fine, Sammy. I just miss Greg. I know he's at work now, so I can't even call him."

"You know, Daphne, he gets off work in like, 45 minutes. That's less than an hour from now."

"Oh, that's right. We're three hours ahead. I forgot about that. Thanks, Sammy." She reached over and hugged me. Then she screamed, "That's my song. Turn it up." She stood up and grabbed both of my hands and pulled me up beside her.

My ear was starting to ring, since she yelled right into it. I was pulling on my earlobe when she grabbed my arm and took off running toward the radio.

Michael jumped out of his chair and started dancing with us to 'Girl You Know It's True' by Milli Vanilli. Then 'Strange Love' by Depeche Mode was the next song to come on. Arturo ran over to me and we started dancing together beside Michael and Daphne.

Tommy and Monica walked out onto the pool deck, and Monica asked, "Are you Depeche Mode fans? I love them," and she ran over and danced with us. When the song was over, she asked, "When did you guys start clubbing?"

"Almost a year ago," Michael, answered. "Well we go to the Spot and it's sort of a restaurant with a dance floor. The music is awesome, and we can be ourselves."

"Oh, I want to go with you guys. Next time I'm in Miami, will you take me?"

"Sure, I would love for you to go with us, Monica."

"Arturo, I want to go to. You never invite me or your sister to go with you."

When Daphne mentioned she wanted to go Sammy, I felt that she was still a little too young. I will make a deal with you both. When Monica comes down for your mom and Guillermo's wedding, we will all go to the Spot."

"What? I have to wait that long? That's crazy. Their wedding is not until August next year. You're going to make me wait over a year?"

"Yes, I am, Daphne.

"Okay, now that's all settled. We officially have plans to go dancing in Miami Beach. I can't wait." Monica said, and she wrapped her arms around us in a group hug.

Monica released us, and Arturo was staring at something behind me. He nodded his head to the side indicating for me to turn around. When I did, I saw Julio sitting by himself at the end of the pool deck. "You should go check on him, Sammy. I think all this talk about Miami is making him homesick."

Everyone walked back over to the table and sat down with Lewis and Tommy. I walked over to Julio and sat down in the lounge chair beside him. He looked as though he was deep in thought about something. Either way I didn't want to disturb him, so I just sat back in the lounge chair beside him.

After a couple of minutes, I asked him what he was thinking about. He said that he was simply frustrated that no one in his family believed him. Instead they believe some liar spreading a bunch of lies about him. I was about to ask him about the lies, but Daphne called out my name.

I sat up and walked over to Daphne. She wanted to go inside the house now to call Greg. She also wanted me to go with her. I agreed to go, and we walked inside.

"Sammy, I have something to tell you."

"What is it?"

"Monica told us that Julio's girlfriend will be here tomorrow. Lewis invited her to the party."

"Wow, does Julio know that? Because he just told me earlier, he didn't have a girlfriend. I wonder how he will explain that to me, when she's here tomorrow."

"Did anything happen between you two?"

"No, but you know something, Daphne? I don't get it. He doesn't lie to me. He may not tell me every situation right away, but he always tells me the truth."

"Really Sammy, well then I guess he intends to tell you eventually about his girlfriend tomorrow, when she's here at the party."

"Why would Julio lie to me about having a girlfriend?"

"You know why. Don't be stupid, Sammy. I know you love him, and I know that he loves you. The long-distant thing hasn't worked out for either of you. I don't want to be the voice of reason, but in this situation, I have no choice. I just can't see you hurt again. Why don't you call Mig?"

"Call Mig? Why would you say that?"

"Don't you see what's been happening Sammy? Mig is always there for you. He always finds a way to pick up your pieces and put you back together. He really cares about you, and he is a good-looking guy. I couldn't understand why you wanted Mig around all the time. Now I do. I realize Mig makes you feel safe. He makes you feel loved without the commitment. I think you should give him a chance when you get home, Sammy."

"I'm really not sure why your talking about Mig all of a sudden, Daphne, but I want you to know that I'm going back outside to the pool now."

When I walked back outside, everyone was gone except for Lewis and Julio. I walked up to the table and asked where everyone went. Julio said everyone went back to his house with Monica. I sat down at the table and Lewis stood up. "I need to call Amy and find out what time I have to pick her up tomorrow." Julio made a face I hadn't seen before. It wasn't pretty but appeared when Lewis mentioned Amy. Lewis gave me a hug and told me, "I will see you at the party tomorrow."

It was now Julio and I sitting alone at the table. He just sat there quietly looking at me. I looked over at him and then toward the pool. I kept thinking about what Daphne said. I wanted to ask Julio about the whole girlfriend thing again. Then I thought to myself, no he already told me he didn't have a girlfriend. Julio reached across the table and grabbed hold of my hand.

I looked down at our hands on the table before looking up at him. "Samantha, dance with me."

"Julio, I don't know about that."

That's when I looked around the pool deck, and he said, "There's no one around, only you and me." He turned the radio off and put in a cassette tape. "Just one song, Samantha." He took hold of both of my hands and pulled me up slowly out of the chair. As soon as the song started to play, I knew it was another one of my favorite songs, 'Alone' by Heart. I looked up into his gorgeous brown eyes and I was mesmerized. When I felt his arms wrap around my waist. I placed my hands up on his shoulders and I continued to look up into eyes. He was wearing a broad smile and I was feeling lost in all kinds of emotions as the lyrics really got to me. We both leaned in toward one another when the song was over. Our lips were about to touch. Right then, my logic kicked in. I heard, don't be stupid, Sammy and I turned my head at the last second as Julio kissed my cheek.

He placed his thumb on my chin, and he gently turned my head back toward him as he leaned in. I pulled my head back and said, "Stop, Julio, Monica told everyone about your girlfriend."

Julio released me from his embrace. "I know you're upset that I know about your girlfriend Julio, but don't be upset. I'm happy for you, and you shouldn't be cheating on your girlfriend."

Julio turned to me and shouted, "Go Samantha run back to your room now, I don't want to ruin your happiness."

That's when I took off running straight to my room. I heard Daphne say, "Greg, I have to call you back." She ran over to me, and I was still standing with my back pressed up against the sliding glass door. Daphne wrapped her right arm around me and walked me over to the chairs. I sat down and she sat down on the ottoman in front of me.

"Sammy, what happened?"

"Julio and I danced to one slow song and I almost kissed him. I didn't though. Instead I confronted him and told him I knew about his girlfriend and he didn't like that very much."

"I'm proud of you, Sammy. You did it. Honestly, I didn't think you could, knowing how you feel about him, I'm proud of you. Sometimes life isn't fair, and we have to think with our head instead of our heart."

"Daphne, when he had his arms wrapped around me, and when he was staring into my eyes, my whole body was humming from head to toe. Every inch of me was finally happy."

"Yes, until you see him with his girlfriend tomorrow. Or worse, you get on the plane with another letter telling you about his girlfriend. No, Sammy, you can't give into that feeling again. It's not permanent because he's not permanent. He lives here now, and you live in Miami."

"It just sucks you know, because I do love him and only him. I know he loves me too. Whenever I see him, I feel like, oh that's what happened to my happiness. It stayed with him. I try, Daphne, all the time, and I only ever feel this incredibly happy when I'm with Julio."

"Look, I know if you both lived in at least the same state, this wouldn't be an issue. The truth is, you don't, and you're both young and need to get on with your lives. That includes dating someone else. Call Mig. I know he would love to hear from you, Sammy."

"I can't call him, Daphne."

"Of course, you can, Sammy. You just pick up the phone and dial the number."

"No, Daphne, I mean I can't call him because it's after midnight in Miami."

Oh, that's not a problem. Greg is sleeping over at Mig's house. I will beep Greg and when he calls back, he can put Mig on the phone." Daphne picked up the phone and beeped Greg. I went into the bathroom and soaked in the tub hoping to relax enough to clear my head and get some sleep.

The next morning when I got up, I saw my mom in the kitchen. She said last night Tommy, Michael, and Arturo helped Monica decorate and set up Pilar's backyard for the birthday party. "That means you girls need to be dressed and ready to leave here for the party by twelve o'clock."

Arturo and Michael ran into our room an hour later. They asked, "What happened between you and Julio last night, Sammy?"

"Nothing. Why? What happened?"

"Julio came back home last night when we finished decorating the backyard."

"Yes, and what happened Arturo?"

"Monica asked Julio to come outside and see what we have done to the backyard. He ignored her and went to his room. He slammed his door shut and turned on his stereo."

"That's great. I guess I should start from the beginning." I told them everything that happened. They both said they were proud of me. They also confirmed that Monica is expecting Julio's girlfriend to be at the party today. They also mentioned Julio did not invite her to the party, Lewis did. Monica and Pilar don't like her and would prefer that his girlfriend skipped the party.

"Wow, I guess you either love her or hate her."

"Sammy, I heard she can be a handful."

"Well, enough about Julio and his girlfriend. Michael, we need to get ready. Can you help me, fairy godmother? "

"Yes, did you remember to bring the outfit, Sammy?"

"Of course."

Michael put my outfit together for me to wear today three weeks ago before he left Miami. That was a week after we found out we were coming back to Anaheim. Michael said he needed to see my closet. We walked into my closet together and he picked out everything. In fact, all the clothes I brought with me were picked out by Michael.

Now I was wearing my hair down with my natural curls flowing to my shoulders. My makeup was light in tan and brown tones. I was wearing little cobalt blue flower earrings. I had on a one-piece jumper that was white with blue pinstripes.

The bottom of the jumper was flared out like culottes. Since the jumper was sleeveless, I was wearing a cobalt blue cotton jacket and matching pumps.

When I walked out of the dressing area, Michael said, "You look perfect, Sammy."

Daphne and Arturo both agreed that today was definitely the day to look my best and feel confident. I admitted that I was nervous, they all assured me they weren't leaving my side. That we would all stick together and get me through this party.

We left the house in three separate cars to go two blocks down the street. It seemed a bit ridiculous when we could walk there, but I just went with the flow.

When we pulled up to Pilar's house, I suddenly had nervous knots in my stomach and a really bad feeling. I prepared myself mentally to stay happy throughout the day. I reminded myself that today I was here for Erika and Monica, not Julio.

Michael and Arturo escorted Daphne and me inside. We walked inside the house behind my mom and Guillermo. We followed them through the house and out to the backyard. Monica ran over to us the minute we arrived, and she pointed out all of the decorations.

The backyard had a big white tent, with sheer white drapes at both entrances. The drapes were pulled back and held in place with large baby pink bows. There were baby pink roses on every table with a baby bottle shaped vase. Off to the side of the tent was a DJ with turntables and the whole setup. In front of the DJ, there was plenty of room for people to dance. Just ask Carmen and Enrique, who were already dancing.

I found the gift table and set my gift down. Once I had my hands free, Arturo said he wanted to walk around and say hi to everyone. We spoke to the newlyweds, Julie and Mr. Sanchez. They still appeared very happy and very much in love. We ran into Alex and Maria. They were staying in the same house with us, but we hardly ever saw them. I asked where they went last night. Maria laughed and said they never left the theatre room.

The four of us managed to convince Alex and Maria to join us on the dance floor. We walked out of the tent and over to the DJ. Michael asked the DJ to play Depeche Mode and dedicate the song to Monica. The DJ smiled and told him it was coming right up, next song.

We all started dancing to the song that was currently playing. It was one of my mom's favorite songs, 'Knowing Me Knowing You' by ABBA. All of the parents were dancing beside us, and I loved it. I started to sing, and I was paying attention to the lyrics for the first time. That's when I realized it was a breakup song. Michael noticed how the song was affecting me. He began to sing along with me as he spun me around a couple of times. By the end of the song, we were singing the song as a duet to one another and I was happy again.

When the song ended, the DJ spoke into his mic and said, "This next song is dedicated to little Erika's mom. Monica, if you can hear me, join your friends out on the dance floor." Monica walked over to the dance floor; Julio was with her. 'People Are People' by Depeche Mode started to play, and Monica ran over to Michael. She hugged him, and they started dancing.

Julio walked up to me, and just started dancing with me. It was a fast song, so I knew I would be fine. The next song to come on was 'Endless Summer Nights' by Richard Marx. I turned to walk away and got as far as one step. When Julio said, "Samantha please." I looked back into his pleading eyes and he bit down on his lower lip the minute we made eye contact. I was weak from that moment on, and he put his hand out to me. I took it and he pulled me into his arms. As we danced together, he sung the song to me every word with such feeling. This song could fit into our lives in so many ways with our past and current experience together. When the song was over, Julio kissed the palm of my hand before walking away.

Arturo walked up to me with a big smile on his face. "Samantha, you let him dance with you for two songs and you're still all in one piece. You see, I knew you could do it. You wasted all of your energy worrying for nothing."

Monica ran up to us as we were leaving the dance floor. She said, "Julio's girlfriend just arrived with Lewis and Amy. I just wanted to give you a heads up. For some reason, she had to come in order for Amy to be allowed out of her house."

"Wait, Monica. Your brother's girlfriend is Megan? The one he slept with less than a month after he moved up here?"

"Yup, that's the one. I really can't stand her. I don't know how Julio can go from a girl like you, to something like her."

I looked up at Monica blinking back the tears in my eyes. Then I looked over at Michael, Arturo, and Daphne. I was so upset, and I said, "I can't believe this girl, Megan, is his girlfriend. After all the pain it caused me to read that letter, where he wrote about his regret. That's his girlfriend now after everything that happened. That's the girl. I just can't believe it. I'm such a fool. I believed him, when he told me how he regretted everything that happened between them. How it was a mistake, and one that he will always regret. Nobody knows just how much it hurt me to read that stupid letter telling me about what happened between them. He kept pleading with me to give him a second chance. I'm so naïve. She was his girlfriend all along. I was the other girl ever since he met her."

"I'm so sorry, Sammy. We'll stick together and have a great time. You'll see." Monica wrapped her arms around me and told me, "I love you, Sammy. We're family. It's going to be okay. Just forget about Julio."

"Thanks, Monica. I'm really glad to be here with you and Erika. Today is a great day, and it's your day as well as Erika's. Don't worry about his girlfriend being here. It should be fine, and I put on a fake smile."

Well I'm just glad you're here Sammy. We had to postpone my daughter's birthday party for over a month until Tio Juan came back from Chile. Now we're all finally here to celebrate her birthday. Although my daughter might sleep through the whole thing. She woke up cranky, so I put her down for a nap before the party starts. That was two hours ago. Come with me. Let's go check on her, Sammy."

Then I noticed two girls headed in our direction with Lewis. As they came closer, I noticed Amy, and the other girl must have been Julio's girlfriend Megan. She was actually beautiful, with long blond hair, a golden tan, and long legs. She didn't leave much to the imagination, wearing a yellow spandex dress, white heels and a tight white jacket with cleavage. She was definitely confident wearing that outfit. I would love to say she looked horrible, but she didn't. She was dressed a lot older than she appeared to be.

Amy walked over to us, and she hugged all five of us. Then her cousin Megan walked up behind her. Michael grabbed my hand and said, "That's your song. Let's go."

Arturo and Daphne followed us out onto the dance floor. Arturo leaned over to Michael and told him, "That was a close call."

The next song started to play, and I froze in place for a second. 'That Was Yesterday' by Foreigner was playing. Michael leaned over me and asked, "What's wrong?"

I whispered, "This is Julio's song. The one he played for me in Miami, you know the breakup song."

Michael leaned back, and his eyes were huge. I laughed and told Michael, "It's alright. Really, I'm fine."

Then I realized Michael was staring at something, or rather someone behind me. I turned around and Julio wrapped his arms around my waist, and he pulled me towards him. "Don't dance with anyone else to one of our songs, when I'm right here."

I took a deep breath and replied, "Julio, let me go. Your girlfriend is right there."

He stopped in his tracks as I pointed to her. Suddenly he had the familiar stone-cold look on his face.

"Samantha, I don't care about her, I only care about you and me."

"Julio," I exclaimed. He raised his eyebrows up at me as he pressed his lips tightly together and shook his head."

When I turned to walk away, Megan walked up to me and Julio on the dance floor. "Why are you here Samantha? You and Julio are done. It's been over. Why do you have to come all this way to Anaheim to see him? Is there a shortage of guys in Miami or is there no one else willing to date you? Either way I could care less. Let me just tell you this now and spare you of any delusion you might have. Julio does not need a girl from Miami coming to see him anymore. He is already dating a girl here in Anaheim and that's me!"

I glanced over at Julio and saw a look of disgust on his face, but he didn't say a word. So, I turned my attention back to Megan. I put my hand up and said, "Just stop, I'm not here for Julio."

"Then why are you here?"

I realized at that very moment her beauty was only skin deep. Her soul and brains were completely missing.

"I'm here for Monica to celebrate Erika's birthday. In fact, that's why we're all here. She crossed her arms over chest and rolled her eyes.

"Don't worry Megan, I know about everything that happened between you and Julio. You can have him. Oh, wait! You already did! On your first date. I know about that because Julio told me everything. Now we all know you're one of those classy girls that people talk about all the time."

Megan's mouth dropped open, but nothing came out. I guess she was appalled by my honesty.

I turned to Julio again and he hadn't said a word. I was angry with him for not speaking up. I was about to walk away when I heard 'Don't Stop Believing' by Journey.

That's when I realized why Julio wasn't saying anything. Nobody believed him including me. Instead everyone believed this girl Megan.

"Julio, it may not change anything between us, but I believe you." His eyes met mine and my throat tightened. I swallowed once and said, "She's not your girlfriend, however she's your problem."

Julio remained silent, but I saw the relief in his eyes. As I walked away leaving Julio to deal with Megan on his own.

The End

Glossary

Translation of Spanish Words into English

Muñeca – Doll

Mi Corazon – My heart

Primo – Cousin

Abuela – Grandma

Abuelo – Grandpa

Mi hijo – My son

Te amo – I love you

Hermano – Brother

Sobrino – Nephew

El amor es una cosa hermosa – Love is a beautiful thing

Chancletas –Flip-flops

Qué es eso? – What is that?

Por favor – Please

Translation of French Word into English

Pénible – Annoying

Book 3 Miami Generation X City of Freedom

Sammy left Anaheim with a completely new attitude. She has a new boyfriend by the time the Sanchez boys come to town for Thanksgiving, and it's not Julio! Samantha's boyfriend has a real problem with Julio and wages a personal vendetta against him. Is it rightfully deserved or is he just jealous of Julio? Tragedy occurs during the Sanchez family stay in Miami causing everyone to be overwhelmed with grief. Everybody starts choosing sides; not everyone has Samantha's back when it comes down to choosing between her and Julio.

For more information on this series go to mgxbook.com

www.ingramcontent.com/pod-product-compliance
Lightning Source LLC
Chambersburg PA
CBHW080814250626